For The Money And The Fun

Jacob D. & Leona M. Deorksen

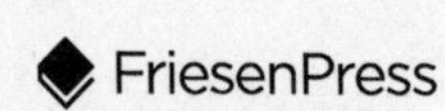

One Printers Way
Altona, MB R0G 0B0
Canada

www.friesenpress.com

First Edition — 2022

Cover Art by Cristina L. Peori

ISBN
978-1-03-912472-1 (Hardcover)
978-1-03-912471-4 (Paperback)
978-1-03-912473-8 (eBook)

1. FICTION, WAR & MILITARY

Distributed to the trade by The Ingram Book Company

For The Money And The Fun

Chapter 1

June, 1943

The whole procedure was not at all what he'd expected. Never before had he felt so exposed. In fact, he couldn't remember ever being so utterly bare before. Although he had always shared a bedroom with his brothers and slept in the same bed with one of them, he'd never stood as naked in their company as he was standing now among all these strangers.

His hands were causing him the greatest difficulty. Where should he put them? They positively twitched with an urge to cover his private parts. Instinctively he knew that would only make things worse. So he strained at keeping them hanging at his sides, casually, as if this whole business was commonplace. His hands knew otherwise. Putting one of them on his naked hip solved only half of his problem. Clasping them behind his back seemed finally to be the best solution because then at least his buttocks seemed less vulnerable. Unfortunately, this relief was offset by the sense that his private parts were embarrassingly thrust forward.

The examiner barked, "Ne-ext!" and he moved another step closer to the fateful moment. There were all kinds of whispers about what was happening at the head of the line, but all he could see was a bare back immediately in front of him. He tried to quell a rising anxiety that had already begun to grip him at the pre-registration desk. *How did I get myself into this?*

Yesterday it had seemed such an easy thing. When he dropped his tools in the repair shop at home his gesture had silenced his father's tirade against the sloth and ingratitude of modern youth. The reverberation of the hammer hitting the plank floor had signaled the end of something more. "I'm going to join up," he'd said, just as if that was the same as saying, "I'm going to get the cows." How sweet had been the sense of power that ballooned in the stillness that followed his words?

Now he tried to summon some of that fine feeling of strength as the line inched forward. Sidelong glances at the other bodies in the lineup raised a fear that the configuration of his own sexual equipment wasn't exactly like theirs. Didn't his testicles seem to hang somewhat lower? What if the medical officer decided that he wasn't a good enough specimen for this elite branch of Canada's armed forces? Why had he been such a damn fool as to announce that he was joining the navy? What if he didn't get in? He stiffened his resolve and attempted to tighten his scrotum. No use. The stupid balls still dangled disconsolately when finally his name was called.

The hand in the rubber glove grasped his pecker and squeezed relentlessly from root to tip. Not a drop oozed out, and, briefly, a flood of gratitude washed over him. He'd made it through the "short arm" test. "Nothing wrong with your dong! Get in line over there." The rubber glove waved him over to the next desk.

Good grief! What now? From what he could see, the men ahead of him in this line were stepping into a shallow tray and then making footprints on the floor for the next examiner. Of this he had also heard rumours, ominous rumours, that not even the army accepted men with flat feet. A peek past those ahead of him confirmed his worst fears. Never had his own bare feet made such kidney-shaped tracks when he stepped from the bathtub onto the painted floor of the farm kitchen.

He curled his feet up as best he could and practiced walking on their outer edges as he moved toward his turn at the wetting tray. "Ne-ext!" bellowed the voice. He held his breath, trying not to hobble while making his six paces across the floor. "OK! Nothing wrong with your feet! Move on to the next line! Ne-ext!"

Whew! This "Flat-Footed Mennonite" had made it past another one! Grateful, the muscles in his legs and toes relaxed as he wiped his feet on the mat. Surely the worst was over now and he'd be able to put his clothes on after the next hurdle.

Arrows directed him along the corridor. His heart sank as he turned the corner to join the next line-up. A long series of desks and a sea of bare backsides extended into the distance. How would he ever get back to his clothes? Would he get his uniform first? What if someone stole the fifteen dollars he'd left in his pocket? Would he have to spend another expensive night in that five-buck hotel before he got into barracks—if he got in at all?

The eye test, the ear test, the nose test. He'd never before been aware of the number of parts belonging to him. Each was now a prospective traitor in this endless ordeal. Relentlessly, he moved from lineup to lineup and then to another line-up. At last he could see the file ahead of him moving out of doors. If only his asshole wouldn't fail him now, he'd be home free. Anticipation of an end at hand made this violation by the rubber-gloved finger almost welcome. "Ne-ext!"

He'd made it at last! No more line-ups. No more tests. With a light step and glowing heart he followed the line. Finding the fifteen one-dollar bills safe in his pants pocket made him feel even better.

As he tied his shoelaces another lot of new recruits was ushered in. Sheepishly they began to disrobe. He took a comb from his pocket and combed his dark hair with a leisurely nonchalance. Poor suckers. How embarrassed they looked as their white-skinned untanned bottoms emerged from their pants. He gave his hair a final pat and moved toward the door with a faint swagger. "Hey, buddy!" One of the newly naked stopped him. "What'd they do to ya in there? How'd you get through?"

"We-ell, all I can tell you is they're tough in there. Nearly rejected me because of my knees, but I made it all right," and he moved to the door with only a wave at the clamour of questions that arose behind him.

Back at the registration desk the officer was already checking his medical report. "Friedlen!" he shouted, as though he were at the far end of the corridor instead of standing immediately in front of his desk. The stark whiteness of the officer's uniform with all those gleaming brass buttons was well-nigh dazzling. How long would it be before he'd be wearing a coat like that, Ike wondered.

"Christian name, Isaac. Is that correct?"

"Yes, Sir!"

"Second name?"

"I don't have one, Sir."

"What do you mean, you don't have one? You've put down an initial. Isaac D. Friedlen. What does the `D' stand for?"

"It, it's just an initial, Sir," Ike stammered. Somehow it didn't seem the right time just now to explain to those brass buttons that second names weren't given to children where he had grown up, and that the initial had become necessary because there were two other Isaacs among his forty schoolmates and one of these had also been a Friedlen. Nor did it seem likely that the steely blue-grey eyes over those brass buttons would take kindly to being told that his last name should rhyme with "free" rather than with "fry".

"An initial has to stand for something!" the voice thundered. The face seemed to be getting redder. "What is it? Speak up!"

"'D' is for -- ah --for --." Vainly his mind scurried about, trying to think of a name that started with `D.' "It, it, it's for Davenport, Sir!"

The officer gave him a sharp look of disbelief but wrote it down on the form lying on his desk. Simultaneously, an assistant wrote it down in a small blue book.

"Nationality?"

"Canadian, Sir."

"CANADIAN????" Ike felt a large blazing question mark embed itself on his forehead. "What was your mother's maiden name?"

"Neufeld, Sir."

"Neufeld! Neufeld! You can't be a Canadian with a name like that. Where were you born?"

"On the farm, Sir. On 19-4-1 West, Sir."

"I don't mean that," the voice said impatiently." Where was your father born, then? In which country?"

"In Altona, Sir. In Manitoba, in Canada, Sir."

"You don't need to tell me where Manitoba is," snapped the officer. "Where was your grandfather born?"

"In Russia, Sir."

"A-a-a-ah!" The steel in the blue eyes gleamed with satisfaction now. "So you're a Russian-Canadian." He began to write.

"Oh no, Sir!" Ike said quickly, trying to stop the hand that with a few strokes on the page was changing the blood in his veins. "My great-grandfather was Dutch, Sir." He knew he was attributing a marvelous longevity on the great-grandfather he'd never known, but he also knew with absolute certainty that the brass buttons did not want to hear about his people's flight from Dutch persecution and the hundred-year sojourn in Russia that began with Czarina Catherine's need to colonize her southern lands. It was enough that "Russian" was being struck out and "Dutch-Canadian" was being printed in its place.

"Religion?"

"Mennonite, Sir."

"Mennonite? What the hell is that?"

"Well, Sir, it-it-it's Mennonite." The officer glanced at his assistant and shook his head. Ike's mind stumbled over the realization that in the gleam of those buttons he couldn't say Mennonites were pacifists. Suddenly he remembered that the man ahead of him had said he was Catholic. "It-it-it's not Catholic, I guess," blurted Ike helplessly. The officer printed "Protestant" on the form and his assistant did the same in the little blue book before handing it to Brass Buttons, who flipped through the pages and added his signature to the last one before handing it to Ike.

"Welcome to the Royal Canadian Naval Volunteer Reserve, Isaac Davenport Friedlen. You are now a second class stoker. Your number is V-63485. Report to the quartermaster for your kit. On the double!"

More arrows promised to lead him to stores and the coveted uniform. A clerk checked his blue book. "V-63485. Here's your stencil and your sea bag." He joined the line that was proceeding past the stacks of bins and had item after item of clothing thrust at him. No time to try anything on. He grabbed each piece and stuffed it into the big, brown bag. Then the bag was full to the top but more stuff was still coming at him. He punched down the contents and added more.

He decided the attaché case and the tin hat box and the boots were just too much, so he tucked the first two under one arm and grabbed the boots in one hand. With the other he guided the bulging bag forward along the floor. At the rack of hammocks he halted. He didn't have another hand in which to grasp this sausage-shaped six-foot long, one-size-fits-all bundle.

"Get all that other stuff into that bag!" barked the officer standing there. Ike stepped out of line punching and pummeling the bag's contents down to make room for the boots. Eventually, he managed to get them in and the clasp closed. He hoisted the hammock to his shoulder. "Move along, move along!"

The lad ahead of him had difficulty lifting the bag that weighed almost as much as he did. These soft city boys needed to put in a few months of work on a farm to build some muscle, Ike mused, smiling inwardly. He braced his 128-pound, five-and-a-half-foot frame and, with only slightly exaggerated ease, hoisted his own sea bag under his arm. With hat box and attaché case in one hand, hammock on one shoulder and sea bag under the other arm, he moved toward the final inspection station.

Finished at last, he stopped outside stores to examine his precious blue book. There it was, stamped, signed: Isaac D. Friedlen, Stoker Second Class, Royal Canadian Volunteer Reserve. Loyal Subject of King George VI. Subject of King George! The words made the world look different somehow.

Until now he'd been a young Canadian farmer, a Mennonite boy who listened avidly to each day's CKY news report about far-off battles for King and Country. Until now he had only imagined what it was like to be fighting to save his country from Hitler's evil fascist hordes. Whatever they were. Now he had a new name, Isaac Davenport Friedlen (he almost laughed out loud at the ridiculous sound of it), a new religion, a new nationality and—what seemed most strange of all—he was the "Loyal Subject of King George VI." He wondered vaguely whether, if the war lasted long enough, he would be able to vote for King George as well as for Mackenzie King.

Chapter 2

Kennedy Street

The afternoon shadows were lengthening when Ike reached the street. He checked the address on his Assignment to Quarters slip. Kennedy Street. Two blocks west. Just an old rooming house! He had hoped to be in HMCS *Chippawa* itself. He might have known the handsome, old, mock-Tudor Winnipeg Winter Club building couldn't hold all the wartime recruits, but in his dreams of being a sailor he had appeared as one of the smartly uniformed men he'd seen rushing up and down those corridors that smelled of floor wax and brass polish. He patted the bag. Never mind. Tomorrow on the parade square he'd look just as dashing as they did. He strode exultantly westward under the arching elm trees that lined the boulevard.

A frizzy-haired woman with chilly, watery eyes answered the doorbell. Wordlessly, she examined his chit and led the way up two flights of stairs. On the first landing, a sailor on his way down hugged the wall to let Ike and his gear get by. Men's voices murmured behind doors on the second floor.

"No girls, no liquor," the landlady declared flatly as she opened the door to his room and handed him the key.

Ike closed the door behind him and quickly dumped the sea-bag out on one of the three narrow beds. White bellbottoms! At last! He pulled them on and chuckled at the flap front. In the mirror he checked to see if his crotch looked all right in this ridiculous rig. Sara would like that, he reflected.

He reached for the long-sleeved top. The label on the bin at the stores had read "Jumper." He pondered the name as he drew it over his head. Considering the tight fit, obviously "jumper" didn't mean you could just jump into it. The square collar with the strings and the dickey should have gone on first, he discovered, but he tucked them into the open neck as best he could, just to see what he'd look like.

Gee Whiz! Was this the same Ike Friedlen that had walked from his father's farm in striped, bibbed coveralls only yesterday? Tilting the little round hat at every angle he settled on a forward slant resting on his right eyebrow. Darned sexy. Yes, but where to fit the little rosette on the ribbon? He'd heard something about Nelson's blind eye, but was it his left or his right eye? HMCS in gold letters obviously went up front. What stared back in the mirror was a far cry from the straw hat he sometimes wore back home in late July heat. Man-oh-man! To strut along Highfield's Main Street in this rig.

The old farts smoking in front of Levy's General Store would not be cheering him on. He knew that for sure. The first recruit to come home on leave in a uniform had had a rough time of it. One of Moses Levy's twelve sons. He changed into civvies for fear of a possible boycott of his father's general store. Joining up to help win the war was not a popular notion in Highfield.

A good Mennonite abhorred war, regardless of its cause, and volunteered for Alternative Service or went to a camp for conscientious objectors. "Winning the war" meant killing. Hard to square with "Thou shalt not kill," the most important commandment in the Mennonite catechism. So, many boys who did enlist said they were in it for the pay. Or for the girls and good times. Those sentiments could be understood, if not approved. Girls and good times went with the natural sowing of wild oats, and every sober adult respected hard cash. Having cash signified just rewards for just living, didn't it? Still, coming from the military changed its significance.

When faced with the choice of being sent to a remote work camp for CO's at fifteen dollars a month, Highfield boys conscripted into the army found their pacifist convictions severely challenged, and gradually more and more of them opted for the alternative: a smart uniform and fifty dollars cash every pay day. Now, after three years of war, the uniform and pay had won out. But the elders still frowned.

Ike's might well be the first navy uniform to appear in Highfield, and the old sidewalk spitters would loudly speculate about its country of origin before grunting about it being too bad that Hendrick Friedlen's boy was going to the devil like so many others. Before home leave, however, there was gear to sort.

Ike put the fifteen bucks into the pouch of the webbed money belt. It was what he had left of the twenty dollars his father had handed him just before he walked out of the house to come to Winnipeg—the first money he'd ever gotten from the Old Man without asking for it. He still felt surprised at the gesture. His father had always promptly paid men hired for harvesting or seeding time, but his sons were expected to work for spending money and it was not freely given.

The belt slid under the flap of his pants and the jumper fitted so snugly over both that getting at his money was difficult. He'd miss the ease of pants pockets until he got used to this peculiar arrangement. Fully dressed he looked in the mirror. Dazzling. He whistled! A completely made-over image. His own man. Never again to scrounge for money.

Ike untied the tapes and examined the small rolled bundle of ticking labeled "wife." Thread, buttons and needles. Other than in the use of a coarse harness needle, he had never threaded a sewing needle in his life.

The image of his mother and sisters suddenly arose as he fingered the skein of black wool and the small pair of scissors. Never, ever, had he given a single thought about the mending they had done for him while he was at home. Patches on his pants and darns on his socks had appeared, like the summer rains and winter snows. He'd give some thought to "wife" later.

The hot, stifling room caused sweat to prickle along his spine. He opened the small window. To keep the uniform looking like new on tomorrow's parade square, he started to undress. Reaching down he grasped the hem of his jumper and gave a heave to pull it over his head, but the dampness of his chest and sweaty arm-pits grounded his efforts somewhere just about shoulder level. He gave another tug. It wouldn't budge. Wriggling, squirming, bending and tugging with increased determination only added to his problem. He stopped to think.

His face, half covered in white drill, glistened with sweat. He moved to the window and bent over, pointing his trapped, extended arms and the open end of the cotton tube towards it, to scoop up more air. His mind groped for a solution. Bit by bit, inch by inch, he was struggling to free his face when the door opened. He turned and peered out of his white cotton tunnel at the long legs, the slim waist, and the broad shoulders that were hiking another sea bag into the room. The sea bag paused. Ike raised his arms a little higher and looked into the puzzled blue eyes that stared back at him.

"Hi!" Ike tried to sound as if walking around with his head in a sack was perfectly normal.

"Hi!" came the slightly hesitant reply. Another pause. "What the hell are you doin' anyway? Gettin' into that thing or gettin' out of it?"

Ike's voice was muffled. "How about grabbing the bottom and giving a pull, eh?"

"Oho! So you're stuck!" His laugh was good-natured. "Hold on a second and I'll give you a hand." Ike heard the new sea bag hit the floor with a thump. A couple of hard tugs and sticky squirms freed Ike to breathe easily again.

"Whew!" He moved to the window and sucked air into his lungs. "Thanks a lot. Friedlen's the name. Ike Friedlen. Thought I'd be spending the night in this rig. Sure glad you came along."

"Len Larsen to the rescue!" A deep chuckle accompanied his extended hand. "Guess you signed up today, too."

"Yeah. If I'd been in longer, I'd have known better than to get into that gear without anybody around to help me out again. Where're you from, Larsen?"

"Interlake district."

"I know where it is. My Old Man used to go up as far as Gimli to buy fish in the winter. I'm from Highfield, south of here."

Larsen pulled a package of cigarettes out of his shirt pocket, lit up, sat down on a bed, and watched while Ike sorted his gear into neat piles. Black socks, white socks. Ike had never had white socks before. For that matter, he had never had this many pairs of any kind of socks at one time, ever. Rectangular dickeys, braid-trimmed blue collars, blue bell bottoms and jumper.

"Good Grief! Will you look at these?" he chortled as he held up a pair of loose, baggy shorts. "This stuff is almost as thick as the material in these bell bottoms. They can't be serious!" They both laughed as he rolled them into a ball and flung them to the bottom of his sea bag.

Suddenly the door burst open and another sea bag came hurtling into the room. A red-faced, red-haired recruit collapsed on top of it, gasping for breath. Ike surveyed the plump buttocks and the pale soft-skinned hands that had obviously never shovelled manure or handled a 12-pound maul. "That bag heavy enough for you?" he asked.

"Jeez! One more flight of stairs and the navy would have been short one sailor. Killed in action. On Kennedy Street." The red, freckled face broke into a grin as he sat up, laughing. "My name's Hogan. Charlie Hogan, Royal Canadian Naval Volunteer Reserve, HMCS *Chippawa*. Guess we're roommates for the next six weeks."

"Friedlen, Ike, speaking. Welcome to the senior service."

Charlie took Ike's proffered hand, hoisted himself to his feet.

Larsen said, "Hi, Hogan," and offered his hand without getting up. "Len Larsen's the name." He took a long pull on his cigarette and inhaled deeply.

Charlie joined Ike in examining the gear on the bed. "So this is what we get to win the war with? Did you get a pair of boots that fit? I hope mine feel better after I've worn 'em a while than they did in the stores. They sure didn't give a guy much time to make up his mind, did they?" He turned toward his own bag, undid the clasp and emptied its contents on the third bed. "Have you tried on anything besides the bell bottoms?"

Larsen laughed. "Should we tell 'im, Friedlen, or should we just go for a walk while he gets into his rig?"

"Tell me what?"

"Well, it's like this, Charlie," said Ike, unconsciously responding to the newcomer's ruddy boyishness by using his first name. "The navy had to find an excuse for bunking us three to a single room so they issued us all with uniforms a coupl'a sizes too small so that each man needs two others to get out of his jumper once he's in it. Larsen barely managed to rescue me just now. Try yours on and you'll see."

"Aw, c'mon. Are you serious?" Charlie's face betrayed real concern. He picked up a jumper from his pile and held it in front of his plump midriff. "My Dad tried to talk me out of joining the navy. Maybe he was right."

"So, did he want you to get drafted into the army instead?" asked Larsen incredulously.

"Well, I guess he didn't want me to enlist at all. He was in the First World War, you know. His outfit ran into a gas attack and he's had lung trouble ever since."

"So, how come you joined up?" Ike was curious.

"I got kinda tired of just listening to the radio about all the action and I've just been waiting for my birthday so I could get into it. They keep sayin' they need more men to finish off the war. My call-up wouldn't've come for another year but I figgered I had to get out there, kind of itchin' to be a part of it. Ya know what I mean? Anyway so, here I am!"

Ike glanced at Charlie quizzically, trying to detect a look that betrayed an ironic intent, but the blue eyes looking back at him were innocent and guileless.

"Hell, he sounds like a damned recruiting poster. D'ya think we can stand it for six weeks, Friedlen?" Larsen's voice was laced with cynicism.

"It'll be tough, but I kinda know what he means. I'd have been called up last year but my Old Man went out and got an exemption for me. At home, every night we sit and listen to news of more casualties, more ships sunk, more planes shot down. The Old Man starts in about how it's all propaganda, how the English were just tryin' to get us out there to fight their war for them again. You should have heard him after Dieppe! I just got fed up with it. Sure, a lot of it is propaganda, but war is war and I'm for winning. So I'm out to do my bit. No more riding around the same darned fields on a tractor."

"Well, I just figgered I'd rather join the navy than get called up for the army," said Larsen, stubbing out his cigarette on the floor. "Damned if I wanna spend my time marching my feet off! Hey! Are you two gonna go on sorting out all that stuff all night? Hell, I'm not! Just lemme find one a' them white uniforms and I'm gonna hit the town."

He reached into his bag, pulled out bits and pieces of gear and flung them over his shoulder until he found a pair of pants and a short sleeved gun shirt with an open, square neck bordered in blue. Quickly he stripped off the slacks and shirt he had on and kicked them under his bed. He pulled on the gun shirt, drew his new bell bottoms up over his long legs and, bending over, pawed through his sea bag again.

"Where the fuck is my belt?" he growled. "The goddam thing'll be right down at the bottom under all this other godforsaken crap!" More gear came tumbling over the edge of the bag as he stirred up its contents. "Aha! There's the son-of-a-bitch!" he exclaimed victoriously and held the belt aloft. He strapped it around his waist, then reached under the bed for his pants. He hauled a handful of crumpled bills and a package of cigarettes out of the pockets and tried to cram them into the pouch. They didn't fit.

"Jeez! Where the hell is a man supposed to carry his smokes anyway?" He slapped the cigarettes on top of the dresser while he buttoned his trousers, then tucked the package into his waistband. Flipping open the lid of his tin hatbox, he took out the white hat and slipped the ribbon around its rim. Then, stepping over to the mirror, he perched it on the back of his head.

"Look out, girls! Here I come!" he chortled, eyeing himself briefly in the glass. "Hey, will one of you guys brush my shoulders? I mean the salt, dammit the salt! I'm ready to go!" He turned to Ike and Charlie. "Are you guys comin'?"

"Gosh," Charlie looked around at the clutter that overflowed his bed, "I think I'll get all my gear stencilled and sort out this mess before I go anywhere. What about you, Ike?"

"Me too. Besides, supper won't be served for another half hour yet. By the way, don't let any officer see you with your hat on like that. Aren't we supposed to wear them tilted forward? Let's look at the manual."

"The hell with the manual. I'm gonna get movin'. I'll get a hot dog or somethin' downtown. And by darn, I'll find me a beer parlour and some dames. I'm dyin' of thirst. See you guys later." He was halfway down to the landing before the door had slammed behind him. Ike and Charlie, ignoring the chaos around Larsen's bed, continued with their own sorting.

"Guess we know now why the navy calls us mess mates," Charlie chuckled.

It seemed to Ike he'd been asleep for hours when a commotion in the hall downstairs woke him. The doorbell rang again and again until suddenly a woman's angry voice complained and scolded. A male voice seemed to answer and after more rumbling and complaining sounds, a set of footsteps came stumbling up the stairs. The door opened and in came Larsen, reeking of cigarette smoke and beer. He didn't turn on the light and closed the door quietly behind him.

"Damn!" he exploded as he bumped into the dresser. Ike remained silent. There was no sound from Charlie's bed. Soon Larsen had finished his fumbling and settled down on the creaky bed.

Ike got up quietly next morning and picked up his shaving gear, aiming for a head start at the bathroom. He'd had enough of line ups yesterday to do him for the rest of his life. He hadn't finished shaving when someone else tried the door. When he opened it, there was Charlie, towel over his shoulder, still yawning as he leaned against the door jamb. Behind him stood two more, waiting.

When Ike got back to his room, Larsen still lay with his head buried in the pillow. Ike deliberately made a clatter as he got dressed. Larsen still lay motionless.

Charlie returned. "Do we wake him, Charlie?"

Charlie looked reluctant. "If we don't, Ike, he's gonna be late. I dunno what the navy does to guys that come in late, but I wouldn't want to find out so soon."

Ike raised his voice. "Wonder when Larsen thinks he's gonna get up." Larsen pulled the blanket over his ears.

Charlie followed suit. "Wonder what happens to guys in the navy who show up late. Looks like Larsen wants to find out."

No response from the body in the bed. "Hey, Larsen! D'you plan to be late first day in the service?" Ike shouted, standing over the bed.

A muffled growl emerged from under Larsen's blanket before his tousled head appeared. "Jesus Christ! What're you guys shoutin' about in the middle of the night?"

"Middle of the night! Look who's talking about the middle of the night! That was when you came back. Look man, it's time to move. Get over to *Chippawa* or you'll be in deep crap."

Reluctantly Larsen threw back his blankets and sat up. "Oh, my God!" He dropped his head in his hands and groaned. "Just stop shoutin' will ya?"

Ike and Charlie looked at each other in amusement. "Maybe you should go on sick parade first thing."

"Yeah," Ike agreed, "D'ya think he'll live, Charlie?"

"OK. Lay off, you guys! I'm up and awake. How much time've I got?"

"None to waste, I'd say," said Charlie. "I'm goin' down for breakfast right now. Wouldn't want to miss that." He moved out the door.

"See you later, Larsen," said Ike as he followed Charlie downstairs.

The landlady's radio was blaring out the morning news: "*From London,*" the announcer intoned, "*Winston Churchill, as though raising at last the bright signal that will send the invading Allied armies plunging forward, quietly told the world today that amphibious attacks are near at hand in the European theatre. 'All is in readiness for this grand assault,' he made clear in a vigorous and heartening report. The Allied submarine position was getting better and better by the day, he said.*"[1]

Ike muttered as he sat in at the table, "They've been promising that 'grand assault' for so long, nobody'll believe it until they actually get some troops over the channel."

"Sh-h! Listen to this," urged Charlie, turning toward the radio.

"*Thousands of additional watches for enemy submarines will be on the alert along the shores of the St. Lawrence River and the Gulf this summer, Prime Minister Mackenzie King informed the House of Commons today. Last year subs sent 29 merchant ships to the bottom in the gulf and river area. In view of the anticipated recurrence of submarines this season, there was a question to whether the St Lawrence route would be served by merchant ships.*"[2]

"See? Just like I told my dad. It's time for us to get out there," said Charlie, hurriedly helping himself to more toast.

They had finished breakfast and reached the corner of the tree-lined street when Larsen caught up with them. A small piece of toilet tissue was stuck over a cut on his chin. He picked at it gently now as they walked along, trying to rid himself of the tissue without starting the nick bleeding again.

"Hey! You guys shoulda come with me last night. You missed a real hot time. D'you know who's billeted right next door to us?"

"Tell us. Who?"

"A whole houseful of girls, that's who. Boy! Talk about hittin' a jackpot! That's how come I got in so late last night. Me 'n this other guy, Wallace, he's billeted further down the street, caught up with these girls on our way back from the beer parlour. We'd sneaked out a coupla bottles of beer so we sat on the porch over there for a while an' finished 'em off an' then it didn't take us long to find out they're a couple of hot cookies, lemme tell ya!"

"Who are they and where from?" Ike interrupted.

"One of 'em is called Doris. She's from—oh damn, I can't remember where—and Betty, the other one's from the same place. We never got 'round to findin' out their last names. Hell, we had hardly finished the beer when they offered to take us upstairs."

"The girls took you upstairs? Their landlady must be a heck of a lot different than ours. First thing I was told was, `No women allowed!' and from the way she said it, I believed her," said Charlie.

"Well, the rules're the same over there so it wasn't easy. We hadda wait till their landlady went to bed before they could sneak us up into their room. The Old Lady over there, she sits in her kitchen at the back, see, where she can keep her eye on the front door, an' she stays there till 'leven o'clock when she locks up.

Well, at 'leven o'clock the girls went in and us guys, we acted as if we were leavin' but we just walked around the block and when we got back, there was Doris, ready to let us in. Meanwhile, Betty was upstairs, flushin' the toilet and runnin' the taps and walkin' around so the Old Lady wouldn't hear us climbing the stairs."

"So, you got upstairs, but how was the necking?" Ike figured Larsen's story sounded like a lot of bull-shit to him. It had taken weeks and months of smiles and soulful looks and hand-holding walks before he had ventured to put his arm around Sara's waist. And this guy was trying to make him believe....

"Neckin'?" Larsen snorted at Ike's question. "Neckin'? Whadd'ya mean, neckin'? We didn't waste any time with neckin'! Look, man, I'm not near dead this morning from neckin'. Hell! I can hardly walk."

Ike felt himself redden at Larsen's tone. He hadn't actually said "dumb farmer" but it was in his voice and that's how Ike felt. "Dammit!" he said regretfully, trying to redeem himself. "If I'd known that, I'd've come along last night."

"Well, there's more than them two dames billeted in that house and they'll still be there tonight."

"Yeah, well, maybe we should check 'em out. Whadd'ya say, Charlie?"

"Thanks, but I'm saving up for when I go home on the weekend."

Ike thought of his promises to Sara, but what the heck, Larsen's story was just a lot of wind. Besides, just going along tonight didn't mean he had to do stupid things, did it? They reached *Chippawa* and all talk about the evening was dropped as they became part of a stream of blue collared sailors moving through its brass-bound doors.

Chapter 3

HMCS *Chippawa*

He moved out of the cool corridors of the administration building onto the parade square, dazzled by the array of white uniforms already lined up in groups of twenty. This time his name served him well. Friedlen didn't have to stand in the first row as his squad formed up. Thank God he'd have someone else in front of him to get the signal from as orders were called out.

Mouth stretched wide open (it seemed to stay open for a long time), the officer bellowed, "Co--Agee-ee-ee – Te-----Shun!" No trouble with that one. Everyone snapped to attention, eyes front. Ike decided to watch the officer's mouth carefully so as not to miss the next order. "Fo-o-o- Mah!" This time he barely caught sight of the officer's tonsils before the mouth snapped shut.

The squad began marching and Ike had to do a quick hop to get in step with the man in front of him. "RI-I-I- Tu-u-uh!" Ike congratulated himself. He'd been pretty sure what was coming because the squad from the opposite side of the square was marching directly towards his own group. A few more times around and the business of winning the war was beginning to look a lot easier. Another bellow from the officer and Ike turned smartly to his right. What was this? He found himself about to collide with another squad! "Co-- eye Ha-alt!"

"Friedlen? Where the hell do you think you're going? Don't you know your left from your right? Get back in line." He wanted to shrink into his boots as he hurried back into place. "That will be one hour of Number 9, Friedlen! When I say `Left turn' you turn left. Or didn't they teach you right from left on the farm?" Ike could have told him the problem was the language being used. English is what he understood. And what in hell was Number 9?

Parade drill seemed to go on for hours. A break at noon and then more drill. When it was finally over, the Number 9 mystery was solved and Ike had time to ponder the language of the parade square as he trotted around it, holding a rifle above his head. Perhaps the language was a form of code. That was it. Didn't want the enemy to understand the orders being given. As the posters kept reminding all citizens, we couldn't be too careful. Spying ears might be anywhere. Good thinking on the part of the navy, but still, they might have let him in on it beforehand. After all, he was on their side, wasn't he?

After half an hour his arms ached and trembled from lack of circulation. Shovelling wheat was easier. Two other unlucky recruits trotted with him. Perspiration trickled down the middle of Ike's back forming rivulets along his legs. His feet weighed a ton. His chest felt tight. He couldn't breathe deeply enough. To his left someone stumbled, righted himself and fell behind. Ike heard his rasping gasps for breath and then a crash! The recruit had fallen to the ground. His rifle skidded along the pavement and his hat went rolling ahead, wheeling around and around in wobbly circles before settling down flat on the parade square tarmac.

Ike and the other survivor continued trotting. As they reached the far boundary of the square a welcome "H-A-A-T!" came bellowing after them. "DISMISSED!" No other command. The man on the pavement lay still. His face had turned to a murky gun-shirt white from his normal, cheery red.

Supper was over and the kitchen closed when Ike got back to Kennedy Street. Charlie was sitting on the edge of his bed, polishing his boots. Ike flopped down on his own bed. "I pinched a couple of slices of bread for you, Ike, but I couldn't get anything else. Saw you on the square. I figured you'd need something when you got back."

"Thanks, Charlie. I don't think I'd have the strength to go out to get anything tonight." He described his experience.

"I figured it wouldn't be any fun. I know the drilling officer. Name's McCurdy".

"Well, he must have escaped from a nuthouse somewhere. Crazy as a loon."

"He signed up about a month ago. Back home weekends, he's strutting like an admiral."

Ike lay with his eyes closed for a little while, then looked over at Charlie who was still polishing his boots. "Y'know him 'n he's only been in the navy for about a month. How in hell did he get to be an officer that fast?"

"Signed up as an Officer in Training. Was in a cadet corps in high school and been to university."

Cadet corps! What in heck was a cadet corps? Ike didn't dare ask. Charlie spoke as if everybody knew what cadets were, but Ike knew only that no such corps had existed in the one-room school he had attended. As for becoming an officer by going to university, what a strange idea! "Poor Benny" was the only one of his schoolmates who had gone off to university and that peculiarity was never spoken of in the community without mention of his fateful accident.

Benny had broken his leg at age twelve and old Doctor Lasken didn't quite get the bones set properly and so he wasn't fit for the hard work of farming. Although Benny was the smartest boy in his class, it was his bad leg that persuaded his hard-driving Old Man to let him go to university.

Until now, Ike had always thought of university students as a bunch of guys who had to keep on studying because they didn't have a hope of making a living otherwise. But by gosh, the navy was making them officers. Before they even got to sea!

Well, McCurdy might have learned a lot of things in university, Ike reflected, but any dumb farmer could have told him he was running that kid too long this afternoon. Surely McCurdy must have seen him stumble several times before he collapsed. The Old Man had always warned his boys not to work a horse too long. He said you might as well shoot an animal that collapsed in the traces. It would never completely recover. Ike hoped the recruit would be OK. Was there no time limit set in Regulations for Number 9's? Did one have to collapse before McCurdy called a halt, he wondered.

He himself would know better when he became an officer, Ike decided. Of course, he was never going to be an officer on a base in the middle of prairie-dry Manitoba. A real ship's officer, that's what he would be. An officer who had earned his rank by doing something more heroic than attending university. He pictured himself in a peaked cap trimmed with plenty of gold braid, leaning on the white rail of a ship, plowing through blue seas dotted with white flecks of curling, foaming waves. How soothing the motion of those curling waves!

The boot Charlie had been polishing thumped to the floor and roused Ike from his half-doze, half reverie. He sat up and reached for a piece of bread.

"Charlie, where the heck is Larsen?" glancing at the disordered, vacant bed. "Has he gone girling already?"

"Yeah, Ike, he's off again. He said if we wanted to catch up with him, he'd be in the beer parlour at the Aberdeen. You want to go?"

"Gosh, no! If I can get to the bathroom and back I'll be lucky." A relief to have an excuse not to go. He admired Larsen's style. That guy sure looked and acted as if he knew his way around—like a real sailor should—and Ike felt the need to fill his own uniform with something of the same swagger. Still, during the day he'd spent some time wondering what he would do if he went out with Larsen and got teamed up with a "hot cookie" too. He didn't really want to get mixed up with any girl like that. After all, he was in love with Sara and had promised to be true to her. He'd just watch Larsen from the side-lines for a while.

"Darn! My neck and shoulders are sore! I just hope Larsen doesn't barge in here waking us up in the middle of the night again. On second thought, I won't hear him tonight no matter how much noise he makes."

He need not have been concerned about Larsen. His bed had not been slept in when Ike and Charlie awoke next morning. It remained empty, in fact, almost every night until they were near the end of their Basic Training. He dashed in, washed up and shaved in the mornings then made his way to *Chippawa*. He and Wallace usually came hurrying along behind Ike and Charlie, barely catching up before they reached the porticoed entrance.

But Larsen, never late for Divisions, always managed to look good enough to escape getting bawled out on the parade square. Ike often wondered how he got along so well with so little effort. He and Charlie spent hours polishing their boots, keeping bell bottoms clean and folded just right with all the seven seas in creases across the bottom, and still McCurdy found a reason to call them out from time to time.

Ike never had to do Number 9's again, but when he made the mistake of wearing his whites home one rainy weekend just because Sara thought they looked so wonderful, and there had been no time to wash out the mud splatters around the hems of his flaring bell bottoms before Divisions on Monday morning, darned if McCurdy hadn't fixed his eagle eyes on the spots as soon as the squad formed up.

"Friedlen! Waddya think this is, a fucking road gang? Get those goddam pants clean and keep 'em clean! Report for half an hour of Number 11!"

On Number 11 he carried a rifle while trotting around the parade square but, unlike Number 9, he did not have to hold it aloft so Ike felt almost as if he had gotten a reprieve this time. Yet the question of how Larsen got away with so little effort troubled him as his boots pounded the pavement. How was it that Larsen could carry on with swearing and drinking and sleeping with strange women without suffering any punishment?

Ike himself had serious worries about what had been happening between himself and Sara. The way she clung to him on weekends now that he would soon be off to war was wonderful, but it sure made it hard to hold back when he got his arms around her. Impossible, in fact. They told each other they would get married as soon as she was old enough, but his mother had always said fornication was fornication and you couldn't hide anything from God. Maybe that's why he was constantly stumbling into trouble. Yet here was Larsen, not hiding anything from anybody and not even trying to stick to every rule and regulation. How come he never got stuck doing Number 11?

Perhaps risking your life for your country gave you a special deal on the punishment business. Fighting Hitler should weigh in pretty heavily on the "Good" side of the scale, shouldn't it? Except that if you were a Mennonite, going to war weighed in on the "Bad" side, right in there along with fornicating. That raised the question of whether he was a Mennonite now. He had learned his catechism along with the rest of his class when he was fourteen, but he'd never quite been willing to take the next step. He'd never applied to get baptized so he wasn't actually a member of the church.

Ike had often thought about joining church. If he had been ready to marry Sara and settle down, they would want to belong. But settling down on a farm, going to church every Sunday.... Well, there were a lot of other things he'd like to do first. That was why he'd started to go to town and hang around with the town boys on Saturday nights. There wasn't much to do in Highfield but it beat listening to the radio at home or going to *jugendverein*, the Sunday evening program for young people. The last time he and Jake Thiessen and Ed Falk had gone to *jugendverein* they'd gone ten miles to Rudnerweide to get in on this hot new kind of entertainment. The Sommerfelder church close to home didn't approve of these programs. It wasn't very long ago that the suggestion of having such a program had been so shocking to most Sommerfelders that it caused a split in the congregation. Members holding to such new-fangled ideas had founded their own congregation and built their first church in Rudnerweide.

That evening Ike and his buddies had chosen to sit up in the balcony at the back of the church and were amusing themselves by making wise cracks about the girls in the pews down below when the minister suddenly stopped in the middle of his homily and said, "I'll just pause for a minute now and let the boys in the balcony say what they have to say before we go on with the program. Which one of you wants to speak first?" He chuckled now at how they had sheepishly slunk down the stairs, out of the church and sped back the way they had come.

That wasn't the only time he'd been rebuked for not being quiet and solemn in church. He could still hear his father saying with sad resignation at the end of an angry harangue, "Well, boy, it seems you still have the wild oats prickling in you." Perhaps it was partly those oats that had got him into Canada's navy.

Ike tried not to think of the tears that had come to his mother's eyes when she first saw him in uniform. Still, she had held out her arms to him when he walked into the kitchen, while his father just cleared his throat and turned to look out the window.

He had not told Ike to get out of the house and to stay out as long as he was in uniform, which was what Ike had half expected, but Ike knew he no longer belonged in the way he always had.

Better not worry about it all, he told himself. Just concentrate on getting through with this darned Number 11. How sick he was of all the routine of marching back and forth, rifle drills, salutings and getting bawled at every hour of the day. He could hardly wait for the end of Basic Training. After all, there were no warships or German U-boats on the parade square and he had joined up to win the war.

* * *

Ike shivered slightly and gazed at the green-blue pool water. He wasn't cold. He was scared. Six weeks basic training and six weeks being shouted at. Might as well be dead in the water. Right here. The grapevine had it down pat. No recruit got sent to sea without passing the swim test. Some of his friends back home had learned to swim in Rempel's dugout, but the Friedlen boys hadn't had time for such foolishness. After all, what practical use was there in learning to swim? No situation on a prairie farm demanded the skill so he and his brothers never learned it.

At *Chippawa*, however, Ike had taken swimming lessons daily along with the rest of the squad, but somehow he hadn't quite mastered the trick of keeping the water on the outside and air on the inside of his lungs while breathing in the pool. He had managed, with a great deal of froth and fury, to get from one end of the pool to the other once or twice, but now he'd have to do it with all his gear on. Word among the ranks was that they'd never yet let a recruit drown in the attempt, but there was always a first time for everything. Then again, they'd pull you out for sure on the second time down. Ike hadn't found time to pray very often lately, but the silent plea he sent aloft now made up in fervour for his recent lapses in frequency. The least he could do to improve his chances.

McCurdy bellowed instructions. Four men at a time, three lengths of the pool for a pass. In at the shallow end, swim to the deep end and back, then finish off at the deep end.

All too quickly the first four were in and out heading for the showers. Ike jumped in along with his mates. Damn it! The boots were heavy. The deep end seemed to recede rather than come nearer with each splashy stroke. Stroke, kick. Stroke, kick. That's what the swimming instructor had chanted. He reached the far end at last and managed to sneak a quick breath before heading back to the shallow end.

Wet as he was, heat and sweat seemed to be gathering under his woollen jumper. On reaching the shallow end he discovered his thighs had turned wooden, numb. "No stopping at the turn!" audible from somewhere, but Ike let one leaden foot sink to the bottom for a kicking start on the last length. If McCurdy saw it, he didn't let on.

Stroke, kick. Stroke, kick. Stroke, splash, paddle, kick, kick. He gasped and choked. Lungs bursting, he fought pool water making its way down his nose. Paddling furiously, all rhythm of strokes and kicks lost in panic, he coughed, gasped and swallowed. Unable to breathe, overcome suddenly by a strange comforting dizziness, he yielded to that gravitational drag, down, down, do-o-ow-own. His own voice seemed to be echoing in his fading consciousness, "Never going to sea -- drowning -- finished -- finished -- finished --." Black dots merged to a burning blackness....

"Are you OK? Friedlen! Are you OK?" McCurdy's voice sounded as if it were coming from a far distance. Ike's stomach heaved. Retching and coughing convulsed his body. He felt the cold tiles of the pool's apron on his cheek as McCurdy pummelled his back. He was alive!

"S--S --Sir!" he sputtered and spat. He was almost glad to feel his nostrils burning and his chest ache. He coughed, spat and blew his nose. Larsen and Charlie, both sopping wet, crouched down beside him. He yielded gratefully to their assistance in getting on his knees and on to his wobbly feet. Coughing and spitting, he staggered past the relieved McCurdy.

"I guess you're OK"

"Sure, I'm OK"

"Well, head for the showers and get into your dry uniform."

McCurdy said nothing about his dismal performance but slowly the pain of what it meant overwhelmed Ike's relief at having survived. His trembling legs could hardly drag his squishy boots across the floor to the locker room where the first lot of men were lathering up cheerfully.

"I guess it's a desk job for you, Friedlen," shouted Larsen when he came in. Peeling off his wet uniform he began to warble,

> He joined the navy
> To see the world
> And what did he see
> HMCS "C" and Kennedy –

Disconsolately, Ike pulled on his dry clothes and tagged after the others, back to the parade square for final inspection. Possibly they'd make him go through another six weeks of Basic Training. More drill on the hot parade square pavement, more being bellowed at about a dirty dickey, a poorly shaved chin, or boots short of a mirror-like shine. Stuck with participating in a tidy, smartly dressed, clean war at HMCS *Chippawa*. The sight of the brown linoleum floors of the main building suddenly depressed him. How damned innocent and naive he'd been to consider the men trotting around on these spotless floors, wafting papers in their hands, as ideals to aspire to.

His chest ached from water he'd inhaled but more so from the very first lines of poetry he had been exposed to, running through his head:

> I must go down to the sea again
> To the lonely sea and the sky...

Ever since the teacher had read them out in class, he had resolved that someday, yes by Jeepers, some day, the day would come. He'd escape, run away from the endless sweep of dry prairie with its monotonous waves of wheat, of oats, of barley, and go to find adventure on a "high ship" with only "a star to steer her by." But he'd failed. Failed the test.

"Co-ane-e-e-T-e-e-e-e-Shun!"

Heels clicked, they stood rigidly at attention, waiting for their fate to be read out to them from a paper the officer held in his hand.

"Compane-e-e has passed Basic Training! You are now fit to proceed with sea service training. Pick up your assignments!" With that the peaked cap and brass buttons turned to walk the brown battleship linoleum in the administration building.

Ike stood stunned. He couldn't believe it. The entire class. He'd passed! He fairly flew toward the lineup for Sailing Orders.

V-63485 Isaac Davenport Friedlen. Posted to HMCS *Cornwallis*. Report for duty on August 5, 1943.

Attached was a forty-eight-hour pass and a railway ticket. Finished with the humiliating Basics! Two more days and he was going to sea!

Chapter 4
The Train

Ike raised the blind. He peered at the parade of shadowy trees and rocks passing by. By "Lights Out" last night the train had passed beyond the flat, open prairies to enter the rocky Canadian Shield. He had only dozed fitfully through the long night, unaccustomed to the rhythmic click of the wheels on the track and the boisterous, boozy celebrations at the other end of the coach.

Saying goodbye to Sara had been tough. Much more difficult than he had expected. He had known she would cry but had not thought that he would too. Only when it had been time to leave for the station had the fact that he would not see her again for months or years become real to him.

Somehow, in the excitement of defying his Old Man, of joining up, of strutting beside her along Highfield's Main Street in his uniform while on weekend leave, the prospect of leaving her behind had seemed way off in some distant future. Now it had actually happened. Now, after fifteen hours of interrupted napping, he still felt that unusual, never-before-experienced ache. A heavy feeling not readily attributable to sitting up during most of the night. How many nights more like this lay ahead? Two? Three?

Larsen and Charlie were still asleep so he was free to take her picture out of his pouch to fix her image in his memory. Gee, she was good looking! Better looking, in fact, than in her picture. He closed his eyes to see her rushing down the stairs toward him when he'd first come home on leave. The look in her shining eyes, even in memory, made his heart thump.

His seat mates began to stir and stretch so Ike hastily stowed the picture away. He wouldn't mind if Charlie saw it, but he couldn't face the kind of comments Larsen would make. He'd probably try to compare her with those girls on Kennedy Street. He shuddered at the thought.

They got up and lurched unsteadily towards the lavatory and on beyond it to the dining car. Bodies in the seats they passed barely stirred at the call for breakfast. They sat down at an empty table and watched, bleary-eyed, as a small pond amid more conifers and rocks slid by the window. Someone on the opposite side of the car shouted suddenly, "Hey, look! A bear! A bear!" but they failed to catch a glimpse of what might have been a welcome change in the endless procession of trees and rocks.

The waiter plunked their plates down on the white, table linen that somehow looked less elegant than it had under the lights at supper last evening. Ike stared down at two egg yolks quivering at him with naked abandon, rhythmically attuned to the swaying coach and clacking wheels. Each golden, staring orb lay encircled by a quarter inch of translucently clear egg white. Was this what CN called fried eggs? His youngest sister would not have set such a plate in front of him at home. Why, even though the men in his family had only been observers of what went on with the pots and pans at home, he himself had been able to baste eggs into a state of decency. At the boarding house on Kennedy, eggs had arrived hard and lukewarm, not to his liking either, but this was going to require courage. He noticed the yokes being G-forced off centre with the coach's sway as it followed the curve of another lake.

He reached for salt and pepper. The generous lashing of black and white particles lent a touch of modesty to the greasy, golden glare of the yolks. It occurred to him that he must get on with it. The privilege he'd had while on Kennedy Street, where he could rely on small cafes only a few blocks away to replace any horrors in the dining room, were not available to him now. Dig in!

A new, uncomfortable thought smote him. Life on board ship was going to be like this. With a pang, he remembered the look on his sister's face when he and his brothers had teased her for letting the potatoes scorch slightly at the bottom of the pan. In memory now, their aroma came back to him as utterly delicious. The warm kitchen and his mother's tearful face the day he left home rose before his eyes and he had to lean towards the window, pretending to see something interesting, until he blinked his own eyes clear again.

He turned back to the eggs. If it had to be done it'd be better to get it over with quickly, he reminded himself. Leaning forward over the plate he briskly pitched an unbroken egg into his mouth whole. Chewed rapidly and swallowed quickly, the egg was gone before he realized that it tasted all right. Trying for a new sensation, he vigorously stirred the second runny yolk into the lump of fried potatoes. He'd win the war yet.

Occasional stops at stations that were no more than huts did little to break the tree and rock monotony. Larsen had stopped at a poker game as they made their way back from the dining car. On his way to the lavatory Ike stopped to see how Larsen was doing. Ike had played many games of whist, cribbage and hearts at home on long winter evenings and had watched his older brothers playing bridge, too. But any card-playing for money had been strictly forbidden, so he didn't know much about poker.

Everyone in Highfield knew of the continuous poker game going on in the back room of Unger's Tin Shop, but he and his friends had always scorned the company of the old geezers who played there. This, however, was a different crowd. Larsen had a pile of coins and several crumpled bills in front of him. His pile seemed bigger than those held by the others he was playing with. Ike watched with keen interest.

"Hi, Friedlen! Shall I deal you in?" Larsen asked.

"Sorry, I'm broke." He still had most of his pay but he couldn't say he didn't know the game or that he wouldn't join in because Mennonites were not supposed to gamble. Besides, he might just try a hand some day when he had a better idea about how to play. He'd been pretty good at cards at home and it would be nice to build an extra pile of money like Larsen. He watched Larsen closely. Didn't take a card every time the deal came around to him, nor did he keep on betting on every hand. Ike learned. All the while, Larsen added to his pile more often than he subtracted. Definitely an interesting game but he'd keep an eye on Larsen for a while longer before betting his own money. It seemed that in cards as in so many other matters, Larsen got ahead.

By mid-day they approached a town of considerable size, the first since daylight. Their coach drifted past a series of fuel tanks and galvanized warehouses. Dispirited filling stations interspersed with seedy looking cafes sporting Coca Cola decals across their front windows and an assortment of nondescript clapboard buildings stared back at them across the street running alongside the tracks. Steel wheels screeched along steel tracks and the train stopped with a jolt. The conductor bawled from the end of the coach, "Nakina! Thirty minutes!"

A murmur of gratitude ran along the car as cramped legs unfolded themselves and creakily made their way along the aisles. Larsen, still stuffing bills into his money belt, came back for his hat. He, Ike and Charlie jumped out onto the cinder bed of the track. Their coach was a long way from the railway platform crowded with uniformed bodies jostling each other among carts full of baggage and mailbags.

Charlie suggested they walk the other way round the caboose of the train. Thirty minutes passed far too quickly and they had to get back on the train. Ike shifted uncomfortably in his seat. "Two more days and nights on this darned train," he grumbled. "My ass'll have callouses an inch thick by the time we get there." After a couple of jerks and jolts, the rhythm of the clacking wheels resumed. More spruce trees, more rocks, more swampy pools of brown water. And he had thought the prairies were monotonous.

Somebody had picked up a copy of the *Globe & Mail* in Nakina and the tattered front section finally made it to Ike's end of the coach. The headline made him sit bolt upright:

Mussolini Fired

Ouster Seen as Step in Bid for Peace

> *In a broadcast proclamation* to the people of Italy from *Rome at 11 o'clock Rome time tonight, King Victor Immanuel announced to the Italian nation that he had accepted the "resignations" of Premier Benito and his entire cabinet. He appointed Marshal Pietro Bodoglio in his place..."to continue the conduct of the war."*

> *Rome radio then signed off for 20 minutes, resuming its broadcast to carry the marshal's proclamation to the nation. It appealed to the nation for calm."*[3]

Ike shook Charlie's shoulder. "Hey! Read this! Looks like great news from Italy."

Charlie rubbed his eyes and grabbed the paper, skimming the print to the bottom of the page. "Yeah! It says Mackenzie King was 'jubilant' at the news. It must be true. It must mean we've got the Italians on the ropes. That's great! Except we're still at war and they're still sinking merchant ships. See the next page? There'll still be lots of fighting before we're through. We'd better get some sleep." He curled up sideways as best he could and closed his eyes.

Leaning back Ike dozed fitfully again, and when he woke, kept his eyes away from the window. A stupor in which time seemed suspended settled upon the coach. Conversation sank to an occasional grunt. Even the poker players gradually drifted away from their table one by one.

Mealtimes came and went and then another night of trying to find space in which to stretch out cramped legs, backs, arms. Ike was so numb he barely noticed when they rolled into Toronto, but he roused himself to get out and stretch his legs while the train sat wheezing beside the crowded platform.

When they fell in on the platform in Montreal the platoon from *Chippawa* shrank to half its original size as some members fell out to report to various bases in Quebec. Like dazed automatons, the rest marched down one set of stairs and up another. Ike realized he couldn't understand the shouts and conversations in the crowd around them. They were speaking French! Then he recalled going to St. Malo with his dad for firewood. The farmer they dealt with there hardly spoke English. There were other towns east of Red River whose baseball teams spoke French all the time when they came to tournaments. He'd always thought it a shame "Frenchies" couldn't speak English. After all, Canada was part of the British Empire so everyone ought to speak English.

They climbed on board another train already partly filled with civilians. Stumbling along the aisle crowded with a ragtag collection of bags and bundles, Ike and Charlie and Larsen finally found three seats together and sank down to endure the last part of their journey, a passage seemingly composed of more screeching stops and lurching starts than of swaying forward motion. By the time they reached *Cornwallis,* many of the other familiar faces had disembarked enroute. Of the *Chippawa* platoon only a handful remained to step off into the slowly falling rain. Amid a troop of strangers they marched up the hill towards a range of barrack huts.

The reddish water trickling downhill alongside the roadway held Ike's gaze. A truck behind them sounded its horn and as they moved to the side of the narrow road to let it pass their feet left its hard-packed surface. "Dammit!" someone behind Ike grumbled. "Damn, it'll take me an hour to bring back the regulation pusser shine to these boots and I'm dead tired."

Ike looked down at his own boots to assess the amount of mud he'd have to clean off before turning in for the night. A narrow rim of reddish sand along the sides of his thick soles! Obviously not real mud at all. It wasn't black nor did it cling in great sticky gobs like Manitoba Red River Valley gumbo.

It was definitely something he would write home about. Farming couldn't be much good around here. His father had often mentioned that whenever their Mennonite forefathers migrated, they had searched for good, black land to start new settlements. Unlikely that they would have settled here to farm.

Chapter 5
Stoker

Plodding through the rain, the platoon passed row upon row of barracks. Their dingy drabness harmonized with the acrid smell of coal smoke mingling with the mist. So this was H.M.C.S. *Cornwallis*! They marched past the huge parade square gleaming wetly in the fading light. The image did not promise many joys but Ike was too exhausted to speculate.

"Compan–ee–ee–ee Halt! Able Seamen, fa--a--ll out!" More than half the company marched off towards a hut nearby. Like somnambulists, the stokers marched up the slope, out through an arched gateway and across a paved roadway towards assigned quarters.

Tiers of double bunks set back to back on either side of the doorway, extended along two sides of the long barrack. Ike and Charlie had been assigned to an upper and lower bunk in the same tier. Larsen bunked on the opposite side further along the corridor near the block of showers and lavatories that tied their hut to its neighbor in H-formation.

Sea bags slung from bunks on the left indicated that the tier was already in use so Ike and Charlie slung their damp bags onto the right side of their tier. Hungry, they made their way through steady drizzle to join the lineup in front of the mess hall. A clatter of cutlery, a drone of men's voices, the smell of wet, woolen uniforms and boiled stew gave a foretaste of what to expect inside well before they reached the shelter of the hall itself.

Briefly the unsavoury odors of scraping a scalded pig flickered across Ike's memory as he picked up his dishwasher-wet metal tray. The image of a raw, steaming carcass, dirt-encrusted, slung by the hind legs from rings in the barn ceiling, doused with kettles-full of boiling water, being freed from bristles and grime in patches of pink that grew under swift glistening knife strokes, had to be resolutely repressed.

He made his way along the counter fronting a line of steaming cauldrons. A ladle of soup, a spoonful of anemic-looking peas and carrots, something brown and fatty afloat in gravy, a clump of mushy potatoes and a gob of a sticky rice mixture were plopped into his sectioned tray. He hoped the dark spots in the rice were raisins.

One spoonful of the soup and Ike decided to sample the other sections of his tray. He cut into the slab of meat. "I wonder what they feed the beef around here to give the fat such a yellow color," he remarked. "Must be corn. Our beef never looked like this at home." In his peripheral vision, the mess hall swayed like the railway dining car. He shook his head to clear away the sense of motion.

"No meat I've ever had tasted like this either," muttered Charlie. "Wonder if it's beef or what."

Ike sniffed at the piece he was lifting to his mouth. "Doesn't smell like anything I've had before." He chewed it and tried to swallow, but found the mass wouldn't go down. He took a large mouthful of water and sluiced the gob down his throat. He looked at Charlie and noticed a greenish pallor extending along his jaw-line. The mess hall was swaying again. "Four days on a train and nothing stands still anymore."

"Down the hatch, boys," said a tall, lean guy sitting across from them. "After youse been here as long as I'ave, hossmeat begins to taste real good."

Ike groaned. "Horsemeat! You must be kidding! We ship horsemeat overseas but, jeepers, not here in Canada?"

"Yeah, in Canada. Nobody in charge o' stores'll ever admit it's hosses, but I was talkin' to a guy who told me he knows hoss meat when he sees it and you're seein' it tonight."

Ike's fork toyed with what was left of the meat on his plate. He thought of Jessie, the horse that had taken the buggy full of his brothers and sisters to school every day for years and years. His fork refused to co-operate. He wasn't entirely convinced about the horsemeat stuff but he hoped there would be identifiable chicken in the cauldrons tomorrow.

"How long you been here?" Charlie asked the stranger.

"Three weeks. Only one more t' go before I gets me a ship, if I passes the bloody exams, that is." He sighed, raising another forkful of food to his mouth.

"What exams?"

"Steam engineerin', and damned tough I'll tell ya. I got through signals and all that crap, no sweat, but all this business of pressure gauges and valves and compression chambers is drivin' me nuts. But I've just got to get through or I'll be in this hell hole for 'nother four weeks."

Ike tackled the rice pudding. He reached for the milk jug, thinned the pudding down a bit and discovered it tasted reasonably good. He resisted examining the brown spots too closely, hesitant to find legs. Legs, and he'd be done for. They tasted like raisins, unwashed raisins he decided as his teeth crunched something gritty. The mess hall still swayed at the corners of his vision.

Ike thought about food, good food, home cooked food. Prepared by Mom and the girls, food the men folks took for granted would always be served on time and be delicious. Never gave any other possibility a thought so they sat down and ate. Now, however, he remembered.

He tried to summon up the flavour and texture of home cured, oak-flavoured, smoked ham. Hams, cold-smoked at home for three to four weeks, then hung from rafters in the hay loft from which they were retrieved as needed all summer long. Baked, fried, or boiled and blended with fresh or bottled vegetables, always superb, as were smoked bacon and sausages. His favourite delicacies, however, had been the pickled pork served cold: tongue, cheeks, snout, ears, head cheese, jaws, hocks and feet lifted out of a 20-gallon pickle crock and most times dipped in vinegar. Oh, for the freshly deep-fried spare ribs and cracklings sprinkled with salt and a fresh, home-made bun in hand to mop them up.

The clatter of his spoon falling into his tray jolted him awake. He had dozed off, sitting up. "C'mon, Charlie. We still have to clean our boots for parade in the morning. See you around," he nodded to the chap across the table as he got up.

"Sure hope I don't get kitchen detail in this place," gloomed Charlie as they stacked their trays on top of the towering pile at the end of the mess hall. Back in barracks they looked in on Larsen. His crumpled uniform lay on top of his blanket. He had crawled in under it, sound asleep. Shoved under his bunk beside his muddy boots lay his unopened sea bag.

A shrill, piercing whistle tore a hole in the misty web of Ike's dreams long before he was ready to face the new day. "Up an' at 'em! Up an' at 'em! Waddaya think this is? A fuckin' hotel or somethin'?" The litany, accompanied by the clang of metal bunk-ends being struck with a stick, made its way along the corridor.

In its wake a chorus of muttered curses and groans arose as bodies emerged from beneath the rows of white, woolen blankets. Ike opened one eye to look at the slit of sky visible through the small window above the bunks. Grey. Uniformly grey. The bedding of his cot felt strangely clammy and damp. Oh yeah, it's what they mean when they talk about "sea air," he said to himself, climbing into his limp PT shorts. "Everything is moist from the sea air." Saying that to himself changed the sensation on his skin from discomfort to something else, something mildly adventurous. Not on board a ship yet, but breathing sea air! He inhaled deeply while trotting out to the parade square in the lightly falling drizzle.

The platoon formed up on the square was blue-lipped and shivering. Ike's squad, finally ordered out toward the gates "O-on the Double!" eagerly ran to warm up.

They ran along the road that paralleled the inshore side of the base and followed it onward as it meandered between fields and farmsteads. They turned a corner and began trotting along a rising slope. Ripening apples dotted with water drops hung just inside a fenced orchard, almost near enough to touch. Cows grazed in the next meadow and up ahead lay a field of red earth turned by a plow.

Oxen! Ike lost his running rhythm at the sight. Oxen hitched to a plow! His father talked of oxen on his grandfather's farm, but now even the horses that had replaced oxen were seldom seen on southern Manitoba farms. His father still had a couple of teams and a dusty job it had been when Ike had last walked behind them and the harrows.

Must have been about twelve or thirteen when he last put in a day like that. Even then his older brothers had been on tractors, doing other, heavier kinds of tillage. Seniority determined who drove the tractors and who had to work with horses and Ike recalled his frustration at the arrangement. Reason argued that a four-horse team was more complicated to handle than a tractor and should therefore have been driven by the older, stronger, more experienced sons. That was not the case. "The boys" operated the tractors. So Ike walked behind whenever horses were called on to supplement the tractors. By the time the youngest son, Ike's brother, was old enough for Ike to bump him to harrowing with the horses they were hardly ever used any more.

On the double they skirted more orchards and fields where oxen plowing left what Ike considered unimpressionable traces. He mentally calculated the futility of starting a day's tillage on the more than nine hundred acres farmed at home were they to employ teams of yoked oxen. They'd be starting fall ploughing there, too, by now, Dad and Abe and Benny. On tractors. With Pete gone to the Conscientious Objectors' camp, they'd have to hire someone else besides. If available. Some kid perhaps too young to be called up or somebody unfit for service in some other way.

The squad turned back in the direction of the base. How many miles had they run already, he wondered. Easy to tell back home where each intersection indicated that another mile had been passed. Here, neither fields nor corners came square and roads branched off at all angles. He could tell they'd gone a fair distance by the lead weight in his legs. He was warm and his breathing had deepened.

Before lining up for breakfast, Ike quickly showered. Charlie, whose squad had started earlier, was already at one of the long tables when Ike sat in. He couldn't see Larsen anywhere. "How's it goin', Chuck?"

"Another mile and they'd have had to carry me. It must have been near freezing, this morning. Will they keep us at it when it starts snowing? In shorts?"

"Let's hope we're both on board ship before we find out."

"Don't get your hopes up. I hear that quite a few of the guys in our hut are into their second time around on the steam training course. If they don't make it this time they'll be stuck in some barracks routine for the rest of the war. Suckers."

"Well, we've bloody well got to make it first time round. It can't be all that tough. An engine's an engine. Some are big, some small. That's how I look at it."

"Yeah, that's easy to say when you know what a small one looks like, but lots of these guys have never touched a motor of any kind. I'm glad I had to work summers in the printery at home. I didn't do that much with the little diesel that ran the works, but at least I know a gear from a piston."

The rain had stopped but a murky haze still hovered near ground level when they fell in on the parade square. The PO's gimlet eyes ran up and down over each member of the squad. "YOU!" he shouted at someone on Ike's right. "Did you sleep in that uniform last night? Waddya think this is? Some godforsaken, fuckin' lumber camp? Fall out! Over there!"

Ike thought it was Larsen who "fell out" but he didn't dare turn his head to check. A shadow of stubble, a wrinkled trouser leg, a soiled dickey—soon half a dozen had been singled out. Ike congratulated himself on his previous night's industry. "YOU!" Ike's heart sank. The finger, quivering with indignation, aimed itself at his chest. The PO had found a trace of red mud somewhere in the creases of his boots. "Didn't they teach you to clean your boots in Basics? Fall out!"

Damn! So his hurried work with his shoe brush had not been enough. Whatever it meant, it wasn't likely to be fun. He stepped out smartly and joined Larsen and the others while the finger-pointing went on. "YOU! YOU! And YOU!" He couldn't tell why these last victims were being separated from the platoon, but since no more were singled out, ten seemed to be the magic number.

Stepping briskly towards this select, small, glum-faced group, PO gave the command. "Report to Hut 19 for coal shoveling detail. Abo-out tu–!! Qui— Maa–a-a-a!!

Coal shoveling detail? What the heck was this all about? Some antique ship tied up close by just to keep the rank of stoker true to its origins? This had to be a joke.

They marched to the perimeter of the square and along a roadway, past a series of shingle-clad buildings. Ike stared intently over the shoulders of those in the lead. Holy Smoke! A black mountain of coal emerged from the mist. It dwarfed two-storied buildings beside it, buildings whose smokestacks betokened the base's power plant. The acrid smell of smoldering coal became sharper as they approached the pile. He tasted it on his tongue. He looked at the pile again. Ye Gods! That wasn't mist rising from its upper slopes. It was smoke! Why weren't the fire alarms sounding? He could see streams from water hoses playing idly over the gleaming black heap, but among the men in coveralls directing them none seemed in a hurry, let alone in panic.

They entered a hut where coveralls and boots were stacked on a long metal table. The choice was limited. Ike rolled up the pant-legs and sleeves on coveralls a size too large. Slowly the detail lined up again outside the hut. Pointing to the wisps of smoke curling upwards from the black mountain's bowels, the officer directing this emergency in what Ike considered a much too casual approach, issued an order in a voice that surely could be heard across the base, "Grab those shovels, get up there and start shovell-i-nngg!"

The detail stared at the officer and then at the mountain. Ten men, ten shovels and a pile of coal as long as a city block. Move it to where? How many years was this going take? Shoveling coal until the war's end? Because his ill-fitting boots had three grains of red soil on them?

"What the hell is this?" Larsen came alongside Ike, both clambering up the glistening, shifting slope.

"Darned if I know, but I'm finding it hard to believe this." Ike muffled his voice and continued to climb. Out of the officer's earshot, the grumbling began.

"Just my goddamned luck," a voice drifted down from those nearing fresh, hot, drifting wisps. "Second time up here for me. Both times, no wind. Damned smoke'll kill ya if ya stand over it. You'd think they'd find a better way to put out their goddamned fire."

"How long has this stuff been smoldering?"

"Dunno. It was burnin' when I got here a month ago. Some guys say it's been a couple a' years. Spontaneous combustion. They bulldozes more coal on top of it each time a load comes in so I guess it'll burn till hell freezes over."

"You've been here a month, eh? I just got here last night. I'm not impressed with this welcome party. Name's Friedlen, from *Chippawa*. Where you from?"

"Saunders, Toronto."

"Where do we start and where do we shovel it to?"

"Don't ask stupid questions. Just start someplace where there's smoke and shovel. Nobody gives a damn where you moves it to, see? Just keep movin' it. Akshally, keepin' the coal movin' ain't the idea. Keepin' us guys movin's the trick, I think."

Ike's thoughts turned back to the time he and his brothers had shoveled a pile of grain that had started to heat because it had been combine harvested before it was dry enough to store. How furiously they had worked trying to limit the spoilage! Even the Old Man had shoveled for a while. There had been a method to that job. They had spread the grain in shallow layers in a number of bins of the granary to expose as much surface as possible to the air. For several days they had shoveled, stirred and shifted until at last they met only coolness rather than a frightening warmth when they thrust their hands among the kernels. This job seemed like what he'd heard of Stony Mountain Penitentiary, except that the rock pile there would be cleaner.

They reached the top of the pile, spread out and got to work, each man flinging his shovelfuls according to his own inclination. Ike shoveled steadily around smoke for half an hour, trying to work downward towards its origin without inhaling the heavy, oily fumes wafting this way and that. He had never minded a shoveling job and the steady rhythm now loosened up those muscles not used during marches. Thrust and throw, thrust and throw. He wondered how far down they'd need to go to find a glow of embers that could be doused with the sprinklers. He stopped to lean on his shovel and looked around. Already the faces of his mates were heavily shadowed with black dust. The smoke seemed to have crept nearer his feet so he shifted his ground and started shoveling again and let his mind wander backwards to the last days of his farewell leave. Boy! How sweet those hours had been! Sara was in his arms again and the coal pile evaporated.

A change of sound broke in upon his reverie. Ike noticed that his was the only shovel still ringing rhythmically. "Time out fer a smoke," said Saunders, leaning on his shovel. The sky had been lightening gradually and now a small breeze sprang up, shifting the smoke away to the north. Suddenly the sun broke through, the low-lying haze rolled back, and there it was—the sea, the real, the actual sea!

The bay did not truly meet his expectations of what the sea would look like. Too closely hemmed in with rising hills. But directly offshore from the base lay a gleaming white ship, a real ship with four funnels! Ike's heart pounded at the sight. His dream of going to sea had seemed to recede ever farther from reach during the past weeks as each long lineup led to another parade square drill or paper chase. Now it was actually in sight! He almost laughed out loud. From where he stood he could see sailors moving about the decks and occasionally a face appeared at one of the portholes. A small motor launch pulled away from her, coming towards the shore-side wharf.

"Hey, Saunders. What's that ship out there?" He tried to keep the excitement out of his voice. Sound casual as if he'd seen a ship every morning of his life.

"That's Buxton. Trainin' vessel. 'Nother week 'n I'll be on 'er instead of on this shit pile. If I pass the damned exam, that is. Boy! I can hardly wait." Saunders spat by way of emphasis. They stood gazing longingly at the clean, white lines at rest amid a low lap of waves now glittering in the sun.

"Get those shovels moving up there!" came a shout from below. Reluctantly they bent to their task again. Thrust and throw, thrust and throw. With the gleaming ship afloat in his mind's eye, Ike gave no more thought to the futility of what he was doing. He'd be on her soon. In the meantime, he'd do his bit towards winning the war by shoveling coal, if necessary. You bet! He paused to shift his position, and as he straightened his back he noticed the awkward, lurching movements of some of the men in the group.

"Jeez! My arms are killin' me already 'n it ain't noon yet," Saunders groaned as he moved alongside.

"Heck, I'm not even warmed up yet." said Ike. "Do you guys from Toronto always do everything the hard way?"

"Waddaya mean, the hard way? You got an easy way to shovel this fuckin' stuff?"

"Well, not easy, maybe, but a lot easier than the way you're doing it. Try to swing that shovel nice and easy so that you only lift the weight of the coal once. You've got to plant your feet apart like this and get your left hand down on the handle about here so's you've got some leverage and then...." He bent down to demonstrate. "Try it, and you'll save your back."

Some of the other men had stopped working to watch. "What makes you such an expert, eh?" sneered one of them.

"Shoveling a boxcar or two full of wheat'll turn anybody into an expert. Even a dumb farmer has to learn some time." Ike's self-deprecating remark brought the group together as they turned back to shoveling.

"Yeah, but maybe it's smarter not to get too good at this," offered Larsen. "Get to be experts and they'll have us up here every goddam day."

At noon they marched to the mess hall in their dungarees, having taken time only to wash their hands and faces before falling into line. The queue, longer than the night before, enabled them to observe the smartly uniformed officers moving towards the officer's mess nearby. Ike looked down at his dungarees and at the ring of dust at his wrists and it seemed that the day when he'd be a smartly dressed first officer of a gleaming vessel like the one in the harbour now lay off beyond infinity.

The afternoon dragged on. Ike looked longingly at *Buxton* more and more frequently. As their backs wearied, the grumbling chatter among the men died away. Shovel-leaning pauses grew longer. Even the officer in the hut below grew tired of shouting at them to keep moving. Finally, the watch over, their coal tarred boots slid and slithered wearily down to the bottom of the pile. A shower had never felt better, unless it came after a day of combining barley, Ike reflected. But barley dust, though pricklier, washed off more easily. After soaping and sudsing and rinsing again and again, his toweled finger still dried black out of his ears.

"I wonder if these blisters would get me into sick bay," he heard a voice to his right.

"If I'm on coal-shoveling detail tomorrow, I'm definitely going to sick bay," came the rejoinder. "Let's see what orders have been posted."

"Boy! Tonight I could eat a horse."

"You will."

"It's another hour before first mess call. Let's go check out the canteen." Larsen was already moving off in that direction.

Ike had intended to head for his hut instead. He had promised to write Sara as soon as he got to *Cornwallis*. But Larsen shouted, "C'mon Friedlen! Let's wash down the fuckin' coal dust so we can tell what they're feedin' us tonight." So he joined the rest and trotted over to the canteen. Before the mess closed, they had time to quickly down a bottle.

Ike couldn't decide whether the hasty beer or the effects of coal smoke caused the corners of the mess hall to undulate while eating his supper. It wasn't chicken, nor last night's ground-up horsemeat, or any other identifiable ingredient in the meatloaf he tackled. He pushed the thought aside. And ate.

He intended to write Sara as soon as he got back to the hut. He'd better do it now. There might be a letter from her tomorrow. She had promised not to wait for his first letter but to write the very next day after he left. He still had to clean his boots and brush his uniform to be ready for tomorrow's inspection. He dug his clothes brush out of his bag.

Charlie cleaned his boots. Ike brushed his rig. He'd thought he looked great in it when he first put it on, but this morning he'd noticed that he and Charlie and other new recruits stood out from most on the parade square. Their uniforms looked bulkier, less sleek than those of men who had been here for a while.

Mitchell, bunked next to Ike, lay stretched out in his uniform, reading. While brushing away, Ike compared the fuzzy serge of his own pants with the smooth-surfaced texture of those that covered Mitch's long legs. Perhaps he'd worn them smooth. "How long you been in, Mitch?" he asked.

"Signed up in May. Been here for almost a month." A month of wear couldn't make that much difference.

"Looks like the navy got a new supply of uniforms between May and June." He held his pants next to Mitch's outstretched legs.

"Hell, no! Ya wanna know how to get yours looking like this? Take your shaver to 'em. All the guys do it. Makes 'em look salty. Just stretch your pants out straight and hold 'em so they don't wrinkle and you can get rid of that fuzz."

"C'mon Charlie, let's get at it." He dug into his sea bag for the shaving gear. Charlie looked skeptical.

"What if you cut into the cloth, Ike? You've got t' pay for the next pair, you know."

"Well, help me hold 'em straight and I'll handle the shaver. After all, it's a safety razor, isn't it? I'm gonna give it a try. If it works, I'll help you do yours."

Doubtfully, Charlie got a grip on the waistband of Ike's bell bottoms and Ike started shaving. "Hey! It works all right!"

"Of course, it does," said Mitch. "Didn't I say so?"

Larsen came in. "What the hell're you guys doin? Don't y'know we gotta get over to the canteen if we're gonna get any drinkin' done before it closes?"

"Heck, I can't leave these pants half done or I'll be on that stinking coal pile tomorrow for sure. Go ahead, Charlie, if you want. I'll manage by myself."

"Nah, I've got stuff to do, too. Some other time, Larsen."

"Jeez! You guys sure can waste a lotta time. Don't you know there are WRENS out there just waitin' to be found? We're not gonna meet 'em sittin' around like fools in this goddam barracks, shavin' our fuckin' bell bottoms!"

"He's got a point, Charlie. How about leaving yours till tomorrow? Can you wait just long enough for me to finish this pair, Larsen?" He hadn't started shaving his pants in order to appear foolish, especially not to Larsen.

A few minutes later, despite Charlie's reluctance, they were all on their way to the canteen. Larsen ordered a round of beer and Ike was about to follow suit when Charlie interrupted with, "Don't order any for me. I'm not havin' any."

"What the hell's this?" asked Larsen. "Just because we hauled you away from shavin' yer fuckin' pants doesn't mean you have to get mad and refuse to have a beer with us."

"Who says I'm mad? Just because I don't drink beer doesn't say I'm mad does it?" Charlie's tone was decidedly hostile. "Look, I promised my Dad I wouldn't drink and so I won't. And if you don't like it, that's just too bad."

"Oho! So we've got Daddy's little boy with us tonight, eh?" Larsen sneered. Charlie rose halfway from his chair.

"Hold it! Hold it! Hold It!" Ike extended his arms over the table to separate the would-be combatants. "Let's stop this before it gets started. I say, if Charlie doesn't want to drink beer, he don't have to drink beer. It's a free country, isn't it? Maybe he'd like a Coke. Dammit, let's sit back and enjoy ourselves. What did you say about WRENs, Larsen?"

But there were no women of any kind in the canteen, so Ike and Larsen had their beer while Charlie drank a Coke.

"Sure as hell goes down good after a day on that shit heap," Larsen lowered his bottle after his first swig.

"I still can't understand," said Ike, "how they're ever gonna get that fire out the way they're going at it. It just seems so damned foolish. Sending ten guys up there every day to shovel a few feet of the stuff back and forth. War'll be over before they ever accomplish anything. If the guys in charge can't figure out how to put out a fire in a coal pile, can we expect to win this war?"

"Look, Ike," Charlie's voice was all patience, "if the guys in charge didn't know what they're doing they wouldn't be in charge. Just because we can't understand it, doesn't mean they don't. It's not up t' us to figure it out either. They've got good reasons for letting that pile burn."

"Yeah!" exploded Larsen. "They've gotta keep it burnin' so's every damn day they can send ten guys up there for not gettin' their boots shined up. Miserable pricks. Can you think of a better way to make a man feel like crap?"

They talked. They listened to badly articulated statements on topics about which they knew little or nothing. They argued in circles until their bottles were empty, then went back to barracks. Till late they cleaned and polished their boots in silence. Then Ike, drowsy, sat over his writing tablet. At the top of the page, "Dearest Sara". He yawned. Where would he start? What would he tell her? Couldn't seem to find a way to begin the letter. Too dead to write. He'd think about it and write her tomorrow.

He awoke in the middle of the night with cramps in his stomach and rushed to "the heads," making it into the only free cubicle just in time. Was it the beer or the fumes he'd inhaled in the coal pile? According to rumbles coming from other cubicles, their occupants too were in deep trouble like he was. Coal fumes weren't the cause then, since he and Larsen were the only ones from this hut who'd drawn coal pile duty. His intestines revolted in sharp agony such as he'd never previously experienced. He was still doubled over in pain on the toilet seat when somebody hammered at the door.

"Hey! Open up! I'm desperate!" said a panic-stricken voice.

As much as he would have liked to sit still till his insides settled down, the multiple groans and curses outside the door forced him to quickly wipe himself and flee. Men crowded into the room; some not able to get into a cubicle, squatted on the floor in desperation. Others clutched their bellies, writhing in pain.

Ike pushed his way out of the stinking room, trying to hold back what was rising in his throat. He rushed outside, leaned against the hut, allowing his heaving stomach to have its way. He spat again and again, trying to clear the sour slime from his mouth before making his way back to his bunk. He needed water but refused to return to the lavatory for some. While other afflicted men, vomiting and groaning, fled the barracks, Ike nursed his unsettled abdomen lying down. His teeth chattered with cold but he turned out of bed to open another window to air out the accumulated stink. The smell of smoke from the coal pile drifted through the open window. Groans, moans and oaths arose from other bunks. He pulled the blanket over his head. Between trips to the toilets, where floors were being constantly sloshed with water, he dozed fitfully until morning.

The sick bay queue was longer than the one at the mess hall in the morning. Ike swallowed the pink concoction handed him, put the tablets in his money belt for use later in the day, and, feeling weak in the knees, walked toward the mess hall.

"What the hell, what the fuck, what the Christ did you guys poison us with yesterday?" The cooks faced abusive accusations, questions and threats as they ladled out sticky, overcooked porridge.

"Don't blame us. The dishwasher didn't rinse the dishes properly, that's all. Too much soap left on the dishes. It'll do it every time. Sure cleaned you guys out, eh?"

"Too much soap like hell," muttered Mitchell in the line ahead of Ike. "It was that goddam meat last night. Rejected by the packing plant in Halifax. You can bet on it. So they feeds it to us."

Unusual gaps around the mess hall tables were readily noticeable this morning. Instead of the normal cacophony of boasts and laughter, a low, resentful rumble filled the cavernous hall. Quickly, however, they became bolder and openly questioned how the war could be won if those in charge were unable to solve the problems of handling grub and extinguishing a coal fire. Eating his porridge soothed Ike's digestive tract somewhat and by evening he and most of the other hands had recovered sufficiently to enjoy genuine beef steak.

Chapter 6
Sunday

PT drill, lectures, uniform brush-up, boot polishing and laundry chore occupied a recruit's time during week days. On Sunday 1030 hours, drums rolled in the parade square, summoning the base to church parade. In brilliant sunshine, personnel formed up outside each hut. After days of mostly soggy weather, the clear sky and warm air spoke of special blessings. Ike's squad stood at ease until groups in front of the other huts had ordered themselves as well. A band struck up somewhere inside the main gate. Strains of "Anchors Aweigh!" swelled and sank as the breeze from the bay gathered gusty breaths and fell again.

Ike's squad fell in, marched across the road and passed through the gate. Gradually the music grew louder as they marched toward the parade square. The tramp of boots keeping time with drumbeats grew steadily stronger as group after group of bell-bottomed uniforms moved out from behind the rows of barrack huts. "Co--a-anee-ee Hutt!"

Reaching the parade square they drew themselves erect as the band major, horns, trumpets and thundering drums marched past. Platoon after platoon followed the band, until finally, they too fell into line. Twelve thousand feet marching in time to left-left-left, down the slope towards the square. Thousands of men moving as the blaze of horns and the roll of drums thundered along the valley and echoed back from across the bay.

Tramp! Tramp! Tramp! Tramp! The earth trembled to the accumulating rhythm, vibrating, burning lofty causes through trembling limbs to throbbing, swelling hearts. Ike's chest grew tight under his tunic at the sense of common destiny. To be in the Royal Canadian Navy. The strength of thousands flowed along his shoulder muscles. Exultation sent a surge of vigor almost like the throb of sex through his marching body. They wheeled left and marched on. Left-left-left, while ahead and behind them horns and trumpets spoke of honour, glory and valor. And he a part of it!

The music stopped. A moment to march to drums alone. Rat-a-tat-tat! Rat-a-tat-tat! And a magnificent booming thundering roll. What glorious drums they were! They spoke of guns, they spoke of might, they spoke of power and battle and the marching feet behind them chorused, yes! Yes! Yes! The cause was just, they had the might, they had the power to set things right.

The horns blared forth again proclaiming the "Hearts of Oak" that were marching off to war! Yes, he was actually off to war now, Ike thought. Let the enemy do its worst! Here was invincible strength and infinite vigor, bravery and courage, honour and glory, noble men in a noble cause! Lucky. Damn lucky. To be a part of it!

The brasses fell silent again and the drums marched the last platoons into place. A sea of men and women stood at attention, sailor hats tilted and braid-trimmed collars draped on square proud shoulders. The band struck up "O, Canada," and six thousand voices sang as one, the dominant, deep masculine tones rising and falling and ringing out their pledge to the skies. What matter now that he was Dutch and Charlie was Irish and Larsen Icelandic and Joe in front of him was Polish and Milo Greek. All Canadian, by darn, a body of dedication on guard for King and for a country stretching from *Cornwallis* to beyond Winnipeg. Tears pricked at Ike's eyelids as voices joined in the appeal for "those in peril on the sea." As the last strains of the hymn died away he noticed that others too were moved by its profound personal meaning for them.

"Compan-ee-ee-ee, A-a-a-R C-ee-ee-ees! Fa-a-all Out!" One by one, here and there, individual figures detached themselves to form an amputated limb that moved to where a priest in vestments stood before a makeshift altar, preparing to say mass, in a far corner of the square. Ike felt a small shock of surprise as Charlie broke ranks to join the small group of Catholics at their separate service. Hogan was Irish-Canadian. Hogan was an RC. He hadn't thought of that before. The feeling of communion engendered by the parade crumbled slightly at the edges.

"Ship's companee--ee–, ha-a-ats off!" Beside the flagstaff on the dais, too far away for Ike to be able to count the stripes on his sleeve, an officer read the lesson. He thought of the services in the little church at home where this very day elders in their black coats would parade towards the front to take their places on either side of the pulpit. Their peerless piety had long since failed to impress him. Not since the day he'd helped the red-faced church elder round up his Jersey cow after she'd leaped a fence in a state of romantic passion for the Friedlens' bull. He wasn't sure where the fine line between blasphemy and nearly innocent epithet lay, but the elder had trodden very near it, that was certain, and those echoes had ever after risen between the pious Sunday face and its intonations. Here, the ritual was unimpeded by banal or comic contrasts, and this Sunday's message reverberated along the fibres of Ike's being.

The padre led them in prayer, first for the Royal family, for the ministers of His Majesty's government, for the commanding officers, for their comrades at sea, for those about to depart for active duty, for their loved ones at home...."

Ike's mind calculated the hours. It was time for morning chores at home. Images of his younger siblings, Ben and Nettie, making their way to the barn. Suddenly the boring bleakness of their lives assailed him. What did they have to look forward to after chores were done? He'd write them this afternoon, he promised himself, and he would tell them about the apple orchards and the oxen here in the Annapolis Valley. He could picture his father, how he would "Hem!" and clear his throat when Nettie read out that part and then he would turn around to lift a stove lid and drop the soggy butt of his hand-rolled cigarette into the fire. He hoped his mother wouldn't cry, although he was sure she would.

Chapter 7

Steam Training

Drilling on parade was overshadowed by steam training in classroom lectures during the next four weeks. In addition, off-duty time had to be spent studying the navy blue *B.R. 77 Machinery Handbook.* Larsen bitched and grumbled that all this goddamned studying left him too little time to find any hot stuff. As though there was any. He usually tossed the manual aside after half an hour and wandered over to the wet canteen or to the movie. Occasionally Ike went with him. Both Charlie and Larsen had the misfortune of more coal pile assignments.

Ike escaped the coal pile. In the classroom setting he discovered that time spent repairing tractors at home had given him a head start in understanding steam engineering. While the instructor explained circles and arrows on diagrams in the manual, representing pistons, valves and bearings, and a host of other mechanical gadgetry that Ike had learned about by cleaning, grinding, and fitting together again, his mind wandered to the workshop back home.

The engines there were all internal combustion gasoline engines. He was too young to recall a time when the big steam tractor had been used to power the threshing machine that moved from farm to farm in harvest time. The steam engineer, as legend had it, always got served first at the supper table, no matter who else might be part of the crew of twenty or twenty-five men sitting down to eat at the big trestle table lit by the Aladdin lamp in the summer kitchen.

He had only been six years old when Dad came home aboard the big gas-powered Minneapolis Universal with its enormous two-foot-wide wheels. Dad, climbing down from the steel saddle seat, had been dwarfed by those wheels, and in the first days after its arrival, all the neighbors came to examine this marvel with which the Friedlen farm was saying farewell to the age of steam power.

Ike reflected on the irony. He'd left home to see a larger, more modern world, to get away from his father's old-fashioned ideas, and here he was learning about old-fashioned steam. Learning that it was not what James Watt had seen coming out of his mother's kitchen kettle, what PSI's were, what the ideal flash point was for bunker fuel and what made the burner produce smoke.

"Friedlen!" The lecturer's bark exploded the calm of his reverie. "Step up here and illustrate on the blackboard how the Steady-flow Feed Check Valve functions."

Ike moved forward slowly, trying to collect his wits. He knew how a feed check valve worked but there were two types shown in the manual. Which one was the "Steady-flow" and which the "Robot"? The illustrations were filed away in his head but which one was which? To gain time he picked up chalk and said slowly, "Well, Sir, the basic part of the valve is a chamber that controls the flow between the delivery from the feed pump to the boiler." He drew these on the board with necessary arrows and while he was doing so his mind fumbled through the pages he had yawned over last night.

To gain more time, he picked up the blackboard eraser and took out part of his sketch and replaced it again, making it look a little more elegant. He still couldn't remember. He turned to look at the rest of the class. Charlie was moving his lips silently. Ike couldn't read the message. Larsen was clearly enjoying Ike's embarrassment.

Ike felt blood rushing to his face. He cleared his throat and repeated carefully, "The basic part of the valve is the chamber that controls the flow ...." As he turned back to his diagram, the image of the page in the manual clicked into place. In his mind's eye he saw the remainder of the valve's functioning parts. Quickly now, he sketched in the needle valve and the control mechanism, explained their function without stumbling, then turned to face the surprised instructor.

"Very good, Friedlen. Thank you."

The guy clearly thought he had caught me, thought Ike as he headed back to his seat. Charlie grinned at him and looked relieved. Ike was surprised to see the almost rueful smirk on Larsen's face. He was studying the handbook closely, as if to find some error in Ike's demonstration.

A narrow escape. Ike decided he'd have to stay more alert, just in case some new bit of information came up amid the stuff he already knew, trivia that might appear on the "Advanced Training Course" exam soon to be faced.

In the meantime parade square drill, classroom lectures, and work detail monotony was lessened somewhat by sporadic special guard duty.

"Oho! Standing guard at some Big Nut's house tonight, eh, Dutchy?" Larsen seemed more than usually interested when Ike told him about it. "Hobnobbing with the upper echelons, eh? That should be fun."

"Something different at least."

"Sure thing." Larsen gave him an odd look, seemed about to say something more but turned instead and headed for the showers.

Ike gave his uniform an extra brushing and his boots a few more than the usual flicks with his shoe rag. He shouldered a rifle and marched down the road toward the large house which sat amid an area of lawns and shrubbery behind the knoll from which the officer's mess overlooked the bay. Ike made a circuit of the white picket fence that outlined the grounds, checking the shrubbery for intruders before complete darkness set in. Someone inside switched on the outdoor lights. He pulled himself even more impossibly erect.

He paced back and forth in front, along the side, around the back, past the garage, and back along the road to the front. Shrubbery screened the windows leaving only a glimpse of a front door flanked by potted geraniums blazing in the porch lights for anyone passing by. Ike positioned himself near the gate so that he had a view of both the road and the grounds.

The tightness in his chest loosened as he breathed in the quiet air, stirred only by the rustle of yellowing leaves in an occasional gust flowing from the inland hills toward the bay.

The long, low administrative buildings nearby were virtually empty and he suddenly realized he hadn't known such stillness since he'd boarded the train in Winnipeg weeks ago. In and around the barrack huts someone or something was always moving, marching, shouting, playing, but the murmur of that noise coming faintly from the distance only emphasized the calm here in the residential section of the base.

He shivered slightly in the crisp autumn air and started pacing again. Back and forth, along one side, across the back, and up the other side again. Indoors someone switched on a radio and "The White Cliffs of Dover" drifted toward him through an open window. It reminded him that he must put his name down for the Mart Kenney concert as soon as he got off duty tomorrow. He and Charlie had seen the posters that afternoon. He'd listened to Mart Kenney on the Atwater Kent A-and-B battery radio at home so often.... What a break to be able to see as well as hear The Western Gentlemen! Who would have thought he'd get such a chance?

It was a sure thing that Pete wasn't getting chances like this in that CO camp somewhere in B.C. Too bad he wasn't here instead. Ike remembered the sessions with Pete and Abe on violin and banjo and himself at the guitar. The three of them played at dances for miles around, before Abe and Pete got married. After that he had taken up the fiddle and Ben the guitar and they'd played at dances too, but it had come to him suddenly one night at a dance in Harder's hayloft that all the other boys were having a great time dancing with Sara while he could only watch her over the movement of his fiddle bow. That cheek-to-cheek waltz with Art Rempel under dimmed lights had finished him. He'd laid down his bow that night and hadn't taken it up since. And to this day he had no regrets. From then on he held Sara in his arms while some other suckers provided music. Besides, Mart Kenney and His Western Gentlemen hadn't had anything to fear from the Friedlen Farm Boys.

He moved along the front of the house again, faster now in order to keep warm. The wind picked up, sharpening the damp chill that always hung near the water. The empty garage reminded him that the Big Nuts must be out and he wondered who was indoors listening to the radio. He glanced up at the house. Must be at least four bedrooms up there. A house two or three times bigger than the eleven hundred square foot one at home.

His curiosity led to speculation about what it looked like inside. The visible lighted kitchen window suggested vast differences from their farmhouse.

Their Big Room had plain white curtains at the windows, but the kitchen had only roller blinds to keep out the summer's blazing heat. Here he could see dotted, sheer ruffles tied back to each side of the window frame, like the ones he'd seen in the Eaton's catalogue.

Suddenly the kitchen door opened. Ike snapped to attention, ready to salute, but the bell bottoms stepping out onto the porch obviously did not deserve a salute. Thirtyish or so he stood under the porch light, stretching his heavily tattooed arms above his head. What's this guy doing here, Ike wondered. No jumper, no hat, no rifle. Clearly he wasn't on duty watch. He came down the steps and sauntered along the driveway towards Ike, who turned to resume his pacing. "Cold enough for you, matey?" One of the tattooed hands reached for the cigarette package tucked into his waistband. Ike said it sure was.

"Have a smoke?"

The package was extended towards him. Ike paused momentarily. Smoking on duty was a no-no. He glanced at the kitchen door and the lighted windows.

"No worry. Nobody home. I'm in charge here tonight. Carter's the name. Ship's chippy, ya know. Bin workin' around the house here for some time. Know him real well by now. Here, put that rifle down and take a smoke break."

Ike took the proffered cigarette, leaned over the lighted match and inhaled deeply. Suddenly he heard his mother's warning on the day he left home: "Never take a cigarette from a stranger. You never know what kind of drugs may be in it." Too late now. He eyed the cigarette closely. In the light from the porch it looked like any other Lucky Strike. Tasted like a Lucky Strike. He wondered where his mother who left home only to attend church and pay an occasional visit to neighbors had heard about drugged cigarettes.

The rather high-pitched voice of his companion went on, pointing out the other homes of top–ranking officers nearby, carrying on about shelves he'd built, repairs he'd done, how this or that one had sat down with him for a beer, how much he was appreciated. Up there by gosh! They had ambled toward the back door during this recital, their cigarettes stubbed in a flower pot on the edge of the top step.

"Tell you what. C'mon in and have a beer. Nobody's back here for a couple of hours. There ain't nobody gonna attack the place if yer not out here in the cold. Leave the rifle beside the door."

Ike felt a queer excitement. Absolutely against orders, but a chance to see what it was like to live big time. Jeepers! He might never have another opportunity. Make Charlie turn green when he hears about it in the morning!

So, he followed "Chippy" into the kitchen, vaguely noticing the door being locked behind them. He looked around, smelling furniture polish rather than food smell. How bright and light it seemed with its white refrigerator and enameled electric stove. They had an electric light bulb in the kitchen at home, but their Wind-Charger and its bank of six-volt car batteries could not have powered that many appliances without interruption.

Chippy opened two bottles, handed Ike one and motioned him toward one of the narrow-backed, white chairs at the white, enamel-topped kitchen table. So different from the dark, pressed-back chairs and the oilcloth covered oak table at home. Must have come out of the Ark, compared with this new looking stuff. Carter sitting at the end of the table near the door continued shooting the breeze about the good guys he knew.

"D'ya know the bloke that lives here?" he asked rhetorically. "I'm tellin' ya, once he gets to know ya, he'll do just about anything for ya, any time." Ike was only half listening, more interested in surveying the room, the house.

A picture of fruit in a bowl and a vase of flowers on the wall opposite. A winter scene on the wall near the window. Pictures, in the kitchen! Not on calendars, but in frames! Sara's mother had a picture of a church beside a river with very dark clouds in the sky hanging over their piano, but in his own home only the oval portraits of his grandparents looked down on guests in the Big Room.

Ike was shocked suddenly out of his bemused observations. A hand was stroking his thigh. He turned sideways in his chair and crossed his knees. The tenor voice went on as if nothing was going on under the table. The anecdote having reached its self-congratulatory end, the voice shifted into a softer, more personal tone.

"You look pretty damn snazzy in that uniform, matey, y'know that? You're quite a guy, I can tell." His tongue slurred slightly over the last phrase. It was obviously not his first beer of the evening. He reached over, patted the square collar and moved his hand caressingly down Ike's back.

"Great to see so many good lookin' guys like you joinin' th' navy. Best service in th' world. Shenior shervice, y'know. A shailor don't hafta stand to toast the Queen, y'know that?" Ike said he'd learned that in Basic Training.

Carter hitched his chair toward the corner of the table, closer to Ike's, and put his arm over Ike's shoulder. Ike recoiled a little from the chippy's beery breath.

"Here's to the senior service. Bottom's up!" He wanted to get the beer down and get out as quickly as possible. But the chippy reached out a restraining hand before Ike could swallow the last of his beer.

"No hurry! No hurry! Hell, we're just startin' t'be friends, ain't we?"

Ike felt a hand fumbling at his crotch. "I'd better get back on duty," he said, trying to rise from his chair. The arm over his shoulder held him down firmly.

"Now, now, Buddy. Let's just enjoy ourselves here. Nobody's gonna know you're not out there marchin' your ass off." The hand was now busy edging the hem of Ike's jumper upwards, trying to reach the buttons on the flap of Ike's bell bottoms. As he pushed his abdomen outward to tighten his belt over the buttons more securely, Ike became aware that the muscles in the arm over his shoulder were surprisingly hard and firm and the exploring hand, increasingly insistent. Strong as hell.

"Okay, okay, let's not rush things here," he said placatingly. "I haven't finished my beer yet and if I'm really going to enjoy myself, I'd better have another." Carter relaxed slightly and Ike squirmed sideways, out of his chair onto his feet, keeping the beer bottle in his hand. "Here's lookin' at ya." He raised the bottle and, to his relief, so did Carter.

"Atta boy! Here's to the Wavy Navy!" Carter tilted his bottle back, emptied it quickly, and belched as he slammed the bottle down on the table.

Ike belched too, then clapped a hand over his mouth and faked a few gagging, strangling swallows. "I -- I -- I'm gonna throw up."

"Hell! Don't get sick in here, for god sake. I told you not to take it so fast." Angrily, he unlocked the door and Ike, making more retching sounds, rushed past him. He grabbed his rifle and bolted for the roadway.

"Sonofabitch!" screamed Carter behind him, aware of the ruse now. Ike heard the kitchen door being slammed hard as he ran along the driveway. He rushed around the corner toward the street light at the front before pausing to look behind him. When he saw he wasn't being followed, he paused in the middle of the road to button his pants with trembling fingers and pull his jumper down over his hips again.

He sucked in some deep fresh, clean air before shouldering his rifle. Be damned if he'd go anywhere near the back of the house again during this watch. Grateful for the cool breeze on his sweaty brow, he began pacing again. The kitchen had not seemed too warm when he followed Carter indoors, but his jumper was damp with perspiration.

So that's what it meant to run into a "cocksucker." He had heard the epithet being hurled in both anger and jest from time to time, but until now it had been just another insulting word. A faint nausea assailed him as he recalled those pawing hands and the heavy, beery breath. No wonder it was never simply, "You cocksucker," but invariably, "You dirty cocksucker" or worse.

As he paced, his pulse stopped racing and he began congratulating himself on having been able to get out without an actual fight. Chippy was a couple of inches taller and at least ten pounds heavier than he was so even if his own arms and hands were strong, he wouldn't have had much of a chance. Especially since he hadn't been in a fist fight since an older boy gave him a black eye in fifth grade.

How would he have explained a black eye tomorrow without revealing the humiliation too? What if they'd had a scrap and banged up the furniture or slammed into that beautiful refrigerator? He wouldn't have had any excuse for being in that house, so no matter what had come of it, he'd have had to keep his mouth shut about the chippy, especially if all those chummy stories about some Big Nuts knowing about him were even partly true.

He stopped in his tracks at the thought. Damn well no truth in it. The man couldn't be in the navy if it was known what he was no matter how great he was at carpentry. All that talk, he'd known it was a pile of bull. Yet, if it weren't true, what reason was there for a chippy being in that house at this time of night? He certainly wasn't building any shelves during evening watch. Why wasn't he billeted in one of the huts like every other rating? Ike refused to allow the thought to complete itself and began counting the paces from one end of the picket fence to the other.

Eventually his relief came on duty and he hurried back to barracks, got under the shower for a double duty lathering. Charlie and Larsen were snoring peacefully. Ike climbed into his own bunk. So, that's what Larsen's funny look had been all about. If Charlie had known he'd have warned me. He fell asleep.

Before Larsen had his eyes properly open, Ike stood over him, towel in hand, ready to administer a few wet flicks to Larsen's bare hindquarters. "You knew, you son-of-a-bitch, and you didn't warn me! Did you think that was some kind of a joke?"

Laughing, Larsen tucked his blankets more snugly around himself. "Hey, just you hold it! I didn't know for sure. I'd heard some scuttlebutt, sure, but I thought it might be just that, no more."

"Well, you could have let me in on it instead of letting me go out there to spend the evening defending myself. Damn near lost my virginity!"

By this time some of the other men had gathered with a chorus of "What happened? What happened?" As Ike continued embellishing, the danger he'd encountered became more menacing and the genius behind his escape more marvelous than in actual fact.

Larsen grinned. "So the big fucker didn't get your pants down. And him twice your size. Gotta hand it to ya, Friedlen. For a dumb farmer, gotta hand it to ya."

* * *

A crowd had already gathered around the notice board, scanning the marks and order sheets when Ike arrived. He could only see the top edges of the pages until some moved away to allow him a closer look. Saunders, standing in front of him, ran a finger anxiously along the alphabetical list. When it stopped, his shoulders slumped. He turned away from the board with a stricken look. Ike had felt sure immediately after the examination that he had passed but now anxiety tightened his chest.

He squeezed his way toward the front. There it was. "Friedlen - 95. Report to HMCS *Buxton* 0800 hours. Monday." To sea at last!! He glanced at other marks on the sheets before giving up his place: 75, 55, 80, but no other 90's. He knew that marks weren't enough for a promotion, but dammit, it felt good to know he'd done so well. He tried to find Charlie's and Larsen's marks but others pushed and shoved. He hadn't seen much of Charlie for a couple of weeks.

Charlie was in his bunk with his eyes closed when Ike reached his hut. He felt a pang. Surely Charlie hadn't failed.

"Hey, Charlie! Seen your marks yet?"

"Yeah. I passed." There was no enthusiasm in the announcement.

"What's the matter then? You don't look like you're celebrating."

"I got posted to Halifax. *Stadacona*. Another dry land ship. I thought I'd get on the *Buxton*."

"Well, you gotta look at it this way. You'll be in *Stadacona* for a few days only. They can't get all of us on the *Buxton* for sea training. Halifax is full of ships. You're just the right guy to be lucky enough to get on one of the big babies."

Charlie didn't buy it. "Don't try so hard, Dutch. Well, I'd better get my gear together," he mumbled. "See you in mess hall."

Mitchell had his kit spread out on the bunk. "Anchors aweigh, me boys! Anchors aweigh!" he sang as he rolled up his whites and stuffed them in the bottom of his sea bag. "Hi, there, Dutch, old chum. How're ya doin'? I made it through that steam course this time, dammit, so it's goodbye to this stinkhole. No more coal shoveling for me. Slackers, here I come!"

"How d'ya know there isn't a coal pile in Stad, Mitch?"

"Hell, if there is, let the guys fresh off the farm shovel it."

Across the corridor, Larsen rummaged through a pile of smelly gear on his bed. Ike watched as he selected several items, flung them into his duffle bag resting on the floor beside him and stomped them down with his boot. He stopped and reached for a cigarette. "God, but I hate packin'. Only good thing about it is gettin' out of this burg. Deader even than where I live. Can't wait to get to fucking Stad. I'm gonna have me a time in Halifax before I get further posting. Where're you goin', Dutch?"

"*Buxton*."

"Not bad. Not bad. But you won't get far in that tub. Escort duty out and about Halifax. Maybe Sydney and back. Never know about that four-funnel job, where it'll take you. I'm hopin' fer a berth in a bigger one, the Hood, maybe. Or even the Prince of Wales."

Ike's elation faded slightly. Until now the sleek lines of *Buxton* had seemed the zenith of all that might be hoped for among the navy's sailing ships. Though the textbooks had black and white photos of all the larger cruisers and battleships, their shapes had never glistened against the blue waters in his mind's eye. It was disturbing to hear that Larsen thought of the *Buxton* as less than the best. It seemed disloyal, somehow.

Although he still had plenty of time to pack up, he too hauled out his sea bag, sorting and rolling up his gear. Only two more nights in barracks! His elation returned. He'd go to the movie tonight. There wouldn't be any of those at sea.

Chapter 8
Buxton

Although Ike had been on *Buxton* frequently during the last weeks of training, it was his first glimpse of the quarters he'd be sharing with thirty other stokers while on board. Four tables with attached benches bolted to the deck provided a surface for eating, writing, coffee brewing, poker playing. This left limited room to pass between the benches and bunks fixed on either side. Two men in dungarees sat near the foot of the ladder, drinking coffee from enameled cups.

"Friedlen, Stoker Second Class, reporting for duty," he announced.

The man across the table got up and held out his hand. "Joe Munden, here. Welcome aboard." His broad-shouldered stocky body, firm handshake and deep voice stirred something in Ike's memory. "Friedlen, your bunk's the top one forward portside. Mine's the lower one. Hope you're not a bed wetter."

"Growing out of it. Ike's the name, but Dutchy most times."

"Snarr here," the tone was almost sullen, the outstretched hand moved reluctantly to meet Ike's for the briefest moment before returning to coffee and cigarette. He took deep drags and exhaled slowly, allowing the smoke to veil his pale blue eyes as he closely examined Ike's features, his build, his duffle bag in turn. Ike felt as if he had just walked into the saloon of a Western movie with Snarr in a black Stetson.

No time for introductions to others playing cards before three more newcomers, sea bags hurtling against the narrow hatchway, came clambering down the stairs. Munden introduced himself to Lennox, Laroux and Olsen in turn, directed each to his assigned bunk, then sat down again. "Standing Orders are posted on the bulk-head over there listing your locker number." He pointed, "Daily duty roster is right beside it."

Olsen, a fair-haired, tall, broad-shouldered stoker who had been in Ike's steam training class, looked at the Order Sheet, then moved his bag along the narrow space behind Snarr. "Jeez!" he exclaimed, looking at the small cubicle beneath the lower bunk. "How'm I ever gonna get all this goddam gear into this locker?"

"If it don't fit, you goddam well throw it out," Snarr said belligerently without turning around. "This is a ship, not a hotel and you'd better get used to it."

Lennox and Laroux unpacked their gear. Ike had seen Lennox in Larsen's company on the base. Like Larsen, Lennox was tall and well-built but his sharp, wolfish features were more striking than handsome. The way he flung his clothes into the locker, punctuating each addition with an oath, reminded Ike of Larsen's habits. On the other side of the table, the short, curly-haired Laroux, black eyebrows knitted in concentration, quickly stowed his stuff. Ike had not noticed him during training, but then he was the kind of a guy you wouldn't notice, Ike reflected, because he went about his business without comment or complaint.

"The *Buxton*'s actually a pretty good ticket," Munden said in an even tone. "She was in mothballs from 1918 until we got her from the Americans through Lend Lease. That's how come you guys are lucky enough to get bunks instead of having to sling your hammocks. The other four-funnel destroyers like this that went to Limeys have had all the bunks ripped out."

"Why the hell would they do that?"

"Tradition. They're nuts on tradition. British sailors slept in hammocks in Nelson's day, so the poor bastards still do."

Ike checked the duty roster. "Looks like I'm on watch at 0800 hours. So are you, Lennox."

"Your first time at sea, Dutchy?" Munden asked.

"Sure is. How long have you been in?"

"Two years, but I've been at sea since I was eight years old, I guess. My Old Man's a fisherman on the west coast, Prince Rupert. Look, you'd better get into dungarees right away. We sail at 0900 hours."

Ike changed out of his uniform and stowed his gear. He noticed that Munden and Snarr were in the meantime washing their cups and trays in a bucket of water set on one of the benches. After Munden had dried the last utensil, he carried the lot to a locker beside the ladder, stowed them in the racks inside and latched the door securely. Snarr wiped the table, wrung out his dishrag and lifting the bucket towards Ike said, "Here. Y'might as well start makin' yourself useful. Dump this in the heads." The surly edge to his voice made the mess go suddenly quiet.

Aware of the challenge in Snarr's pale blue eyes, Ike paused a moment, tucked his shirt into his pants carefully and deliberately, settled his collar and checked the buttons on each cuff of his shirt before reaching for the handle of the bucket. "No sweat," he said amiably. "I'll do you the favour, since I was going to the heads anyway." He caught Lennox's eye and its enigmatic look as he moved toward the ladder. Glad it's Munden in the bunk below mine rather than that bastard. With these thoughts he made his way upwards. Ten feet of mess space isn't enough, but it's better than having him just below me like Lennox does.

He got back with the empty bucket in time to report to the boiler room. Munden led the way. He saluted the Petty Officer at the door. "Leading Stoker Munden reporting for duty, sir." He introduced Ike and Lennox to PO Simpson who logged them in.

"You've been on board before so you know the boiler room is pressurized. Each air lock door must be closed securely before the other will open. "Lennox, you and I will go down first." Munden and Ike waited for the far door to close before following them into the pressurized chamber, down the ladder into the boiler room. Ike surveyed the six-foot-high bank of burners and their dials behind which the boilers breathed easily. Only two burners were lit, he noted, but within a few minutes of their arrival "Slow ahead!" came down through the voice pipe.

"Friedlen, fire Number Three burner. Lennox, fire Number Eight!" Munden called out. The boilers shuddered as they leaped into flame. Ike watched his gauges, adjusting air flow and oil delivery, ensuring the clean, smokeless flame he'd been taught about during training. Engines throbbing, the ship moved slightly under his feet. This was it! Too busy adjusting cocks and levers to savour the moment.

As the boilers superheated, a smell from the hot, freshly painted pipes that crossed and re-crossed the space above their heads became stronger. He could only guess at the nature of the ship's movement from their enclosed cell, but his imagination turned her bow toward Digby Gut, the mouth of the Annapolis Basin, into the Bay of Fundy. Oh, to be on deck! He had looked forward to this moment for so long but never had he been encased, sealed below deck, when visualizing his dream. The last of the rocky headland slid past but his eyes didn't see it.

Skipper signaled for more steam. Certain that the gut had been cleared, Ike thrilled as the speed of the turning screw sent its vibrations through the steel deck. "Full speed ahead!" They leaped to fire the last two burners. A virtual small explosion rocked the room as Number Ten burst into flame. The panel in front of the fire chamber pulsated madly and the growl of the burners increased to a roar. Eyes glued to the steel panel, certain that the whole bloody thing was going to burst from its moorings and come crashing in on them, Ike felt his heart pounding.

"Too much air! Too much air in Number Ten!" shouted Simpson above the din. Ike wished he could cover his ears as the pressurized air rocked with the noise, but his hands were in constant use to control burners in his care. Vibrations and pulsations challenged his confidence in what a bolt could withstand.

Munden leaped over to where a white-faced Lennox stood with his hand seemingly frozen to a lever, shouldered him aside, and pulled it downward. His big hands moved quickly and confidently among the controls, adjusting the mixture of air and oil until, gradually, the banging, slamming, screaming noise settled back to a steady, vibrating roar. He moved over to Lennox who clung to a handrail. "You OK?" he shouted. White-faced, Lennox nodded dumbly. "Sure you are!" He slapped Lennox on the back and exchanged looks with PO Simpson. He came over to Ike eyeing the dials. "Everything OK with you?"

"Yeah, sure."

Hot water suddenly spurted from a joint overhead. “Damn! Friedlen, the spanner, quick!” He leaped up the steel steps and clamped it on the coupling. “That other one too, and grab this son-of-a-bitch and hold it while I tighten ‘er up.” Hot water sprayed in Ike’s face and over his shoulders so he couldn’t see Munden’s work, but the increasing stress on his arms as he held the spanner counter to Munden’s tightening motion promised eventual success. At last the cursing stopped, the spray diminished, then stopped completely. “You got ‘er.” He relaxed his grip.

Looking down from the upper cat-walk had made him aware of the heaving, heaving, heaving deck below and a sudden fullness rose in the back of his throat. He got back down to the boilers, checked each burner carefully, and by concentration on their functioning, tried his best to ignore the uncomfortable sensation of the boiler room heaving up and down, back and forth. At the other end of the deck, PO Simpson pointed to various levers and dials. Lennox, having regained some composure, nodded in response.

Ike longed for an easy, glorious belch to rid himself of an uncomfortable lump in his throat. He swallowed hard instead, afraid a belch wouldn’t come up clean if allowed to rise past his gullet. Powerful paint fumes from hot blazing pipes blending with heated, heavy bunker fuel odors added to his discomfort. Munden’s attempt at tightening and wiping joints that oozed bunker fuel because of the excessive vibrations they had endured was to a large degree futile. Ike suddenly needed air. He longingly, furtively, looked at the overhead fans whirling at high speed. If only they’d bring in some fresh air! He couldn’t quite come to grips with why he felt so god-awful, so suddenly don’t-give-a-damn awful. Rotten smells -- motion -- heat -- heaving deck -- air----- air....

“Get up on that catwalk and check those pipes up there,” Munden’s voice said in his ear. Gratefully, Ike clambered quickly up the ladder and moved slowly along the walk, eyeing each joint. The flow of moving air near the fans diluted the smell of oil and paint and his queasy stomach settled down somewhat. He tried to tell himself he wasn’t getting seasick. He’d considered himself immune. Barely out of the Bay of Fundy and he, the invincible, cocksure Ike, was being forced to acknowledge that god-awful tasting lump reappearing in his throat! Over and over he told himself “It’s got to be the paint fumes, only the paint fumes.”

His breakfast was still with him when they tied up in St. John, but it had sat precariously near the back of his throat for the last hour of the crossing. His watch wasn't over when the engines slowed to a stop, and with the cessation of motion, the smell of the boiler room became bearable again. At a signal from the voice pipe, the PO suddenly started up the ladder, beckoning Lennox to come along. Ike looked at Munden questioningly.

"Grog time. We take turns when on watch so we'll go when they get back. You're issued two ounces of Pusser rum every day you're at sea. Helps keep the engines oiled," he grinned.

They stopped at the mess for mugs and when their turn came, lined up amidships where an upper deck officer ladled out to each crew member a portion dipped from the copper bucketful that had been drawn from a wooden keg beside him. With their mug of rum the men sat down or stood leaning against a pipe, or walked about sipping until the grog was downed, then went to their own mess.

Ike had never cared much for rum. His queasy stomach didn't increase his enthusiasm, but the hand of tradition was on him as he sat down and quickly gulped his two-ounce tot. A shot of fire flowing down his gullet stopped his breath instantly. Choking, he coughed and spluttered while the mess roared at his discomfiture. Munden pounded his back. "Hey! You've gotta take it easy with the stuff, Dutch. This is Pusser rum, the Royal Navy's own 160 overproof special. The strongest rum in the world. It's not meant for gulping. Sip it slowly."

Ike wiped his streaming eyes and gasped, "Now you tell me!" He rubbed his midriff where the searing sensation seemed about to burn a hole in the lining of his stomach. He'd know better next time. On their way back to the boiler room, Munden stopped in the stoker's mess and Ike saw that his mug wasn't empty. He watched Munden stoop down, remove a half empty bottle from his locker, and pour what was left of his grog into it. "As I told you, Dutch, you're supposed to drink your tot up there before you leave the mess. Watch what goes on. You'll see most men faking it to save up for a bash when we hit shore. Or some guys sell theirs. It's against regulations. If you think of trying it, don't get caught."

As he passed through the air lock again, Ike realized suddenly that the lump in his throat was gone. What was more, the boiler room atmosphere didn't bring it on again. A credit to tradition.

The mess was full of high spirits when they came off watch. He and Lennox gathered up soap and towels and headed for the showers. "Don't be long about it," Munden warned. "Cookie won't keep that mess open forever. Not when we're in port."

"What say we head right for town, Dutch?" Lennox called over his shoulder. "They tell me there's a coupla hot spots and I'm ready."

To hear him, you'd think we'd been at sea for a month. "Sounds good, but let's eat first. No sense spending our money on food ashore. Might as well save it for beer."

"Now that's what I call thinking, but it ain't only beer I'm looking for when I go ashore. Was ever a place more dead'rn Digby? Here I'm lookin' for hot stuff."

They picked up their trays from the locker and headed for the galley. "Hey! I'm glad you thought of this, Dutch. These guys get real beef!" Lennox exulted as the cook slapped two thick slices of meat into his tray followed by a mound of mashed potatoes, a spoonful of peas, and a ladle full of gravy.

"Yeah, makes that stuff in *Cornwallis* look like garbage, doesn't it?"

Munden greeted the cook with introductions. "Friedlen and Lennox here have just joined ship's company. This is Lynch, not a bad cook as cooks go. Looks like one of his better days."

"Watch your tongue, Munden, or the crew may be getting funny looking cutlets for supper tonight." Lynch brandished his carving knife in mock menace. "These the guys sending smoke signals all the way across the bay? Tie'm up in that boiler room before they get us sunk when we hit open water. You guys signaling to U-boats or what?"

"Aw, c'mon, Lynch. You mean you don't recognize a good smoke screen when you see it? You gotta admit, no U-boat could have seen us once we got those boilers bouncing this morning." They hastily headed down the ladder to their mess.

"You two are on wash-up detail," Munden announced when they'd finished. "Laroux and Olsen, sweep the deck before you go anywhere. The broom and buckets are in that locker over there."

Munden dressed while the mess was being cleaned and headed up the ladder. "See you up top." Dutch counted his money. He still had twenty dollars left of his last month's pay but there was another week to go before next payday. He put ten dollars in his belt and the rest back in his locker.

"C'mon, c'mon! St. John awaits the King's nay-vee! Let's not keep all those girls waiting."

On the upper deck a group in dungarees were playing crap. Snarr, Laroux and Olsen, all in uniform, were watching. "Y'comin' along?" Munden called out.

Laroux and Olsen moved to join them but Snarr, dice in hand, said, "Nah! I think I'll play with these babies for a while first."

The wooden planks of the jetty leading towards town had been warmed by a bright Indian summer sun. "What a great day," Ike murmured, pausing to watch a sea gull coast gracefully downward to the water.

Munden stopped beside him. "Yeah. A day like this and you almost wish you'd signed up as an Able Seaman, but there are plenty more when the boiler room looks a whole lot better than topside." They hurried to catch up with the others.

"Which way do we go?"

"For beer, over there if you want to start drinking, but in St. John you have to see the Tidal Bore. This away men! Follow me."

"What in hell is a Tidal Bore?" Ike listened intently as Munden explained the way in which the Fundy tidewater rushes into the mouth of the St. John River, forcing the river water to reverse its natural flow until at neap tide the sea water retreats back into the Bay.

"Sounds like a great big bore to me." Lennox guffawed loudly at his own wit.

They sauntered in the direction of *Brunswicker*, peering into shop windows as they went along. Chains, hooks, pulleys and other ships' gear stared back at them in the first block. Gradually housewares and clothing shops replaced the chandlers. A group of girls with schoolbooks cradled in their arms came towards them.

"Well, well, look at this!" Lennox tipped his hat a little farther forward and stopped before they came abreast. He whistled appreciatively, eyeing intensely the one nearest their group. "Hello, hello! Haven't we met before?"

She paused briefly, looked at him, then turned back to her friends. Giggling, they moved on quickly, leaving Lennox to look after them. They kept on walking, but after a few paces they peeked back over their shoulders and giggled some more.

"C'mon boys. Let's follow them," said Lennox.

"Aw, you're wasting your time," said Olsen. "I thought we were goin' fer a beer."

Lennox turned reluctantly and they resumed their amble towards the canteen. Other groups of sailors wandered in and out of shops along the street. Well before reaching the doors of the canteen, they could hear the clink of glasses and loud voices coming from behind the curtains hiding occupants from the view of passersby. Two girls in high heels and very tight, short skirts stood near the lamppost on the corner, a few paces from the door.

"To me it looks red hot," chortled Lennox. "Who's with me for a go at these two?"

"The blonde could do with a retread," Ike said, eyeing her peeling high heels. Aware of their speculative notice, the girls smiled bright, red- lipsticked smiles. Hands in their jacket pockets, they turned to show the bulging fullness of tight sweaters underneath.

"Maybe they'll settle for getting their valves reground," chortled Lennox.

"Oh, oh!" groaned Olsen. "There's only two of them and five of us. Wadda we do? Flip a coin for who goes first?"

"I'm too near broke," said Laroux. "I've gotta settle for a beer."

Ike, not wanting to admit he wouldn't know how to approach the girls even if he wanted to said quickly, "You guys go ahead. I'll have a look at the Tidal Bore first, for inspiration. Meet you for a beer later. Which way did you say, Munden?"

"I'll come with you. C'mon with us, Laroux. We'll have plenty of time to drink later."

"OK. Let's go." Lennox plucked at Olsen's sleeve impatiently and they walked over to the girls.

When they got back from sightseeing, the two girls were standing on the same corner. Ike stepped into the blue haze of the dimly lit interior. He sniffed at the smell. Beer and piss, just like the beer parlour at home. He felt a heaviness inside. Most tables were full, some with young men in uniform, others with men whose middle-aged faces spoke of many years in wind and weather. They were about to sit down at a table occupied only by empty glasses sitting in pools of spilled beer when Lennox's voice haled them.

"Hey, *Buxton*! C'mon over here!" Flynn, another of their messmates, sat with Olsen and Lennox.

"Hey, Lennox," Laroux said as he sat down, "Dem girls are still out dere. I t'ought you guys'd still be in the sack wit' em."

"Hell, no! D'ya know what they charge for a room here? For only an hour? Two whole bucks! Ya'd think it was the Ritz or sump'n. Dirty bitches."

Ike had often wondered about the details of sexual commerce. "So you didn't take them upstairs?"

"Oh, sure we did, but it was about the poorest piece of ass I've had in a long time. Jeez! Nothin' turns me off like a woman pretendin' to get hot when she feels like the North Pole in midwinter!"

"What about you, Olsen?"

Olsen smiled slowly. "No complaints. When I'm looking for a quickie, I don't expect no True Romance stuff, like Lennox here. Just wiggle it in, wiggle it out and wipe it off. That's good enough for me." Even Lennox managed a smile among the general burst of laughter.

They had ordered a round when Snarr suddenly appeared, half empty glass of beer in his hand. Nobody invited him to sit down but he pulled up a chair anyway and lowered himself heavily into it. Ike thought he moved like a man in pain.

"So, what you guys bin doin'?" He scowled across the empty glasses on the table.

"Oh, Lennox and Olsen have been getting themselves laid while the rest of us walked around, seein' the sights."

"Hope all you got was some ass," he said, looking at Lennox. "I hear some of the boys picked up a dose somewhere on this run a coupla weeks ago."

"They didn't get it here in St. John?" Lennox's worldly wise look changed suddenly to concern.

"Dunno where they got it exactly. Coulda bin here. Coulda bin Sidney or Halifax."

"Never mind, Lennox. You ain't a real salt until y've had the clap," said Flynn. "It's like one of them service badges. Only it don't show."

The sun had set and night was falling fast when they stumbled out of the canteen heading for the ship. They turned off the main street and walked toward the harbour. Ike and Olsen, reaching the jetty ahead of the others, looked around, puzzled. *Buxton* was nowhere in sight "Holy Jesus! Did she sail without us? Wadda we do now?" There was rising panic in Olsen's voice.

"Maybe we're on the wrong jetty," Ike suggested, although he was certain they had come down the same street they had turned out of earlier. They peered anxiously along the length of the darkening harbour front that had seemingly been deserted by all of the vessels tied up there when they left the *Buxton*. Munden, Snarr and Laroux caught up with them as they stood there, uncertain what to do next.

Olsen's large blue eyes were larger than ever as he turned towards the others. "Hey! *Buxton*'s gone without us. Wadda we do now?"

Munden and Snarr burst into uproarious laughter that continued until both had to pause, gasping for breath. "He says *Buxton*'s gone..." began Munden weakly and that set them both off into fresh gales. Ike shrugged his shoulders at the others, "Damned if I know what's so funny about facing a court martial when you've only been out to sea for four hours."

Finally a coughing fit struck Snarr and Munden's hilarity subsided enough for him to speak. He caught his breath, wiping his eyes. "The tide, you idiots, the tide. If you weren't so pissed you'd see the mast. She's down there at the end of the jetty. Because the tide's out, she's lying thirty feet lower than she was when we tied up this afternoon. Don't you remember, Dutch, we talked about the difference between high and low tide when we walked over to the Reversing Falls this afternoon?"

The laughter and the beer they had drunk added hazards to their trip down the long gangway to the deck below, but no one fell and they felt comradely as they headed for the mess to change into dungarees. Munden and Snarr had barely hit the lower deck when they told and re-told their story to the loud and gusty amusement of all hands. "What I'd like to know, if you guys can stop laughing and be serious for a minute…" Ike noticed his tongue was thicker than usual so he spoke very slowly, "…what I'd like to know is where does all the extra water come from when the tide comes back in?"

"Hell," shouted a voice from one of the bunks, "We'll tell you that when you tell us where the extra meat comes from when you get a hard on." And the mess roared again.

"Dutch wouldn't know about that," countered Lennox.

Somewhat fuzzily it dawned on Ike that he'd better not ask stupid questions again even though the whole business of tides was puzzling. In fact, he'd be careful not to ask questions at all, if he could help it. Or be careful of whom he asked them, and Lennox wouldn't be one of those. He looked longingly at his bunk. It would be so nice to lie down to sleep off the dizziness but there wouldn't be time for that and grub, too, before the next watch.

Later, when they came off watch, he asked Munden what would have happened to them if the ship's sailing orders had been advanced while they were ashore. "Oh, we'd have heard about it. All the canteens and movie houses and cafes get rung up. Announcements are made for ship's personnel to report back immediately."

"Yeah, but supposing one of us had gone to visit a girl somewhere in a private home?"

"Well, Dutchy, the ship's supposed to know where you are. When you decide to do that, let your buddies know where you're going before you go ashore, just in case. The excuse that you didn't know she was leaving wouldn't be enough to keep you out of the brig. And, if you'll take my advice, you'll be careful about the kind of dame you shack up with. You heard what Snarr said."

Chapter 9

Halifax

Dimly aware that his bunk was swaying, Ike awoke to an incessant banging. He found himself in a world where nothing was still or quiet, where throbbing engines and pumps below deck struggled against the thud and surge of seas the ship was ploughing through. Every joint creaked and groaned. In a metal locker, something dislodged from its moorings clanged with each dip and roll. He looked over at the bunks opposite. Lennox, Snarr and Laroux were still asleep. He considered swinging his legs over the edge of his bunk.

Munden came down the ladder, towel draped over his shoulder and soap dish in hand. "Wakey! Wakee-ey!" he called out reaching into several bunks as he came down the length of the mess. "Wakee-ey! Wakee-ey!" He leaned over Ike's bunk, pretending to wave a lantern in his hand. "Time to milk the cows, Dutchy! Time to milk the cows!"

Ike sat up, swung out of his bunk and found the deck suddenly coming up to meet him. Momentarily he lost his balance. The ship lurched with shuddering vibrations. He grabbed the edge of the bunk to avoid falling against the table. His trip to the heads helped to explain the reason for railings and hand holds. Wherever she was going, he reflected, *Buxton* was certainly out of the Bay of Fundy. On the open sea.

In the galley the cook was cracking eggs into a large, six inch-deep, open pan where an inch of fat bubbled and sputtered. With the ship's sway, hot fat flowed back and forth over the eggs evenly basting the entire panful. Untroubled by the motion, Lynch lifted out two at a time with a long handled spatula and slid them onto each tray that filed by him. A few slices of bacon from the griddle and toast taken from a stack on a counter accompanied the eggs down to the mess.

Ike sat down on the fixed bench by the mess table. He began to eat with his knife and fork. Suddenly his tray blithely skidded the length of the table to the ledge at the far end. He dropped his knife and retrieved his tray. The moment of calm in which he might use both knife and fork to cut up his bacon did not come. One after another he folded each piece with his fork and thrust it into his mouth whole. A twenty-mug pot of coffee, secure within the hot plate rails, brewed constantly at the far end of the mess.

He marvelled at the skill with which others half-filled their mugs and made their way back to the table without spilling a drop. He longed for coffee himself but didn't dare the risks of getting it until Lennox sat down beside him. "Hang onto this for a minute for me, will you?" Although each step demanded forethought, he made it back with his mug unspilled. Lennox, he noticed, looked green.

"Too much beer or too much ass yesterday, Lennox?"

"Never too much ass for this lad. Must be the beer. Wish I had a bottle this morning. Nothin' like a hair of the dog that bit ya, eh, Olsen?"

Both Laroux and Olsen sitting across the table had shovelled down their eggs and bacon but Lennox's tray was still half full. He chewed slowly on a piece of toast and suddenly bolted for the ladder. "Oh, oh! One breakfast for the sea gulls," chuckled Munden. "Just as well he gets rid of it before going on watch. I hate the smell of puke in the boiler room."

On return, a paler Lennox showed darker green streaks along the jowls. "Never mind," Munden consoled him. "You'll find your sea legs in a few days. You're bloody lucky we've got good weather for breaking you in."

Ike congratulated himself on how well his own breakfast behaved as he and Munden passed through the air lock to the boiler room. Below, however, the super-heated oil and hot paint fumes became overpowering. His senses revolted against the deafening noise created by forced air rushing through slots to feed the battery of bunker fuel burners. He swallowed hard, desperately trying to clear a lump building in his throat. He grimly clamped his jaw shut and got to work.

Munden, he noticed, was eyeing him curiously, so he strove to look as normal and casual as possible. He puckered his lips to whistle, but gave up the effort.

"If you've got to spew, Dutchy, don't do it on the deck. Use that bucket." Munden had hardly finished pointing when Ike made a lunge and grabbed the pail from its hook. Bacon, eggs, toast and slime shot from him like a geyser. He wiped his face with his handkerchief and turned back to the boilers. Lennox grasped the handrails at his end of the boiler room with eyes tightly closed.

"Jesus! Now there's two of you," Munden groaned.

The smell of vomit pervaded the enclosed space but for the moment Ike felt better. "Put on that Mae West and empty that bucket up top," said Munden.

Gratefully, Ike filled his lungs with fresh air and returned to his post. He couldn't hear what Munden said to Lennox, but noticed him pointing upwards. As though by major effort, Lennox, his face by now a mixture of puke-ish hues, loosened his grip and slowly, hand over hand, made his way to the air lock. He came back carrying a clean bucket.

The four-hour watch seemed endless. Although his breakfast was long gone, Ike bent over his bucket from time to time, retching and heaving bile. He had an overwhelming urge to lie down. On the steel deck plates. Anywhere. But the surging sea forced him to constantly make adjustments to burners, to water pressure, to bilge pumps. He stood his watch. Standing up.

On relief, Ike left the sour, oily stench and went topside. A fresh, cold wind cut through his shirt as he leaned over the rail to retch some more. Sea spray left his shirt clinging to his skin, making his teeth chatter with cold as he made his way down below again. His messmates had returned from the galley and the aroma of spicy grub greeted him. "Better get something into that stomach, Dutch," called Munden. "You've got to have something to bring up, and besides, chile con carne's one of the cook's specialties."

Ike took one look at the steaming red-brown mess of beans and meat in Munden's plate and lurched for a bucket. Some laughed, but Snarr growled, "Get that fuckin' bucket outa here. You're puttin' me off my dinner."

"Guess you weren't ever seasick, eh, Snarr?" someone asked. Ike headed back up the ladder again and Snarr's reply was lost in the general din and the buzzing in his own ears. He avoided looking at any food when he returned to the mess. He stripped off his wet clothes and crawled into his bunk. To keep from rolling out of it, he wedged one knee against the bulkhead, braced the other foot against the front ledge, and pulling the woollen blanket over his miserable head, he fell asleep.

He dozed fitfully. Dimly aware of the ship heaving and plunging onward, he dreamt he was on a horse in the pasture behind the barn at home. His father and older brothers stood in the doorway of the barn, watching as the bronco bucked and circled as it tried to throw him. The reins had slipped from his hands and the pommel on the saddle had disappeared. He strained this way and that, trying to keep his balance, and then found himself being thrown in a great arc of falling, falling, falling. He awoke just before landing amid the plumes of foxtail grass growing in clumps along the pasture fence. The image of grass, vivid with colour, more clearly outlined than he had ever seen it when walking among it at home, stayed with him after waking. How beautiful those arching plumes tinged with purple swaying gracefully in the breeze! He clung to the sensation, the feeling of home, trying to slip back into the dream, but its benefit was all too swiftly overwhelmed by the grinding, crashing groans of his actual surroundings.

He had no idea how long he'd been in his bunk when the ship's motion seemed to assume a less frantic rhythm. The slamming waves seemed to come at longer intervals and the roll that threatened to pitch him out of his bunk became less severe. Beneath his diaphragm lay an area of leaden ache linked to the knot in his throat, but its pressure eased slightly.

He opened his eyes cautiously and turned to face the room. Lennox and Laroux were still in their bunks. Munden, Snarr, Morgan and Flynn were playing cards. A poker game went on at the other table. His bladder demanded a trip to the heads. He considered the many separate motions required. It seemed like such an immense journey. He decided to wait a bit longer. His clothes weren't dry yet and he couldn't think of bending down to haul dry ones out of his locker. Not yet. He closed his eyes and dozed again.

When he woke again he knew he had to roll out. Munden and Snarr were packing up cards as he gingerly swung out of his bunk. A miasmic sour smell seemed to hover over his sticky skin. A shower would make him feel better. He reached for his soap and towel.

"Well, looks like the farm boy is gonna live," remarked Snarr. "The bigger question is, will he stay on his feet during his next watch. Boy! It looks like you drew a coupla doozies this trip, Munden. You're welcome to 'em."

"Oh, we'll get ourselves sorted out pretty soon, don't you worry about it," replied Munden evenly. "By the way, Dutch, you're lucky Action Stations weren't called while you were in your bunk. From now on you'd better sleep with your clothes on at sea and keep your boots and Mae West handy, or the hatch will be slammed on your head before you can get out of here."

Ike struggled with supper. Momentarily his stomach seemed grateful, but after half an hour in the boiler room, he retched. Munden nodded to his questioning look so he headed up the ladder to empty the bucket again. He leaned on a rail for a few minutes gulping lung-fulls of air. In calmer waters for certain now but still too dark to see anything except the ship's pale wake and the whitecaps in the near distance. His stomach reacted unfavourably to the sight so he headed down.

Back on watch, with every move a giddy haze of wretchedness, he stayed on his feet by stern effort. Intervals of leaning over the bucket alternated with periods dominated by a determination not to do so.

At midnight back in the mess, Munden set the teapot on the hot plate and put two slices of bread in the toaster. When they were done, he handed one to Ike and one to Lennox. "You'd better eat these or you won't be able to get out of your bunks tomorrow. Take small pieces at a time and chew each one slowly. It'll stay down." Dubious at first, they found he was right. Ike felt much better after half of his slice had gone down. Munden poured himself a mug of black tea from the pot steaming on the hot plate. "Want some?" he asked. Ike shook his head. At home, tea came pale amber in tea cups and was considered unfit to drink if allowed to boil in the making.

"Thanks, but I'm crawling in. My guts are still not settled." Lennox nodded in agreement and they stumbled toward their bunks. Exhaustion dropped Ike into a sleep too deep for dreams as he closed his eyes.

When he stepped out on the upper deck next morning, a long line of ships dotted the horizon. He joined Munden leaning on his elbows at the ship's rail. "So that's what we're doing out here. Picking up a convoy. I wonder how far we're going. I hope it's right across the puddle. Always wanted to see England."

"Well, you won't get there on this run. We'll only feed these vessels into the main convoy where another lot of escorts takes over. The convoy goes over to Londonderry, but the escorts only go halfway or so. There they rendezvous with one made up of returns coming from the other side. They bring those back here."

"You mean we never get to go all the way across?"

"That's right. Early on in the war our ships went all the way, but now they've found it's more effective this way."

A disappointment coming on top of seasickness. Ike looked down at the grey water churning away from the side of the hull but raised his eyes quickly again. So all of this misery for what? A few more stinking beer parlours and more grey seas. Ruefully, the chorus he had been teased with on his last leave came to mind:

He joined the navy
To see the world
But what did he see
He saw the sea....

Well, he had refused to believe it then and he would refuse to believe it now. After all, the *Buxton* wasn't the only ship in the Wavy Navy. He turned and went down to the galley to pick up some breakfast.

For some much-needed relief between watches, Ike spent time on top deck in the fresh air. Still, the fundamental overwhelming discomfort of his entire being remained until they tied up in Halifax. Even there the ship had been tied up for an hour before all defensively clenched mechanisms relaxed. He was off watch till 2400 hours and though supper was served during their gradual approach to the jetty, he skipped it.

Ike hauled out his writing kit. Just had to write Sara before going ashore. Within a few minutes of tying up, those that had been off watch during their approach clanged up the ladder to disembark. Lennox, still in his bunk, began to stir. He had barely managed to drag himself to the boiler room and out again during the last two days at sea. At times it seemed his mind was not too clear.

“C’mon, Lennox,” Ike called out, “the girls are lined up out there, waiting for you.”

Lennox slowly opened one eye, then the other. He stared at the bulkhead above his head for several seconds as if trying to assure himself it was no longer moving. He groaned, and turned over on his side. Ike saw that his face had lost some of the pasty colour it had worn during the days at sea.

“What’s that you said, Dutch?” He yawned, stretched and sat up. “Did I hear you say ‘girls’?”

“Yeah, but you’d better get in the shower and scrub. You smell. No, dammit! You stink.” A chorus of agreement came from messmates still jostling each other, getting dressed to go ashore. Lennox slid down to the deck. He rummaged in his locker and, finding soap and a grubby towel, disappeared up the ladder. Ike sat down to write:

> Dearest Sara,
> Well, I got to sea at last and I’m telling you it wasn’t exactly what I had figured it would be. I can’t tell you where we are or where we’ve been. I can tell you I’ve spewed more in the last few days than I did in all my previous 19 yrs. Apparently it takes a few weeks to get one’s sea legs and overcome minor seasickness.

He paused, wondering whether he should mention St. John and the Reversing Falls. No sense writing something the censor would ultimately black-line. He would have liked to tell her about them “losing” their ship.

> The food on board is pretty good so far, I think. I haven’t been able to eat much of it yet. There are over a dozen men in the stokers’ mess and most of them seem OK. A bunch of us are going ashore today and I’ll tell you all about it in my next letter. From where we’re berthed it doesn’t look like much because we can’t see anything except jetties and warehouses and ships.
> I miss you very much. Wish you were here. We will get mail today and I am hoping for a couple of letters from you.

His pen doodled around on the inside cover of his writing tablet while he tried to think of how to tell her how he wished he could hold her in his arms again and.... That censor's eyes kept getting between his pen and the paper so he sighed and signed off with

Love, Ike.

then folded the letter and put it into an unsealed envelope.

By the time he'd finished writing, Lennox, Olsen and Laroux were in their uniforms ready to go to town. Lennox by now was in great good humour. He slicked his sandy hair back in front of the small mirror in his dressing case, perched his hat cockily over one eyebrow and surveyed his image smugly. "God! How will they ever resist, eh, Olsen?"

"Are you coming, Dutch? Good God, you're slow. Forget about writing that girl of yours. She's forgotten you by now anyway!"

"Go on without me," said Ike. "I'll catch up with you somewhere. Are you off to the Clock Tower?"

"Not me," said Lennox. "A stroll along Barrington Street will do me just fine tonight. OK men, let's go!" and he bounded up the ladder.

Munden, still in his dungarees, chuckled. "By God, listen to Lennox. Salty Old Nelson himself, now that we're tied up." He and Ike got dressed and, joined by Merant who until today had either been asleep or on watch whenever Ike had been in the mess, they sauntered ashore.

Passing along the harbour apron, they were struck by its bustling activity. Wagons and carts stacked with pallets of material either being loaded or unloaded crowded the quay-side while officers and men in and out of uniform scurried back and forth, shouting orders to one another. They walked up the slope to Barrington Street for a streetcar to city centre. Traffic of all kinds clogged the street and people jostled each other on the crowded sidewalks.

At Duke Street they stepped off. Munden pointed out where Ike should stop if he wanted to go up to the Hill. Both Merant and Munden had been to Citadel Hill before, but then they'd been all along Barrington Street plenty of times too so, what the hell, they might as well go up the Hill along with Ike.

The climb left them breathless but the sensation of stretching their legs after too long confinement in cramped quarters made up for it. "Ike, that clock's three hundred years old," Munden pointed out. Gosh! Nothing on the prairies had been there for a hundred years. "Old" suddenly took on new meaning. Compared to the city centre they now looked down on, Winnipeg's Main Street seemed brand new. Out in the harbour the water shone a sparkling blue in brilliant sunshine. Why it wore such a sullen tone on the open sea was a mystery.

They turned towards the squat stone walls. "Hey, Merant! Imagine what the guys endured who stood watch when this place was first built."

"Betcha they stood there wishin' they didn't have to. Like us on watch in the boiler room." He stopped and scuffed his boot on the pavement, trying to dislodge something grubby and papery stuck to the sole. "Good God! It's gett'n so you can't walk anywhere up here without stepping on the bloody safes! Used to be they were only thick among the bushes!"

"It gets a bit crowded over there after dark." How did Munden know?

"Hell, some of `em don't even wait 'til its dark. Look at those two over there."

With an arm around the waist of a slim, long-haired girl, a salt bent back the branches of the shrubbery on the far side of the hill. A couple, one of many lying on the grass nearby, called out to the disappearing pair. Boy! Not even Lizzie Letkeman about whom they made many a smirking joke in his home town would have gone into the bushes with a man. That is, not in broad daylight!

Down from the heights they made their way along Sackville Street to the Public Gardens for a brief stay. They walked to Spring Garden Road past a multitude of uniformed men with their arms around their girls occupying every park bench in sight. A light breeze sent cascades of rust-coloured leaves down from the tall trees, leaves that crunched under their boots as they ambled along the sidewalk. When they reached the campus of King's College they found a spot of grass in the sunshine and stretched out for a while. Students walking back and forth among the various buildings looked incredibly young. "I wonder how many of those kids would be in uniform if they weren't here in college."

"Yeah, Ike, some people have all the luck," Merant grumbled. "First they get an exemption from service. When they're done they step right out into an officer's uniform even if they don't know an armature from their own assholes. If my Old Man had the money to send me to university, I wouldn't be spendin' my days down in that stink-hole of a boiler room."

"Aw, c'mon now, Merant," Munden drawled. "You'd have never made it through university and you know it. Those lectures in Advanced Training nearly drove you nuts and they only lasted a couple of months."

"They don't have it all that easy either," Ike said. "There was this guy McCurdy in *Chippawa*. Seemed like such a kid, giving us a hard time in parade drill. Kept us at it to the very last minute of every drill. Put me on Number 9 one time for having a splash of dirt on my whites. Well, when we got to *Cornwallis* I saw a bunch of junior officers getting it on the parade ground. Holy Jesus! Talk about a hard time. Drilled right into the ground. I didn't mind seeing them sweat, I gotta admit, but it changed my idea of an officer's easy life, let me tell you. Not that I'll refuse the promotion when it's offered to me." They laughed at the notion.

"Well, I'm heading back to town." Munden got up and brushed leaves and grass off his uniform. "You guys gonna stay here all afternoon?"

Ike and Merant got up too. They passed the Lord Nelson Hotel with its brass trimmed doors and uniformed doorman. "Hey! Let's go in here for a beer."

"You won't get a beer in there, Merant. This town is dry. The only place to get a beer is in the wet canteen at Stad or the army canteen on the Hill. Me, I'm on my way to pick up my new uniform. The tailor's shop is just around the corner. You guys go ahead."

"New uniform? What for?" From what Ike saw there wasn't anything wrong with the uniform Munden wore.

"Wait'll you see it and you'll know." When Munden came out of the fitting room Ike knew that before long he'd have a uniform like that too. The fit was perfect, the fabric was so fine it made the naval issue look like burlap.

"How much?"

"Depends on the cloth you choose. This one's setting me back eighty-five smackers."

Merant let out a slow whistle. "Eighty-five bucks! Hell, that's more'n a month's pay. That'd buy a heck of a lotta beer."

Whatever the cost, Ike decided it was worth it, but he knew he'd have to save for quite a while yet. Christmas was coming and he intended to buy something special for Sara.

"OK," said Munden, tucking the parcel containing his old uniform under his arm. "Now I'm all set to go to the Lord Nelson. It's just about tea time there too." As they approached the hotel, they discovered Munden was serious about going in. He led them up the steps and through the handsome, old, oak doors.

Inside, Ike murmured to Munden under his breath, "Wadda we do now? You been here before?" To their left small tables were placed among potted palms where waiters hurried to and fro with trays of cups and silver teapots. A small group of ladies picked up their gloves and handbags at a table near the door and as soon as their perfume had wafted past them on their way to the door, Munden led the way to the deserted table. The white jacketed, grey haired waiter clearing away the dishes paused, looked at Munden frostily, "There is a café just around the corner, sir."

"Thank you, but we would like to have tea here," Munden said firmly.

Pale blue eyes surveyed them and their uniforms slowly, then registered the look in Munden's steady eye. "For three, sir?"

Munden looked pointedly at each of his buddies then back at the waiter and said gravely, "Yes, by my count there are three of us. How many do you get?"

"Right. Tea for three, sir." Not a muscle in his face moved as he made a note on his pad. "Anything else?"

Munden's eyes had wandered about, noting what was being served at other tables. "No, tea for three will be just fine, thank you."

Ike dared not look at either of his mates as the waiter hurried away, for fear of bursting out laughing.

"Stuck up old prick," murmured Munden as they sat down. "If we're good enough to fight for King George, we're damned well good enough to have tea in his admiral's hotel."

"For a minute there I thought he was going to kick us out," Ike said, recalling his experience in Manitoba while in Basics. "I'd been drinking in the local beer parlour for years even though I wasn't twenty-one yet, and nobody ever questioned it. Well, the first time I walked in the beer parlour at home in my uniform, do you know what the son-of-a-bitch of a waiter did? He came over and asked me how old I was. Well, I didn't think he was serious so I said, 'nineteen.' You know, the bastard refused to serve me a beer. There I was, out to win the war for that silly prick and he wouldn't serve me a beer. Now I think that was kinda funny, but I didn't feel that way then."

"That don't make no difference to some people," agreed Merant, "but I'd a' liked to see this old bugger try to kick us out."

Ike felt uncomfortable at Merant's tone and focussed on something to say to clear the air of its belligerence. While they waited to be served he looked around at the brass floor lamps with their little silk shades, the oak panelling, the shiny brass ROYAL MAIL plate on the mail slot and the carpets that softened every footfall.

"Just like our mess, eh? Needs a bit of puke, spit, stale smoke and bunker oil smell to make it feel homey." Other good natured comments restored them to good humour but the hatted dowagers sitting at nearby tables turned questioningly at the sound of their levity.

They finished their tea quickly. "Now y'know what it is we're fighting to defend," said Munden as they stepped out onto the street again.

"Like hell I know," Merant firmly disagreed. "Lemme tell ya a helluva lot of things is gonna be different when this war is over. Like this here hoity toity tea business. When we finish with the Germans and the Japs, we'll tackle places like that. I wouldn't mind pushing that old geezer's face inta one of them potted palms."

"What for? He's just a waiter. Pushing his face in wouldn't make a damned bit of difference. It's the like of those old biddies with their pearl necklaces and the old men making enough money out of this war to buy them more earrings that burns me up when they turn their noses up at guys like us."

Ike readily agreed to Munden's suggestion that they stop by at the K of C canteen near the water on the way back to the ship. They entered to find most tables fully occupied with men from all services. The matron behind the counter to whom they had given their order beamed as she handed them the sandwiches. "Anything else you'd like? We've just brought in some home-made pies today." How could they refuse?

"Helluva good pie," mumbled Merant, his mouth full.

"Yeah, and not a single palm tree or silver teapot in sight. Can't say I miss 'em." Ike fished a couple of nickels out of his money pouch and walked over to the jukebox. They sat back to listen and the general hubbub in the canteen died down while Dinah Shore sang "Always" and "I'll Walk Alone". As the last notes died away, Munden crushed out his cigarette in the ashtray. "I'm heading back to the ship. Got some gear to wash before we go on watch." Ike said he'd go along.

As they walked toward Barrington Street to catch a streetcar, big, bold headlines at the corner news stand caught their attention. "Hey, guys! Look at this!" They crowded around the paper. "Allies Invade Italy – Canadians in Spearhead."[4] Mentally, Ike quickly reviewed the list of men from Highfield that might be out there on the beaches. The paper said it was the Canadian 1st Division but that didn't tell him much. The last he'd heard was that most of them were still "somewhere in England." In the picture Montgomery was standing on an amphibian "duck" saying, "The Canadians were terrific on the beaches and on the attack inland."

"They don't mention casualty figures," muttered Munden. "But look down the page there: 'John J. McCloy, United States Acting Secretary of War, estimated that the Japanese evacuation of Kiska before the American-Canadian force landed August 15, spared the "invaders" from 5000 to 6000 men.' Invasions don't usually come cheap, not even on a small place like Kiska. God knows how many didn't make it onto those Italian beaches."

"Where the hell is Kiska?" asked Ike.

"Up in Alaska, one of the Aleutian Islands. The Japs seized it last year about this time, I think. That they're out of there is damn good news. They were getting too close to our west coast for comfort. Hey! All this good news calls for a little private splicing of the main brace. Let's get back to the ship and see what we can find in our lockers."

* * *

Four hours on, eight hours off, four hours on, eight hours off. HMCS *Buxton* plied the seas along the Atlantic coast, picked up tankers, carriers, and cargo vessels at St. John, Halifax and Sydney, escorting them to join convoys destined for England. The breaks offered at ports of call varied. A stay in Sydney for more than a day or two was unusual, but not unwelcome. Olsen said it for them all, "Not much to do but they smile when you're doin' it." St. John had numerous places to drink and more girls willing to give solace to the homesick sailors coming ashore. As a port of call Halifax had one important feature in its favour—mail from home.

The historic sites of Halifax soon became commonplace to Ike and he spent more time with the others, wandering along Barrington Street. They lined up to see the latest movies. They gazed into shop windows but had too little money to buy the furs and jewellery on display. They searched for good quality socks and underwear. Both were hard to find and very expensive. More than a buck for a pair of dress socks! Ike wished he had an Eaton's catalogue. He'd get three pairs for that price, he was sure. He bought a zippered leather case for his shaving gear but he was still saving for a "tiddly" uniform like Munden's so he never took all of his cash with him. Still, he avoided becoming a piker so he carried enough cash to stand a round or two in the wet canteen at Stad. His dreaded chronic seasickness was good reason not to get drunk.

The monochrome monotony of November descended on the North Atlantic. An endless procession of days in barely distinguishable variations of grey went by. Grey skies, grey rain, grey seas dotted with grey ships afloat amid grey-green seasickness. Lennox gradually stopped throwing up on every watch and started eating again, but Ike avoided the galley except to beg a loaf of bread to carry down to the boiler room with him on watch. He nibbled at the crust. Gave him something to throw up.

Particularly fierce weather on this run drastically slowed the escorted freighters. Ike's wretchedness brought him to the brink of despair. His knees were shaky when he climbed the ladders and his mind became so confused he had lost track of time when calmer waters at last heralded their approach to land again. Petty Officer Simpson stopped him as he stumbled off duty the day they entered Halifax harbour.

"Friedlen, tomorrow at 600 hours report to the Engineer Officer's mess. You'll serve as steward to that mess until further orders. Your duties'll be assigned by the Chief Engineer."

A reprieve from the sickening, sour smell of bunker fuel in the boiler room. As steward, he brought the officers their meals from the galley, washed their dishes, cleaned their mess. He was on duty from breakfast until the galley was closed in the evening and stood one four hour watch in the engine room during the day. Gradually his seasickness subsided. A faint biliousness still haunted his hours at sea, but he ate more than bread crusts and his vomiting spells became sporadic.

The food locker in the stoker's mess had seemed to be overflowing with good things to eat when he first came aboard from *Cornwallis*, stocked as it constantly was with generous quantities of bread and butter and jam for those who wanted to snack between regular meal times. The officer's mess, however, offered more than mere plenty. Real cocoa, creamed cheeses, bottles of pickles, mayonnaise, tinned meats and smoked oysters. Ike's dungarees which had begun to hang baggily on his gaunt pain-racked frame began to fit snugly again.

There were other differences. In the stoker's mess, a poker game was in progress almost around the clock, but in the officers' mess bridge games filled off-duty hours. Ike had rarely been invited to take part when he watched his older brothers and their friends play bridge at home. Now he had the chance to refresh his memory of the game while serving drinks and he soon realized that the game being played here was much more sophisticated than what he had seen at home. There, covert signals between players who knew each other only too well raised recurring complaints. Watch as he might, he could not detect such behaviour here.

"You know how to play, Ike?" asked O'Brien one day when they found themselves short a fourth. Ike said he'd played a game or two. "Sit in. We play a dollar a corner per rubber." With some inner trembling, Ike sat in. The cut partnered him with Taylor. From his "kibitzing" Ike had a fairly good notion of Taylor's style. He didn't bid rashly but he never underbid either.

Between them, with the help of a few good hands, they walked away from the game with a few extra dollars each. It doesn't matter much to Taylor, thought Ike, but those bucks'll make a difference to my next shopping trip in Halifax. He was asked to play quite often after that and although there were days when his bundle of dollars shrank considerably, he was well ahead by the time the ship nosed into Halifax harbour again.

Although Ike still slept and ate in the stokers' mess, he was not as much part of its daily pattern of feuds and friendships as he had been. He noticed, however, a growing friction between Snarr and Flynn. Snarr didn't seem to have many supporters among his messmates. Besides being surly, Snarr was slovenly. Flynn had not been a ray of sunshine from the time Ike first came aboard either, but now he was belligerent.

"Goddam you, Snarr!" Flynn would launch into a tirade. "Waddaya think this is, some fuckin' two-bit whorehouse? Why don't you clean yerself up for a change and wash them goddam dungarees. The godforsaken things are so thick with oil they're ready to walk out of here by themselves." Snarr didn't get any neater or cleaner.

Two days in Halifax and most of the men felt the effect of too much time spent in bars and fleshpots of the city. Ike came down after finishing his midday chores. Snarr, dressing to go into town, hung his dungarees over a pipe. Flynn stirred in his bunk awakening from a deep sleep. He opened one bloodshot eye, then the other. His gaze met Snarr's oil-soaked dungarees hanging close to his bunk. He roared out of his blanket, grabbed the offending dungarees, flung them into Snarr's bunk and sent a flood of practised invective after them. The legitimacy and probity of Snarr's mother, his father and his forebears to the fifth generation were denounced. A legion of saints and potentates were called upon as guarantors of the incendiary fate awaiting the unregenerate Snarr.

While Snarr had stubbornly borne many uncomplimentary remarks about his standards of personal hygiene, this attack was utterly void of even the smallest grace note that might have permitted him to pass it off with his own brand of surly flippancy. He straightened himself up from tying his shoes and turned toward Flynn slowly and menacingly. "That's it, Flynn. You shut your fuckin' mouth," he roared, stopping Flynn in mid-rhetorical flight. "I don't need to take that kind of shit from you. Shut up!"

But Flynn was just hitting his stride and paused only long enough for a breath. "Who the hell d'ya think you are, telling me to shut up? You scum of the goddam earth." And he was off again, continuing his tirade as he pulled on his boots and stood up again. Snarr took a step toward him with fist clenched. He was heavier than Flynn by at least twenty pounds, although most of that weight lay in the slight paunch thrusting against his grimy undershirt. "I'm tellin' you, shut your goddam face and stop actin' as if you're better'n everybody else on this ship."

"You low-down bastard! Anybody's better'n you. Hell, your mother pisses on the fire wagons when they go by. Hell, even the goddam fuckin' dogs're better'n you. I know what you are!" Flynn's fist shot out so fast, Snarr was sent backward from surprise as much as from shock of the impact. Before he could gather his reflexes to retaliate, Flynn had landed another blow.

Just then Munden came down the ladder. Manoeuvring his way quickly between tables and benches he got behind Flynn. "Okay, okay! Let's settle down here!" His voice was loud but calm. "Back off, Snarr," he said. "That's enough." But Snarr had got himself wound up and landed a fist that sent Flynn backwards. Munden caught him and whirled him around, interposing himself between Flynn and Snarr's advancing fists. "Flynn, you're due on watch in two minutes. Get down there."

Snarr's punch had reduced Flynn's enthusiasm for more. Besides, his fury had expended itself somewhat in the blows he'd landed on his adversary. "Yeah, I'm goin' down, but get that fucker to clean himself up. I don't hafta live with his shit and if you don't get him to clean it up, somebody else will."

"Awright, awright," said Munden soothingly, "I'll take care of it, but you get yourself outa here."

Flynn clumped up the ladder angrily and Snarr reached into his locker, found his shaving gear, and left the mess as well. The mess was silent for a moment after they'd gone. "Guess some guys are nuts about clean dungarees," ventured Ike, "and I can't say I blame 'em."

"Yeah, but I wouldn't have thought Flynn was one of 'em. He don't always smell like roses neither," remarked Olsen.

"We-ell," offered Merant slowly, "the smell that Flynn's got stuck in his nose don't come from that pair of pants. Those guys used to be great buddies. Used to hit town together all the time. A while back, Snarr got a dose somewhere, but he didn't let on to Flynn right away and the next time they got into port, he passes it on to a bitch that Flynn had a go at too, so then Flynn got the clap too. He's madder'n hell since he figured out where he got it."

Ike looked at Lennox. "What's he so mad for? Wasn't he the guy that told us we wouldn't be real sailors until we had a dose?"

"Yeah, but I guess he figured his pecker didn't need that extra service badge."

Ike ate his lunch slowly and then began sorting and reorganising his locker so that he wasn't dressed for going ashore when Munden, Merant and the rest were ready to leave. "I'll catch up with you at the canteen," he waved them on. Alone, he dressed and caught a streetcar for downtown. He paused a moment in front of a jeweller's window. Yes, that was it. That's what he'd send her; the heart-shaped pendant with a naval crest in the centre. She couldn't wear it without thinking of him because of the crest and that shape. Definitely, the right gift. He bought it without a thought to cost. He knew the "tiddly rig" would wait for him. He wanted to make sure she would too.

Three hands were intent on a poker game and the others who had stayed on board were in their bunks asleep when Ike returned. Without attracting attention, or so he thought, he wrapped the gift for mailing. That very evening, however, when Merant asked, "Hey Dutch, what happened to you? Didya get lost or somethin'?" Matheson, who had feigned sleep, rubbed it in.

"Nah, Dutchy wasn't lost, were ya, Dutch? He just had more important things to do than go out with you guys. He was playin' Santa Claus, an' you should a' seen what he was packin' up."

"Aw, c'mon, Dutch. Ya don't mean to tell me you spent good money on some dame you can't even get your hands on for God knows how long?" Lennox sneered.

Ike knew he dare not let them see any of this bothered him, so he said cheerfully, "Well, you know how it is. Gotta have somebody keepin' the home fires burning. How'd you guys make out downtown?"

Of course, their account of the afternoon ashore was typical of every shore leave they had spent in Halifax, except that this time someone had picked up a rumour about the St Croix, a sister ship to the *Buxton*. She'd been sunk on convoy duty in the North Atlantic. A British ship had picked up her survivors and then she got sunk as well. Only one guy from the St. Croix survived.

"What I heard was that the whole convoy had a bad time of it. Seems the Gerries've got some kind of a new torpedo. It's a real sonofabitch," said Olsen. "Once they get it aimed at a ship, she's a goner."

A babble of questions broke out but no one who'd been ashore had any further information.

"Well, my idea is it's better not to listen to that kind of talk. We haven't read anything in the papers or heard anything on the news so I say we should forget the whole thing. Maybe it's just a rumour being spread by the enemy to lower our morale. Besides, didn't Churchill say just a few weeks ago we were winning the war against the U-boats? As for the *Buxton*, she's not getting out very far into the North Atlantic on these runs so it's not our worry."

"Good thinking, Munden." Lennox offered, and murmurs of assent followed, but the mess became unusually quiet until the poker players took up their unending game.

Christmas day in Sydney Lynch cooked up as fine a turkey dinner as might be expected from any ship's galley, but in the stokers' mess the meal was eaten in silence. Not the daily portion of grog or the fact of Christmas produced any of the usual light-hearted banter. Over *Buxton*'s static-filled loudspeaker system, they listened to carols and to Bing Crosby crooning about a white Christmas. As the day wore on, homesickness set in. Listening to "Silent Night" and "Joy to the World" for the fourth time got Merant. He shot out of his bunk and shouted up the ladder, "Will somebody tell that son-of-a-bitch playin' those records to stop it? Stop it! I'm tellin' ya it's gittin' to us. Damn well enough for one day."

Ike wrote home. His first Christmas ever away from the farm brought thoughts of his mother's roast goose baked with a dumpling batter stuffing. The large flock of geese would have been slaughtered in early December for the Winnipeg market. He remembered all too vividly his trip to Eaton's purchasing room with last year's birds in the back seat of the Whippet. They had to remove the upholstered seat and the back rest to hold all the birds and since there was no heater in the car, both he and the birds were chilled to the bone on arrival.

He had been deeply resentful at the buyer who examined each bird for the tiniest of imperfections—a small tear on one, a small bruise on another. He couldn't downgrade them for anything else, since they were plump and firm and had been plucked with the greatest of care. There was no arguing with his judgments. It was "take it or leave it."

Still, he thought he had brought home a nice bit of cash from the transaction and he had done all right, judging by the fact that his Dad had made no complaint. Only cleared his throat when he counted the bills and then asked if he'd had any trouble with the car on the way. Three of the best looking geese had been held back live, to be slaughtered just before the Christmas feast.

At home today they would have begun the day with the usual chores but immediately after breakfast everyone would have gathered in The Big

Room to hear Dad read the Christmas story in German, a language they all understood, having learned it in school and heard it in church regularly. Then Mother would read the story in English and after that the gifts would be distributed. They were usually items of clothing, although when he was very little, a toy had appeared occasionally, but he had never counted on getting one.

Then it was off to church for the parents and some of the older brothers and sisters. He wondered if Nettie would have stayed home alone this year to keep her eye on the goose and to get the dinner on the table. When he was younger, there had always been several sisters to do that. All married now, they would come home for dinner after church bringing their husbands and children. What a crowd they had been last year! Dinner had been served in two sittings because even their huge table that could seat fourteen had not been big enough for them all.

The men of the family ate first, of course, with the eldest of the women filling any vacant spaces. When they were seated, Dad would signal others to ask the private blessing. This year he would be sure to pray for the boys who were far away from home, for Peter in CO camp and for Isaac in the war. Ike's eyes moistened at the thought. He knew his father did not approve of going to war, but for sure would not leave his wayward son out of his prayers. He forced his mind past that image. Once the food was passed the hubbub would begin, everyone talking and laughing, talking and listening at the same time, or trying to.

The meal would start with borscht. He tried to recall the fragrance of those spices—bay leaf, star aniseed, allspice, dried red chilies, and parsley—added to the rich beef stock before the cabbage and potatoes and tomatoes went in. Still, the goose was the main treat, served with mashed potatoes and brown gravy and carrots and parsnips and onions.

Dessert would be layered chocolate and vanilla milk pudding topped with heaps of whipped cream. No seasickness would mar their enjoyment and here he was, still struggling with a sick gut each time they left the wharf. Well, he'd lick that problem yet but it would take a bit of time, it seemed. He sighed and decided to think of something else.

He shouldn't be indulging in this homesickness, he told himself. He was lucky compared to the poor bastards fighting in Ortona.

He wrote Sara and reread her most recent letters. She said a few of the boys still stationed at Wainwright and Portage la Prairie expected to get Christmas leave and he wondered whether his gift had reached her before they did. To change direction of his thoughts, he sat in on the poker game and lost five bucks. On duty he read a book.

The officers having gone ashore, clearing away after supper was short work for Ike. He took time to relax in the best chair and considered the future. Steward's duty had made his dream of becoming a skipper himself both more compelling and more distant than ever. He was still only a Second Class Stoker. Three months service on this sleek four funnel destroyer chasing freighters on the eastern seaboard of Canada made for less excitement than dreams of great battles. Yet he felt a certain satisfaction in contributing to winning the war.

In spite of the risks, secretly he had yearned for open action with U-boats, a hit, a save. Enhance his credentials. Make news headlines at home. "Friedlen in Major Sea Battle Somewhere in Atlantic!" "Friedlen Saves Ship!" "Friedlen's Rise in Rank a Certainty!" But *Buxton*'s run was more troubled by bad weather and by mechanical and structural weaknesses than by subs reluctant to expose their position. Logic convinced him that it wasn't likely to change much. So, he'd ride out the storms on her and begin his advancement by going for a First Class Stoker's rank. He got up from the comfortable chair, and cleaned the officer's heads before retiring to the stokers' mess below.

CHAPTER 10
Stadacona

Early in '44 the *Buxton*'s effectiveness as an escort vessel came to an end and she was detailed to become a permanent naval training vessel. "Report to HMCS *Stadacona*," appeared next to Ike's name on the Orders board. Not *Stadacona*! Any ship but *Stadacona*! He cringed. Maybe the transience of its population accounted for the lack of spirit embodied in its nickname, "Slackers". He wanted a ship, not a land base. Yet once again he was packing his stuff into a locker in a barrack that held hundreds of men, all supposedly awaiting transfers as he was.

"What the hell kind of third rate cockroach is that?" he complained aloud as he stomped on a leggy, brown insect currying along the floor.

"Waddaya mean third rate? They're pedigreed. Bred for sophistication, you might say. What's more, they're trained. They never puke except in the toilet and they go there for their get togethers, too." The man in the next bunk grinned. "Welcome aboard."

"Thanks. But you guys haven't seen nothing till you see *Cornwallis* cockroaches. Plumper, scalier, hungrier, and a richer red colour."

A combination of voices from surrounding tiers drowned him out. The *Stadacona* roaches had earned Canada-wide recognition. They were merely waiting for the Canada Mint to strike a medal to honour their heroics. Ike had to submit. Moreover, he could not defend *Buxton*'s roaches either since she had only been taken out of mothballs in 1940 after the "Ships for Bases Deal" with the USA. They had not yet been bred to a strain worthy of a boast. In fact, they were so little appreciated that just before Ike got his transfer, the ship was abandoned at the jetty for twenty-four hours to enable exterminators to evict the undesirables. Of course, the first new hands drafted aboard would, no doubt, bring a fresh contingent to fill the vacancy.

Musing on this exchange later, Ike recalled that farmers' talk invariably turned to the weather. So much depended on the weather. They planned according to seasonal weather patterns. Each day's activities depended on the weather that day and the outlook for tomorrow. Here, weather was immaterial to the tasks at hand. Duties had to be carried out regardless. So no one talked about weather.

But cockroaches made for a common topic. The feel of scrambling feet across one's face at night produced an instant loud alert to the entire barracks. Biggies lurked in the heads and only a man with nerves of wartime steel dared to sit down and dangle his dong into the deep after sighting cockroaches clinging to the inner rim. *Stadacona* definitely was worthy of special honours.

Ike's new orders came quickly, the very next morning, in fact. He was to pick up a pair of coveralls in stores and report to Work Duty Station B at 0800 hours on the following day. An ominous order. Work duty assignments in *Cornwallis* had not been pleasant. Surely to God there was no coal pile in *Stadacona*!

Transported by truck to the Navy Yard gates, six stokers—a mixture of First and Second class, one Leading Stoker and one Petty Officer—made up the work party. Ike, a new recruit in the party, learned while on the way to the yard what task awaited them. The rest of the crew had been at it for a month or more. "It's fuckin' boiler cleaning. The dirtiest goddam job in the whole fuckin' navy." The speaker wore his navy hat tilted back, showing his high forehead and dark, almost black hair.

"Nah, it ain't the worst and it ain't even the filthiest. Wait'll you get to cleanin' bilges. That's class, by God."

"Aw, c'mon now. You know damn well the bilges on these ships can't be cleaned. They're so gummed up with shit and oil and all kinds of crap not even a rat could stay in there."

The Leading Stoker seemed to be enjoying the exchange. "Listen, you guys. All I'm sayin' is that when you're in the bilges, you've arrived. That's rock bottom. And when you get there, treat the rats with respect. They've learned to survive in there and you gotta learn too."

"Screw the rats!"

"Holy Sweet Fuckin' Father of Abraham, Isaac and Leading Stokers, deliver us from bilges."

"Amen!"

From the gates of the yard, dressed in their blue coveralls but wearing their navy hats, they marched in proper drill parade fashion to a destroyer tied up at the jetty. Ike decided this must be one of the low points in his life. Why were they not allowed to arrive in less conspicuous fashion? Why march in coveralls? Or if those, why the hat? The combination did not bespeak heroism. Bloody humiliating and degrading.

"Work crew coming on board!" the Petty Officer called out.

"Proceed," came the quartermaster's reply.

Since the boilers were shut down completely they walked through an open air lock to Boiler Room #2. "Friedlen, you're on the port boiler. The rest of you take up the same positions as yesterday. Now, get to it, men!"

Cleaning boilers had not been one of Ike's burning ambitions. However, it was another one of those challenges a sailor on the rise had to face; learning to accept a dirty job with gratitude. Fuck the gratitude. First off, since he hadn't done it before, he watched his mates.

The six stokers broke up into three groups—two men for the port, two for starboard and two for the upper boiler amidships. Ike was teamed with Jack, the dark haired sailor who, now that they stood side by side, loomed above him, taller by more than half a foot.

Like all the other four-funnel destroyers built by the Americans in 1917-18, this one was fitted with a Yarrow boiler, a boiler of quite simple design. Three horizontal drums sat in an A-frame configuration. Hundreds of iron pipes connected the top drum with the bottom two and these pipes were heated by burners below. Heating the water in the pipes turned it to steam in the top drum and became the ship's power source. These pipes became dirty and rusty. While only pure water was used in the boilers, somehow dirt, rust, scale and salts accumulated over time, reducing their conducting efficiency. So they had to be cleaned.

Ike's team mate got into the bottom drum, head first and wriggled to the far end. "Friedlen, you're next. In you go!" No time for questions about what to do once inside or how to get in. Dammit. Just get the hell in there. The sixteen inches wide by twelve inches high oval opening looked awfully small. One arm and head in, Ike forced his shoulders through by holding the other arm behind him until the elbow was clear. With both arms inside he scrabbled forward in the tubular cavern. He pushed with his arms. He wriggled. He scratched. He squirmed. Finally, his knees, legs and feet followed him through the opening. He was in, but he foresaw a problem. The drum was only thirty to thirty-six inches in diameter. How would he get out quickly? Obviously, he'd have to back out. He'd worry about that later. For now, this goddam war had to be won.

Jack's feet touched Ike's head. "What do I do now, Jack?"

"Just take it easy. There's no rush. You just lie there until the guys in the top boiler push a flexible steel cable down one of the tubes. They'll signal when the first one comes down. When it comes, grab it and pull it right into this boiler until the steel brush attached halfway along the cable comes through. Then you give it a jerk. That signals the guy on top to pull it up again. You do this three times. On the fourth haul-up, he'll put the cable into the next pipe. Got it?"

"Yeah, Jack, but how do I get outa the way of the dirt comin' down the tube?"

"You don't, man. Got it?"

"I don't want it."

He felt a need for ventilation in the drum. He couldn't turn around. He lay on his back, performing His Majesty's duty in coveralls with his eyes full of rust, dust, and sweat. Three hours of this without a break. And there'd be three hours more after that.

He thought of gophers. How he had enjoyed hunting gophers at home on the farm. They also lived in narrow caverns like hollow drums and tunnels, but always these were connected so as to provide an escape route. No dust in there, by Cripes! The life of a gopher in a prairie farm was in that way better than that of a Second Class Stoker in the RCNVR. A gopher could turn around in his drum. He sat up on his hind legs, clean and proud, his fore-paws almost in a gesture of supplication, waiting for a 22 calibre bullet to whack him squarely in the chest. A nice, clean way to go. None of this backing out of the drum with all the soot and dust clinging to your coveralls, your face, your hair, your shoes, your hands, and a Petty Officer waiting to march the crew across the naval dockyards as if on parade.

At the end of the day they marched out of the yards and off the site as quickly as possible. Thank God, the navy's truck was on time to take them back to barracks in relative privacy. Only the rear end of the truck was open and Ike turned to face towards the front so that no one following would recognize him. But then, what the heck! All five feet six and one-half inches of him were all of the same colour anyway—black. No telling where shoulders or neck ended and head began.

A shower and change of clothes made a difference but he still felt depressed when he headed for the mess hall. It would take weeks to clean this set of boilers and there would be another ship waiting in line after that. And another after that. His only hope of reprieve was an assignment to a ship.

Because he had just been transferred, the prospect of a letter from Sara to lighten his mood was unlikely. From the smell and appearance of the vats in the galley, the food promised to be no better than he had experienced at *Cornwallis* and those who slapped it into his tray seemed surly and resentful at being forced to provide even this much for the lowly likes of him. Utterly dejected and diminished in spirit, he sat down and stared at the mess in his plate. Only the potatoes were recognizable. The brown stuff was gravy with what was passed off as meat in it, but the mushy, greenish gob alongside defied identification. Perhaps at some time in the distant past it had been cabbage.

"Don't look at it, that's my advice," offered Jack cheerfully as he sat down beside him. "If you look at it too long, you may see little legs in there that never belonged to a cow or sheep. Down the hatch, is the only way to survive. It'll fill a length of gut. At any rate when we're done, we go to the canteen. Boiler dust needs something to wash it down."

The wet canteen was as rank as all the other beer parlours Ike had encountered. Tonight he overlooked its shortcomings. He and Jack ordered beer after beer and before long were in the mood to join in lustily when a group nearby began to roar out,

Roll along Wavy Navy roll along,
Roll along Wavy Navy roll along,
Though we joined for the money and the fun,
Though we joined for the money and the fun,
Of the money we've had none
And the fun has just begun
Roll along Wavy Navy roll along.

They lurched out of the canteen and stumbled back to their barrack. Jack, still in the mood for another verse of "Bangin' Away at Lulu" was cautioned by Ike. "Down Jack, or we'll be up on orders tomorrow an' never get outa this hell hole."

"Thass right, Dutch. Yer damn well fuckin' right. Gotta be careful so's we c'n get outa here," he agreed groggily. They were barely back in time for Lights Out.

Next day's boiler cleaning went the worse for their evening's jollity. "Listen, Jack," grumbled Ike after their first hour inside the boiler, "don't ask me to go drinking beer again before the weekend. This place is bad enough without you farting all over my head."

On the second week Ike got shifted to the top boiler. There he lay on his stomach. A welcome change and big improvement in that for the most part the dust went downward. That which billowed upwards could mostly be kept out of his eyes. Doggedly, while hating every minute of it, he performed each day's work. New oaths were welcomed into his vocabulary as the only weapon against the foulness of his circumstance.

He worried, too, about not having heard from Sara for several weeks. In his mind he listed all the boys that had gone to war or had found work in the city and wondered which of these might have come home at Christmas time to charm her with tall tales of valorous exploits. He knew her dark eyes would sparkle with excitement at their telling. She'd toss her long curly hair, laugh and ask more questions. Dark images of betrayal swirled amid the dust and dirt that enveloped him day in and day out.

In Ike's third week a new recruit was sent in first into one of the bottom boilers. Jack followed him. No sooner was Jack in than trouble began. "Lemme outa here! I can't take this shit! Lemme out! I'm gettin' outa here! I can't take it!" The panic-filled voice echoed in the drum. "Jack, goddam you! Get me outa here, quick, quick! I gotta get outa here! Lemme out, out, I say OUT!"

He screamed, he kicked, he pounded, he moaned, he begged. Terror filled the boiler room. With no time to manoeuver out of the way, Jack was trapped, pinned down in the drum as his mate scrambled and kicked and clawed in a frenzied determination to escape. When the recruit's feet emerged, the Leading Stoker grabbed them and began pulling but getting the man out wasn't easy. His shoulders jammed in the opening and he was too hysterical to remember how to shift one arm down to ease his way out. Eventually, they got him out. A new recruit took his place next day.

Finally, Ike received mail—two letters from Sara which he put aside, almost afraid to open them—and a letter from home. They hoped he had had a Merry Christmas. They missed him very much and prayed for his safety. The Christmas dinner had not been quite as merry as usual since two sons were now away. Peter was now serving his second year in the camp for Conscientious Objectors at Riding Mountain. And, of course, there was Ike, the sailor. Pete's wife had come with her babies but had to leave early because she was now alone to tend all their livestock by herself.

The dinner itself had been different, too. All except the breeding geese had been sent to market and the extra cash had gone towards War Bonds. But they had chicken and plum mousse and fresh buns. They had not exchanged gifts. Some money had been sent to Peter. He was only receiving fifteen dollars a month while in camp and that would not keep him in clothes and cigarettes. "All the same," wrote Mother, it was a day of rejoicing for all of us who honour Christ as King. His birth has made a difference for almost two thousand years and nothing will happen to turn our hearts from him now. Keep him in your heart, too. Our prayers are with you."

One of Sara's letters had been written before Christmas. He read it through quickly. She said nothing about his gift. He tore open the second envelope. "My dear Sweetheart," it began. Ike's heart sang. She had not called him "Sweetheart" in any letters prior to this. The pendant had arrived on Christmas Eve. She said it was the most beautiful gift she had ever received and she would wear it every day until he came home again. The parties during the holidays had not been much fun for her because she had missed him too much. Ike's eyes blurred at the thought and he put the letter away quickly.

He would read all of it over later. For now it was enough to know his hopes were intact.

Ike was put in charge of a crew cleaning a Babcock and Wilcox boiler on a corvette. A much easier cleaning job. Here, outside panels were removed to access a large chamber from which the crew comfortably cleaned tubes. Still, he exulted at new orders awaiting him on return to barracks on Friday: "Report to HMCS *Kamsack* K171 on Saturday 1100 hours. A navy vehicle will be at Station `A' for transport." Yahoo! Only extreme insanity would compel a man to want to stay in this hell hole. He began packing immediately. He shared his good news with Jack, the only one of the work party with whom he felt any kinship.

"Ike, I'm jealous as old hell. By God I hope you like your new ship. Best of luck." They shook hands on that.

"Thanks, you old bugger. I'm pullin' for you to get a ship too, and soon."

"Hold on a minute. We'll have a drink on that. My roaches tell me there's a wee bit o' rye in my locker, waiting for the right occasion."

"Great guns! That's fantastic."

Chapter 11
Kamsack

K171, a Flower Class corvette, was berthed alongside three other corvettes at Pier #5. Ike dragged his gear across their decks, a welcome exercise considering his eagerness to escape boiler cleaning and Slackers. "Friedlen, Stoker, reporting for duty." The *Kamsack* quartermaster checked his log.

"Welcome aboard. Gear goes down t'the stokers' mess. Report to Leading Stoker Barnes." Ike pulled his sea bag forward through the seamen's quarters to a hatchway and turned to go back for his hammock. A seaman stopped him. "Hi! I'm Wilson, leading hand of this upper deck mess. You comin' on board?"

"Sure am. Friedlen's the name, but just call me `Dutch'. I'm on my way to the stokers' mess."

"Welcome aboard." They shook hands.

He stumbled down the ladder with his bag.

"Dutch! You sonofagun! How'd ya do it?" Good old Charlie!

"Put 'er there, man!" A grip warm and firm as ever.

"My God, but it's good to see you, Charlie! How long've you been on this bucket?"

"Only ten days. I spent a couple of months on another tub doin' the Quebec Sydney run. How 'bout you?"

"Tell you all about it later. Who's the leading Joe around here? I gotta report."

"Right here. Barnes. Welcome aboard."

"Thanks. Ike here. Most times 'Dutch'. Where do I dump my gear?"

"Sea bag goes in Locker #7. Number's on the front. Sling your hammock over the mess table on the same side as your locker. When ship's in port, all hammocks are to be lashed when not in use."

Charlie had already made one round on the Triangle run—Halifax, St. John's, New York—and considered *Kamsack* to be "a pretty good ticket". In the corvette's crowded stokers' mess there wasn't much chance to catch up on all their experiences since separating in *Cornwallis*. She was smaller than the four-funnel destroyer *Buxton*. Certainly more crowded and all astir now with him and two other new recruits coming on board.

Slinging a hammock seemed medieval to Ike but he was too elated to mind. Off to sea! Screw the barracks. He undid the lashings on the giant bologna that was both bed and bedding. He released the slings and tied them to rings in the bulkhead, adjusting them to raise the hammock well above the aft starboard table. He'd be sleeping right above other hands sitting down to eat! That'd put a crimp in any urge to fart, but By Jumpin' Jeez! He was eager to have her sailing. Farts or no farts!

She slipped off at 1300 hours. Ike wrote Sara to give her his new address and posted the letter on board, open, for censorship by the ship's officer. Aware of those intruding eyes, he hadn't dared to get mushy, to tell her how he'd like to get her in the back seat of his Dad's car again. This was war and that could come later. His watch was posted as 1600 hours to 2000 hours and 0400 hours to 0800 hours. Anderson, another new man on board, would be standing watch with him.

Kamsack made her way out of the harbour in a brisk wind. On deck, Ike watched the collection of vessels tied up at the piers as they slid by them. Small craft, barges, patrol boats, ferries, crisscrossed the harbour, dodging freighters and other large ships lying at anchor, lending an air of urgency to the entire scene. A rush to get on with winning a war.

Ike's sense of wearing a layer of dirt, the accumulation of his weeks in barracks, disappeared with the wind in his face. By 1600 hours, however, the time to go down on watch, he began to feel queasy. At first he dismissed the feeling as a normal signal for his body to adjust to the sea. He assured himself it could hardly be as severe as what he had gone through before.

Barnes took Ike and Anderson down to introduce them to *Kamsack*'s boiler room on this their first watch. "Oh yeah, I've met one of these before. Got to know it from the inside out, you might say, during my boiler cleaning days at Stad. Cleaned one before I got my transfer," said Ike.

As the two men being relieved squeezed past them on their way back to the mess Anderson ventured, "Well, I ain't cleaned one of these babies, but we learned about it during training."

Nonetheless, Barnes coughed a bit to clear his throat and launched into a lecture about the intricacies of the Babcock and Wilson boiler and then took them through the most elementary steps of their boiler room duties. Having done so, he stood back and watched for a while. Finally he said, "D'ya think y'can handle her now?" Ike and Anderson chorused assent and nodded enthusiastically.

Barnes left the boiler room and had hardly reached the top of the ladder when Anderson began to throw up. No damn wonder, considering all that shit he'd filled up on. After lunch, he'd chomped down a bag of peanuts and a chocolate bar he had picked up in the canteen. He'd learn. Just as Ike had. Eat lean and you'll still spew but not as soon or as long. He, after all, had several months sea time under his dickey while Anderson was on his first ship.

As the watch progressed, the sea became more severe and Anderson increasingly more incapacitated. He lay on the steel plated deck like a sack, face drained of all colour, repeating over and over, "Dutch, I'm sick. I'm so sick. I'm so god-awful sick. I'm not gonna make it."

Unlike the *Buxton*'s, K171's boiler room was not pressurized and only two stokers stood watch at a time. Ike stood over Anderson's prone form. "Can you make it up to the catwalk? Get up there and get some fresh air coming in through the hatchway, but don't leave the boiler room, goddammit, or you're in shit!"

Anderson clambered slowly up the ladder, desperately clutching at each rung, making gagging, retching sounds all the way up. There he lay for the remainder of the watch, feebly vomiting now and then with nothing to vomit into. Down through the open mesh of the catwalk came what was left of his day's bread. Ike could manage the boiler by himself and was glad to be fully occupied to divert attention from his own inner torment. He felt dizzy and weak in the knees. Anderson's addition to the usual boiler room smells suddenly triggered his own shot at the bucket.

Ike felt better for emptying his stomach and got back to work. He rationalized that Anderson's puke flying all over the place had finally done him in. But he admitted that it must be jeezly rough out there or he'd have been all right. His own contribution to the bucket didn't smell much better than Anderson's but he vowed to remain vertical. Fuck the rough sea. This ship would continue to sail. If only his cocksucker of a head wasn't so damned dizzy. He swabbed the deck, climbed up and, stepping over Anderson, dumped the bucket contents over the side. He retraced his route to the boiler room.

At 2000 hours Barnes and Charlie came on duty stumbling over Anderson who still lay on the catwalk, comatose. "Everything OK, Dutch?" Barnes was first down the ladder.

"Sure." Charlie came down the ladder. "Don't you look like the white angel of death's creepin' over you, and you without a shave? You seasick or something?"

"A bit," said Ike and quickly started up the ladder. He got his arm under Anderson's head. "C'mon, our watch is over. I'll help you back to the mess." Anderson responded sufficiently to get on his feet. They stopped at the heads to throw up before going all the way down to the mess. Ike saw he was only bringing up white slime by this time and Anderson wasn't doing much better.

Back in the mess, he helped Anderson into his hammock, found an empty can to put into his hands for catching the inevitable. He gave a brief thought to his supper and decided the galley was just too far away. Too miserable to care about eating, he washed up and, can in hand, got into his own hammock. Its sway helped to offset the ship's roll somewhat, but it did nothing to sooth a stomach sensitive to the sharp vertical motion of the ship heading into the waves. Up, up, up she went until her prow stood exposed and dry, only to slam down in a shuddering belly flop. Then she did it again, and again, and again....

The stoker's mess, abutting the anchor chain locker, took the full force of a rough sea. Too ill to care about the occasional clang of the anchor chain, Ike lost consciousness with the thought of riding a roller coaster. He dozed fitfully until he heard Barnes and Charlie coming down at the end of their watch. They were deciding whether or not to eat.

"You don't seem to be the least bit seasick, Chuck, and it's pretty rough out there tonight." It was Barnes's voice.

"Well, it's not exactly the same as being tied up at the wharf, but my stomach's OK."

"Well, you're a born sailor, like me. I've never been seasick in my life. Been at sea for more almost three years, steady. I say, let's eat."

"OK, but what've we got. Galley's been closed for hours."

"I've got just the right thing. Get out that hot plate, plug 'er in and hang onto 'er so she don't get thrown off the table."

Ike heard the hot plate being set down just beneath his hammock and the sound of a pan being set on it.

"Barnes, you sonofagun. Where'd you get that fresh meat?"

"Charlie boy, The Lord works his wondrous fresh pork into the stokers' mess in many different ways. One way is to get on the good side of Old Moss up there in the galley. He agrees with the rest of us old salts that initiating new hands properly is part of the war effort. Frying this wee bit o' pork will make those chaps in their hammocks drool to share our repast."

"Barnes, you're a dirty bugger. I'd never have thought of it."

Ike's stomach was hurting and he had a fuzzy feeling in his head as if its contents were being sloshed back and forth. He didn't think he had slept much but he wasn't really awake either, and now his semiconscious senses were assaulted with fried food odors. Oh, God, not food! He couldn't take it. This strong overpowering heavy, greasy smell of frying meat. He could actually taste it and it made him retch. He groped for his can but couldn't find it. He stumbled out of his hammock, almost putting his foot right on the hot plate and fled up the ladder to the open deck. Clinging to the rail, he retched and retched and nothing came up except slime. The noise of his own torment drowned out the sea until finally the spasms died away. It was damned rough out tonight, he could see that much. He returned to the mess.

"Dutch, would you like a bit of fried pork? Chuck and I are having some and you're welcome to share it with us." Barnes' eyes were laughing although the rest of his face wasn't.

"Gosh, that's good of you, but no thanks. I'll just wait for breakfast. Gotta get some sleep now." Ike rolled into his hammock and released a big fart as he lifted his backside over the edge. The bastards!

The next watch, 0400 to 0800 hours, did not go better. The storm had increased significantly. Anderson again ended up on the catwalk while Ike attended the boiler. On being relieved, Ike went out on deck. The storm still partially obscured the view, but he could see that the corvette was accompanying dozens of freighters traveling in convoy formation. They had congregated somewhere off the eastern seaboard, coming from far off places like Central and South America, some had come through the Panama Canal, some from New Orleans, New York, Boston, Quebec, Sydney, Halifax. All had been escorted and shepherded to a precise spot in formation at a precise time by the escort group under command of Western Approaches in Liverpool.

Ike could tell they were loaded, lying low in the water, laden, he imagined, with guns, ammunition, food, vehicles. Supplies to conduct a war. In need of the escort's protection, freighters, regardless of their capacity for greater speed, steamed in a disciplined formation to accommodate the speed of the slowest of their number. Some were armed with a few depth charges that could be rolled off the ass end and others had a small cannon on board for use should a U-boat surface to have its picture taken. Without the escort they'd be easy pickings for U-boats. Ike's chest swelled at the thought of his part in the protective force.

He skipped breakfast and drank water instead. Since hands coming off watch were responsible for cleaning the mess, and with Anderson already in his hammock, Ike finished the job by himself before crawling into his hammock too. He managed the day on water and didn't miss a watch. On the third day out, Barnes put it straight to him when he caught him bent over a bucket, spewing blood. "Dammit, Dutch, you've got to eat something or you'll spew your guts out. Now, go down to sick bay before you get into your hammock. The Doc'll give you some pills to help you hold something down."

The pills might have helped, had they stayed down, but they didn't. Ike recalled Munden's cure and nibbling on bread crusts continuously kept him from bringing up more of his stomach lining. On the fifth day the storm abated somewhat. In mid-afternoon when Ike got out of his hammock for a go at the heads, he was surprised to feel less ill. He went up to the open deck.

Cripers! He still felt lousy, but at least the contents of his head had stopped sloshing about. That the storm was passing spelled great news for his tortured insides, but dire news for the convoy. A likelihood of more sub activity.

By next night they sailed in calm waters. When Charlie gave him a determined shake Ike felt he had only just barely fallen asleep. "Time to roll out, Dutch. Ten minutes to go. See you down below and don't be late to relieve me. I'm bloody well beat and want to hit the sack." He disappeared up the ladder. Ike had difficulty waking Anderson but they made it down to the boiler room on time. Seventeen minutes later, the bell clanged Action Stations! In tonight's darkness and calm waters an alert operator had spotted the unwelcome evidence on the radar screen.

Down in the boiler room, Ike shouted to Anderson, "Get your life jacket on and up that ladder to batten the hatchway. Hang on tight! We've got Krauts calling tonight!" The ship swerved sharply to starboard. More hot bunker oil to the burners set them pulsating to the urgent command down the voice pipe: "Full steam ahead!" Ike could only imagine the battle from the erratic movement of the ship, the pattern of explosives resonating on her hull, the crucial need for steam to co-ordinate with engine requirement on demands for: "Slow ahead. Dead stop. Slow astern. Ten Ahead." Ike's imagination struggled to fill in the gaps.

He could tell that the men shut up in the signals room were tracking the U-boat, trying to get positioned above her. The detonated depth charges sent deafening shock waves through the hull. His feet tingled from the vibration absorbed by the steel deck beneath them. Jeez! It felt as if the goddam deck itself was coming up into the boiler room. Time and again the TNT-filled charges exploded beneath them.

"Dutch! This damn ship is coming apart," shouted Anderson, his face white.

"The hell it is. Just keep those fuckin' burners going and listen to that sweet sound of steel plates buckling." Ike didn't feel that confident himself. The *Buxton*'s boiler room had been an island of calm compared to this, even when the convoy encountered U-boats. He remembered what he'd heard about the *Arvida*, how in a battle with a sub one of her depth charges had not been set properly and went off so close it loosened her plates, flooding the boiler room. For God's sake, you guys up on Action Stations, watch what you're doing.

"Dammit! How in hell do we get outa here if she gets hit amidships?"

"Don't ask such stupid questions, man! Just keep those burners going. More fire, Anderson. Just more fire all the time while this metal coffin gets blown straight to heaven in a cloud of smokin' chicken shit! At least you won't do any more pukin' after we get hit amidships."

It occurred to Ike that unless the escorts scored a direct hit, the Germans in their tin cans probably suffered a lot less than did the stokers in the boiler room of a corvette. Every pattern of charges dropped formed an envelope around the corvette and so she took the shock waves from one side after the other as she zig-zagged between port and starboard charge and the hunt went on. For all the tons of explosives tossed overboard in the war so far, relatively few subs had actually been hit.

The battle continued for over three hours. Barnes and Charlie relieved them at 0800 hours. Both had been on Action Stations since 0417 hours, both on the port side depth charge station. Since they had only fourteen minutes to change into dry clothes, they came on duty without breakfast. As with all battened-down mess hatchways so, too, the galley. Moss, the cook, had been out on his battle station with the rest of the crew.

When Ike and Anderson got off watch they got the story from all sides. Every corvette in the escort group had, it seemed, been on top of the bastards at one time or another. Radar, ASDIC, and whatever else was operating as a detection device had assisted in the sub detection maneuver. Every means of destruction had been flung at them. Pure, unadulterated TNT had been rained on them like manna from heaven. The subs had still escaped. But next time.... By Christ!

The fact was, there was no strange oil slick on the water at morning light. No subs had surfaced showing the white flag, but then they weren't expected to exhibit such civilized conduct, the dirty, sneaking bastards. No Carley floats bearing swastikas were there to be plucked from the waters by gleeful victors. No special message had come saying, "Auf wieder sehen." On the other hand, the convoy had lost four freighters, each one hit by an acoustic torpedo.

Still there were advances. Anderson had not been ill up on the catwalk throughout the watch. And he even helped with cleaning up the mess after breakfast.

When Charlie and Barnes came off watch, Ike sat down with them for lunch. Barnes told and retold their part in the battle, how every depth charge had been wrestled into place on the thrower, how clumsy a shipmate had been at helping Charlie here with the block and tackle that hoisted the charge onto the launcher. Yes, and by darn, he had just barely managed to get the detonation pin set for 80 feet when the order to fire rang. But he had done it, by God! Even though he'd had to hang on for dear life as the skipper veered to starboard with the engines going Full Speed Ahead.... Yeah, sure, that's how we win battles, thought Ike. With a lot of bullshit.

"What's this I hear about acoustic torpedoes? I mean why an 'acoustic torpedo?' A torpedo is a torpedo. Right Barnes?"

"Not right, Dutch. But let me explain." He cleared his throat for the lecture. "Ya know 'acoustic' has ta do with sound, don't ya? Well, the principle of the acoustic torpedo is simple. It's guided by the sound waves coming from a ship's propellers. They just set off their torpedo in the general direction of these waves and it'll land like a homing pigeon, right bang on the ass of the ship. Like a tomcat following his little kitten. Once he's dug his nose into her sweet, pearly patoot, the end result is certain. BANG!!" He slammed his fist on the table for emphasis.

"Sounds like one helluva severe enema," said Ike.

"Yeah, that'd clear all the pipes in one split second," agreed Charlie. "Whammo! No time to even shit in your pants and you're gone."

"That's right, Charlie. The Germans have got it and we're still tomcattin' around." Barnes looked grave and took another sip of coffee. "Scuttlebutt says that one a' them that got it this morning was Greek, two were American, and one was Canadian. That's top secret a' course." He sniffed, pulled his chin in and lowered his voice, "I got it from one a' th' officers' topside."

"Fuck the Germans. Eventually they'll run out of torpedoes, and for now it's full steam ahead." Ike stretched and yawned. "Think I'll take a nap in case the buggers come back before I get another chance."

"Me too," said Chuck. "We didn't get any sleep at all and I was bushed when you guys came down at 0400 hours. This side of the water seems to be crawling with Krauts lately. They say we take a different route each time we take a convoy out, but they seem to find us anyway. I guess it's hard to hide a hundred ships, even in an ocean as big as the Atlantic."

"Well, you maybe didn't notice with all the crap and corruption goin' on, but we're out of range of the air escort from either side out here. Those U-boats know it, too, so they're swarmin' around this Black Pit in mid ocean and the freighters are almost like sittin' ducks. Keep yer fingers crossed another wolf pack doesn't find us before we turn around."

Ten hours later they met a return convoy in mid-Atlantic where both escorts changed course 180 degrees. One headed ENE with the responsibility to safely deliver the loaded freighters to Britain while the other set course to WSW where eventually the largely unburdened freighters would fan out to North and South American ports. Return freighters running high on the water were attractive enemy targets. However, a submarine's foremost function was to prohibit goods from reaching any active war theatre and hence U-boats pursued loaded convoys more aggressively.

Shifting course made little difference to Ike. From his first day at sea he had always sailed westward, regardless of changes in course he was told about. Sailed west escorting Europe-bound loaded freighters, and west with less laden ones to North America. He became comfortably accustomed to a sun's idiosyncratic way at sea, always in keeping with his sense of Westward Ho!

Kamsack was running low on bunker fuel, on fresh water and other provisions, so she took a short break away from the convoy to head for St. John's, Newfoundland. Ike kept his seasickness in check in another heavy gale as they approached Newfoundland's rocky coast. Suddenly a three-masted schooner in full sail was sighted off the starboard bow. Word spread quickly and soon all hands except the stokers on watch crowded the rail to catch sight of her. She identified herself as a fishing schooner bound for St. John's with a hold full of fresh cod. An unusual sight for the predominantly inland crew who had seen pictures of sailing ships but had assumed that all sea going vessels nowadays were equipped with engines. Skipper granted special permission to take pictures.

They came upon St. John's harbour with unexpected suddenness. They had approached a seemingly impenetrable expanse of fissured rocks when suddenly this gap appeared. A narrow opening between a mighty rock off starboard and a slightly lesser one to port. Signals from K171 were acknowledged and since she was known from previous calls, clearance to proceed was quickly obtained.

Wilson, who stood at the rail beside Ike as they made the approach, explained that there was no getting into the harbour without it. A steel mesh curtain had been drawn across the entrance at the narrowest point of the channel to keep out aliens bent on the destruction of the city. St. John's had good reason to be on the defensive. U-boats had been sighted in Portugal Cove just a few miles along the coast. When friendly vessels asked permission to enter, the mesh could be lowered, as now was being done for *Kamsack*.

Once past the barrier the ship entered what Ike thought must be the most beautiful, most peaceful harbour in the world. Gone was the heaving and tossing, the pitching and weaving, the lifting and falling and corkscrewing of their passage outside. Here their only motion was forward. Here was utter calm and it was utterly beautiful. Ike's heart sang at the sight of the brightly painted wooden houses rising from the harbour front. They seemed infinitely blessed, resting under the protection of the twin towers of the cathedral that dominated the starboard skyline.

In a few hours' time he and Charlie and Anderson would slip ashore for a spell. He would have a short period of land sickness, but then he'd be able to enjoy a bit of sightseeing and they might find a pub somewhere for a quiet beer before heading out to sea again. Because of their watch schedules so far, he hadn't yet had a chance to talk to Charlie without Barnes being there to offer opinions on every topic.

In darkness they clambered over three other vessels to which they were tied and stepped onto the finger wharf. Only a short walk up from Baird's Cove to Water Street where a street car was making its way eastward. A recent snowfall had been turned to slurry by heavy rain. Walking in it was tough on their shoes, but they had come to walk. Besides, they had no idea where the streetcar would take them or even where they wanted to go. The few lit street lamps were fitted with shades to reflect their light downward and most shops were closed. Charlie said there was a K of C servicemen's canteen somewhere nearby but he wasn't exactly sure where they'd find it.

After stumbling along the street until their feet were thoroughly soaked, they stopped at a corner, wondering which direction to take next. "Hey, listen, Charlie. Don't you hear music?"

"Yeah, and it's coming from over there. That's what we're lookin' for. Come on."

Up a steep side street and around the corner they found the source and entered. The place was booming. Food and drinks were being served at tables around the perimeter of the hall while the space in the centre was filled with dancing couples. They were lucky to get a table when an American serviceman and his girl got up to leave. Ike and Anderson ordered beer while Charlie asked for a Coke. Anderson tapped his feet with impatience. After a few minutes he bent forward and said in conspiratorial tones, "Look, you guys. This is all very nice and homey, but I'm going to get laid tonight and this ain't the place to get it."

"So why don't you go out and find yourself a whorehouse and let us enjoy the evening."

"Damn you, Dutch, I don't need a third rate whore. What I want is to provide great pleasure to a nice Newfie wench who appreciates a set of balls that've seen lots of salt water."

"I agree with Dutch. A whore is what you're describing. Fuck off, Anderson, you reprobate," Charlie waved him away amiably.

"Don't forget to get back in time," Ike called after him. He leaned over towards Charlie. "OK, now I want to hear all about what's been going on with you since *Cornwallis*. How long were you in Stad?"

"Only a couple of weeks but it seemed like years. That place has got to be the absolute worst godforsaken base in the country. If there's any place in the world designed to make a man feel like shit, that's *Stadacona*." The word "shit" registered in the back of Ike's mind. It was a word he'd never heard Charlie use before.

"I was put on work detail scraping decks and painting ships in for refit and stuff like that. That was OK but then I got to cleaning bilges. I'm telling you, it's no picnic."

"Yeah, I heard about that when I was at *Stadacona* cleaning boilers. I thought that was bad enough. Did you run into any U-ee's on that run?"

"Oh, yeah, almost every run. If Canadians knew how far those bastards come into the St. Lawrence, there'd be shit hemorrhages across the country. Did ya know Mackenzie King closed the St. Lawrence to overseas shipping last fall 'cause we lost so many ships? The U-boats were practically tying up at the Hotel Frontenac! We never got one though and we had a damn good skipper. A Newfoundlander named Skinner. Tough as nails, but knew what he was doing. How about you?" Ike got going about the *Buxton* but was interrupted.

The job of the canteen hostesses was to entertain and they did so with cheerful goodwill. Now two of them came over and asked them to dance. Dancing meant talking, too, but the conversation was always more or less the same. "What's your name? My, but you're a good dancer. Where are you from? Oh, dear, you are a long way from home, aren't you? I have an uncle in Toronto. Would you like a sandwich? My husband is with the army in England. Are you married?"

Anderson had been right. These girls were not there to provide what he was looking for, and that suited Ike just fine. But they gave themselves over to the dancing and he in turn responded. It felt good to have his arm around a girl's waist again, having her come closer at the slightest pressure on her back so that they could move as one, cheek to cheek, thighs snugly touching with each step, until at last, "Thank you for the dance. That was beautiful."

The lights were dimmed for the third dance, a slow waltz, and Ike sensed that both he and his partner did not want to talk. Silently, she gave a bit more of herself as they circled the floor. Ike's thoughts turned to Sara and he found himself holding his partner very close when she whispered, "Do you miss her very much?"

"Yes! Do you miss him that much too?" She nodded and on his cheek he felt her tears.

Ike and Charlie allowed themselves half an hour to get back onboard, just enough time to change and get down to the boiler room. Ike was on the graveyard shift with Anderson who scrambled on deck with only two minutes to spare. Ike met him rushing down to change. "Hi, Dutch. I'm here! Hold the fort for me, will ya buddy? I'll be there in a coupl'a seconds." Dutch held the fort. The *Kamsack* would sail at 0100 hours.

The boiler room was quiet, warm, and comfortable with only one burner fired to maintain heat, electricity and hot water for the ship while she lay tied up in port. Using their life jackets as cushions, Ike and Anderson sat on two upturned buckets to review the evening's events.

"Well, did you guys meet any dames in that joint?"

"Sure, Charlie and I did quite a bit of dancing."

"Make any mileage with any of 'em?"

"Depends on what you mean by mileage, but from the short time I've known you, I'd say the answer'd have to be `No'."

"My God, Dutch. Why do you guys waste all this time? You should've been with me. You'd have had somethin' to write home about."

"Like what, Anderson?"

"Like how to come up with one helluva fine piece of ass. Jeez, Dutch, she was good and I let her have it till I thought she was ready to beg for fuckin' mercy."

Ike nodded, laughing, "Or maybe until you were like a rag and couldn't get it up any more? Like, after the first time?"

"Bullshit, buddy. I can keep going' forever, but I had to get back to this tub."

"Guess you'll keep in touch with her if you liked her so well. You'll be writing her so that you can see her again next time we're in port."

"Fuck that noise. You know better'n that. It was cunt I needed tonight. Not a pen pal."

"Well, at least she'll be able to use you in her list of references."

"Look, I'm not stupid. I know hundreds of matelots have been into 'er but it's still goddam good to see her squirm when a real salt fills 'er up."

After two hours at sea, Anderson was lying on the catwalk, terribly seasick again. Ike nibbled on bread crusts to fill the vacuum left each time he had to throw up and managed the watch by himself. He had made up his mind to beat this seasickness bitch. He would not lie down. Keep your head up. Nibble on bread crusts. Think of winning the war and shake the fuzziness out of your brain. Nibble on more bread crusts.

CHAPTER 12
New York

New York! New York! They steamed past the Statue of Liberty. A city with its welcome mat spread out. First class. First rate. Ike had read about the statue and heard about it on radio but had never expected to have its greeting apply to him personally, to inspect it while passing, to be so thrilled at doing it. It disappeared from view and its impact was overshadowed quickly by that of the city itself, the harbour and the frenetic activity wherever he looked. Spellbound, he wrenched his eyes from gazing when shipmates dressed for shore leave came on deck.

"Let me tell you guys a few things about New York," Barnes had said last night. "When you go ashore, for God's sake, wear your Canada badge on your shoulder. Make sure ya got one on both your tunic and your coat."

"What the fuck for, Barnes?"

"Well, Americans can't stand the bloody Limeys. Since our monkey suits are exactly the same, they'll take you for a juicer. Once they find out you're a Canadian, boy, you've got it made. So get yourselves some extra Royal Canadian Navy shoulder badges and, dammit, sew 'em on everywhere."

"OK, OK, we're not stupid. Sew Royal Canadian Navy on your fly," Anderson had spoken for the group.

Ike hadn't found extra badges so, reluctantly, he left the deck. A boisterous crap game was going on in the seamen's mess. He paused to watch the gambling table surrounded by players who had an hour to roll before berthing at Pier 29 on Staten Island. Enough time for a few to be cleaned out. Ike had noted that these games generally ended with big bucks in the hands of one or two players.

By now, several guys had already pulled out, claiming they had lost their shirts and had to keep a few bucks at least for going ashore. No matter. They had made a sizeable contribution as could be seen on the table. Three officers were playing, too. It was difficult to get a good crap game going in the wardroom so they frequently came down to play with the ratings. Ike forgot about the badges. He nudged his way into line.

His turn came and he put a twenty on the table. He took the dice and rubbed them between his hands, talked to them, kissed them and rolled them gently, pleading for sweetheart to be there. She was there with a four and a three. His heart leaped. He left the forty bucks in the pot and continued. This time he rolled an eight. Odds on matching this were longer. Three more throws and two fours showed up. He left his winnings on the pile. After a few more throws his stash had increased to well over a hundred so he took some off the table.

Ike kept on playing a cautious game, not covering more than he thought it prudent to lose at one throw and opening the pot with modest amounts on his turn. He had over two hundred bucks besides his current month's pay to play with.

With only fifteen minutes of play left before docking, they agreed that the eight players still in would each take a turn at the dice. Ike was number eight.

One by one the players took their turn and as each one finished the chorus became louder. "Get this bloody game over with." "What the hell is the hold up?" "Let's move on and go ashore." Lieutenant Whiley was Number Seven.

"OK, you big shots. Here's a hundred bucks. Cover that and weep!"

Ike was first to place. "I'll take it." He could lose a hundred and still be ahead.

"Ten on Dutch!"

"Twenty on Whiley!"

"Anyone else for ten on Whiley?"

"Here!"

Whiley talked to the dice, threw a five. Crapped out on his third throw. Two hundred dollars in the pot. "Shoot it!" said Ike. About ninety dollars were covered in small amounts around the table, and Whiley covered the rest.

"Be there baby! Baby needs a new pair a' shoes! Come to me, Mama! Be good to me, Mama! Seven or eleven, be there, Honey!"

Ike threw. "Honey was there, men! What you sees is what I shoots!" He continued to roll them bones. At game over he was more than five hundred ahead.

Within an hour after the game, he had become the J.P. Morgan of the lower decks. Doled out three hundred of it to guys who "didn't have a dime to go ashore with," who "couldn't even make a phone call," who "couldn't take a shit in one of those public places, if it came to that?" others asked plaintively, "Gonna send all that money home?" The heaviest loser was Lt. Whiley. Didn't ask for a loan. Good loser that.

Barnes had been in The Big Apple before and was only too happy to show Ike and Charlie around on their first evening in New York. "The Yanks are very generous to service men and women so there are plenty of free tickets for anything you wanna take in," he told them as they started for the ferry.

"You mean movies, Barnes?"

"No, hell, lots more'n that. You name it. Opera, ballet, recitals, art shows. Go to the USO on 42nd Street and it's all there. This place is in a separate class, lemme tell ya. There's sightseein' tours, all kinds a' them. You c'n even put your names down to go to people's homes for a meal—breakfast, lunch, dinner. Now, tonight, I think we should get tickets for Radio City Music Hall."

"What about churches, Barnes?" asked Charlie. "I mean, about attending."

"Well, you put your name in for somebody to pick you up to go to any church of your faith and get you back to the ferry later."

Ike kept his eyes glued on the Manhattan skyline as the ferry took them across. Barnes led the way to the El station for a train downtown. The El. A veritable marvel. To Ike the trestles on which the track was laid seemed much too slender for the train to speed on. Through dusty windows he viewed a new world as the El wound itself along crowded streets where cars below traveled unimpeded by the train's hurtling pace. With the eyes of a thirty-foot giant he saw the buildings flying by.

Gradually it came to him that second and third floor windows were much dirtier than those at ground level. Some were dressed to catch the eyes of El passengers and many large billboards were obviously for the same purpose, but the effect was a bit shabby. Momentarily this realization dampened his spirits. Still, the trip was exhilarating. What problems could be overcome by building on these stilts! No black gumbo in rainy weather, no snow to shovel from the track in winter, no dangerous crossings, no seasickness. Barnes suddenly said, "This is it!" They disembarked and walked.

Seated in Radio City Music Hall Ike attempted to recall, without success, what his vision had been of a concert hall while listening to the radio on the farm. He conceded that the battery operated Atwater Kent had let him down. No amount of careful adjustment of each of the three tuning knobs had conveyed a sense of this place. It had not prepared him for this experience. Even before it rose, the immense, rich curtain impressed him with his enormous distance from the farm. Yes, he really was watching the organist handling the keyboards and the symphony orchestra rising from the pit. The Atwater Kent radio had delivered wonderful music, but not with this clarity and depth of resonance. This was pure sound with no static or interference.

It was over all too soon. They rode the El and the ferry in silent meditation until boarding K171.

"Look, I'm for a cup of tea and I'll make some if anyone wants t'join me," announced Charlie as his feet hit the deck of the mess. A chorus of agreement rose all around.

"How about a little less of that transmission oil texture that you usually end up with. Something a bit more like, you know, tea?" came from a hammock.

"Did I hear you say you'd make it?" Charlie asked. He lifted the twenty-cup grey enamel pot, peered into it and took it up the ladder. When he came back he set it on the hot plate, dumped a half cup of loose tea into its steaming contents, and sat down to wait for it to boil. Inwardly, Ike groaned. Undoubtedly Charlie would leave it there for fifteen to twenty minutes, having heard his view that it required that much time to make real pusser tea, according to KR and AI, *The King's Rules and Admiralty Instructions* manual that governed their official duties.

"Well, how did you two enjoy that for a concert?" asked Barnes.

"For me," said Ike, "that was the finest performance I've ever seen and I'm going to spend a lot of time there while I'm in this port, I can tell you."

Barnes glowed as if he had created the concert himself. "Well, it's what I told you guys. New York's in a class by itself and you ain't seen nothin' yet."

"I thought that organist was great," Charlie chimed in. "My God! How many keyboards and gadgets does that machine have? Never seen anything like it."

"For me, that orchestra rising out of the pit was the cat's ass. You know, we used to listen to the Philharmonic concerts on the radio at home, and I thought the music was some kind of a gimmick, that no one orchestra could come up with all that music at the same time, and then, tonight. Now I know. What a night!"

"You guys must be gettin' soft in the head," groaned Barnes. "Neither of you has said a thing about the Rockettes! Here I take you to see the greatest chorus line in the world and you guys go on and on about the trimmings!"

"Look, Barnes," said Chuck, pouring out mugs of tea, "there's only so much an innocent, young Christian boy like me can take in properly in one night, regardless of how many milky white legs are waving 'Come here, Charlie' at me."

"You're right, Charlie, it's too damned much to digest all at once, and then to get this as the grand finale!" Ike stared into his mug. "Tell me, you got an undertaker's license?"

Barnes stirred and dipped frantically into his mug. "Yeah, Charlie, my front teeth damn near dropped off with my first sip. Next time you go to confession, ask for forgiveness for this hellish-tasting bitter fruit. You'll end up in eternal fire for doin' this to us, you rotten sinner you."

"Now listen, you bilge rats, flattery gets you nowhere."

"We've heard all the good stuff about New York, Barnes, what's the bad side? It can't all be like Radio City Music Hall."

"No really bad sides, Dutch, but there are restrictions. Like in every big city where bums and thieves and rapists like you guys are out on the loose."

"We can't wait, Father Barnes. What restrictions, exactly?"

"Well for one, Harlem is out of bounds for all military personnel, regardless of country of origin."

"Harlem!" said Ike. "I've heard about Harlem, but I can't remember what."

"C'mon, Dutch! Is pulling cow's tits the only thing you ever learned down on the farm?" Did your mother never tell you about niggers and whores? For God's sake, man, Harlem is New York's black district."

"Meaning the Negro section."

"That's right. They live in a separate section of the city. They're not allowed to live in the white districts."

"But they can work in the white districts, am I right?" asked Charlie.

"Right."

"But I still don't understand the restrictions," said Ike. "Why does that make Harlem out of bounds for us?"

"Look," said Barnes impatiently, "You're big boys now. It ain't my responsibility to explain the rules that Americans put in. I'm just makin' sure everybody in the mess knows about 'em. Harlem's outa bounds. That's it!" He slammed his open hand on the table to end the topic.

Just then Anderson and Leach hurtled down the ladder, reeking of beer and jollity. Anderson set a soggy paper bag on the mess table. The smell indicated its contents. "No Alcoholic Beverages Beyond This Point" posted at the Shore Patrol gate had been circumvented. A chorus of approval resounded the mess.

"Hey, hey! That's what I call good tea!"

"Where did you guys get that?"

"How did you get it through?"

"Howdja do it, you sons-a-bitches?" asked Barnes with grudging admiration.

"Aw, hell, it was easy," said Anderson gleefully. "Me 'n Leach stopped at that little pub down the road there on the way back from the ferry. We figgered those guys at the gate are just like the rest of us. You know, wouldn't mind a beer or two themselves. So we got the bartender to pack up two a' these bags, see? We got him t' put these two half-gallon paper cartons in this big bag `n then we got him to put a one-quart carton in a smaller bag. I carried the big bag and Leach took the little one. When we got close to the gate we were talkin' an' laughin' like we didn't have a worry in th' world.

'Halt! Who goes there?' the patrol shouted like they always do an' I says, `Anderson and Leach, Royal Canadian Navy, seeking permission to pass.'

`What do you carry?'

"Distilled water for RDF I says, an' I shook the bag a bit so's they could hear it was liquid, y'see."

"Yeah," interrupted Leach, "and you shook it so much the damned beer started to foam up and leak outa the top of the cartons."

"Anyway," Anderson resumed, "then he asks Leach what he's carrying an' Leach says, 'A quart of-of-of-Schlitz beer.'

'No beer allowed past this point,' he says. An' Leach says, 'Dammit! Oh, the hell with it. I'll just set the damned stuff right here. Is that OK?'

'OK. Proceed.' An' all the while my brown paper bag is getting wetter and anybody could've smelled the beer from a mile away!"

"All I can say," said Barnes, "is that if I'm gonna be forced to forget that I know about this beer, I'll just hafta drink some of it."

"Sure thing, Barnes, anybody that wants to chip in is welcome," said Anderson tipsily, and began to pour as mugs were hauled from the locker and coins clinked onto the table beside him.

K171's four days tied up to Pier 29 gave Ike enough shore leave to continue his adventures in what he now knew for certain to be the greatest city in the world. New discoveries at every turn. The ticker tape in Times Square had him rooted to Forty-second Street pavement for long periods in spite of the February chill. News of the war seemed to be flowing towards this centre from everywhere:

> *800 Japs, 286 Yanks killed in the Marshalls*
> *Russians wiping out trapped Huns in 2 Ukrainian pockets*
> *Nazi troops massing to attack Anzio beachhead*
> *Deadlock below Rome worrying for Britons*[5]

It sounded like a stand-off but then he hadn't yet had a chance to make his contribution felt. That would change soon, he was sure.

During the past three weeks, radio blackout and censorship had kept the crew in isolation. Now they could catch up. Newspapers were brought on board and the radio was there for those unfortunate to be on watch rather than roaming the city streets. At times the news elicited elation; at other times, apprehension. How much of what was broadcast could be believed? Ike wondered. Charlie had told him about the merchantmen they'd lost in the Gulf of St. Lawrence, but that story had never been mentioned in the papers or on radio. Didn't they matter? Or didn't the War Office want the public to know?

Whenever he and his buddies went ashore and felt they'd had enough looking, they frequented the pubs. Not merely drinking holes like the men-only beer parlours at home where patrons spent hours alternately licking salt off the backs of their hands and swilling ten-cent beers to be farted off in an atmosphere that became increasingly foul as the day wore on. These pubs had class.

Barnes, Ike and Charlie (who didn't drink but came along for protection) set out to sample them all one evening. One drink at a pub and then on to the next. They soon discovered that a drunken sailor was not tolerated in the pubs they liked best, regardless of his shoulder badges, so they began ordering soft drinks or simply left their glasses untouched. Good pubs had entertainers. A piano player, a singer or someone on a sax. This was the life. Being suitably entertained while sipping a drink with friends.... with no crudity or vulgarity. Small wonder the preachers at home had held forth against alcohol so loudly and so long. That kind of drinking was a sin.

They headed out to sea again for three rough days of pushing, squeezing, luring, cajoling freighters into convoy formation. It reminded Ike of herding the farm flock into a pen for the annual goose kill. There, too, selecting the best (those to be saved for Christmas) came first, then herding the bigger part of the flock that was to go under the knife into the pen and, finally, reserving the gander and two geese to make more goose dinners for the governor's table next year. Penned up, the geese did not resist. Since they were disciplined by the gander to stay in formation while in the pen, they went to the kill without a fight. Not so with the escort or its flock. Davy Jones would demand its share on this run as with every other that had sailed from down south. But not without meeting resistance.

Ike received his First Class Stoker's rating when K171 reached Halifax. Proudly, he snipped off the Second Class badge and sewed the new one in its place. My God, but he was moving up the ladder fast! Less than a year in the service and already he'd reached First Class rank. Surely at this rate a skipper's rank was within reach. A moment's mental calculation gave him pause, however. Resolutely, he pushed aside the realization that the war would have to go on for another six or eight years at least for him to achieve this. Let not such a thought put a damper on the flaming glory of this moment. He was now First Class! And there was no indication the war would end soon.

Sorting his fresh mail, he put aside a letter from his parents, dated in November, to read at sea. A letter, too, from Sara. He put that aside for a moment of privacy. They had orders to sail at 2400 hours compelling most of the crew to stay on board. Like Ike, they were mingling thoughts of home with every line of the letters being written. In his own case, with the news about his promotion, hopes, prayers and the love that flooded over him as he wrote.

The meditative atmosphere of the mess was broken suddenly as a sea bag came hurtling down the ladder and landed on deck with a thud. It was followed by a pair of very large boots, a long, long pair of legs and the rest of a sailor, well over six feet tall, hauling his hammock after him. Even before his head cleared the hatch, all minds registered dismay at the prospect of a hugely more overcrowded condition in the mess.

"Hello everybody. I'm Jack Jeffries." He announced.

"Jack! Dammit! Welcome aboard!" Ike leaped up with outstretched hand. "Jumped ship to get out of boiler cleaning, or how did you do it?"

"No tricks, no strings pulled except a big prayer every night, hard work in the daytime, and keepin' my nose clean—well, as clean as possible while cleaning boilers, and Holy Shit! I made it!"

"I c'n see all of those three must've been damned difficult, but it's good t' see ya. Barnes, here's your new man." And Barnes went through the business of introducing Jack to mess orders. It struck Ike that Jack was a very handsome man—dark complexion, black hair, high cheekbones and a nose reminiscent of a portrait of an Indian chief in a history textbook at school. Dirt of boiler cleaning days had obscured his good looks back in Slackers, but now, moving about getting settled, every muscle, fold, joint and sinew seemed in perfect harmony. Damn good to have him on board despite his bulk.

His gear stowed, Jack sat down at the table across from Ike and Charlie. "OK, Dutch, tell me all about this bucket. How does she act?"

"Well, she's a cross between a roller coaster and a duck. If you're standin' watch with me, don't be as seasick as I've been since coming on board. Otherwise, she's a good ship. Lots of new activity, too, on the upper deck lately. Latest scuttlebutt has it we're being fitted with some brand new detection device that'll have U-boats crying 'Uncle.'"

"About time we came up with something to make a difference in this war." Charlie offered. "Right now, it seems we're just standing still."

"If it's a worthwhile gadget, it has to have somethin' to do with the boiler room. If they came up with somethin' that would automatically fire a burner that would be great, eh?"

"Dutch, you miserable prairie gopher. Don't you understand you'll be firing burners in eternity? And with you there, why have automatic gadgets?"

"Well, if you ask me," said Barnes with his all-knowing sniff, "I don't think they've got anything new. But y'see the public of Canada needs a morale booster, so maybe they'll feed a line of bullshit to the press and everybody at home will piss right up the wall for joy. Meantime the war drags on."

"If another weapon or device comes on board, you can bet my mother's boots that some politician in Ottawa has it for sale and it won't work worth a damn."

"Jack, y' don't know what you're talkin' about. This tea party is not a Canadian election we're fightin'. This is war."

"Same thing."

After less than twenty-four hours in port, K171 sailed again to rendezvous with another main convoy. It became clear to the crew, once on open sea, that a new anti-sub device was operating on board. Barnes had heard from his buddies topside that a new man, who wasn't replacing anyone, had come aboard in Halifax. Trained in handling the new instrument which was, according to Barnes, "an anti-getting-hit-in-the-ass-acoustic-torpedo device."

Speculation ran high. What did it look like? Where had it been installed? Each man in the mess had seen some activity somewhere on board that pointed to the location. Was it in the control room? On the bridge? Surely, it had to be in a place where its secrets could not be readily copied and passed on to the enemy. For once the Canadian Navy would be ahead of the Gerries and we wouldn't want them to perfect an anti-anti-acoustic-torpedo-getting-hit-in-the-ass device, putting the navy back to square one.

Ike felt relief as he went down on watch. One menace of the war would soon be removed. He had not allowed his fears to surface and no one in the stokers' mess talked about it much either, but each man going down on watch knew that if the ship were hit, no one from the boiler room stood a chance of surviving.

His relief did not last long. It struck him that if the acoustic torpedo were made useless to the Germans, their only recourse would be to return to their earlier strategy of surfacing, sighting, and firing their torpedoes dead broadside. On a corvette, the bull's eye sat on the boiler room.

They seemed to be heading into a storm and in no time the boiler room turned cold. Unlike the *Buxton*'s pressurized space, this boiler room was open to a ventilator shaft extending up beyond the upper deck. Anderson and Ike put on extra jackets, mittens, socks and their life jackets but still shivered. Being tossed around by the heavy sea, both men turned sick. Ike was into his sixth month of spewing, spitting and gagging. As always, that dizzy instability accompanied the seasickness. He forced himself to stay upright and not succumb to the temptation of sleeping on the catwalk. The war had to be won standing up. Moreover, he was getting better at controlling his behaviour during these spates of illness. He practiced new techniques. It almost became a game, a diversion. The inevitable eruption, however, continued to come as a strangulating, painful climax.

Off watch, Ike went up for fresh air. He faced the cold, north-westerly gale drawing across the ship's stern. Hanging on to a depth charge rack he gazed aft, watching the ship's wake. A wake so effectively used by subs in the past to guide torpedoes. Now however, somewhere on board the secret device, perhaps a little black box, transmitted commands to torpedoes, "Do not touch!" He noticed a light steel cable being dragged from the stern as though it held something in tow. He shouted up to the oilskin-clad watch on the Oerlikon anti-aircraft gun platform, "What the hell is that line for?"

"C'mon up here. I can't hear you from there." Ike climbed the ladder.

"That line's hauling the new CAT gear, the Canadian Anti-Torpedo device that's supposed to make any torpedo fired at us go crazy."

"How the heck's that?"

"The line goes out several hundred yards and at the end of it is tied a metal boomerang that swishes back and forth, side to side. It creates confusion for the torpedo."

"But how is it controlled? Who is in charge of setting it in motion? Did we get anyone special on board to handle it?"

"Nah. Look at it, Dutch. You see it all. Hey! You'd better get down to the mess where it's warm. You're soaked, Man, soaked."

Ike's teeth rattled. A rough son-of-a-bitch of a sea out there and the Oerlikon anti-aircraft gun platform no more stable than the boiler room. But it was in the open. In earlier days at sea, to protect himself from the elements while on deck for fresh air, Ike had sat in a ventilator shaft's hood with knees pulled up under his chin. Secured to a depth charge cradle with a rope and free from bunker oil fumes and vomit stench, he dozed.

One day in a rough sea the rope had saved his life. The clanging of Action Stations had wakened him to the sight of heavy seas washing across the deck, sloshing and foaming among the depth charge emplacements. Seamen and stokers in life jackets were groping for handholds as they lurched toward duty stations. Ike had hit the deck to join them when a huge wave came crashing over the ship's bow. He was lifted off his feet, afloat and gasping in froth and foam, and felt himself being sucked down and hurled against the ship's rail. Unable to gain a hold, he was swept by a more vicious surge aft along the deck. With an abrupt jerk, the rope, still in place, stopped his course.

After that experience, Ike abandoned the ventilator shaft. From then on when the seas were rough he ignored the open deck and put up with the heavier atmosphere in the mess when he was off watch. Simply getting through each day without slacking off on his duties became an almost overwhelming ordeal. Whatever else he might be too sick to care about, he was going to make damned sure no one in the mess would be able to call him a shirker.

Among the men he had grown up with, no one was spoken of with more contempt than the guy who failed to do his share of the work in hand. Pulling one's weight almost belonged among the Commandments. He could still see his mother, sitting and stroking her apron over her knees on a day in which one of her splitting migraine headaches had kept her from her work for a few hours. "Today I've stolen a day from the Lord," she'd say dolefully, and work that much harder the next day.

Now as he retreated to the mess he thought with admiration of the man on the Oerlikon platform. True, he didn't have to breathe bunker oil fumes and got plenty of fresh air at his post. But it was wet; it was cold. From there the watch scanned the sky for aircraft approaching from any direction. He had his work cut out for him. Watch the sky, watch the sea, watch for ships in distress, watch for submarines, just watch, watch, watch and don't close your eyes.

That device out there gave his work a new dimension. Now, too, he could watch for a bewildered torpedo as it neared that twirly wriggler. He imagined how as it approached the ship's wake it would veer to starboard, then to port, stand on its tail trying to sort out its confusion. Meanwhile the watch would sound the alarm, "Crazy Torpedo Astern," and by the time the crew had reached action stations, the silly fucker of a torpedo would have taken a nosedive.

The great storm continued on, tossing around more of that peril stuff on which the mariners' hymn was based, the one they had sung with such emotion during church parade at *Cornwallis*. There, as a dry land sailor, Ike had been comforted at the thought of God's promise to calm the storms and protect them from the raging seas. Now there seemed to be a different need, one not as clearly defined in that these stormy seas were turning out to be a blessing.

Ike worried about this mixed blessing. If he couldn't beat his seasickness soon, he might be sent back to some kind of shore duty. He knew he's been close to that fate before getting posted to steward duty on the *Buxton*. How he'd hate to end up back in *Stadacona*! Made it tough to know what to pray for but, in balance, anything that kept the torpedoes at bay seemed to carry the most weight.

The weather, to be sure, was brutal. Not a step could be taken anywhere without a secure hold on a stanchion or handrail. Swabbing the deck in the stokers' mess had to be done with less than half a pail of water held between the legs while sitting down, one hand hanging on somewhere and the other performing the mopping chore. Even then, the water spilled over the edge of the bucket at times as the ship lurched from side to side.

Meals became an acrobat's test of skill that led many to go without rather than endure the struggle. Ike was made constantly more aware of the ocean's might and her power to affect every breath and motion of his body. He clung to the handrail in the heads, trying not to roll too heavily into the urinal. At that moment the ship plunged downward, God only knew how many feet, forcing back into his body the stream of urine that only a second earlier had flowed freely from him. "Piss on it!" a wry comment on unappreciated wonders of the sea.

Not a single ship in the convoy was lost in that raging storm, a fact that could not be attributed solely to the installation of the new wriggler. Jack had summed it up at poker, "No need to be concerned about a U-boat attack today. Only mad dogs and us crazies would go out in this storm. The Germans don't quite qualify in either category. I'm for non-stop storm. If life's too goddam miserable for any you on the water, go back to boiler cleaning."

Jack got his wish, the storm continued. Ike had time to reread the mail they had taken on in Halifax. He hadn't really appreciated the significance of the news in Sara's letter. She said Ernst Bartfeld's mother had heard from her daughter-in-law in Jamaica that a letter from Ernst had come through from Hong Kong. No one in the family had ever met the girl he married during his short posting to Jamaica before being shipped to Hong Kong. They kept in touch with her by mail but all had given him up for lost since there had until now been no word from him since Hong Kong fell three years ago. Ike decided there were even worse things in this war than facing the furious storms of the North Atlantic. Things like a Japanese prison camp.

To pass the time, he played poker. A game, with limits, going on somewhere at all hours. Five cents a card and two raises of ten. Not much money was lost or gained in these sessions, but they diluted the boredom and made life endurable in the small space to which they were confined.

Eventually the poker players, too, played out because of the storm and cashed in their chips. Crew members stumbled out of their mess only when duty called them to go on watch and wearily climbed into their hammocks on return. Only Jack Jeffries seemed unaffected by the exhaustion that gripped the rest of the stoker's mess. He, in fact, seemed to be enjoying life. "A storm is a storm is a storm," he announced cheerfully as he came down the ladder. Not even a grunt came in response. "A storm is a storm is a storm," he repeated, hoping to provoke some conversation. "Do you salts know who wrote that famous line?"

"Jack, for fuck's sake, don't give us that pile of horse balls. You know damn well, nobody would write such crap," Anderson growled.

"Yeah," Ike chimed in grudgingly, "the line doesn't go that way at all. It goes, `A piss cutter is a piss cutter is a piss cutter.'"

"Well, Dutch, it's one hell dammer of a gale out there to be sure. I noticed the new Engineer Officer that joined ship in Halifax is having a hard time with his guts."

"Yeah, I haven't seen him around much. What's his name again?"

"I think its McCurdy."

"McCurdy. What's his other name?"

"Don't know. Just heard McCurdy."

Charlie leaned his head out of his hammock. "Did I hear you say 'McCurdy'?"

"That's right, Charlie, you son of a whoring mermaid. How come you're alive all of a sudden?"

"Never mind the suck-holing, Jack. You're not getting any favours from anybody with that line of bull. Where's McCurdy from?"

"Manitoba, I believe. Some small two-bit joint infested with, I can't recall exactly, mosquitoes or Polacks or something. Why?"

"Only curious, Old Man, only curious. I used to know a guy named McCurdy. Remember McCurdy in *Chippawa*, Ike? Wonder if it's the same guy. I can't seem to shake him. He was in charge of the work party when I was cleaning bilges in Slackers. Gave us all a hard time but he seemed t'get a special kick out of nailin' me for every little thing. Acted as if he didn't know we grew up in the same town. I hope it's not him. This is an awfully small ship."

"I hear he's tough as nails on discipline and tidiness," came from Barnes' hammock. "Have you guys seen the engine room? My God, the place has been cleaned up for a change."

"As I heard the story," said Jack, "he went down to the engine room, looked around, walked around. Al Morgan's there, sitting on a bucket, watching gauges and bridge signals and not saying a fucking word to the new brass. McCurdy, silent as sin, goes on looking, staring, and then he stops at attention, within three feet of Morgan, and shouts at the top of his voice, 'MORGAN!'

Well, Morgan moved his ass a bit more quickly than it was used to. As he jumped up the bucket tipped over. It rolled the length of the deck from engines to bulkhead but above the din of engines, the sea and clanging bucket, you could hear Al's faltering, 'S-s-s-s-sir!'

'Morgan!' with every syllable loud and clear, 'Morgan!' I want this shit house removed from the engine room and returned to the upper deck heads where it belongs. In forty-eight hours.'"

"Sounds like a bit of a prick to me," said Charlie.

"The hell, a prick," said Barnes. "Even though Morgan is one of the best goddamn engineers in the navy, he's just never left home. He's in a fog, dreamin' that his mother and his wife are still sweeping the floor for him. McCurdy'll do him good."

"McCurdy's still a shit," maintained Charlie.

When the gale finally subsided, they lost a freighter. Not by the kick-in-the-ass treatment but by the straight, old fashioned way. Surface! Aim! Fire! The tons of depth charges released while in action during the storm had produced no results. The sub had evaded them all and gotten the hapless freighter within range of her torpedoes. So, on with the job.

The escort exchanged convoys with their opposite escort group and headed west. In St. John's, K171 provisioned and refueled. For Ike, the stop was critical for his health. During the storm, he had been reduced to eating bread crusts from bread that had become moldy in ship's stores. Barnes brought fresh, crusty bread down to the mess and its fragrance was a relief regardless of what it promised for Ike's physical condition. He immediately tested a slice to see if his stomach could tolerate it.

On the next leg of the run, the weather improved. The ship moved with the rhythm of the long, rolling, ocean swells which, long before land was sighted, presaged the approach to even quieter conditions. Ike was surprised to find he could even enjoy the ship's motion. He'd get his sea legs yet.

Chapter 13

Harlem

As once again they headed into New York, his favourite port of call, Ike did not get ready to go ashore when *Kamsack* sailed past the Statue of Liberty. Earlier in the day Charlie had come to him and asked with some embarrassment, "Would you mind takin' my watches for me during the next two days? I'll trade you whenever you want the time back."

"Sure thing, Charlie, but what's up? There's nothing on in Times Square that lasts two whole days, not that I know of anyway."

"Well, I met this girl at USO canteen last time we were here. She wrote me. Asked me over to her place. I'd kinda like to go. But she's in New Jersey. A long way out there and back just to stand a few hours watch and then go out again."

"I see. Well, you'd better leave me a phone number in case sailing orders get changed before you get back to town."

So Charlie took off for New Jersey. Ike pondered over the chances of this new attempt at romance. He doubted anything much would come of it, but Charlie, figuratively from Missouri, had to see for himself, had to be sure, to think, to decide. An Annapolis Valley girl had caused him such grief on leaving Cornwallis that he had spent endless hours thinking about her while awake in his fart-sack. Eventually he got it right. She was not for him. Had never mentioned her since he and Ike met again on *Kamsack*. Now he was out visiting Marlene, meeting her family, brothers and sisters, dog and cat.

His extra time on board gave Ike a chance to do his laundry, a job too difficult while in the North Atlantic with *Kamsack* bobbing, weaving, rolling and bucking like a wild bronco. A toilet plunger and a bucket of hot sudsy water on the top deck soon cleared the sweat and grime out of the clothes he'd worked, ate, and slept in since they were last in port. A good rinse and they were ready to hang over the pipes in the boiler room. Here was one advantage stokers had over seamen, Ike reflected. They always had a warm place to dry their clothes.

After two days standing watch for Charlie, Ike was very happy to see his stout figure coming along the pier toward the ship. "How'd it go, Charlie? Have a good time?"

"Sure did. They've got a real nice place out there and the Johnsons are a nice family. But Jeez! I'm beat. Marlene and I danced until three-thirty this morning. I don't think I got more than about three hours of sleep since I left."

"Tough luck, man. That's what women'll do for you once you start getting serious. Now you'll be punished for your sins. You've got to keep your eyes open for eight long hours. You're on until 1600 hours. Barnes said he'd relieve you for a half hour lunch break at 1200 hours. OK, Chuck?"

"OK, Dutch, but when will you be back?"

"Our sailing orders are 1900 hours. I should be back by about 1700 hours."

Ike took his liberty by himself since the rest of the mess had already gone ashore. Since he had no one to drink with, he decided to stay cold sober. Nothing was more devastating than to begin fighting the sea with a hangover.

After getting off the Staten Island ferry on the Manhattan side, he stopped for a hot dog. The open air stand, always popular, dished up the best dog anywhere. Nowhere else was there as much butter on the bun and no other stand served a mustard like theirs. It made the dog. The difference. Today he was not disappointed. He hesitated for a moment after taking his first bite, trying to decide whether to wipe the juicy mixture of butter, mustard and wiener dripping down his chin with the paper wrapper or to give it the finger job. The finger would give him the chance to lick the full ten cents worth, but the dignity of his position and the paper wrapper won the day. The hot dog was either late breakfast or early lunch. He'd flip a coin later to settle the question

The eleven o'clock movie, *Casablanca*, starring Humphry Bogart and Ingrid Bergman, seemed right for his mood. He settled in toward the back of the theatre with his popcorn and opened his pores to sentiment, nostalgia, loneliness, heartbreak, all the tender feelings that could never be expressed on board ship. He cried a bit and was thankful to be alone. Nobody in the movie house cared and it was not embarrassing to sit with his handkerchief in his hand. Sara reached over for it, too.

He stepped into a bar restaurant and ordered a large slice of cheese cake and coffee. He ate slowly, savouring each bite, thoughtful of its flavour and texture, of its fragrance. For once there was no hurry, no one with him to urge him to get going to the next place or event. As he leaned on his elbows, sipping the last of his coffee, his thoughts turned to the future. There was more to life than Moss's roast beef, mashed potatoes and canned peas. He paid the bill. Ninety cents. A little more than he had expected, but then he had asked for a large piece. He left a ten cent tip and went back to the street. Regardless of these delights, the war had to be won. On the *Kamsack*.

Back on board at 1500 hours, he slung his hammock for a few hours of sleep before supper and drifted into a confused dream in which Anderson and Chuck and he were on a wagon and the horses were running away but then he was holding the dice in a crap game where all the other players, all Mennonite preachers dressed in black, withheld their bets. Now Sara tried to hold onto him but the road was steep and he slid away from her and he swayed from side to side and up and down and out of the sea rose a porpoise who announced that "The Bells Are Ringing," and then another emerged with a school bell in his hand, shaking it madly. He fought them off and then Chuck was diving into the water and Ike dived in after him. As he hit the water, horns blared and bells rang interminably.

Action Stations! Ike groped for his life jacket, his boots. Not there. "Jeez! Who's got my fucking life jacket?" With one hand on a stanchion he groped blindly. He had to get out before the hatch clanged shut. He stumbled toward the ladder and reached it before waking completely. He stared down at his pusser shorts. He looked around. Good God! They were still in port. There wasn't anyone else in the mess. Why the bells? Those jeezly bells! And what in hell was all that other noise going on up there? Had the Germans come into New York harbour? He dressed in frantic haste, found his life jacket and raced to the upper deck where he encountered utter confusion.

Black smoke billowed from K171's smoke stack. Holy Shit! This tub was on fire. Through a darkened skyline Ike saw fireboats racing toward the ship, water spouts spraying, ready to douse the fire from a distance. Sirens sounded at full volume from every converging boat. On ships nearby, bustle, action and panic, captains and crews fully aware of the dangers of a fire out of control on a Canadian corvette. Unless contained, farewell to a section of the harbour. Her cargo of depth charges would make one helluva bang.

Ike looked around the deck for the skipper. Then he remembered. Captain Crowley had gone ashore for a haircut leaving McCurdy in charge for an hour. He scanned the wharf and saw the captain getting out of a taxi at the checkpoint. Skipper paid the driver and identified himself to the security guards, seemingly unaware of K171's state of peril. He tipped his hat and turned to see the spiral of smoke—black, very black smoke—rising from Pier 29 and rushed towards his ship. From behind him came the sound of fire engines. Glancing over his shoulder, he saw a fleet of red fire trucks racing to catch up with him.

Ike saw the skipper come on board to be recognized by Quartermaster, who stood his ground throughout all the commotion before making a dash for the bridge. Why the bridge? Ike wondered. Cowboys stopped to put their boots on before dying; perhaps captains had to die on the bridge.

Kamsack's pumps were delivering water with hoses turned overboard since the location of the fire had not yet been determined. Ships moored forward and aft of K171 had their firefighting hoses in action, wetting down their own decks, hosing down anything that might catch fire or explode. Preparing for the worst. Fire trucks on the jetty extended their telescoping ladders and men in slickers on small enclosed platforms stood at the ready with hoses in hand.

In the distance as far as his eye could see through the smoke and water spray, boats continued to come like so many reserve troops, ready to fill the gap should the first assault capitulate. The shrill, eerie, piercing sirens continued. Surrounded, K171 was destined to be destroyed, Ike thought, if not by enemy fire then by the water that was about to be pumped into her. He could see the rescue craft standing in readiness to drag her out to sea. Lines had already been cast on board. The steel cable was firmly secured to haul her out.

All the while the black stream of soot and ash belched out of her stack as if it were fed by hell itself. Ike rushed toward the boiler room hatch and looking down, saw Charlie attempting to make a point with a very excited fire chief who seemed to be insisting that he was going to stick his hose into one of the fire chambers. Like everyone else on deck and on the pier, Ike couldn't tell the origin of the smoke, but he had a suspicion. It was borne out later when Charlie reviewed the day's events, recalling them in chronological order for the benefit of his puzzled messmates.

"I was relieved by Barnes for lunch. At 1230 hours I went back to the boiler room. Barnes left. The port burner was operating; steam was normal. At 1300 hours I reduced fire in the port burner; steam was on the high side. At 1315 I cut out the port burner; steam was on hold. At 1400 hours, steam was down a bit so I cut in the port burner."

Here Charlie stopped to question his memory. It was customary when steam was down and all burners were out to turn on the fuel valves on two burners at the same time, then light the torch and insert it first in one burner and then, when it was burning, remove it to insert it into the second burner which by this time would be ready for firing.

Charlie wasn't certain about events at this point. Had he turned two burners on? Had he forgotten to light the starboard burner? And, worse yet, had he then forgotten to turn off the fuel valve? Or had Barnes done this?

Whatever the case, he was sure he had only dozed for a minute. When he woke up, steam was too low with the port burner functioning at Low burn. At 1510 hours, he fired the starboard burner, turned it on High burn. Steam was low. At 1520 hours, Action Station bells were ringing all over the place. He checked the burners. Starboard burner was a bit hazy, but going strong. Steam was normal.

"Then I heard cries of 'FIRE!' 'FIRE!' 'Where's the FIRE!' They came from the upper deck and I started up the ladder to see what was going on. Just then McCurdy came crashing down the ladder shouting, 'Fire! Fire! We're on fire!' I was on my way up shouting 'Where's the fire? Where is it?' I stuck close to the rungs of the ladder and tried to paw my way up and I felt these boots and legs and finally a belt scraping the back of my head. Then

McCurdy was hugging me and pressing me to the ladder as if he loved me, I'm telling you.

We both came to our senses at the same time. `Sir!' I said. And McCurdy shouted in my ear, 'We're on fire, dammit. Where's the fire down here?' Well, we both let go of the ladder at the same time and crashed down on the deck and picked ourselves up to find the bloody fire. We checked the burners. I guess the fuel valve that had been left open for I don't know how long had filled the bottom of the fire chamber with about five to eight inches of bunker fuel. Hell, there must've been about a hundred gallons of stagnant fuel in there, burning without enough oxygen to produce a clean burn. I knew it'd take an hour or more to burn it off.

About this time the water hoses began to come down the ladder. McCurdy started up the ladder to keep them from pumping water into her and the Fire Chiefs started to come down. 'Where in hell's all the smoke comin' from? Where's the fire?'

I said, 'It's in the boiler, where it's supposed to be.'

'Don't get Smart Alecky with me, buddy. This god-damned ship's on fire! Where in hell is it?'

So I took him to the starboard burner and pointed to the air slots so he could see the inferno inside. Well, you should have seen his face, Ike. 'Holy Christ!' he said. 'Bring that fire hose over here. Hey, you there!' he shouted to the firemen above who were pulling the hose and a couple of them came down into the boiler room. I'll tell you it was getting crowded down there.

I told him, 'You can't put cold water in there, sir. You'll crack the boiler and cook us all like so many chickens.'

'But you've got a fire in there, goddammit! It's gotta be put out!'"

"I heard that part," interrupted Ike, "while coming down the ladder to see what was going on. He was determined to shove that damned hose right into the burner. What a steam bath that would've made."

"Anyway," continued Charlie, "I had just about persuaded him that everything would be all right if we just let the oil burn off when the safety valve at the top of the boiler blew open! That runaway burner had increased the steam pressure, lemme tell you. The sound of the steam blasting through that valve rattled the bulkheads and to make it worse, when that steam hit the atmosphere in the boiler room, it filled it with white condensation. The fire chief thought it was the pall of death coming down on us all."

Ike laughed. "From the look on his face, I'd say you're right. God, he was shit scared! I had been watching the gauge so I knew what was coming, but even so, that blast was a shocker."

"It sure was." Even Charlie was beginning to see some humour in the ordeal he had just gone through. He smiled ruefully and went on. "The Chief hollered, 'Jesus! We're all sunk and we can't even find out what the hell happened. Bring that fire hose, goddammit!' McCurdy stopped him, but only by standing in front of the burner so he couldn't get at it. He pointed to the safety valve and shouted in the chief's ear and finally he understood. God! I'll tell you, I was more scared about what he was gonna do than about the fire."

Hanson, one of their messmates who had been on shore leave, came rattling down the perpendicular stairs. "What the hell's been goin' on around here? There's fireboats runnin' all over the harbour and I musta seen a dozen fire trucks pullin' away from this jetty on my way back from the ferry, and just now I saw the Captain takin' a bunch of firemen to the wardroom. Can't I leave this tub for a coupla hours without you guys gettin' into trouble?"

So the story had to be told again and the smoke got blacker and the drama in the boiler room more intense with its retelling. Ike went up to the galley for his supper and found Moss busy fixing a tray of snacks. "Hey! Is that what we're getting for supper? I didn't know this place had turned into a fancy tea room."

"Some fancy tea room with you guys fillin' it up with smoke and shit. Just look at the stuff that's floated into this galley." He wiped his hand over the lid of one of his big steam kettles. It came away black and he wiped it on an apron that had obviously already done that service several times before. "First you guys damn near set the place on fire and now I gotta fix up a party so Captain Crowley can get out of trouble with all them fire chiefs up there. You can damn well wait for half an hour for your supper today and you're lucky you're gettin' anything at all."

Ike went topside to wait out the delay along with the rest of the crew. They stood at the rail, watching the last of the fire trucks reel up their hoses. Black smoke still belched from *Kamsack*' stack, but it seemed to rise with less fury than when it first raised alarms. In a few minutes, Moss made his way to the Captain's cabin, bearing his tray covered with a white towel. A clink of glasses could be heard coming from the same direction. Whiley came over and stood beside Ike. "Tell me, Dutch, what exactly was going on down there this afternoon? You guys had us scared shitless. Not to mention the New York Fire Department."

By the time Ike had given his version of the problem with the starboard burner and the stand-off with the Fire Chief, the peace negotiations in the Captain's cabin came to an end and four fire chiefs emerged, their faces somewhat flushed, presumably from the heat of the day. There had, after all, been a fire on board. Each one carried a bottle of 160 over-proof pusser rum barely concealed under his slicker. "Fuckin' good ships, these Canadian corvettes," one of them remarked jovially as the group made its way down the gangplank.

At 2100 hours they were back at sea, the supper of Moss's Special was out of the way and the dishes and deck had been washed. The mess was still abuzz with speculation about the day's events. "There'll be shit to pay by somebody for this fracas," Barnes asserted.

"Yeah, you just can't send out smoke signals without some chief noticing, no matter what tribe you're from, Charlie," offered Leach.

"It's a helluva lot easier fighting the war than fighting the New York firefighting brigades, I'll tell you," Charlie said regretfully.

"Who in hell pays for today's special? The Canadian Government?" asked Jeffries.

"No fuckin' way the government pays," said Carpenter vehemently. "It's part of the US contribution toward winning the war."

"The bloody hell it is. You know who pays? The goddam Germans will pay and why the hell shouldn't they?" Barnes asked.

"I think it ought to be the Engineer Officer. He was in charge when it happened. McCurdy's gonna take the rap," Jack said emphatically, and several hands echoed agreement.

"That's right! McCurdy's got to take the fuckin rap. You're damned right."

Charlie spoke up angrily, "Listen, you guys don't know your ass from a hole in the ground and much less what you're talking about."

"Oh, Yeah?"

"Yeah. It's me, Charlie, that's who's taking the rap. Six days shore leave denied in the port of New York. And I'm not bitching about it, see? And you're not going to make a damn thing about it, see? Now get all that shit back up your fat asses and let me go to sleep!"

At sea again, the fire provided material for discussion, comment, and jokes. Charlie, however, did not see the humour. He kept to himself as much as it was possible in cramped mess quarters. He felt the burden of blame keenly and though Ike tried to make idle conversation about other topics, Charlie's unresponsiveness was discouraging. Ike saw him reading over his letters from Marlene and knew why the loss of six days of shore leave was casting such a pall, so temporarily Ike talked less to Charlie and played more poker.

Approaching the Newfoundland shore, *Kamsack* signaled for permission to enter St. John's for refueling. She tied up on the south side and took on fuel syphoned from storage tanks located high on the hill. Ike went ashore with Charlie, Jeffries and Barnes. When in the company of Jeffries who soaked up beer like a sponge, overindulging by the other three seemed obligatory.

As a result, Ike's seasickness on the leg into Halifax was compounded by a terrible hangover. He vowed to mend his ways but when they tied up, Charlie had to stand watch and Jack was all set for another carouse. Ike persuaded him to see at least one movie before hitting the wet canteen, so they went to the Capitol where Errol Flynn and Alexis Smith were playing in *Dive Bomber*. Ike enjoyed the movie, but Jack was annoyed when they came out.

"Those goddam airmen get all the glory. You'd think they were the only ones fightin' this war. Jeez! That story was a pile of bull. You'd think somebody'd make a movie about the guys that get the fuel across so those pretty fly boys can sport around among the clouds playin' tag with the Germans. Hell, if it weren't for us holding off the U-boats, they might as well pack up their fancy airplanes over there. C'mon, let's go for a drink."

"Whaddya mean, go for a drink? You know there's no place to buy a drink in this town and I don't wanna go all the way to the canteen at Stad for a lousy beer. This is Halifax, man. Not New York."

"An' don't I know it. You ferget, Dutchy Boy. I was stuck in Slackers long enough to learn a few things besides boiler cleanin'. Just follow me an' we'll find us a blind pig."

"What the hell's a blind pig?"

"Just stick with Old Jack, Dutchy, an' you'll get wise."

They turned down a narrow side street and into an alley, then knocked on a door. A small hatch opened. "A coupla dry ratings, Canadian Navy," Jack said, and the door opened. Up a narrow stairway they entered a noisy, smoke-filled, steamy room crowded with civilians and servicemen in damp uniforms, clammy from a heavy mist that hung over the city.

While Ike nursed his beer, Jack downed his quickly and ordered more. *Dive Bomber* still rankled. He began to express his resentment in louder and louder tones. "I'm telling you, Dutch, there isn't an airman alive that doesn't think his shit don't stink. Walkin' around with noses stuck up in the air. I'm not gonna kiss their fat asses."

"Aw, c'mon Jack. You don't need to brown-nose nobody. So they're stuck up. Can't blame em. Nobody gives a damn. You think your pretty shit-hot yourself sometimes. Get off it and drink your beer, you silly prick."

Jack laughed uproariously. "Hey, that's good, Dutch. Chickening out, eh?" He turned toward an airman seated at the next table. "Hey! Is it true you guys have to hose out...."

"Jack, god-dammit, let's get outta here." Ike was glad to note that the airman was at least six inches shorter than Jack, but he did have two buddies with him. For a moment it looked as if all three were going to get up to answer Jack's unfinished insult, but were stopped when two bouncers loomed over their table. They settled down to their drinks, pretending to ignore Jack who stood nearby.

"OK, Jack. Time to get back to the ship. Let's go." Ike got up, put his arm around Jack's waist, tried to keep his voice low enough that only Jack would hear. "Man, let's get out of here. I can handle a couple of airmen but I'm not big enough to take on those big bruisers too." Jack looked down at Ike whose head barely reached his shoulder.

"Jeez! You're right, Dutch, ole buddy. Let's go." He chuckled, patting Ike on the head. "Gotta get you back to the ship. We gotta win this war, right?" They made their way to the door under the baleful gaze of the bouncers and Ike breathed a sigh of relief when they reached the street. He had some difficulty persuading Jack to board the streetcar, but eventually they both got on and Jack promptly fell asleep. As they rumbled back to the ship, Ike decided that in future, when going ashore with Jack, he would persuade others to join them.

Kamsack clipped past McNab Island and nosed directly into a formidable storm. Ice built up fast on her upper decks where seamen had to keep hacking at it lest it outweigh her ballast. While chipping away, Ike considered himself fortunate not to have this task as his main job. Although in critical circumstances, stokers had to assist with clearing ice, the stokehold was a haven to return to. It, too, was cold, but dry. Everywhere else wet clothes, wet boots, dripping bulkheads and leaky pipes made for soggy, damp misery.

U-boats, usually so prevalent on this run, respected the storm and left the convoy unscathed. During the run, one old freighter failed to retain its position and collided with another, but damage was minor and she made it back to port.

The ferocious storm had wreaked havoc all along the north Atlantic seaboard. It delayed the assembly of another convoy off New York, causing an extended layover for *Kamsack*'s crew. The relative calm of their approach to the jetty and their arrival in brilliant sunshine revived weary spirits and ship's company with leave credits tumbled ashore as soon as hawsers were made secure. Even Charlie's glum face could not quell Ike's sense of elation as he, Barnes, Jeffries and Leach hurried away from the pier.

At the ferry dock, The Gold Star Mother embraced them warmly and they stood at the rail enjoying the bustle and clamour of the harbour during the crossing. "What the hell kind of name is 'Gold Star Mother' for a ferry? Anybody know?" asked Leach. Nobody, not even Barnes, knew.

"I'll tell you what," said Ike. "Let's ask the skipper. He's gotta know. Why don't you go and ask, Barnes?"

"Like hell. It was your idea. You go and ask." So Ike made his way to the wheel house.

"Yeah, it's some name alright," said the skipper in reply to Ike's question. "She got this moniker when Mayor La Guardia got the notion that women should have more babies, what with so many men getting killed and all. So he started this contest, y'might call it, for having the biggest family, see? The more kids, the higher the award; bronze for so many, silver for so many more, and a gold star for the most. Why he hadda name the ferries, I dunno, but it was just for the publicity, I guess. So we're stuck with this stoopid name. He's a great guy, but boy, does he get crazy ideas!"

"Well, maybe he was trying to give the passengers some ideas about what to do to pass away the time on the crossing," laughed Ike.

"Hell, plenty of 'em had that idea already."

The story only served to heighten the good spirits with which the group launched their assault on city delights. Hot dogs were a unanimous choice for a change from the seafaring, moldy bread sandwiches Moss had made these last few days. A pub crawl downtown was in order.

Ike tried to stick to his "fewer drinks" resolution, but what the hell. They had a couple of days in port to recover and the bars were as captivating as ever. One bar, one drink and on to the next, melting to the mood of the piano, the singer, the clarinet and feeling dry and warm and welcome. A middle aged man joined them at one bar and asked the bartender to "bring these hee-roes a drink". His order was graciously welcomed by already over-primed recipients.

"Too bad about Charlie," said Ike. "He'd only order a Coke, I know, but that 'hee-ro' stuff would make him feel good."

"Yeah, poor Charlie. Here's to Charlie."

They repeated the toast at the next spot and then Barnes proposed, "How about one for *Kamsack*," and they all drank to *Kamsack*. From then on, they had to have two drinks in each bar and before long Ike found it hard to keep his head up. Dimly he realized that Barnes was trying his best to organize their return to the ship and Jack becoming progressively louder and more belligerent.

"What the hell's the matter with you, Barnes. It's only one o'clock an' we got overnight leave. What's this fuckin' idea 'bout gettin' back t' the ship. Y'know what? Yer jus' startin' to ack like an ol' woman, Barnes. Y'know that? An' y'know somethin' else?" Jack paused, seeming to lose the train of a complex and portentous thought. "Y'know that nobody, but nobody tells Jack Jeffries when it's time t'go back t'the ship." He lurched slightly as he turned to resume his course along the sidewalk.

His head wanting peace and quiet, Ike longed for his hammock. Sensing trouble coming, he put his hand on Jack's arm. "Hey, Jack. Ol' Dutch here needs some shleep. How 'bout givin' me a hand back to the train, ol' buddy," and he leaned heavily on Jack's arm. "We c'n hit another bar or two on th' way t' the station, OK?"

The next thing he knew, he was lying on a cold, hard bench and someone was shaking him. "Hey! You guys wanna get off or d' you wanna spend th' night at the dock while we tie up 'till morning? This is the last trip to Staten Island until 0730 hours." Ike raised his head. It seemed to weigh a hundred pounds. Barnes and Leach sat up, but Jeffries was still lying face down on one of the benches, one long leg dangling to the floor.

"C'mon, Dutch. Help us get him up. You're the only one he'll listen to."

Ike felt incapable of helping anyone other than himself, but he rose to the task and between the three of them, they got Jack moving. The ferry crew waited patiently until Jack's long legs got untangled and down the gangway.

Too miserable to think of leaving the ship, Ike vowed over and over to cut out drink. Forever. Still in the sack after a full night's sleep, his head bursting, threatening to explode with every sharp sound, he noticed Jack was his usual sprightly self. Ready for more carousing. Fleetingly he speculated about drinking. A sin or not a sin. Whether his condition was punishment for overindulgence. Seeing Barnes and Leach in like condition he dismissed the thought of his individual guilt and wondered if perhaps by late evening he'd be ready for an hour ashore.

On their last day in port Ike and Leach set off together. "Now, listen, Leach. No boozin' it up again. We just gotta make it back before that damn ferry shuts down or *Kamsack*'ll sail without us. Sober's the word, Leach, you got that?"

"Suits me fine, my head isn't ready for another jeezly hangover."

"So what do we do with the day?"

"How about a movie and then let's just walk around to enjoy the solid ground underfoot. My legs begin to feel as if they need a good stretch after a trip like the last one."

"Sounds good to me."

They stuck to the plan. After watching a movie, they ambled about aimlessly. Suddenly Ike became aware that all the faces around them were black. "Hey, Leach," he said in a low voice, grasping Leach's elbow. "Are we in Harlem?"

"Hell, I dunno. But now that you mention it, I think we are." They paused at the next corner to read the signs.

"D' you think we should get the heck out of here?"

"Nah," said Leach nonchalantly. "Let's just walk a few more blocks to see what it's like. Doesn't look dangerous to me."

"Sure. Why not? Everything I've heard about it has made it seem kind of mysterious. And what the hell. You only die once!"

"One thing though, Dutchy boy. We agree not to make any passes at the females in this place, OK?"

"Couldn't agree more. From what I hear these black guys'd rather castrate you on the spot than wait for apologies if you as much as say 'Hello' to one of their women."

"I wouldn't mind trying out a pub or night club if they'll let us in. Whadda you say?"

"Fine. The guys on board say the entertainment in here is the greatest. How in hell they know beats me. It's out of bounds so nobody gets to go."

They maintained a casual air as they penetrated further and further into forbidden territory. Black faces met them, black faces came up from behind and, in passing, turned to take a second look. Ike felt whiter than the white of his dicky, as if his face was flashing like a neon sign. A man stopped to watch them approach and shook his head in disbelief. But the only threatening moments came when they passed a group of teenagers lounging in a doorway, spilling out onto the sidewalk.

"Fuckin' Limeys."

"Bringin' the clap in here, the buggers!"

But the voices were kept low, only loud enough to be heard, but not loud enough to demand response.

Darkness was falling and they passed more pedestrians. Some girls in tight skirts and sweaters like in other ports. Girls with polite fetching propositions. "You lonely tonight, sailor?" "Need a little lovin' baby?"

"No thank you, Ma'am."

"Maybe another night. Thank you just the same."

The rest blended with the night. Only Ike and Leach stuck out as if lit up.

"We'd better find someplace to get off the street for a while," Leach suggested, sounding a bit worried.

A well dressed, middle aged man came toward them.

"Excuse me, sir. Can you tell us where we could find a nice night club around here?"

"Well, let me see. How can I give you directions?" After a moment's thought, he suggested a place only three blocks away and ended with, "Now have a good time."

They hurried toward a street much more brightly lit than the ones they had been following. Turning into it, they felt relieved to be among a moving mass of cars and people. They found the club, its bright multi-colored neon sign flashing a warm welcome.

Ike noticed a couple of pedestrians stopping to watch these two sailors make their way up the steps to the door of the club. The noisy clamour within faded before them as they crossed the threshold. Every face inside turned to stare. The voice of the head waiter echoed in the sudden silence.

"Good evenin', gentlemen. What c'n ah do fo' you?" The words were polite but the tone was otherwise.

"We'd like to take in your evening's show and if you serve dinner we'll have that, and drinks. Is that possible?"

A long pause suggested refusal was being considered. "This way, please."

They were led toward the back of the large room in which several dozen tables filled the centre of the floor and a stage occupied the far end. A pianist sat with his hands motionless on the keys. Many of the tables were already occupied. "The waiter will come to take your orders in a minute."

"My God Almighty!" said Leach in a hushed voice. "We're the only whites in the place. I'm feelin' a bit shaky. How about you?"

"I've had better moments, but my pants are still dry."

"I have a notion it's gonna be a bit rough. I think we need a stiff drink. Scotch or rye, what'll it be?"

"Let's wait and see what the waiter's got to offer. Here he comes now."

A huge bulk loomed over them. About 260 pounds, Ike figured.

"OK, what'll you Limeys have?" he asked in a surly tone that reminded Ike of the bouncer of a racy night club in a recent movie.

"Sorry, sir, but we're not Limeys," Leach said politely.

"Look, man. Ah knows the Brittania Navy uniform, so don't tell me who's a Limey an' who ain't a Limey. Now, what'll you have?"

Ike and Leach cleared their throats at the same time.

"I'll have a rye and ginger," said Leach.

"I'll have the same."

"Ice?"

"Ice."

While their drinks were prepared at the bar, more customers arrived. Their table seemed to warrant special attention from each new arrival as well as from those already seated. "Jeez, Dutch! Some of these women know how to dress. They look all right."

"Yeah, they're definitely not the low end of society. But let's not stare or we'll end up with our nuts in a wringer." The waiter brought their drinks.

"That'll be two-fifty."

Ike handed him a five dollar bill.

"Look, Mistah. This ain't no good in the U.S. This here's a Canada five."

"Sorry. I'm a Canadian and got my money mixed up with my US stuff." He took back the bill and replaced it with an American five.

The waiter returned with the change. "How come, if you're Canadian, how come you guys're wearin' a Limey uniform?"

"We aren't," said Leach. "This is the Canadian Navy's uniform. See this badge on my shoulder? Royal Canadian Navy. Here's to the Canadian Navy!" He raised his glass.

"To the Canadian Navy!" echoed Ike as he handed the waiter a fifty cent tip.

A few minutes later the waiter returned to say, "What would you like to eat? Food will be served during the entertainment."

"Like what?"

"Like steak and baked potato."

"Sounds good to us."

"Rare, medium or well done?"

Both Leach and Ike asked for medium. The listening crowd seemed to approve of their choice. The piano which had fallen silent when they walked in began tinkling softly and conversations were resumed in low voices here and there. Ike breathed a little more easily.

They sipped their drinks slowly. "So far so good, eh buddy?" said Leach.

"Yeah, but I still feel like pissin' my pants."

A big bosomed, sequin-clad singer came on stage. Their steaks were good and her voice was deep and throaty. They applauded when it seemed appropriate but tried not to overdo it. Leach whispered, "First class!" Still Ike's apprehension grew. Where in hell were they? How to find their way out of Harlem when the show was over? How many dark streets to walk before the nearest subway station?

At intermission, patrons headed for the washrooms. Ike felt the need as well but all he could see was a door for "Ladies." Men passed through a door from which the food had come. He and Leach considered their options and Leach said, "Hell, if you gotta go, you gotta go, man." They decided Ike would be first to venture into the unknown. He stood up just as a waiter was passing their table.

"Could you tell me, where's the washroom?"

"Right through that door, sir."

Ike passed through the swinging door and found himself in a long, narrow room with cutting and preparation tables along one wall and a cooking range at the near end of the tables. Startled, he stopped in his tracks.

"Where you goin', Limey?" He was the blackest Negro Ike had ever seen. Like the other three working at the tables, he seemed to be a giant. He wore no shirt and his skin glistened in the heat. His tone of voice abrasive.

"To the washroom. Which way is it?" Ike's voice sounded anemic in his own ears.

One of the others turned from the cutting table and pointed with what seemed like an enormous, two-and-a-half-foot knife. "That way, man. Out that door an' make it quick 'cause we ah busy!"

The door was at least a mile away. With watery knees, Ike walked along behind the row of knife-wielding cooks, keeping as far from them as the narrow space would allow. Each one turned from his work to watch him pass. A spot between Ike's shoulder blades tingled with dreaded anticipation and he felt the hairs on the back of his neck rise as he moved down the line.

At last he stepped through the door and found himself in bright starlight! Several other patrons were lined up against the fence. Scanning for it, Ike located a spot in the lineup where he'd less obviously be the white horse. He lowered his trouser flap, and pulled out his dick. It seemed to glow with a pale white light. He cupped it with his white hand. Relief at last! He glanced along the line and mused, "Holy Shit! At least what's coming out is all the same color."

Comments from above the line of emptying bladders were familiar, too. They would be at home in any latrine he had ever visited. "Wonder what that gal doin' the jazzy piece would be like in bed, eh?" And a chorus of appreciative laughter. "Ah'd eat a mile of her 'you know what' just to see where it come from, ah would!" "Yeah, she's sure got her tits jazzed up, eh? Boy, what I could do for her without goin' on stage!" At each off colour remark, with shoulders thrown back and peckers thrust closer to the fence, raucous laughter filled the starlit pissing patch.

Ike felt he could have contributed to the camaraderie with a one-liner or two but he held back. Anything he said might be taken as derogatory and at best he'd get pissed on for punishment. He was already getting enough splatter on his bell bottoms from sheer quaking fright.

When the rest of the lineup started moving back toward the kitchen door, Ike wasn't finished but he cut it short. He was not going to be trapped alone in that back yard with four big Negroes and four big knives between him and Leach. He marched through the kitchen with the rest of the crowd. Back at the table he told Leach about the gauntlet he'd have to traverse in order to reach the "lavatory." Leach decided he could wait until they got back to K171.

As they left, Leach asked the doorman. "Our ship is berthed on Staten Island. Which way do we go to catch the El or get a subway to the ferry?"

The doorman stepped out to the street with them. "Take this street and go that way for five blocks. You'll see a big subway sign there. The station's jus' half a block round the corner. Good night, gentlemen."

0030 hours and five blocks to go—the longest walk they'd ever walked. All warnings in the mess had been dire. Harlem, absolutely Out of Bounds. Anyone venturing in deserved castration. Equally foreboding were thoughts of possible arrest by a US Shore Patrol if discovered in this zone.

One block. Two blocks. Three blocks and they were still all right. A group of young blacks lounged under the light at the next corner. "Hey! Looka what's here to see da sights?" a voice rose from the gaggle. "Looks like the navy's landed," offered another.

"I think this is where we cross the street," said Ike in a low voice.

"I'm right with you, buddy."

They dodged through traffic. A glance over his shoulder told Ike the corner boys were staying where they were. Whew! Another block and as they turned the corner they could see the subway sign. Bright lights shone ahead but they weren't home free yet.

"Holy Hell, Leach! Isn't that the US Shore Patrol comin' at us? Now wadda we do?"

Before Leach could reply, they found themselves face to face with four uniformed men with wide, white bands on their arms. One of them raised a whistle to his mouth.

The patrol approached, swinging batons.

"Good Sweet Mother of Cunt! They've got us by the short hairs," groaned Leach.

"Look here, you two. Don't you Canadians know you're in a danger zone?"

The second wasn't as polite. "You idiots are lucky to come out of there with your heads on. What the fuck made you do such a stupid thing?"

The third put in his oar. "You're just lucky somebody called us to report that they'd seen you entering here or we might not have found you at all. Did either of you get hurt?"

"No, we're fine. No trouble at all," said Ike.

"Mighty bloody lucky!"

"Jeez, men, but you're lucky you've still got your heads and your balls."

Transported to the Staten Island ferry and placed on board with one of the patrol accompanying them, they were taken through the checkpoint and marched back to *Kamsack*. "Reporting two Canadian sailors rescued from Harlem and delivered safely."

The quartermaster looked astonished. "What? Dutch and Leach rescued? Are you serious?" He seemed to think it was a joke. Leach turned to the patrol.

"Thanks. We'll look after the detail." They exchanged salutes and the patrol marched away.

Ike and Leach quickly started for the mess. Behind them the quartermaster muttered, "Look, you two. What the hell kind of a stunt are you pulling now?" but they decided not to hear. In the mess they undressed hurriedly and crawled into their hammocks. Ike lay back and counting his manifold blessings, fell asleep.

Back at sea, the mess, furnished with new ammunition for discussion, continued to raise questions. "What's this about being rescued in Harlem?"

"Say, Leach, how does it feel to be scared to death?"

"Dutch, did you really shit your pants while down in Harlem?"

"How long did you say the cook's knife was, Dutch?"

"Listen, you guys, can you imagine your mothers receiving a telegram saying, 'Wounded in action on the Harlem front'?"

"Aw, his mother would only say, 'Well, screw him.'"

To counter the razzing, Ike and Mitch took to the offense. "Greetings, men. I'll take your questions about the American Fortress Harlem one at a time. The line forms on the left," Ike would announce on entering the mess. Or Leach would say, "Hi, you salts. I'm here to tell you all about Harlem." For a while the joking simply took a different tack.

"Tell us, is Harlem one of your Lend Lease bases?"

"Are we fightin' for you or against you in this war?"

"How would you compare Harlem with Cape Breton (or Quebec)?"

"I guess you guys'll hafta eat separately from now on?"

"And serve the coffee while the rest of us play crap."

"Don't use the white man's heads. You can piss over the side."

"Not into the wind, mind you."

But gradually the questions became more serious. They were, after all, very curious about what lay beyond the invisible line marking the mysterious territory that was Out of Bounds. Some, it seemed, were rather disappointed to hear that their evening in Harlem had resulted in no real harm. In time, their mates became weary of trying to find fresh jokes and both Ike and Leach became weary of responding in kind.

One day at supper after a difficult, U-boat-ridden watch, Ike turned on Carpenter, one of the most persistent of his tormentors, "Look, you'll have a hard time convincing me that it's a good idea to be fighting Hitler as long as we have such archaic ideas as yours on our side." He knew it was a low blow. Carpenter was the oldest man in the mess, a man who had served in the merchant marine for years before the war and one whom Ike actually held in considerable esteem for his steady calm under all conditions.

"Waddaya mean? If you're gonna give us a lecture, make it snappy. I've gotta go on watch."

"Well, look at it this way. The whites in the U.S. consider themselves to be the superior race. So the Negro is pushed into a corner called Harlem. In practice, he has no rights other than the right to serve the Big Brains.

He comes out of his night closet in the mornings to serve coffee to the crap shooters and when the midnight hour arrives, he goes back to be locked into his box. How would you like to live like that?"

"Well, maybe that's all he's good for. If he hasn't got the guts and brains to stand and fight for his rights, he deserves what he's got."

"You don't know the meaning of brains," Leach joined in, raising a chorus of, "Hey, hey! Watch what you're sayin', Leach."

"OK, but let me tell you, the show we watched at that club was as good and maybe even better than anything we've seen in the rest of New York. The food was better than plenty we've had, and everyone behaved as well as anywhere else we've been. There's no reason to think they'd behave any worse if they were allowed to get into any of the places we've visited in the rest of the city. The problem is dividing the city into separate territories. To say they don't deserve any better just shows you don't know the meaning of democracy."

"Temper! Temper!" intervened Hanson in a falsetto voice and a bit of laughter here and there cooled the air. "You know damn well that Harlem is an exception and the Americans have their reasons for the arrangement, and they'll work it all out just fine."

"Like hell, it's an exception," interrupted Kowalski who rarely spoke unless spoken to. "Why do all of us have to name our nationality and our mother's too when we join up, if we're not obviously English? It's because the fuckin' English think they're so damned superior to everyone else."

"Well, they should. They damned well are superior," said Barnes emphatically. "They fought fair and square on the Plains of Abraham and beat the shit out of Montcalm. They have to keep control and they will because they're better!"

"I agree," said Carpenter. "If you know you've got it, if you know you're superior, there's absolutely nothin' wrong with puttin' yourself in the Head Cheese role. And there's clear evidence. Look at all the possessions Britain has. I say leave the system alone. It works. Don't destroy it." He pulled on his life jacket and started up the stairs. Hanson followed him and the argument seemed ready to die away. Then Chuck spoke up.

"Got a letter from my Dad and he says the CCF is advocating giving the vote to native Indians, to the Chinese, and even to the Japs. Now that's equality and I think that's worth fighting for."

"Ah, C'mon! This CCF party you're talkin' about's nothin' except a bunch of Bolsheviks," countered Barnes vehemently. "Canadian Commonwealth Federation," he sneered nasally. "What the hell does that mean anyhow? You goddam Irish have all kinds of funny ideas. Can't be satisfied with bein' either Liberal or Conservative like the rest of us. How'd you get into the country anyways?"

"We sneaked in because we're white. We fooled the English and stupidly fought the Indians for them."

"Listen, you Western Canadian grasshopper. Take your CCF socialist garbage and stuff it into the boiler next time you go down. And I don't know what all this shit has to do with fightin' the war anyway. Makes me feel like takin' a crap." He started up the ladder, muttering, "Miserable Irish pricks," as he went.

"Well, I don't exactly know either," said Ike slowly as Barnes disappeared, "but here we are, fighting the Germans and what their Master Race notion means, and when that's done what'll we do in Canada to be more civilized?"

"I say, let the Brits carry on as they like and the Americans too, but we Canadians have got to pack in the ties with the British Super Master Race if we're gonna have a real democracy."

"Hell, Chuck, I don't even know what the word 'democracy' means. I just want to be treated and to behave as an equal to other Canadians. Right now, I'm second or third class, I don't know which, but compared to the Negro in Harlem, I'm way ahead."

"Yeah, but we've still got to make it better. My Dad often talks about the Irish in Ireland losing the will and the heart to fight. That's why they emigrated to North America. They expected here it would be possible to make it better. I think it is getting better all the time."

"You know, my mother came from the Southern United States and she used to say that the Negro there was treated as though he didn't have a soul. That's a step behind not having heart or will. She said it was un-Christian, the way they were treated."

"Of course it is, but then I guess it isn't Christian to kill, kill, kill."

Action bells clamoured as Chuck finished his sentence and they both scrambled for their life jackets to get on with winning the war.

Chapter 14

A Casualty

Reaching Halifax, home base for the Triangle Run, provided time to get the clothes washed and dried that had been worn throughout the heavy storm. There was mail from home as well and that made everyone in the mess happy. Even Anderson, who rarely showed any excitement about the mail, let out a whoop while reading one of his letters this time. "Hey, you guys! Will ya listen to this? My Old Man's got himself into the army, the old bugger. Lied about his age to get in, and he's stationed in Truro! He's comin' to Halifax on leave this weekend. Would ya believe it? Now there's a guy knows how to enjoy himself. I can hardly wait to show him around town."

He rushed about, getting his gear in order and getting dressed for another assault on the delights Halifax had to offer. He was giving his boots a final lick with a cloth when word came down that he had a visitor at the gate. "I'm off," he announced. "See you guys around town maybe. I'm off to have me a time."

Ike was in no hurry to go ashore. After New York, Halifax seemed tame. He took time to read the newspapers that had come aboard and smiled wryly at the headline: "*Tension Grips all Europe as Invasion Plans Mature*"[6]. Hadn't he read that story before? Every week the same. Still, the Russians seemed to be taking back the Crimea and the Allies were making progress on the Anzio beachhead. On the Pacific, too, the US forces were pushing the Japs off more little islands. Maybe the Good Guys were actually winning the war. Slowly. But *Kamsack* still had been forced to fight off a pack of U-boats on the last leg from NewfyJohn and he was sure she'd have to fight off more the next time out.

He spent some time writing letters while Charlie stood watch. Together, they went ashore to see *Mrs. Miniver* at one of the movie houses. When it was over they started for the K of C canteen. Suddenly they bumped into Anderson with a soldier leaning heavily on his shoulder. Both were clearly far from sober.

"Godammit, Dutch!" Anderson roared. "C'mere an' meet my Old Man. Him an' me've been seein' the town an' I think he's had a bit much to drink. This here's my pal, Dutch and this's Anderson Senior who's the bes' sport in the whole worl."

The Best Sport gazed closely at Ike and Charlie out of red-rimmed eyes. He, like his son, was tall but had lost the other's loose-limbed, slender shape. His flushed face, though still handsome, showed the signs of an extra twenty years of hard living. "Pleased ta meetcha both." He took his right arm off his son's shoulder in order to shake hands but that was a mistake. He nearly fell over before Charlie's hand could meet his and hold him up with his firm handshake.

"I think we need a cuppa coffee," declared Anderson. "We gotta sober up a bit or we won't be any good for the girls we're gonna find in a few minutes. C'n you guys give me a hand with the Old Man an' we'll get him sumpin to eat too."

Ike and Charlie suggested they all go to the canteen which was nearby. "But you gotta act sober when we walk in or they'll ask us to leave," Charlie warned. "So just don't say anything. Just keep quiet an' Dutch and I will get you to a table."

Luckily, a table near the door was empty. After coffee and sandwiches, both father and son looked less flushed and spoke more clearly. "Lemme tell you boys," said the elder Anderson, "I'm havin' the time of my life. This war c'n go on forever as far as I'm concerned. A man gets sick an' tired of goin' ta work day after day an' not havin' any fun or gettin' sour looks and arguments every damned time he wants ta go out with his friends. Now I c'n do as I damn well like an' I'm doin' it. An' there ain't nothin' like a uniform to attract the girls, I've found out. An' I'll tell ya' another thing, have fun while ya' can. That's what I always say."

"And that's what you always do, you old sonofabitch," laughed his son.

"Yeah, an' I tell you it's high time you an' me had chance to go out together, boy. At home, your mother, who's a very fine woman," he paused and looked sternly at his son, "your mother's a very fine woman an' don't you ever forget it...." He seemed to lose his thread of thought and searched the bottom of his coffee cup for it. "Your mother is a fine woman, but she's always tryin' to make a pansy out of you. Me, I want my son to be a man, dammit, an' he's doin' all right." He reached out an unsteady hand to pat his son on the shoulder. "He's doin' OK."

"You guys wanna come with us?" asked Anderson Junior. "I'm takin' my Old Man to see some of the ladies up near The Hill after this."

"Keep your voice down, for Christ's sake," hissed Charlie. "I think I'll head back to the ship myself, but Dutch may want to tag along." Ike fully appreciated Charlie's helpfulness.

"No thanks, Al. Maybe some other time. I still haven't caught up on all the sleep I missed at sea so I'll head back with you, Charlie. Nice to have met you, Mr. Anderson."

"Hell, never mind the Mr. Just call me Jim." He held out his hand in farewell.

They left the Andersons and made their way back to the streetcar stop. "Boy," exclaimed Ike. "I can just see my father going out to a whorehouse with me!" and he laughed at the very idea. "He never let on he even knew about such places, although I'm sure he did. If so, the subject certainly never entered the dinner table conversation."

"Yeah," agreed Charlie. "It's not exactly what we called family fun at our house either."

The second day in port was pay day and Ike was able to collect some of the loans he had made in New York, and get to the tailor's shop where he had gone with Madden the first time the *Buxton* called in at Halifax. Charlie, who didn't drink or gamble and therefore always had money, came with him and they both got measured for new tiddly suits. Feeling considerably poorer after this exercise, they went back to the ship for supper. Anderson was out with his father again and, except for the men on watch, everyone else was in town for the evening as well.

They had just finished cleaning the mess after supper when the sound of stumbling boots and loud voices cursing and complaining came from above. A minute later, Barnes came backing down the ladder, trying to help Jeffries' boots find each rung as he followed, complaining loudly all the way. Leach at the top was steadying Jack from above. "Grab the goddam rail, Jack, so you don't fall down on top of Barnes, damn you!"

"I'm all right, I'm tellin' you guys. I'm just fine. Are you tryin' ta tell me what to do, you little sonofabitch? I'll teach you ta tell me how ta get hold of a goddam rail."

For a moment it seemed Jack would start up the ladder again, but Leach said soothingly, "Hey, c'mon buddy. This is your shipmate, Leach. Let's go down to the mess, OK? Let's just go down t'the mess an' find a cuppa tea." Jeffries paused for a bit to think over what Leach had said and started downward again. Reaching the bottom, he sank down on the bench nearest the ladder and cradling his head in his arms on the table, fell asleep. Leach came after Jeffries with only slightly less difficulty.

"Jesus Christ!" he exclaimed. "I thought we'd never get that guy back here alive. He was fightin' the goddam war all along Barrington Street."

"If he wasn't so goddam big it would have been easier," said Barnes. "When he got mad and started throwin' punches at that airman with those long arms of his, it was a good thing he was too drunk to land a real good one or that guy woulda been gone. I was scared to get near him myself. We were just lucky to get him outa there before the Shore Patrol came along."

"I was glad he fell asleep on the streetcar," said Leach. "When we got on, I thought for a minute he was gonna go after the conductor. He's some wild man when he gets a coupla drinks under his belt. You won't believe this," he laughed, "but that crazy bugger thought the conductor was a German an' kept tellin' him we'd beat the shit outa him and his buddies yet. He'da started on him too, if we hadn'ta bin there."

"Wanna help me get him into his hammock?" asked Barnes.

"Hell, no. Let him sleep there for a while. He ain't hurtin' nobody an' he's too damned heavy to lift."

The long weekend of carousing was apparent in many pale, worn faces when they hove anchor again. The convoy under escort was one of the biggest K171 had joined since Ike was on board. Barnes said 163 ships. They were slow feeding them all coming out of Bedford Basin into formation. For a change, the Atlantic was less turbulent, but a heavy fog and mist compounded the difficulties of maneuvering. Ike felt they were participating in one of those dreams where ones limbs are burdened with an inexplicable weight and no matter how one struggles, every step is in slow motion. They seemed to be barely clear of Sambro light when Action Stations broke the trance. "What the hell's goin' on?" shouted Barnes over the sound of the bells. "What're them Krauts doin' on this side of the pond?"

"Trust the buggers to surprise us," Ike responded as they dashed for the starboard launcher. "A lot of nerve, comin' right into our front yard. Let's get the sonofabitches this time."

For the next four hours they had no time for conversation. *Kamsack* had picked up a ping and the zigzag hunt for the U-boat was on. Depth charge after depth charge in a pattern synchronized to follow the boom-boom-boom of the hedgehog volleys. Again and again the drums were hauled onto the launcher and shot over the side.

Then suddenly it was Slow Speed Ahead. ASDIC had gone silent. No sign they'd hit anything. She was simply gone. *Kamsack* with other escorts circled back, trying to re-establish contact. No use. Reluctantly, the crew left the depth charge station and went below. Barnes sank heavily onto one of the benches and wiped his brow. Although the temperature topside was near freezing, everyone on depth charge duty had worked up a sweat.

"I still can't figure out why we're runnin' into U-boats so close to home. Up until now, they've been waitin' for us out there in The Pit and comin' at us in packs. I didn't see any sign of other escorts bobbin' and weavin' like we were. Not that ya c'n see much on Action Stations. But it seemed to me we were huntin' a lone wolf this time."

"Maybe what the Big Nuts are sayin' lately has some truth in it," offered Ike. "Maybe we *are* winning the U-boat battle. We've tossed so much TNT at 'em in mid-ocean the bastards've changed their tactics and stopped providing us with closely packed targets."

"Nah, that ain't it at all. Didn't you notice we had some air cover last time we were exchanging convoys?" Charlie asked. "We never used to get that in The Pit, and only the flyboys can see those U-ees when they're runnin' just below the surface to close in on us. That new schnorkel they've got is hard to spot in rough water, but from above.... A warning makes it easier for us escorts to fight 'em off. Remember we didn't lose a single freighter on the last run. Too bad *Kamsack* hasn't made her kill yet. It's darned frustrating." He slapped his palm on the table by way of emphasis. "Anybody for tea?"

"Only if you can make it quick. Me 'n Anderson have to hit the boiler room in ten minutes."

At St. John's where they made a brief refuelling and provisioning pause before starting on the last leg of the Triangle Run heading back to Halifax, they heard the *Valleyfield* had been torpedoed just off Cape Race. Another attack close to a safe harbour. Clearly, the pattern of combat was changing and the Battle of the Atlantic was far from over yet.

Ike noticed that Anderson didn't perk up at all during their time in harbour. True, he had been pretty sick during the last storm, but previously the hawsers had hardly been wrapped around the bollards before he was ready to hit town. Although the next few days brought easy weather, Anderson still lay about both during and off watch almost as much as when his seasickness first assailed him. When rough weather struck, he barely kept on his feet during Action Stations. Ike carried most watches in the boiler room singlehandedly.

Finally, when he and Ike went down on watch Ike asked, "What's wrong, Al? Got woman trouble? For days after our last call at St John's, you kept on talking about that "hottest thing on earth" you'd found here. This time you didn't even go ashore to see her."

"If I had, I'd a' beaten the shit outa her. I think I'm in deep trouble, Ike. I think I got the clap from her." He sank down on an upturned bucket and held his head in his hands.

"God, no!" exclaimed Ike, and sat down nearby. "Are you sure about this? How do you know? Have you seen Doc?"

"No, I haven't seen Doc!" Anderson said angrily. "I don't need to see Doc. It'd be too embarrassing to see him. I know how I feel, dammit. I know how it looks, feels. My Old Man told me enough about it, bragging about it, that

I'm certain it's what I've got. I gave myself the short arm test and I've got a green one all right."

"Well, you've still gotta go to see Doc. How else are you going to get rid of it?"

"I dunno, Dutch, but I'm sick of this whole shit. I don't know what to do or where I'm at. Worst of it is, I met this really nice girl in New York last time we were there, and look at me now."

"Another of your quick and easy tricks, Al?"

"No, she was different, and I actually thought I'd like to see her again. Now I'm scared to. Damn the luck. Why did I hafta get into this jam just now?"

"Jeez, that's really tough. Of course, you could have picked it up from the ladies you visited on Hollis Street in Halifax. If you got it in St. John's, you had it when we tied up in Halifax last time and I guess that means it's not only you that's got it, but a helluva lot of other people, too, including your nice girl in New York."

"Goddammit, Dutch, stop pushing at me. You're not making me feel any better. God knows I feel lousy enough without you reminding me of that."

"Well, you might as well go to get checked out by the Doc. He'll do a short arm on us all one of these days anyway, so there's no point waiting for it, is there?" Anderson grunted in morose agreement and Ike turned to check the burners. He knew that for the rest of their watch Anderson would probably stay as he was now, immobilized by dejection, too wrapped up in self-pity to take on his share of the boiler room duties. Well, let him sit. I can only feel sorry for the guy. What can you expect, with parents like he's got? Suddenly, his own father's face with its smitten look rose between him and the burner valves, but what he felt was something other than a sense of power.

Had Anderson told him or was Barnes seeking confirmation of his guess, Ike wondered as Barnes greeted Anderson on his return from the little cubbyhole Doc called "sick bay." "So, what's the word, Al-Boy? You got clap or worse?"

Red with fury, Anderson turned on Ike. "Dutch, you bugger! Can't you keep your mouth shut about anything?"

"Whatever Barnes knows, you must've told him yourself. I never breathed a word."

"Aw, c'mon. Don't blame Dutch," said Barnes placatingly. "Any guy that screws everything in sight every time we hit port and then suddenly starts walking around as if he's been hit in the nuts just has to have caught a dose. That's as simple as it is. And when you go to see the Doc and come back looking as if you've been whipped, it ain't very hard to figger out what's wrong. So, what's the verdict?"

Anderson sat down heavily on one of the benches against the wall. "Well, he gave me some stuff for the clap, but he's given me an order for a blood test when we hit port, too. He thinks maybe I've got syph too."

"Holy Hell!" "Good God!" "Jesus Christ!" A litany of groans and curses rumbled among the hammocks and bunks.

"Just see to it that you clean that goddam latrine every time you use it from now on," Kowalski bellowed, waggling his finger in Anderson's face.

"Smarten up, Kowalski," said Barnes. "You know you can't catch a dose from the heads or the toilet seat."

"That's what you say, but I say it's better to be safe than sorry."

Barnes turned to Anderson. "I guess you know what you're in for, if it's syph," he said with his knowing sniff.

"I guess they'll give me more pills or injections or something," Anderson said dully.

"Hah! Injections ain't nuthin', dear boy. If you've got syph, you get the Hockey Stick Treatment. Ain't you heard of it?"

Several heads appeared over the side of the swaying hammocks. "No, I never heard of a Hockey Stick Treatment. What the hell is that?"

"Well, y'see," Barnes leaned over towards Anderson but spoke loud enough that all could hear, "you won't find it in that little handout about VD ya got from Doc, but they've got this thing, this instrument, that's shaped like a hockey stick and they shove it up your dick right into your balls and ream everything out."

Anderson turned white. "I don't believe it. You're just tryin' to scare the shit outa me." He cupped his hand over his crotch protectively.

"If y'don't believe me, ask Doc."

"How come you know so much about it, Barnes?" Carpenter asked from the far end of the table. "Sounds as if you've had the treatment."

"Never mind how I know. I just been around long enough to know a few things, that's all."

"Well, I'll be damned if anybody's gonna shove any hockey stick up me," said Anderson vehemently. "Hell, that's worse than what I've got already."

"But it ain't worse than what you're gonna get if you don't get treated, and don't you forget it. If you wait and let those little bugs get into your brain, you'll be spendin' your time cuttin' out paper dollies somewhere."

"Except you won't be able to hold a pair of scissors," Carpenter laughed ruefully. "There was an old guy used to stumble down the street in my hometown. He'd get to the beer parlour, but he could'nt get a glass of beer to his mouth without spilling most of it all over himself. We kids used to make fun of him and he'd get mad and try to chase us, but he couldn't even walk properly. They finally put him in the mental."

Anderson groaned.

When they reached Halifax, Anderson had his sea bag packed. The shore patrol was waiting for him at the gangplank.

Chapter 15

Shore Patrol

Springtime toned down gales and storms but the ice cold North Atlantic waters engulfed K171 in a tooth-chattering chill until she came well within reach of offshore breezes. Ike and Chuck leaned on her rail, soaking up the warm mid-May sunshine as *Kamsack* pulled up to the Staten Island jetty. Chuck, having served out his penalty for the notorious fire, was itching to go ashore. Both he and Dutch had drawn first watch in port so they watched enviously as their messmates dashed for the ferry. "You heading out to New Jersey again when you get off watch, Chuck?"

"Nah. I wrote Marlene two letters and never got an answer. Sporting around with some other uniformed man I guess. Don't know exactly what I'd like to do, but why don't we skip the bars for a change. We get off watch at 1200 hours and it's too nice a day to be sitting inside."

"Like maybe just sit in Central Park. In the sun. Watching all the girls go by, as the song goes."

"How 'bout putting our names down for one of the hospitality offers for a change?"

"Itchin' to find a New York version of your Annapolis Valley dame?"

"Hell, no Ike! One's enough to last me the rest of my life! But why not try for some good home cooking?"

"OK, I'll go for that. You talked me into it. Take care of the details and I'll hold on down here below."

They showered and dressed with extra care when they came off watch. From the tempo of Chuck's whistle, Dutch could tell that he was anticipating something special from their venture. The mood was infectious and he, too, felt a quiver of excitement as he set his cap at a jaunty angle. Still, instincts urged caution.

"Listen, Chuck, let's not mention that we've got a weekend pass until we see what we've gotten ourselves into, OK? If I get stuck with something that was rejected by the Sally Ann, I'm coming back to this tub."

"OK. OK. Don't worry. It'll be all right." They looked anxiously toward the chain link fence as they walked to the gates of the dockyard but there were no long-limbed, beautiful girls in sight, only an elderly gentleman, leaning on a walking stick. Chuck groaned. "If he's got any daughters, you can bet they're over-ripe."

"Thought I'd come over here to meet you boys rather than take the chance on missing you on the Manhattan side." The voice was cheerful and the handshake warm. "Seward's the name."

They introduced themselves. "This is awfully good of you, Mr. Seward," said Chuck.

"Oh, it's my pleasure. I try to do what I can for you young fellas. I fought in The Great War and I know how it feels to be far from home, fighting in miserable conditions. Now, I don't know what you've seen of our city so far. Or is this the first time you've been in New York?"

"Oh, no," said Dutch, "but most of our time has been spent around Times Square." He decided he wouldn't mention Harlem.

"Well, I thought we'd take my car and I'd show you sections of the city a bit farther away from the centre. We'll have dinner after our drive. How does that sound?" he asked as he led the way toward a group of cars parked near the gates. When he moved to open the door of a long, low, light blue convertible, Chuck, gaining Dutch's attention, gave a long low whistle. "Sounds just great to us. We've got passes for the weekend so we don't need to get back early."

Chuck climbed into the back seat and Dutch sat in front. He leaned an elbow negligently out of the open window, trying to create the appearance of having been driven around New York in long, low, light blue convertibles every day of his life.

"Since it's such a nice day, I thought I'd keep the top down," said Mr. Seward. "Let me know if it gets too breezy for you."

Chuck laughed, "That's not likely after the North Atlantic, sir."

Mr. Seward eased his car into the heavy Manhattan traffic. Dutch's head was in overdrive. "Oh Boy! If only Sara could see me now! She wouldn't believe it. I don't either. Too good to be true!"

They drove through Central Park and as they crossed one of the low bridges, Chuck said, "Mr. Seward, could you stop here some place for us to take some pictures?" Dutch decided to get several shots with his own camera even though film was expensive and sometimes hard to find. But what odds? He'd never have a chance like this again. They took turns at posing with Mr. Seward in front of his car and exchanged seats for continuing their drive.

For several hours they were driven through the city. Mr. Seward pointed out historic buildings, cathedrals, monuments, took them over bridges into suburbs, through parks and past Yankee Stadium. Obscured by skyscrapers and by tall buildings on either side of the streets they traveled, the sun could be spotted now and then. It was low when he turned the nose of the convertible back toward the centre of town. "You boys must be hungry by now, so let's stop at the Plaza for something to eat."

Mr. Seward nodded to the doorman who greeted him with "Good evening, sir," as he opened the door. Dutch could see palm fronds ahead as they climbed the steps to the main lobby. He remembered the Lord Nelson, its dark, heavy furniture, and the frosty waiter.

"If you boys want to freshen up, the washroom is over here." They followed him through the heavy, brass trimmed door. Marble, thought Dutch. That's what it is, marble. In the heads, yet. On the floor, on the walls, on the counter. What a change from the battleship linoleum and damp, mildew-stricken walls of the pissing trough on board ship. Somewhere from a gramophone in the back of his mind, a tenor voice sang, "I dreamed I dwelt in marble halls." I'll bet the poor bugger wouldn't have dreamed there could be marble in a toilet as well. Brass taps, too. Darn, wouldn't like polishing all the brass around here.

Washed, combed, and smelling like Park Plaza soap, they stepped along the passage to the entrance of the bright, summery green and light of the courtyard where white wicker tables and chairs clustered among the potted palms. "The dining room is further on," (Dutch caught a glimpse of stemmed glasses on white tablecloths beyond a stiff white-jacketed waiter) "but I thought this was a better place on such a fine evening." Chuck and Ike agreed.

Ike noticed the array of cutlery. As much set out on the table for three as they had in the mess for twenty men. "I guess we shouldn't complain about not being able to get any French wines, considering what's happening over there," their host said, "but dinner still doesn't seem quite right without it. I got used to it when I was in France." The waiter leaned over and said something in a low voice the boys could not hear.

"Wonderful! First rate," said Mr. Seward and the waiter scurried away.

They studied the menu. Ike fervently hoped that Mr. Seward would recommend something. He had never before held a menu that consisted of more than a single sheet of paper with a few plain headings: SANDWICHES, SOUPS, MEALS, DESSERTS. Now he was faced with HORS D'OEUVRES and ENTREES. Jeez!

"I think we should start with a half dozen oysters," Mr. Seward suggested, relieving Ike's state of panic. "Do you boys like oysters?" Ike had encountered smoked oysters in the officers' mess on the *Buxton*.

"Well, we don't grow many of those things on the farm, but I'd be willing to try them," Ike offered. Chuck looked doubtful, but he didn't refuse.

"After that a sirloin steak would look good to me." Chuck looked much more cheerful at this suggestion.

"Make mine rare," said Mr. Seward. "How would you boys like yours?"

Ike thought rare seemed to go with oysters and palm trees. "Rare for me as well," he said.

"I'll have mine well done," Chuck announced firmly, closing the door on any further gastronomic adventures.

They leaned back and looked around while waiting for their food. Ike admired the tall mirrored screens reflecting fading light from above. Musicians played somewhere out of his range of vision. Violins and a piano, a cello and a bass viol? Couldn't tell what they were playing, but it was incomparably lovely, floating among the greenery, the low voices and light tinkle of glass and cutlery.

The waiter delivered what looked to Ike like a wide-mouthed milk bottle and poured a small amount into Mr. Seward's glass. He swirled the pale gold liquid about and held it near his nose for a moment before taking a sip. "Not bad," he sounded surprised. "Not bad at all. The Plaza still has a good pipeline, it seems." The waiter smiled.

"Well, a little comes through now and then."

He poured Ike's glass. Chuck put a hand over his. "No, thank you. I don't drink. I promised my father I wouldn't."

Mr. Seward looked astonished. "You must be one in a million. You must have some father."

Dutch was glad his own father had not asked him to promise such a thing. Not that he would have obliged. The Old Man knew better than to ask, he thought. Involuntarily that smitten look over the workbench on the farm rose in his mind's eye. He regretted the look but not what was happening now.

The oysters arrived. Chuck took one look at the quivering, grey globs in the barnacle-encrusted shells and reached for his water glass.

"Now, Dutch, you said you hadn't grown these on the farm so let me show you how to eat them. Squeeze a bit of lemon juice on one, then take that little fork to loosen the oyster from the shell, if it's still attached somewhere. That's it. Now you can spear the thing and pop it into your mouth, but I prefer to lift the shell and let the oyster slide into my mouth from the rim." He demonstrated. "I guess it's not quite as polite as using a fork, but you get all the salty juices that way so I say, what the hell!"

Ike was a bit startled to hear Mr. Seward say "hell." but then he kept telling them about being in World War I, and communication in trenches couldn't have been any more elegant than in a stokers' mess. He tipped an oyster. Momentarily he gagged on the slithery texture. He decided against trying any chewing and let it slide down with surprise at how easily it happened. The taste of lemon and salt was rather nice, too. Chuck had not touched his plate. While Mr. Seward and Ike dispatched their remaining oysters, Ike asked what business Mr. Seward was in.

"Oh, I'm retired now, but I was in the insurance business before the war and got back into it when I was de-mobbed. They asked me to come back now that the war has taken so many young men away to fight the Japs so I go to the office for a few hours a couple of days a week. Mostly, I spend my time training young women that we've taken on. Never used to have any except the president's private secretary and she was old. It seems strange to see that office full of females now. They're all young. I enjoy going in just to look at the pretty ones." He chuckled. "They make me wish I was young again, like you boys. Except then I wouldn't be in the office either. I'd be out there in the jungles like most of our boys. Guess you lads have girl friends back in Canada, eh?"

Chuck said, no, his girlfriend had found another sailor.

"That's too bad. Maybe I can arrange for you to meet some of the pretty girls from the office. Most of them are lonely nowadays. They complain like Betty Grable did in that song, "They're either too young or too old," about the men that are left. What about you, Dutch?"

Ike looked around the Palm Court for a moment before replying, "Well, I don't know if I've got a girl or not. I haven't had a letter from her for quite a while and I haven't seen her for almost a year."

"When you get to New York next time, call me and I'll try to arrange something with the girls." He looked over at Chuck's plate of oysters, still untouched. "Tell you what, Chuck. If you don't want those, Dutch and I will gladly finish them for you."

Dutch realized when he saw his steak that rare meant something quite different in New York than it did on board ship where Moss always reserved the slightly pink centre of the roast beef for Engineer Morgan and the First Mate. This steak still oozed bloody red stuff! He hesitated to begin, while Chuck cut into his meat with enthusiasm. Mr. Seward slowly sipped his wine before attacking the steak so Dutch did too. Perhaps the beast would cook in its own heat a bit if he waited.

The wine did not resemble anything he had tasted before. But then, he had never had wine with a meal before. Certainly this was a shade superior to the gallon jugs of Bright's Catawba they used to buy when they went to dances at home. It had invariably left him with a terrible headache the following day, even when he used restraint. He put that thought aside firmly as he lifted his knife and fork. It was not going to make this steak easier to dispatch.

They talked over cheesecake and coffee. Mr. Seward told them stories about the Great War and his experiences on the Italian front. His memories seemed filled with scenes in which muddy roads and impassable mountain routes blended with scrounging food and wine from reluctant villagers. Dutch asked if there hadn't been any good times.

"Oh hell, yes! There was lots of wine wherever we went and there were always girls and somebody in every little place could play music of some kind if we wanted to dance. But the nice girls from good families were kept hidden away, you know, and the ones that were on the loose were, well, loose. I guess that's the way in every war."

After the meal, they moved on to the Algonquin for the cabaret. Mr. Seward pointed to the round table in the lobby where many famous writers were often seen. He mentioned names, but Dutch had never heard of them before, and Mr. Seward could not recognize any among those gathered there this evening. The floor show was so much better than any they had watched in bars around Times Square. Ike and Chuck insisted on paying their way. Mr. Seward stood his ground. "No, boys. This is my treat all the way. It's the best I can do now. You've got weekend passes so why don't you come home with me for the night. I have plenty of room and I would enjoy your company."

Dutch expected a long drive out to the suburbs, but after a few blocks along Fifth Avenue they pulled into a side street and stopped in front of a tall, brick building. A grey-haired man in a dark jacket and trousers let them into the lobby. Mr. Seward handed him the car keys. Dutch wondered about that. He only had time to notice the large vase of flowers on a side table and a bronze bust on a pedestal opposite before they stepped into the elevator, and were whisked upward. The faintly perfumed, lemony smell of furniture polish told him, however, that the place stood a notch or two above the Lord Nelson.

Judging by the size of the entrance hall and the large living room, Dutch reckoned the apartment was bigger than their house on the farm. Imagine that! He had never been in a block of apartments before. "Come in and we'll have a nightcap before we turn in." The boys sank down among cushions on the sofa.

On the mantel piece stood a framed picture of a middle aged couple, obviously Mr. Seward and his wife some years ago. Another picture of a young girl in cap and gown stood on a corner table next to a porcelain lamp. Mr. Seward explained that his daughter was married and her husband was serving in the Pacific so she had moved to California. "They wanted me to move to the West Coast, too, but I've lived here for almost all my life. I'm staying."

Mr. Seward handed Dutch a short-stemmed glass with a bit of amber colored liquid at the bottom of its fat bowl. What the hell, thought Ike, if he didn't have enough liquor to fill the glass, why did he offer drinks in the first place?

"Could I get you something else, Chuck? A glass of juice or something?"

"A glass of milk would be fine. We don't get much fresh milk at sea."

Ike sniffed at his glass. Holy Hell! Brandy! A sudden queasiness seized him. Brandy was the only liquor they ever had at home. There was always a bottle in the corner cupboard in the Great Room where his parents entertained their guests on Sunday afternoons. Not that the guests ever got any. It was there in case of an emergency such as whooping cough or flu or other bothersome childhood diseases that brought on fever and delirium. Now the smell brought back something of the terrible, all-encompassing misery that called for a teaspoon of brandy in hot sugar water. He set his glass down on the table beside the sofa. Good thing Mr. Seward hadn't had enough to fill the glass.

Their host came back with Chuck's milk on a tray. He sat down in an easy chair opposite the sofa and sighed, "Ah-h-h! Nothing like a bit of brandy at the end of a long day." He swirled the brandy round and round, cupping the bowl in his hand. Ike, watching, did the same. He was ready to swallow its contents in one gulp when he saw Mr. Seward pause, sniff and start swirling again. Dutch swirled his brandy, too. The smell and the swirling had a most welcome effect. Mr. Seward took a small sip, swallowed and sighed deeply. Dutch took a sip, swallowed, and bent over, coughing. He sensed a burning line down his chest to his stomach. A warmth spread through his insides. The queasiness gone, he sipped some more. A thimbleful was all that was needed. Powerful stuff. Like pusser rum.

Mr. Seward talked about the war in the Pacific where his son-in-law served. He talked about Europe and wondered how long until the Allies would be able to invade. He spoke of relatives over there, a sister and a nephew in Austria when the war broke out. "What were they doing over there?" Ike asked.

"Oh, they didn't emigrate when my parents came over. My sister's husband had a business there and he didn't want to leave. We tried to get them over when things began to get bad but they didn't make it. The Nazis wouldn't let them out."

Ike looked at the candelabrum on the sideboard in the dining room. He had seen one like that before, once when he delivered a Christmas goose to the Altmans in town. The Altmans owned the general store. So, Mr. Seward was a Jew! A New York Jew! One of those his father sometimes blamed for starting the war.

"Well, now let's get some sleep." Mr. Seward ushered them down the hall to a room with two single beds. "I hope you'll be comfortable." The blankets had been turned back. On each pillow lay a pair of pajamas, folded neatly. They looked at the pajamas and looked at each other.

Thanking their host, Ike closed the door and turned to see Chuck on the bed, contorted with suppressed laughter. Ike held the paisley bottoms across his front and sashayed around the foot of the bed. "Jeez! I've never slept in pajamas in my life." At home it had been long underwear in winter and nothing at all in summer. No stoker on board ship would have dared to confess owning a pair of pajamas. Paisley or whatever.

"I guess we'd better wear 'em," said Chuck. They helped each other out of their tunics and Chuck donned the striped pair. He surveyed himself in the mirror. "I may not be able to sleep in `em but I sure look classy."

"Yeah, just like those pretty guys in Eaton's catalogue. I'd hate to think what the guys in the mess would say if they saw you now." Ike got into the second pair and looked at himself, too. "Too bad there isn't a long mirror so we could get the full effect. Hey, how about if I take a picture of you, Chuck?"

"Like hell you will." Chuck hastily got into bed and covered up.

"Chicken!" Dutch put out the light, crawled in and lay back, thinking over the day's events. Wondered what it would be like to live the high life. Soft carpets to hush every footfall and velvet drapes to muffle street noise. How it would feel to step into an elevator each time you wanted to go out. Live like this with Sara? Then, for sure, he wouldn't be wearing pajamas.

Amused at the thought, he drifted off into a dream in which he walked along a marbled corridor with brass doors opening off on either side. At the far end he saw palm trees waving gently in the light. He hurried towards them because he knew Sara was there waiting for him, but no matter how he hurried the palm trees and the courtyard seemed to be ever farther away.

Next day, Mr. Seward took them on more sightseeing and to see Jimmy Durante in a matinee performance on Broadway. Still in high spirits, they said goodbye at the ferry in late afternoon. "Remember now to call me when you get back to New York," he said. "I'll try to arrange something for you with younger people, too."

They leaned on the rail, crossing to Staten Island, "I think we should keep Mr. Seward's invitation to ourselves, eh, Dutch? Can you see some of those guys in that living room?"

In spite of their resolve, they were bursting to tell of their great weekend, but K171 buzzed with other dire news. Jack Jeffries and Kowalski hadn't returned from shore leave. When Hanson last saw them, they had been set to clean out a bar near the ferry terminal. Barnes, Hanson and Leach had barely made it out the door in time to avoid a US Shore patrol on the way in.

"Dammit, Barnes, how did it start?" asked Dutch.

"I don't know. We're all feeling pretty good when we got back to the ferry and then Jack and Leach decided we had time for one more before it was time to get back so we stepped into this little place and ordered another round. I went to the heads and when I got back, here's Jack and Kowalski swinging at a couple a' Limeys and the bouncer tryin' to break it up. I saw the owner behind the bar talkin' on the phone so me and Leach got outa there. Hanson was ahead of us."

"Yeah, I could see what was comin' when one of them Limeys made a crack about Canadians fightin' the war with tomahawks," said Hanson ruefully.

"I guess they musta cleaned 'er up pretty good," offered Leach. "I could hear chairs and tables smashin' after we got out. They say Jack and Kowalski are in the brig."

"Why didn't you stop the fight before it got going?" Dutch asked. Suddenly, the elation he'd brought back from his shore leave evaporated. If he'd been there the whole thing might have been avoided. Although Jack was so much bigger and taller, Ike had begun to feel as if Jack was a younger brother, someone he needed to look after, someone who needed help in keeping out of trouble. The good humor that made Jack such a bright note in the mess when bad conditions had turned the rest of the crew surly seemed to desert him after a few drinks. That's when something hidden beneath his usual good cheer broke out, looking for a fight.

"Barnes, let's go over there and get 'em out!"

"Are you kidding? You're talkin' about the US brig. Now it's up to the boys in the peaked caps, not us. McCurdy has been talkin' to the Captain and they'll go on over to see what can be done, I suppose."

The missing men were not released that night and, with sailing orders posted for Monday 1300 hours, Ike rolled into his hammock fully expecting them to be left behind. At 1000 hours, however, they came rattling down the ladder into the mess. Jack carried his hat in his hand. It wouldn't fit over the bandage he wore like a turban. One eye was closed, the other bloodshot and blackened. Kowalski's swollen mouth protruded from beneath a bandage on his upper lip.

"Jack, you old son-of-a-bitch! What the hell d' you mean comin' back on board looking like this? Can't you go ashore without getting into trouble?"

"Yeah, Dutch, I shoulda waited for you an' Chuck," groaned Jack as he sank down on one of the benches. Gingerly, he ran a hand over his bandaged head. "Them Shore Patrol fellas don't stop to argue, let me tell you. I was just tryin' to tell this one guy where to get off and the next thing I knew I was in the brig, bleeding like a stuck pig. I dunno how many stitches I've got up there but my head feels like a pumpkin."

"You shoulda seen Jack here pile into those Limeys though," mumbled Kowalski through his swollen lips. "They hardly knew what hit 'em. It'll be a while before that one smart ass gets lippy with us again."

The story would be told and retold all the way to Halifax. Beside it, Chuck and Ike's sky blue roadster and striped pajamas story was utterly lacking in drama. Clearly there would be no difficulty keeping the prospect of another visit with Mr. Seward to themselves.

Hanson came down to relieve Ike and Carpenter at 1400 hours. "Jack is still in his hammock. He looks in pretty bad shape, but he won't go up to see the Doc. See what you can do with him when you get up there, eh, Dutch?

I can handle it here as long as things are as smooth as this, but we could be hitting heavy seas pretty soon."

By the time Ike got to the mess, Jack was rolling out of his hammock. He clung to it as his feet hit the deck, unsure of his balance. "Hell, but I'm dizzy, can't seem to stand up." An image of Jack swaying back and forth among the blazing hot pipes of the stokehold rose in Ike's head.

"Look, man. We won't lose the war just because you miss one watch. Can you get up to see the Doc? He could give you something for your head. I'll go back down and help Hanson out until you get yourself in shape to come down." He gave Barnes a shake. "I don't think Jack Jeffries is fit to stand watch, especially if we run into rough weather. See what you can do about him, will you? I'll go down till you get the watch sorted out." Barnes must have gone right back to sleep and Jack stayed in his hammock, confident his watch was being covered.

In Halifax, *Kamsack* gained another man, bringing her stoker complement closer to par. When Alan Morrissey's curly head and baby face emerged from the hatchway, Ike suddenly felt like an old veteran. The new arrival necessitated a watch reassignment. He was teamed up with Chuck. A quiet person like Kowalski, he contributed little to the mess arguments and banter but quickly gained the respect of the stoker crew for his serious approach to issues. An RC, he joined Chuck in going to confession when possible. On arrival in New York again, Chuck and Ike took Alan ashore with them.

Tied up at Pier 29, Chuck sought out the nearest phone booth. He came back beaming. "C'mon, you two! We're having lunch at Lindy's on Fifth and Forty-seventh. Mr. S. is meeting us there."

Mr. Seward led them through the crowded restaurant to a table towards the rear. He introduced the three girls at the table explaining his need to be in the office at one to meet a client, and that he had taken the liberty of ordering for them all. Edna, the girl opposite Ike, had long, gold-blonde hair done in a roll at the front. Pat, who sat next to Chuck, had heavy, dark, curly hair, freckles, and the curliest eyelashes Ike had ever seen. Doris was a tiny little thing, as dark as Alan was fair.

"Tell me, Chuck, how's the war going?" asked Mr. Seward jovially.

"Well, sir, I can't tell you any secrets, but we've just brought through a convoy with fewer losses than ever before. We're feeling pretty good about it."

"I'm not asking for secrets, my boy, but I am glad to hear what you're saying. The radio keeps telling us we've developed new and better tanks and new and better planes and new and better guns, but the war just goes on and on and on. Here we are, almost three years into it with no end in sight. We've stopped believing the good news and we've never believed the bad. The first is always too good and the bad usually turns out to have been a lot worse than we're being told. Glad to hear some real advance is being made."

Ike thought Chuck should have kept his mouth shut about the convoy. Weren't they always being told not to talk about what they were doing? Mr. Seward didn't look like a spy, of course. Neither did Edna who was smiling at him and asking him where he was from. He started telling her he was from Manitoba and found that she hadn't the faintest idea where that was. He drew a map for her on a table napkin.

The girls giggled at names like Manitoba, Neepawa and Saskatoon, which was Alan's home town. Then he found out that Edna came from New Jersey and he broke into a chorus about "That Little Black Shack Back in Hackensack, New Jersey" and teased Edna about it being her home. He could only recall one line of the song, but Mr. Seward sang the rest of the chorus in a fine baritone to their applause. They were having a fine time and had seemingly just started to find out about each other when Mr. Seward left. Chuck asked quickly, "Couldn't we all meet again when you get off work?"

"You won't need me tonight. Count me out."

Although they knew what he said was true, they protested. Edna told them where their office was and said they would be in the lobby at five. Pat, who clearly had her eye on Chuck, said, "Yes, why don't you come and we'll all go over to The Hut?" Nobody explained about "The Hut," but it sounded exciting.

To pass the time till five, Ike, Chuck and Alan picked up free movie tickets and watched Esther Williams and Van Johnson diving and gliding in a touchingly beautiful water ballet and then, finally, it was five o'clock.

Emerging from the elevator in their office building, the three girls kept the boys standing in the lobby for a while as their co-workers left for the day. Each group alighting from the elevator hesitated briefly, smiled broadly, and exchanged comments before departing through revolving doors to the street.

Ike hoped his collar was perfectly straight. He was glad they had stopped for a shoe shine while walking back from the movie.

"Let's stop for a soda before we go wherever we're going," suggested Ike and they all squeezed into a booth at a nearby café. Somehow, Edna sat next to him and Pat sat next to Chuck. Ike wondered how the girls had decided which one to corral for the evening. Clearly, they were doing the maneuvering.

Pat made a try at conversation. "So Chuck, you're winning the war now."

"Don't answer her, Chuck. Remember what the posters say: `You never know who could be listening!'"

"Right, Dutch. Come to think of it, she does look like a spy."

"Oh, Mata Hari, no less," laughed Edna.

"I thought The Dragon Lady was more my style." Pat pulled her eyes into an Oriental slant. "Me Dragon Lady, you Terry?"

"You bet!" Chuck handed her a straw from the dispenser. "Your cigarette holder."

"Trouble is, I can't hold my eyes and that, too. Now what to do?" Her thin, high voice ended in a tinkling laugh.

"OK, if Chuck is Terry, who are you?" Doris asked, looking at Morrissey.

"You mean you don't recognize Clark Kent when you see him?" Chuck pretended incredulity.

"Yeah, sure. Where's my phone booth? Where's my phone booth?" asked Alan, half rising from his seat.

"What about Dutch?" asked Edna.

"That's easy," laughed Chuck. "He's Li'l Abner."

"You're talking about the muscles now?" Dutch asked.

"Well, actually, it was more the hayseed dripping from your boots, I think."

"Tell me, Chuck, does he play hard to get, too?" Edna asked.

"None harder".

"Absolutely," agreed Morrissey. The boys exchanged glances, holding back remarks that would surely have followed if they were back in the mess.

"Yeah, he's voting for Senator Claghorn, too, in the next election," laughed Chuck.

"Don't you guys start on politics again, or I'm going to sit in another booth," warned Morrissey. "You should hear these guys on board ship. With the election coming up, you'd think it was up to their votes to decide the fate of a nation."

"But you've still got a king," piped up little Doris. "How can you have an election if you've got a king who is king just because he was born a king?"

"That's something I've always wanted to know too," said Edna.

"Oh, it's like this. If King George doesn't get enough votes, we'll put him on boiler cleaning after the election," Dutch said and then launched into an explanation of the Canadian electoral system about which he knew very few details. The argument for and against a monarchy took them past the sodas and time to move on.

The Hut turned out to be a canteen operated by Knights of Columbus. Its juke box was pumping out a swing tune at top volume when they entered. The small dance floor was crowded already. Most of the men were in uniforms representing branches of US and Allied services. "Hi, Edna!" "Hi, Doris!" and "Hi, Pat!" Greetings came from dancing couples as the newcomers made their way to a table. At a counter along one wall, matrons dished up sandwiches, so Ike and Chuck went over to pick up a plateful for their table. By the time they got back, Alan and Doris were dancing.

"Hey, Dutch, will you look at that!" said Chuck in amazement. "Did you know Morrissey could jive like that?"

Ike put down his sandwich and turned to watch. Alan and Doris danced as if they had been partners forever. He twirled her under his arm and she twirled back to be spun around again. Her short skirt flared out from her neat waist and she smiled at Alan as she moved back toward his arms. Gradually, the other couples stopped dancing and gathered to watch, clapping their hands to the beat. Back and forth, around and around, perfectly synchronized, a delight to watch. The record stopped and when they came back to the table, Doris's eyes shone.

"Look man you've been hiding things from us," accused Ike. "You should've told us you were King of Jive?"

"Well, the two of you haven't been much by way of partners, you know," said Morrissey, a bit out of breath.

In the mood,
You've got me dancin'
In the mood,

You've got me prancin'
You've gotta do some dancin'
When you're in the mood...

The evening slipped by very quickly. At midnight, Morrissey and Doris were still swinging and twirling, Chuck and Pat danced a more mundane style, and Dutch, talking to Edna, watched the clock. "Look, Edna. We've got to get back to the ship in about an hour. We should be taking you girls home, I guess."

"An hour? You'll never make it if you take us home first. Never mind. People here we know will see us home."

"All the way back on the subway, Morrissey kept humming "In the Mood," "Boy! Can she dance! Did you see her?" he smiled to himself and hummed some more.

"Yes, yes, we saw her, Morrissey. We saw her, we saw you, we saw you together, we saw you dancing together, we applauded. What more do you want from us?" Ike asked.

"Yeah, for God's sake, find another tune if you have to sing or hum. Better yet, shut up," said Chuck, leaning back and closing his eyes. "Boy! Am I tired! And we've got to go on watch as soon as we get back."

Jack had a mug of tea on the boil. Chuck and Morrissey scrambled into their dungarees. "Damn it, Dutch. You're bloody cold sober! What's this? They'd better give me shore leave next time we hit this town. Can't let you go ashore without me. One trip without me and you go all to hell. I've just gotta look after you." He poured the tea.

"I'm tellin' ya, I stood watch for so many guys today, this ship'll hafta be tied up for two weeks before I have to stand watch while we're at this jetty. Brace yourself, buddy. They can't keep me cooped up on this bucket forever."

Ike got out his writing materials and started a letter to Sara but he couldn't seem to find much to say.

In the mood,
You've got me dancin'
In the mood....

He decided he wasn't in the mood for letter writing. He'd finish it tomorrow. For sure before ship left port. But when *Kamsack* sailed out past the Statue of Liberty, Ike realized that for the first time since he'd said goodbye to her that there was no letter for Sara on its way from his port of call.

Four letters from Sara awaited him when they reached Halifax. The first must have arrived just after the ship left on its last call there. He put them aside. Although he knew it wasn't possible, the thick, battered packets seemed to exude an air of recrimination. The letter from his sister told him about spring seeding and that his father was appealing for the release of Pete from CO camp. It certainly sounded as if he needed help.

When at last he opened Sara's first letter, he found she had sent a few snapshots. Mostly they were of herself and a new girlfriend. They must have taken a whole roll of film. He looked at the pictures again and again. Somehow in most of them, Sara didn't look quite like the Sara he remembered, but there was one that had been taken before she had time to look at the camera. He savoured a momentary overwhelming urge to reach out and touch her.

He read and reread. Mostly, Sara rambled on about being bored with school and how she was looking forward to being free of books to the end of term. No mention of dances or parties. Her latest letter, however, contained a paragraph that troubled him:

> *Aunt Dorothy and Uncle Pete came out from Winnipeg last weekend. She says there is a job opening in the fur department at Holt Renfrew where she works. They are offering $8.00 a week and she wants me to apply. I could live with them, she says. Mother won't let me go. She says I can't leave without finishing Grade XI and that I can't live on $8.00 a week. It sounds like a lot of money to me but she worked it all out with pencil and paper and I guess she's right.*

It had never occurred to him that Sara would be anywhere than right where she had been when he went away. He hoped no other chances to go to the city would come up before he got home again. There was something about city girls that he didn't think would fit Sara.

Ike remained on board ship during the two cold and foggy days she got tied up in Halifax. He played craps and lost a few bucks. He switched to poker and won enough to pay for the tiddly uniform, but by that time it was too late to fetch it. He went up on deck to watch the ship get underway and saw Chuck and Morrissey come dashing up the gangplank just as it was about to be raised.

"Do you know what we did on shore, Dutch? You won't believe this, but I'm telling you it's true. We spent hours in the railway station! And d'ya know why we spent hours in the station? It was because this lame-brained idiot here got into a phone booth and spent hours trying to get through to New York! That jitterbugging skirt's got him twirling around her finger. The poor jerk spent twenty bucks. I had to keep running around for more change so they wouldn't cut him off."

"You know what, Chuck? You've got a great big mouth. Bigger'n your fat ass. Now shut up!" shouted Morrissey. "You'll be glad enough to come along again next time we hit New York so shut your goddamned mouth!"

Ike was surprised at Morrissey's vehemence. He did seem truly offended. "Wouldn't mind going along myself, Alan." He said as mildly as he could. "Have you got something lined up?"

"We'll see when we get there," said Morrissey, still flushed and angry as he stomped off toward the mess.

The convoy going out was especially slow, burdened with a few rusty antiques that could barely keep their boilers going. Then, two days out of port, the U-boats found them. Ike was off watch when the alarms sounded and dashed up just behind Jack Jeffries to his action station at the starboard depth charges. For three hours they circled and dodged and hunted. Obviously, the skipper did not give a damn about the boiler room, or for that matter any other part of this boat, judging by the way he had her veering sharply to port and then so abruptly back to starboard that she virtually lay on her side. It was the only way to avoid the blasts of her own depth charges being launched from starboard and port launchers alternately in quick succession.

He could picture the goings on down below where a step on the steel deck among pumps and hot pipes with steam flying and fires roaring was like venturing among hot coals, always with one hand holding on somewhere. Each depth charge he and Jack launched overboard rocked them as it exploded but what was a solid jolt on the upper decks would seem about to destroy the whole dastardly ship down below where deck plates heaved at every blast.

Between launchings, Ike watched the activity on the bridge where the skipper stood shouting into a voice pipe and listening to reports from radar and ASDIC operators that gave some clue to where the enemy lurked down below. No time to be concerned about the stokehold. Avoiding a torpedo up the ship's backside was his preoccupation. Strike and blast away regardless of whatever discomfort down below. And so the order came for more firings, some set to trigger near the surface, certain to cause stress on boiler room joints, pipes and welds, others set to sweep the ocean clean of U-boats lurking with deadened engines on the bottom.

Excitement mounted at Action Stations as *Kamsack* circled and zigzagged, probing the ocean for an enemy certain to be somewhere. Surely this time she'd make her kill. But then weather conditions began to deteriorate rapidly, decreasing the chances of either sub or corvette making a hit, so skipper gave up pursuit and turned her into the wind. Damn! Ike felt let down.

As All Clear sounded, a giant sea crashed over K171's bow and bridge, further drenching the already soaked bridge, gunnery and depth charge crew. Ike saw the awesome wave strike in time to grasp a handrail near the doorway. His feet swept from under him, his arm stressed to the breaking point, he clung desperately. Something heavy banged into and bounced off his back. He gasped and swallowed water. He choked, lungs bursting until the wave retreated.

Scrambling to his feet, he saw where further aft other bodies crawled and scrambled up from among the gear. He lunged for the doorway. Still coughing, he stumbled over the coaming, landing on his knees while other boots and bodies hurtled past him trying to escape the next deluge. Retching from the salt water, he went to the heads. Barnes, already there, spitting and coughing into a sink, "Jesus Christ! That's a son-of-a-bitch!" Ike could only cough and retch in reply. When his inner revolt had died down, he followed Barnes down to the mess. There they discovered that Jack Jeffries was missing.

CHAPTER 16

R&R

Heavy storm damage to main deck gear made it necessary to lay over for five wet, foggy days in St. John's getting temporary repairs. It was June 6th when they reached New York. Only limited shore leave was permitted, so Chuck, Ike, and Morrissey headed straight for The Hut, expecting the girls to be there waiting. Both Edna and Pat, however, were dancing intimately with other men in uniform when they walked in. Doris was helping the ladies at the sandwich counter. Morrissey moved toward the sandwiches as if he were a starving man.

"There you see it, Dutch, Old Boy! What do you make of it? Ya think its true love stuff like the movies have it? Morrissey's lookin' pretty hot to me."

They sat down at a table and watched while Morrissey made his play. Doris laughed and blushed. The record stopped. Edna came over to say "Hi!" and moved on. Pat waved from where she sat with the airman. Chuck sighed. Ike tried not to admit how disappointed he was.

"No point waiting around here for Morrissey to remember we're here, too, so Chuck, let's get the hell out of here. We've got better things to do than watch guys on the make."

They wandered along Seventh Avenue towards Times Square. "Holy Hell!" Dutch stopped in his tracks, "Look at the ticker tape, Chuck! We've landed in Normandy!" People crowded the street to watch the news. "By dammit, Chuck! We may get this fucking war over yet. C'mon, let's get a paper and have a drink!'

Disappointed in their inability get into any bars which were jammed with people celebrating, they returned to their ship. News of the landing had been heard on the radio but to see the headline in print added authenticity to what they had heard. "Let's see the paper." Some men were joyous, others turned somber like Carson. "There'll be a helluva long casualty list out tomorrow. I know a couple of guys that are probably out there." With this latest excitement, Morrissey got away with overstaying his leave by two hours. He tumbled down the ladder into the mess as *Kamsack* cast off.

"Where in hell were you," asked Chuck. "Sure's hell McCurdy's down in the engine room, screaming for you. What happened?"

"I figured I could take Doris home and make it back here in time, but she lives a helluva lot farther out than I thought." He scrambled into his dungarees, buttoning his shirt as he started up the ladder.

Ike shook his head as he watched Morrissey's boots disappear. "Boy! That kid has a bad case." He felt a touch of envy. If Sara were within reach he knew he'd not get back to ship on time either.

"Yeah, I know how he feels," said Chuck. "I just hope he don't get his ass kicked for his pains."

Before long, *Kamsack* was ordered into St. John, New Brunswick, for a minor refit. Seven days leave suited some, like Leach and Barnes, able to travel home and back in that time. Ike and Chuck envied them. They applied for an extra week. Were refused. Like others, they accepted a week of R & R at a fishing camp. A better bet than hanging around St. John playing cards or shooting crap. Morrissey packed his ditty bag and took off for New York.

Owned and operated before the war by a pulp and paper company for the entertainment of their important customers, the camp had been seconded for wartime use by the military. A handful of log cabins and, closer to the river, a large lodge in which they took their meals. The deep quiet of the woods was a startling change from roaring boilers, deafening depth charges, pounding seas and the bustle and noise of an ordinary shore leave. Relief from the crowded mess. No more privacy was offered but the cabins were sufficiently roomy to move about without forever jostling one another.

In small groups, formed according to inclination, they walked along the stream to pools reputedly teeming with trout. Inexpert though he was, Ike managed to catch a few to add to the cook's fry for supper. Often, however, he left the others to do the fishing and searched for a spot among the rocks to lie in the sun. He had not realized how utterly weary he was. The dampness of pine needles and the smell of decaying leaves produced by a burning sun, worked on him like a narcotic. He slept.

On the one day it rained, Ike wrote letters and re-read again the latest ones from home. The War Office had sent notice that Buz Bargen was missing in action since D-Day. Sara wrote that one of the Gertzich boys serving with the RCAF in England was temporarily invalided to a hospital in Scotland under psychiatric care. She was going to Winnipeg to get a job as soon as school was out. The news was all bad, it seemed, but there wasn't anything he could do about any of it. He was overcome by a strange lethargy. He dozed on his cot, declining invitations to participate in the inevitable poker and craps games continuing in the lounge between meals. Simply couldn't rouse himself from his lassitude.

At the end of the week, families from the nearby paper town came out for "a boil-up" on the beach. Loaded with lobster and crab, clams and mussels, salads, cakes, pies and a keg of beer, they proceeded to impress these prairie sailors with Eastern cook-out hospitality. A fiddler and accordion player struck up tunes, raising the spirit of revelry to a louder pitch, while inexperienced sailors cracked lobsters on exposed rocks along the river bank. Later in the lodge a group gathered around the battered piano for a singsong. They sang WWI songs. They sang, "Roll Out the Barrel," "I've Got Tuppence," "White Cliffs of Dover." When they got around to the old country melodies and sang, "Home, Home on the Range," Dutch got misty eyed and walked out. To the dock.

Small shadows of wavelets broke the pale surface of the water and a host of frogs conducted a chorus somewhere nearby. The cry of a loon came from the far side of the water. He sat down, dangling his legs over the edge. "Silly ass," he told himself. There had never been any damned deer or antelope playing anywhere near the farm he'd grown up on. Not in his time anyway. No reason at all for that stupid song to make him think of home. Home.

They would be haying. A task he had despised. And his brother in a CO camp not there to help either.

Sara's letter said that she and her sister were going out to work in the sunflower fields after school and on weekends. So were a lot of the other girls they used to go around with, earning a dollar a day plus meals. He pictured her slim body bent over the hoe, thought of the banter that flowed when the work crew gathered at the end of the field for the afternoon coffee. Good thing there were no boys left around Highfield to weed sunflowers. The men's baseball team had folded, she said, so they had organized a girls' team but had trouble getting to tournaments because of gas rationing.

Buz, a great pitcher, had been the first of the men's team to enlist. During his embarkation leave he and his steady had danced the night away. Handsome couple on the floor they were. He tall, curly-haired with laughing eyes and she willowy and beautiful. That night they had moved with special grace. "Missing in Action." In a few days, that would be followed by another telegram: "Presumed Dead." For her there had never been any other man.

He wondered about Sara. Would she have changed? Would he ever see her again? For darned sure he would not see Jack again. Jack and his carefree, two-fisted, laughing approach to life. He rehearsed those horrifying moments on *Kamsack*'s deck. Could they have rescued him? Could anyone have noticed sooner that Jack was not among those lying among the gear on the after deck? Why had he not noticed? Common sense told him no one swept into the churning, heaving deep could have been found. Yet, the nagging questions continued.

Ike shivered in the chilly air and retreated to his cabin. He fell asleep as soon as he pulled up the blankets. A sleep troubled by dreams from which he woke with a start.

The truck came early morning for the return to St. John. *Kamsack*'s gear had been put in order, her plates had been checked. New armaments graced her forward deck. With other seamen, Ike and Chuck gathered around the installation for inspection. They saw an unimpressive, steel plate of modest size mounted at an angle on the deck. From it, spikes protruded, pointing skyward. Impaled on each spike, a canister filled with explosives. Whiley explained.

"What you guys see here is a hedgehog. The Limeys have had hedgehogs on their ships for over a year. Now us Canadians are finally getting fitted with 'em. When this hedgehog is detonated, the canisters are shot out in fan formation over the bow. With depth charges catapulted over the side and more rolled from her stern, we'll be laying a pattern of charges all around the ship. There won't be a square inch in which a fucking U-boat can hide. The explosive they're made of is a helluva lot more powerful than straight TNT too."

"Holy Hell!" someone piped up. "They've found out they couldn't sink us with depth charges alone so they had to try something else. You realize we've gotta steam right over these bastards after they're fired?"

"But those things aren't depth charges," said Whiley. "They're supposed to explode only on contact."

"So if we hit a sub, we still blow the bejeesus out of our own bottom."

"Well, they're supposed to fall so far ahead of us that the ship can turn to avoid the target area and the blast will be over and done with if the ship passes over any part of it."

"We hope," said Ike.

They went down to the stokers' mess which neither looked nor smelled as it had when they left. Chuck opened the food locker to check on supplies. Completely empty. He looked in the tea canister and the coffee tin. "Hey! What's this? I'd better get up to Moss and start stocking up. Barnes may not get back today and there's not a thing here for us when we come off watch."

He scurried up the ladder and came back laden with a tin of jam, a block of cheese, a loaf of bread and some tea. "You know what? They fumigated this tub while we were at camp. No wonder the cockroaches weren't scurrying out of the way when I opened the locker door."

"Fuck! Gotta arrange our own gear from now on. Place is goin' to pot."

By day's end, those who had gone home during refit straggled back to the mess. All except Morrissey. At midnight when Ike and Chuck went down to stand watch the word was out. "He ain't makin it back". They sailed at 0100 hours.

"Wonder what they'll do to the kid," Ike checked the burner.

"Whatever it is, I'm glad it's not me," Chuck said fervently. "The girl's got him going in circles, but Jesus Christ! He's gotta have a damn sized better reason than that when he catches up with this tub."

Test-firing the hedgehog in open water substantiated Ike's prophetic fears. In addition to the thumping clangor raised by depth charges, they were now subjected to a series of short bursts in rapid succession. Like boom-boom cannon fire striking the hull. On watch in the boiler room, Chuck and Ike eyed each other apprehensively and held their breaths when the first charges exploded. *Kamsack* rocked and rolled in the aftermath.

The PO came down on the All Clear signal. "Check the bilges. Make sure nothing's popped open. In this shallow water, those buggers banged off before we got away."

"If we didn't pop something, those guys in dry dock must've done a helluva job welding her."

Riveted and welded seams had remained intact. In the stokers' mess, however, opinion about the new device was sharply divided. Some boasted that *Kamsack* would get her "kill" at last. Others were certain it wouldn't make a damned bit of difference. "One thing we know for sure," Carson said gloomily. "It won't make it any easier standing watch down below while the skipper's up there turning this tub on a dime. Hell, we'll be passing over our own charges two or three times at the rate he keeps moving."

"Hard on the balls that's for sure".

In Halifax, military police escorted Morrissey on board and marched him directly to the wardroom. His shipmates held their breaths, waiting to hear his fate. It came without delay.

"All hands on deck. Rig of the day: Number Ones."

"What's happening, Barnes?" Ike asked as he changed into his uniform.

"Court martial, that's what. You can't jump ship and get away with a slap on the wrist. KR and AI, *King's Rules and Admiralty Instructions* is what's being followed, that's all."

The crew fell in facing the forward deck. Officers stood near the new hedgehog installation. "Atten--shun!!" Ike realized he had not been called to attention like this since he had finished cleaning boilers at *Stadacona*. He had not missed it.

The Captain strode briskly forward and took his place in the centre of the group of officers. Morrissey, bareheaded, emerged in the custody of the quartermaster. In total silence they moved forward to face the assembled crew. After a great deal of saluting among the stiff-backed officers, the charge was read and a few questions were hurled at Morrissey standing at attention. His quiet answers did not shed any new, favourable light on his case. An officer stepped forward, ripped the rank badge from his shoulders and read the sentence—a month in the brig. To Ike, once the badges had been torn away, the sentence seemed anti-climatic. Morrissey held his head high as he was being marched away.

* * *

In Ike's view, the sea wasn't fit to sail on, let alone calm enough for the hazardous operation of transferring bunker fuel. Yet they were eighteen days out and four days short of St. John's, the nearest refueling port for K171.

A tough convoy, this one. After several months of relative quiet, German U-boats had constantly attacked with renewed ferocity and the corvettes had fought back furiously. Heavy seas or no, every torpedo seemed aimed out of a determination to prevent the fates from switching sides in a battle that had seemed to be theirs to win for many years. Losses in the convoy had not been heavy. It was not because the attacks had been few but the corvettes, including *Kamsack*, with newly installed cat-gear and hedgehog armament, had rendered U-boat strikes less effective. Now it was Christmas Day and she was running short on fuel. For the first time since Ike had come aboard, K171 would be refueled at sea.

After several unsuccessful attempts, a flexible fuel line was transferred from a tanker, secured to *Kamsack*'s intake, and valves were opened. Semaphore signals were dispatched to proceed with pumping and new life flowed into her. To avoid being torn apart, both tanker and corvette maintained a difficult but steady and precise course amid the heaving waves.

Off watch, Ike observed these Christmas Day activities from the ship's prow. Very impressive. Turning toward the bridge, he saw skipper, cool and possessed. A word to the helmsman, now an order for slightly more or less speed, looking here, observing there, completely in control. Oh, to be a skipper! Control of oneself and a ship. He'd learn to be captain by watching the skipper. By observation. He'd garnered the basics of playing bridge by watching his older brothers, looking over their shoulders, observing. Then again, learning to be captain could not be accomplished if one was constantly down on watch in the fucking stokehold.

At 1300 hours the umbilical cord was unscrewed and the long, flexible six-inch copper hose sucked back into the tanker. *Kamsack* steamed on to fight the war. One more day. With all fires down during refueling, lunch had been delayed but was in full progress by the time Ike went below. Moss had been grumbling for days that his larder was "damned near empty," but he came up with a special Christmas Day treat. Balogna sandwiches. No fresh beef or pork until reaching port, and with these sandwiches the last of the balogna was gone. Tinned goods—Klik, Spam, sardines, and salmon would be the order of the day from here on. So they ate their sandwiches with special Christmas reverence.

For Ike, balogna was not deprivation. He had seen the production line at Canada Packers in Winnipeg and knew it to be good quality, old bull meat, ground, spiced and rammed into huge horse gut, then smoked for curing and flavour. After all the long months on board he found it more palatable than another round of aged roast beef, mashed potatoes and canned peas. The blessing he secretly asked as he sat down to eat was accompanied by appropriate thanks.

No extra time off on Christmas day for ship's company. Four hours on, eight hours off, the same old routine. Ike and Charlie stood the 1600 to 2000 hour watch together with hardly a word spoken. Neither felt a need to encroach on the other's private, sentimental connection with home.

They checked their timepieces frequently and at ten to proceeded to set things in order for the change of watch. Ring! Ring! Ring! Action Bells exploded!

"Holy Shit!" Charlie shouted. "Not on bloody Christmas Day!"

A four-hour hunt, sounding, testing, firing, then suddenly, all quiet again. All except the North Sea. A sea oblivious to Christmas.

Moss served supper delayed by the action at 0100 hours. He managed to steam up an Argentine corned beef hash, for which only Barnes and Carson got in line. Ike and Charlie settled down for pusser rat trap cheese, boiled tea and jam from the stokers' mess, still well supplied with these basics. They cut crumbly, thick slices of Canada's best, uncolored cheddar from a large, white, well-aged round, slapped them on stale and moldy bread. Some mess mates considered the cheese too strong and too dry in texture, but Ike and Charlie ate with enjoyment. On the cheese they spread pure raspberry jam dipped from a two-gallon pail held firmly on the deck between their legs. Charlie insisted the tea be boiled the K171 standard ten minutes before allowing Ike to wash his food down with it for this Boxing Day breakfast.

St. John's harbour was more crowded than ever when they finally reached its blissfully calm waters. "Wonder what's goin' on?" mused Charlie as *Kamsack* edged alongside three other corvettes tied up for refueling at the South Side pier. Charlie and Ike made their way over the intervening decks and walked toward town, heading into a stiff wind sweeping down from the hills that formed the northwestern backdrop to the city. From time to time they turned and walked with their backs to the wind for a few paces.

"If it weren't for the water, this place would remind me of home on a day like this," Ike shouted, holding his hat with one hand and tucking the other into the warm pocket of his Burberry.

"If I wasn't so sick of the smell of our mess after all this time at sea, I'd've stayed on board," Charlie shouted back. The distance to the bridge at the inner end of the harbour seemed twice as long as usual and they were especially grateful for the shelter of Water Street on reaching the northern side. A thick, grey-blue haze of smoke hung over a crush of navy blue uniforms in the wet canteen.

"Hell, this smells almost worse than our mess," Ike muttered as they stepped aside to let some sailors pass them to get to the door. They slipped into still-warm benches, nodding a greeting to men on the opposite side.

"Stay here, Ike, and I'll get something to drink. Want, a beer?"

"No! I've gotta wait'll this room stops pitching and tossing before I start drinking. Bring me a coffee if there is any, or a Coke."

"You guys just get back from Derry?" A poster above the speaker's head warned LOOSE TALK CAN MEAN LOST LIVES. Ike paused and eyed the speaker's shoulder badges carefully before answering. They seemed as genuine as his own.

"Nah! Just another fucking convoy from the east coast to the middle of nowhere. Triangle Run. Out on that goddam water three weeks. U-boats coming at us from all sides. We keep hearin' the war's just about over but we sure didn't notice any signs out there."

"Know what you mean. I was sure happy when our tub got transferred to the other run, just for seein' the other side, but by damn, as far as U-boats go, makes no matter where. First trip across we lost a coupla tubs in the Irish Channel. Them guys don't think they're licked yet. Did ya hear they sank the *Clayaquot* Christmas Eve? Practically at the mouth of Halifax harbour."

Charlie brought two sandwiches and two Cokes. "Fresh bread! Never better than in St. John's. It'll be ambrosia after that moldy stuff we've been fed." Ike tried his sandwich. Out of the corner of his eye he could see the floor rising and shifting. His stomach heaved in harmony. He bit into the sandwich with angry determination and quelled his inner turmoil by staring the floor into submission while the conversation proceeded around him. Inconsequential comments, unanswered questions, boasts and counter exaggerations between sips, farts, and drags on fags left Ike cold and uninspired.

"It was a treat to see somethin' other than the old familiar stuff around here, and there's good times to be had in Derry, even if you've got to look a bit harder for it, eh, Buddy?" the speaker nudged his neighbour who was peering boozily into his empty glass.

"You can't tell me it beats New York though," challenged Ike.

"Hell, nothin' beats New York. But after all, Derry's part of the Old Country and that's what makes it worthwhile gettin' over there."

The thought fed into Ike's general unease. He vaguely heard Charlie's query about the escort make-up.

"How many Canadian ships now on the Derry run? Any Limeys escorting?"

"No. Pretty well all our ships. Has been, I think, for over a year. A few Americans on this last run, but the Limeys are busy convoying stuff across to the Continent, I guess. Most of us were Canadian.

"Look, Charlie," Ike said, standing up. "The heat in here is getting to me. I'll wait for you outside," and he pushed his way toward the door.

"Be right with you," Charlie shouted after him.

Outside, leaning against a lamp post, Ike gasped in the cold air, struggling with a bout of nausea. Charlie came up behind him.

"Hey, don't tell me that sandwich wasn't any good. You look sick as a dog."

"I am," groaned Ike. "Land sick I think. Christ, you'd think after all the months of puking I've done on the water I've had enough. Let's walk around a bit and I'll get my land legs back. Sitting in that place was bad for the stomach and listening to those guys turned me off. Made me wanna puke."

"Why for God's sake? They're just tryin' to be friendly. That's all. Ike, I think you're sick in the head, not the stomach."

"Yeah, maybe I am. I'm sick and tired of every day bein' the same as the last, only worse, and I didn't want to hear about how great it was to get to Londonderry or Murmansk or Gibraltar or anywhere else we'll never get a chance to see."

"It gets boring all right, but think of all the mail there'll be waitin' for us when we hit Halifax. Besides, maybe *Kamsack*'ll get transferred to another run one of these days. The war isn't over yet. C'mon, let's go over to the Caribou Hut. Maybe the girls there can cheer you up."

Chapter 17
Bermuda

On May 7, 1945, K171 in Liverpool for minor refit to upper deck gear lay comfortably berthed for a well-deserved respite from steady sea service. Her one and only radio transmitted daily news from shore side stations. On this day it sounded too good to be true.

> *Germany surrendered unconditionally to the Allies today, completing the victory in the European phase of the Second Great war – the most devastating in history.*
> *Prime Minister Churchill will proclaim the historic conquest 3 p.m. (9 a.m. E.D.T.) tomorrow from 10 Downing St. and simultaneous announcements are expected from President Truman...and Premier Stalin....*
> *The crowning triumph [comes] just five years eight months and six days after Hitler invaded proud but weak Poland and struck the spark which set the world afire....*
> *German troops were fighting on in Czechoslovakia after General Ferdinand von Schoerner...repudiated the capitulation announced by Grand Admiral Doenitz. Russian forces were also reported swiftly surging towards the capital from the east and north.*[7]

"We've got the bastards by the balls." gloated Barnes. "I always said we'd beat the shit out of 'em. Still, it's hard to think of what it'll be like, not havin' to scramble up that ladder on Action Stations again."

Some expressed concern for the delay in getting a complete ceasefire. "Hell, it sounds as if the Allies are just sitting there. Waiting for God knows what, while the Russians are galloping across Europe. Claiming territory. They'll hang onto it. You would too, eh?"

"Dutch, don't you worry about that. Let Eisenhower handle it. Ike knows what he's doin'," Barnes sniffed. "You just start thinkin' about what you'll be doin' with yerself when the end finally comes. Or are the cows just waitin' for ya back home?"

"I know where I'll be going. No questions asked. Since you're so cocksure about everything, what about yourself?"

"Well, we haven't beaten the Japs yet and, hell, as far as I'm concerned this war could go on forever, it'd suit me fine, except for Action Stations. I've gotta find a job when I get back. What about you, Charlie?"

"I've got no problems. My Old Man's been a printer for years. He'll get me in the business. I'll be fixed. Only thing is, I'll be a lot older than most apprentices I'll be bumping. They won't like making way for us vets. So what does a guy do?"

"God, you guys are serious about this." Carson chimed in. "Me, if I get outa this thing alive, and it sure ain't over yet, I'm gonna go on one helluva toot, just to get the smell and feel of this ship outa my system. Lights out for me for a week at least."

"Not me. I'm gonna screw the first broad I see. I'm just gonna have me a time! Later, one helluva lot later, I'll start worryin' about where I'm gonna go and where I can get a job. One thing's for sure. I will absolutely never, never ever, set foot on a goddam ship again for the rest of my life."

"You can say that again," from one of the hammocks. "Me, I'm goin' home and I'll get locked up in a room with my little woman. Orders, by god, for no one to open the door until she comes out to announce, 'He's dead.' And when they come in, they'll see me smiling." A chorus of laughter indicated general approval.

Next morning, confirmation came. The war in Europe was over! The loud speaker system conveyed the Captain's order to "Splice the Main Brace." The entire ship's company fell in forward to receive an extra ration of rum in recognition of the great achievement. They had won the war! Whistles blew, horns blared, bells rang, hands clasped. Some men cried and others laughed hysterically. Some drank their tot quickly and easily found more grog in the pleasant state of disorganization that enveloped the ship. No one seemed to mind when a matelot, already three sheets to the wind before the splicing, stumbled over a piece of gear to go sprawling amongst the officers posing for a picture. Why worry? The war was over at last! With victory in Europe, the real war had come to an end.

"Ship's company dismissed." An order with ceremonial significance only since everyone was standing very easy by the time it was given. The First Mate's voice came over the loudspeakers. "We have a bulletin from the Liverpool authorities: In recognition of VE Day, no liquor will be dispensed at the local liquor stores and all establishments that normally serve alcoholic beverages will close their doors until further notice."

A loud groan that seemed to come as one voice resounded throughout the ship. Complaints in all the messes grew spontaneously. "What the hell is this?" and "They can't do this to us!" and "The fucking bastards." And "That's not what I bloody fought for."

For the moment, there was still a liquor supply available in private lockers and anyone known to have a bottle of rum stashed away was pressed to pass it around. Still, by late afternoon the ship was dry. Only one place from which to restock. By 1800 hours the word had spread. Booze at the liquor store. Ike and Leach rushed out along with the rest to do their share. Why not? Hadn't they just won the war? Stoked up with a tot of rum in the morning, a hefty toddy while splicing the main brace, then repeated toasts to the victory from private bottles that had leaped from mess lockers, plus the high excitement of the day, their blood quickly reached the boiling point.

Arriving too late, they witnessed a confused withdrawal from the liquor store premises. Men running in every direction, some with bottles in hand, others trying to hide bulging items as best they could, in their trousers, under their tunics. From a distance, Ike and Leach stopped dead. "Better turn back before we get nabbed," said Ike.

"Yeah. I see Shore Patrols over there and local cops. Funny, they aren't arresting anybody!"

"Not yet, they're not, but I'm for getting the hell out of here before they start!"

Back at K171 the celebration continued. Without any bottles in sight, men got merrier as the night turned into morning. Nobody seemed to tire of congratulating his fellow man on the job well done. His Majesty's senior service had practically won the war single handed. F****** --- the army! F****** --- the air force! F****** --- all the Wrens! (Loud cheers!) By god! They couldn't have done it without the Canadian corvette navy, the best god-damned navy in the bloody, fuckin' world. Yeah!

Sailing orders came at 0800 hours. Holy Hell! Many of the crew were still in a stupor and had to be picked up bodily from where they had collapsed. Those that were on watch were tidied up and helped to their stations. But where the hell was *Kamsack* going? The war was over! Nothing could be urgent enough now to put to sea less than twenty four hours after the war had ended! Still, within two hours she was at sea and rumour had it her destination was Halifax where she would await further orders. That skipper had pulled out of Liverpool to avoid embarrassing apologies for the behaviour of those of his men who had misused their shore leave privileges was more than speculative scuttle butt. From the upper decks, too, came word that the Captain was fuming! So they were putting to sea although most of the officers were still in less than ship-shape condition, having exercised copiously the privilege of their rank in toasting King and Country in their private mess. While sitting down.

Skipper, having issued No Shore Leave orders while still hot under the collar, must have felt his anger tone down somewhat on reaching Halifax. Whatever damn fool mischief his crew had been up to in Liverpool was child's play compared to what he saw in that port. A city sacked by both civil and military personnel angered by a decree prohibiting sale or issue of any alcoholic drinks on VE Day.

Restrictions on shore leave were lifted next morning. Ike and Charlie took a street car, one of the few still on the tracks, for a short run to explore the shambles of Barrington Street. What had been smashable was broken—lights, windows, doors. Automobiles and streetcars still lay where they had been overturned. Some had obviously been burned. They wandered down towards the K of C canteen, peering between boards that had gone up in place of broken show windows at interiors of shops containing nothing but litter. A woman's shoe, shiny and new, lay near the door of Wallace Bros. amid a pile of battered shoe boxes, broken glass, and trampled tissue paper. Ahead of them a clean-up crew swept the sidewalk.

They wandered over to the unexpectedly boarded up Green Lantern. "Let's check out the K of C canteen. If anything's open, it'll be the K of C," Ike vowed. They pushed their way into the canteen and struggled past crowded tables toward the counter. "A Coke and Orange Crush, please," he asked. Leaning on the counter, they sipped and joined in conversation with others near them.

"Some mess out there, eh?" came from the soldier who stood beside them.

"Sure is. You here when it all happened?"

"Not really. Me and my buddy only got downtown for a coupla hours the first day and then went back to our canteen at the barracks. That was before they looted the liquor stores. By the time we got down there next day, the place was a shambles."

"What happened anyway?"

"Well, I figger the city got what it deserved. Y'know what them Big Wigs did? On VE Day? Ordered the jeezly movies closed and liquor stores too. Cafes all shut tight. Here we was, wantin' to celebrate, an' not a drop of booze to be had anywhere. Y' couldn't even buy a Coke anywhere except here at the K of C, and thousands out on the streets wantin' to whoop it up. Didn't take long, the crowd went for the liquor stores. And sure raised hell!"

"So lockin' everything up backfired. Stupid!"

"Me an' me buddy, we went up far as the cemetery. This here bootlegger, he'd laid a gravestone 'cross coupla others t' make him a counter an', Man, was he sellin' drinks all day. Roarin' business he did." He chuckled at the thought. "It was wild, lemme tell ya. Guys layin' down all over among them graves, dead drunk. Won't be rememberin' much about VE Day."

"Who smashed into all the stores?"

"Hell, I dunno who started that. We got down there 'n everyone was pickin' up much as they could haul. Lotsa women, too. Men went fer heavy, big stuff like furniture an' women fer clothes. *Stadacona* guys is gettin' big shit for it all, but the lootin', that was mainly civilians done it. Hell, what could a serviceman take an' hope to get away with it? They mainly went fer the liquor. Where were you guys?"

"At sea, yeah, we were at sea," Chuck said quickly.

"Yeah," Ike confirmed with alacrity, "we spliced the main brace up on the forward deck and then drank what we'd stashed in our lockers. It's a good thing we weren't in here though. I'm sure we'd have been right in there like a dirty shirt."

"I'll tell ya', it was somethin' to see. Sofas dumped outa the window at Eaton's an' guys sittin' out on the street drinkin', just like they're right at home. But we didn't see hardly nothin'. Sure would've liked seein' them two gals in uniform stagin' a contest to see which one could take on the most men. Right there on the grass. Damn! Right on the grass."

"You're kidding!" exclaimed Chuck.

"Hell I am! It was goin' on all over the place. Every fuckin' inch of Citadel Hill in motion."

Their soft drinks finished, Ike was itching to go, "Let's get outa here, Charlie. This place is as crowded as our mess. Nice talkin' to you," nodding to the soldier.

Sailing orders came that evening. K171 would sail in the early morning, escorting a Red Cross hospital ship. Tropical gear would be required. Their destination was revealed after an hour's sail out of port. Bermuda! Cheers!

Standing watch in a corvette boiler room while sailing in the north Atlantic in the month of May was a reasonably pleasant experience. A comfortable work station. The big vent turned into the wind scooped up steady flow of air into the boiler room maintaining a comfortable temperature well above the near-freezing conditions prevailing from December through to March. The vents, however, were not intended for comfort. Basically they provided the necessary draft for clean combustion in the burners, and could never be shut entirely, regardless of how cold it was. Or how hot.

There had been occasions when the bridge sent down orders to stop laying smoke screens and that smoke must be made only upon orders received to do so. Smoke on the horizon provided too much evidence for U-boats to spot convoys. Stokers could freeze their nuts off, but smoke there would be none!

Warmer air flowing through the vents had always made Ike and his messmates aware of crossing the Gulf Stream, even when they were confined below deck. Now, heading south meant a boiler room constantly warmer than they had previously experienced. In fact, it became very, very hot! Before long, stokers on watch were ordered to take alternate turns of twelve minutes below and twelve minutes on the upper deck to cool off. No one had ever questioned whether Canadian corvettes were suitable for serving in extreme climates. Simply designed to sail under any conditions. That their crews might not survive had not been a consideration. And, what odds? The corvettes had won this bloody war.

The war in the Atlantic over, escorting this hospital ship was a slow business for several reasons. There was no urgency. Waters through which they sailed changed from a thrashing, threatening, grey to a blissful, calm, emerald blue. No need to hurry. Stretch out this voyage. The feeling inhabited every crew member and was carried out as though on an order from the bridge.

At 1300 hours on the second day out, to no one's surprise, the engine room reported a problem with one engine, forcing reduction to slow speed. Several hours later the captain ordered a full stop for repairs. The hospital ship slowed to a crawl. A cheer arose when permission to go for a swim came down the voice pipe. Ike dashed for the upper deck, feeling hardly a moment's qualm about Charlie and Leach who were unlucky enough to be on watch at this time. A dozen or so seamen had already gone over the side. Ike looked down at the sparkling waters dubiously. Sea water as he knew it was always cold. He would wait to hear the reports from those already diving in.

"Wow! This is great! Come on in. It's warm as a bathtub."

Ike thought back to the swimming pool at *Chippawa*, but what the heck! He could always stay close enough to the ladder. His feet, dangling in the water from the bottom of the ladder, sensed the delight of cool water on his skin. A shout came from above. "Sharks! Sharks! Sharks!" He climbed back up again, hurrying to get out of the way of bodies scrambling after him in a state of panic. Looking out over the water he could clearly make out several rippling V-shaped patterns heading for the men who were swimming furiously towards the ladder.

A rifle crack came from the bridge and then several more shots rang out. Ike watched with his heart in his mouth as the distance between the dorsal fins breaking water and the last of the men grew shorter. "God!" muttered the man next to him at the rail. "The last two are going to come up half-assed for sure!" With the next volley of rifle fire the sharks veered away and with a few more strokes, the men reached the ladder.

"Jesus Christ! – I didn't know – I could swim – that fast!" gasped one of them.

"That was breaking the world's record for sure," laughed one of his mates. Relieved and shaking slightly from the realization of what might have happened, Ike picked up his clothes and went down to the showers.

At 1600 hours, the engines pulsed in tandem again and K171 picked up speed. Carpenter, coming down the ladder with his supper tray that evening, announced that the sea was like glass.

"Why in hell are we still rolling like this then?" demanded a voice from a hammock.

"Hell, what do you expect," offered Barnes cheerily. "A Canadian corvette rolls in a heavy dew."

"Let 'er roll," chortled Ike. "I'm not seasick and nobody else is seasick, we've got no worries about U-boats, for once we're not freezing and wet and the war is over. So what if the old girl rolls around a bit. She sure came through for us this afternoon."

"Yeah," agreed Barnes, "you measure a ship by its ability to perform under extremely adverse conditions and she did it today. Never before have we had engine problems that the engine room boys couldn't repair without loss of speed. Not even in heaviest seas. Never when we were out there freezin' our nuts off. She's a damned durable ship, a helluva fine ship, and she came through again today." General agreement supported this assessment.

"By gosh I'm thinking...," Ike started to say.

"About time, Ike. For a change you used your head for something other than napping and sex."

"As I was saying, if the guys swimming today had had their asses chewed up by the sharks, would they've been given a medal? Say for heroism?"

"Nah," decided Barnes, "same category as clap, chronic seasickness, or the DT's. Hell, them guys don't get medals. Or sympathy."

The sun came up hotter and the water turned glassier. . Boiler room watch was rescheduled for ten minutes down and ten minutes on deck. At 0900 hours when Ike took his ten-minute cooling off on the upper deck all hell broke loose. Action Stations! Bells rang and whistles whooped. What the hell? The war was over! They were supposed to have seen the end of this. Ike realized suddenly that he was on deck without a life jacket on for the first time since he'd joined ship. He dashed down to the stokers' mess, got his life jacket and dashed up the ladder to find the hatch banging down on him at the top step! He stepped out and let the hatch cover fall in place behind him. "Damned near gotcha that time, Dutch!" shouted the seaman on duty.

The action was for real. A sub attack. Two torpedoes aimed on the corvette had missed. Since there was no convoy and the hospital ship would not be fired on, the corvette escort was a logical target. K171 let fly with her arsenal. Depth charges set and delivered at various depths. Hedgehogs blasted away. All gun stations were manned and ready for firing should a strike be made. "Damn it," Ike muttered after they had been dropping depth charges for half an hour trying to finish her off, "if we didn't damage her somehow that captain must be awfully good at maneuvering."

But no oil slick surfaced and no swastikas were waving in surrender, nor did a U-boat crew provide any other souvenirs for K171, proud ship of the third largest navy in the world. "Wonder when those fucking Krauts will get the message that they lost the war? No radio on their tubs?" grumbled Morgan who was on station with Ike.

"Maybe they're without wireless, or maybe they wanted one last chance to make a kill before giving up the fight. We've been the enemy for almost six years. Gets to be a habit. One thing for sure, Morg, I won't get caught without my life jacket ever again, VE Day or no VE Day."

On deck as they approached Bermuda, Ike was struck by its contrast to other ports of call. New York at this time of year first appeared as a long jagged skyline of different shapes, mostly grey, before the gleam of the Statue of Liberty welcomed ships into the harbour. Halifax was approached along a seemingly endless, low shoreline of greenery that gradually gave way to the grey of concrete commercial buildings. The first view of St. John, New Brunswick, might be from far below or from above its wharves and warehouses, or it might hardly be visible at all, depending on two factors: tide and fog. Reaching St. John's, Newfoundland usually meant a grey approach—much hard water and then all of a sudden the harbour entrance behind which lay the foggiest, greyest city of them all. But here they were sailing into something different. Bermuda was pink! Pink bungalows with shiny, white roofs set among green palm trees. In the brightest sunshine. It hardly seemed real.

In white tropical hats, shorts and middies, they hurried ashore. The days of sunning themselves on deck during the voyage had done little to camouflage their shockingly white knees. First they checked out the usual important landmarks. Where the booze was sold and where the girls hung out. Ike however had his own plan, "I don't intend to spend my time inside a bar and let this sunshine go to waste."

"Me, too," Charlie was quick to agree. "Let's find a way to see something of the island."

"I'll go along with that," Carson offered so they set out to find some means of transportation. Reality faced them. No taxis no automobiles. The dozen or so cars on the island were there for the Governor General, ambassadors and other important personages. "We'll rent bicycles," announced Carson who had gone on reconnoiter detail. "We can see the whole island by bicycle they say, and in a few hours, too."

"I can't believe this, no cars? How can they get along without them?"

"No real roads either, Ike. You guys stop looking as if this is the end of the world. We'll go on bikes like everybody else does here. So what's the big deal, eh?"

Ike's dismay, though he wasn't ready to admit it, was caused by the fact that he had never been on a bicycle before. He felt the very thought of peddling one's own vehicle smacked of insult. He could ride a horse, drive an eight-horse team, handle any tractor on wheels, drive trucks or cars. At the age of eight he had secretly driven (even if only for a few feet) his brother's 1928 Whippet and had encountered only one small problem—that of stopping it. Since the car faced the barn when he started it up, the problem was soon resolved, even if somewhat abruptly.

At fourteen, his father had concurred with his view that his driving abilities were much better than those of many older persons and had, for reasons of his own that involved getting the grain hauled to the elevator, taken him for a driving test (which he had passed) and had allowed him to claim he was really sixteen, the legal age for obtaining a driver's license.

Now he was faced with this foolish bicycle. Damn it all anyway! He had not shirked the challenge of the swimming test at *Chippawa* and he had overcome seasickness in the line of duty, and he would now damn well learn to ride this two-wheeled toy, regardless how his nuts got mangled by that stupid looking seat.

He did not tell his buddies of his ignorance, but a few minutes down the road made it abundantly clear that Ike was either hung over from the few drinks they had had last night or else he couldn't ride a bike. "Something's wrong with this bike," he claimed loudly, but that did not wash with the gang. How he wished for the large Mexican saddle he was accustomed to at home in exchange for what he found to be the most uncomfortable seat he had ever sat on.

On the other hand, it would have been so simple to do the tour by the Governor General's limousine or the military commander's vehicle. It was certain they had never learned to ride a bike either, he reflected. Their uniforms were not designed to look good on a bike. By the day's end his pride was bruised and so was his backside but he had seen most of the island.

They went overboard for a swim when they got back to the ship, having been assured that sharks were not a problem in the harbour. In the warm salt water Ike felt at ease doing his dog paddle alongside the ship's hull. He floated easily on his back, looking up at the pink houses amid the gently waving palm trees on the hillside above the harbour. The sounds of loading and unloading along the wharf had died away and quiet tranquility descended with the sunset. Perhaps not having any cars on the island was not such a bad idea after all.

Next day the crew faced a new announcement from the Naval High Command: men who had volunteered for the duration of the war could now volunteer to continue in His Majesty's service to fight in the Pacific. Those who did not do so would be demobilized immediately on their return to home port.

"Where do I sign, that's all I want to know," said Barnes loudly. "I'm in no rush to go job hunting." But others in the mess were in a turmoil.

"If I don't take the chance to go home," muttered Hanson, "I don't know what my wife's gonna think. Hell, I'd like to stay in, but….."

Ike lay in his hammock, watching the smoke from his cigarette curl upwards among the steam pipes. His skin still held the memory of that warm water and behind his eyes the white roofs of the pink houses still glinted in the setting sun. And then there was Sara who had promised to wait for him. Try as he would, he could not get her face in focus in his mind's eye when he was awake. Only in dreams did she seem as real as when he had held her close. Would she wait until the Japs surrendered? One thing he knew for sure, he'd never have another chance to go to the Pacific, perhaps to sail through the Panama Canal, to go ashore somewhere else where pink houses with shining white roofs nestled among gently waving palm trees.

Chapter 18

Skeleton Crew

A noticeable change had come over Halifax during K171's voyage to Bermuda. Their approach to tie up, which normally caused some delay, now seemed effortless. The usual frantic movement in the harbour and along the waterfront was gone. Small craft plied Bedford Basin leisurely and the ferry went back and forth to Dartmouth at her normal pace, but other activity seemed to proceed at half speed. No delay in refueling K171. Bedford Basin shipping, usually on the move, lay at anchor in its sheltered waters. Similarly, escort vessels, ordinarily frothing and fretting at preparations for the next assignment, lay still on slackened hawsers.

In no time flat, K171, too, was traumatized. Orders arrived on board for her to be decommissioned. An immediate reduction of ship's officers and men to a third of her normal strength. Reassignment to other duties for some. The rest, discharge.

A majority of corvettes had already been dispatched to the Royal Canadian Navy's graveyard, if not already there. K171 was among the last to receive her decommissioning orders. Finished for this war. What ultimate fate awaited her and other ships being sent to Sorel, Quebec, was a matter of conjecture.

Within hours of their arrival at the Navy dockyard, the list of personnel to be transferred to H.M.C.S. *Stadacona* was posted. By 1600 hours ship's company was down to twenty-eight men. Farewells were taken over quick tots of rum poured from locker bottles stored too long and a few addresses were exchanged. They left without complication, tears or regrets. Navy trucks stood ready for transportation and, one by one, these navy vets made their way up the ladder, out of the mess and out of each other's lives. Burdened with a sea bag and a hammock, a few struggled with additional small mementos. Essentially they were leaving with only their allotted baggage. It was all they owned.

At 0700 hours, the ship sailed out of Halifax Harbour on her way to Sydney where her complement of men would be further reduced. Ike and Charlie from the upper deck watched the familiar shoreline slip past. "I don't know whether to consider this a punishment or a reward."

"Ike, I don't mind having one last fling with the old girl," said Charlie. "You gotta admit, she's been a pretty good ship. Me...I'd like to sail her up the St. Lawrence. I'm sure the other guys is wishin' the same thing. Sure can't all be lucky."

"Whiley's telling me that after Sydney only a skeleton crew will be left. He says only the best."

"Damn! Guess that'll leave me out. The brass won't forget the boiler fire in New York harbour." Charlie spat over the side.

"By gosh, you never know." Ike tried to sound convincing, but he had his own doubts. "You're dependable. You don't get drunk. You silly prick don't even swear. Officers appreciate your kind. They don't know better."

"Well, it's too much to hope for. I'm not placing any bets. Sure as hell hate going back to Stad though."

"Me too. It's a shit hole. Can't believe it'll be any better than when I was on boiler cleaning." They fell silent, peering pensively at the rapidly fading outline of McNab Island.

"Aw, c'mon, Charlie. Let's stop this and enjoy just one more run. It's a glorious day for it. I guess we should go down and lash our hammocks. Just in case. Might have to carry them ashore in Sydney. If we stay on board, we'll sleep on the lockers."

"Seems like the Queen Mary down here," Charlie remarked as they made their way down the ladder. A mess suddenly enlarged. Adequate room to haul their sea bags and gear out of the lockers in comfort. They dumped their gear on top of a mess table. Ike had only begun filling the bottom of his bag with his heavy winter sweaters when Charlie swept his gear back into the locker and started for the ladder.

"I'll do this when I have to and not before. Too much fine weather up there just now. See you later."

Alone, Ike lit a cigarette and took out Sara's picture. Since registering for the Pacific in preference to an immediate discharge, he hadn't written her. Simply had not yet found the courage to let her in on the choice he'd made. There had been a letter from her when they got back to Halifax, full of the excitement about VE Day and counting the days when Ike would be home again. She had been writing less frequently since she'd gone to work in the city and he had wondered if she'd care very much about his decision to sign on for further service. Her VE Day letter, however, just assumed he'd be as happy as she was that the Atlantic war was over. He put down her picture, ground out his cigarette in a tin can and resumed packing.

When Charlie came back he had the latest. Word had been passed along that while enroute to Sydney, K171, without risking her seaworthiness, was to be thoroughly gutted. "Guys up there ranting about scrap dealers in Sydney, Montreal and Toronto buying up all ships' gear. Making a killing. Ike, you gotta hear them blowing off steam. That all this stuff is already paid for. By tax payers. Madder'n heck somebody's making a fast buck. They keep asking each other, 'Why in hell should this be?' So they're dumping stuff overboard. Right now. C'mon!"

Ike followed him, half agreeing with the logic. No denying what they say. Damn right. On deck, the crew was hauling paint pails out of storage. Red lead, white lead, grey lead, you name it. A spike driven into each bucket, then dumped overboard. He and Charlie joined in the wanton destruction. Guns blazed for a final practice session. Brass casings were ditched, depth charges were fired and rolled off K171's stern. Small tools vanished into lockers, sea bags, hammocks. A small representation of each item was left in place – enough to satisfy the buyers, or as expressed time and again, "those pricks," waiting in Sydney.

Although he went about the jettisoning as briskly as everyone else, the process bothered Ike. All that paint. More had gone overboard than it would take to paint all the buildings on the farm at home. At lunch he expressed his doubts to Charlie.

"Y' know Charlie, it'd have made more sense to give all that stuff to somebody in Sydney that needs it. I don't mind all that ammunition part. But it bothers me to waste good paint and stuff."

"Yeah, it kind of feels that way to me too. But then could you stop it from falling into the wrong hands?"

Ike wasn't too sure who the "wrong hands" might be, but he kept the thought to himself. The deed was done now anyway. He raised the subject again when they went up to the forward deck for a smoke with the rest of the crew. "I keep thinking there should've been another way to get rid of all our stuff than just chucking it overboard. Maybe it could have been donated to a Vets organization."

"Well, that might've been a good idea, but I just figure nobody ought to get a franchise to make a bundle on it all. And from what I hear, that's what's going to happen," said Whiley.

"The government ought to set up a sales office to sell the stuff. Fair and square to everybody. Then take the profits for vets' pensions," suggested Charlie.

"Might be OK for selling paint and dishes and small crap like that," interjected Morgan, "but you ain't gonna get rid of a four-inch gun that way. Or the shells or radar equipment. Ordinary people don't buy that stuff."

"Yeah, you gotta face facts." agreed Ike ruefully. "Corvette equipment wouldn't quite fit on the store shelf beside a monkey wrench."

"Yup, I guess these junk dealers will have their way with what's left," said Charlie. "They'll be on board too soon to suit me."

At 1300 hours they hit port and by 1600 hours it was all over. Anything saleable, valuable, moveable and not required for the trip up the St Lawrence had been grabbed and removed. Ike felt as if he'd watched the rape of K171. In the water, stark naked.

A further twenty-one crew members received orders to report to shore base H.M.C.S. Protector in Sydney. Ship's company reduced to a seven- man skeleton. Ike and Charlie among them. "Put 'er there, Ike!" Charlie reached out his hand, smiling. "By God! It's more than just luck. They said the best men would sail her to her grave. Didn't they now!"

"Damn right, Charlie! If we hadn't been on this tub, war would still be going on. Imagine, though. No more heavy seas to plough through. No more spewing."

"No more being tossed out of your hammock at night."

"No more dishes to wash."

"No more sleeping on your dungarees to keep the crease in."

"No more hitting the sack with your boots on."

"No more of that Moss roast beef."

"Hey, you know Moss stayed on board with us. Brace yourself."

"I can take it. Just a few more days and it's all over. But I need a shower. Funny I never felt this before. Charlie, what in hell did that bastard want to look in our lockers for?"

"Yeah, what for. Time I've been on this tub, no officer ever demanded a look into a locker. Fuck him anyway, whoever he was. I told him lockers were none of his business. Keep his dirty hands off. Gee! Did he turn red!"

"Wish I'd seen that."

"Well, he darned near burst a blood vessel when I told him that if he insisted on looking in my locker he'd have to wash his hands properly first."

Ike found that amusing. "I heard you tell him he wouldn't find any dirty underwear to sell in Montreal. Not in these lockers anyway. My God, they can give a man a creepy, crawly feeling. It's like some stranger coming into your house. Lifting all the pot lids on the stove."

"Get in that damned shower, Ike. You not only look dirty, you're thinking dirty."

"I'm going, Man, but Chuck-boy, you saved me from an embarrassment. I won't get a medal for it either, but in that locker of mine there rests the last of *Kamsack*'s white ensigns to see salt water. I rescued her from the briny deep. Tomorrow, look for a new flag flying." As he dashed off to the shower he heard Charlie muttering something about "a lucky bastard."

At 0500 hours she was off! Goodbye, Sydney! Goodbye, east coast of Canada! Goodbye, North Atlantic. Nothing spectacular or visibly different about the water on the first leg of the journey. Choppy and murky as always. The ship rolled and tossed. After passing the craggy outline of Perce Rock entering the Gulf of St. Lawrence she began to settle down. For several hours they sailed upstream in sight of the southern shoreline. Eventually the northern shore, too, was visible.

His thoughts turned to junk. An image of accompanying his father on a trip to Winnipeg. Impressed with what seemed acres of junk of every conceivable kind. A dealer handling junk that nobody else wanted to be bothered with. Old motors, frames, fenders, wheels, lights, motor parts, seats, axles, harnesses, wagon parts, buggy wheels, saddles, mattresses, beds, chairs, watches, chains, cable, sinks, lamps. No end, as Ike recollected. All of it old junk.

The fact was that such a trip was usually well worthwhile. Cheap stuff. Pick your own pieces and try to buy only junk in useful condition. His father had saved money that way. Not a bad friend to have, the junk dealer. Perhaps then, something to be said for allowing a junk dealer to collect a ship's removable gear. He'd think about that. See what Chuck and others had to say.

The St. Lawrence became narrower as K171 slid westward. Leaning on the rail in the gathering darkness, Ike could see lights in widely spaced settlements on either side of the ship. For a while he had the illusion of actually moving on a level higher than the land itself. Gradually, river banks became more discernable as hilly contours rose and fell against the fading light of the western sky.

On the second day upriver, the engineer had engines shut down for a minor repair. An estimated six-hour job. With anchors dropped, *Kamsack* faced westward into the current, as was fitting to Ike's mind. The entire ship's compliment gathered on deck for lunch, leaving both engine and boiler room unattended. Repairs would commence after lunch. "Do you think you can repair this tub by yourself, Al?"

"No doubt about it, Chuck," Al grinned. "We're shorthanded but I've looked her over and with a bit of help from you stokers, I'll make it."

"A stroke of luck to have the engines know enough to save their trouble until we got around the Rock."

"Well, it's like playing craps, fellas, and talking to the dice. You've got to talk to these engines. Nine times out of ten they'll perform. Mind you, sometimes, you crap out, but this time my engines listened good. Isn't this one hell of a fine place to have an engine breakdown? Who wants to be down in the engine room anyway, when the rest of the crew is up here enjoying the scenery?"

"Al, we know you're the best engineer in the Canadian Navy but is it at all possible to repair that feat of modern engineering down there so it'll hold together for a few more nautical miles? Or can we look forward to a few more of these stopovers before we reach Sorel?"

"Ike, you leave the engine room to Good Old Al here, and you worry about blowing off enough steam. Just remember to save some of it for the engines."

"Are you actually repairing those engines, or are you stripping all the brass to sell to the natives in Quebec City or in Sorel? If we ever get there."

"The hell, I'm stripping brass! Chuck me lad, the bastards we met in Sydney are getting it all. The problem is that there's no brass I can take before the engines are permanently at Full Stop. If I could, I'd take and dump it all overboard. To hell with them."

"Now, now, Al!" Moss responded as though offended. "Talk about blowing off steam. What the hell difference does it make to you who buys the damn brass for scrap? It makes bad sense to leave it all on board and see the rest of her rust off around it until she sinks. That's not benefitin' anybody."

"Don't tell me what I know! We've gone over this a dozen jeezly times since we left Halifax. I'm sick of the topic. I'm still sayin,' why should any single person profit from what all of us taxpayers have paid for? I just don't want those damned dealers to benefit from anything I've tried to keep spotless and in good working order for winning a war. That's all."

"Well, Al, you got an alternative to offer?"

Al munched on his sandwich, pondering the question. They looked at him in anticipation. Struggling. To simply answer "No," would never do. The crew respected him for his abilities as an engineer and expected him to measure up in a rational discussion. Finally he swallowed the mouthful he'd been chewing, followed it with a sip of tea. "Sure, I have an alternative. It's no good throwing stuff overboard. I know that. But I'm tellin' you it's even worse to let only a few individuals at it. What do we do? Well, probably the answer is to form a government company." He set down his mug firmly as if that finished the matter.

Chuck, who had been leaning back with his legs stretched out lazily, sat up suddenly. "I can't believe what I'm hearing, Al. Did you say 'government'?"

"Yeah, Chuck, I've been thinking about this business quite a bit since the ship's been moving toward decommissioning. First, the government is already in business in certain lines—the CNR, Trans Canada Airlines, the Post Office. So why not a postwar corporation to handle these ships, turn them into a national shipping company, for instance. Corvettes could be converted into some kind of cargo vessel, manned by ex-navy men. Of course, more money would have to be poured into the venture, but the people would support it with bonds. You'll have to admit that kind of scheme is far superior to what is happening now—giving the damned stuff away for practically nothing, if what we hear is true."

Al got up as if he could now go down to the engine room, but Chuck stopped him cold. "Hold on, Al. What you're proposing smacks of policies like what you've argued against. I suppose I wouldn't find it hard to support that. But, Al, you were arguing for the Conservatives in the last election. They'd shoot down your idea real quick. You can't have it both ways, both a Tory government and a government corporation. It's like demanding a pregnant virgin."

Moss couldn't wait to get a word in. "You're both sick in the head! How in hell did you guys pull the wool over my eyes for all these months? I thought you guys were smart. Now I realize you've had too much pusser rum. It mushed up your brains. Now stop and listen. The CCF tries to make everyone equal and that means my head will be as addled as yours. That's not for me. The Conservatives are getting their back twisted and their ass out of gear, looking to the past for some medieval approach to force on the people. I say the Liberals under MacKenzie King are the only solution to our problems."

"But what in hell are you suggesting that we do about Al's brass?" asked Ike. "You're not offering any solution. You're only throwing more monkey wrenches into the gears here."

"Screw Al's brass. It's not important," replied Moss, testily. "For all I care, he can shove it up somebody's ass or let the junk dealers at it. When I get to Sorel, I'm giving my dishes and kitchen gear to the locals and if they don't want it, I don't care who gets it. I simply don't want it and I don't give a damn!"

Now Moss doesn't give a damn! Ike wondered at this. At their Halifax-Sydney tea party, he was up to his navel in stuff he was chucking overboard.

Amazing what the St. Lawrence can do to a guy! For a man who was adamant that no bloody Jew should put his hands on his kitchen gear, the change was dramatic. In a few days he's changed his mind completely and doesn't give a damn.

"Moss, you silly prick! You sound as though you don't know what you want. Please, please, don't go into politics when you get home. I can stand to eat your Red Lead and Bacon but I wouldn't be able to swallow your politics. So you don't give a damn. That's how we went through the war, but that's over. In another day or two you'll start thinking and giving a damn because you'll be finished sucking the navy's tits. In two days' time Moss, if you're lucky, you're finished with this outfit. You'll be scratchin' your head about what to do next. Now, tell me. What's that going to be?"

"Gosh, Ike, I don't know for sure. The wife's working now but she'd like to quit and start raising a family. The problem is, I don't have a job to go to and the cook's training I got in the navy won't be much good in a restaurant or a hotel. I just don't know what I'll do. Guess it's too early to start worrying about it today. Enough time in two days from now."

"Join the crowd. You're one little fly speck out of about a million who in the next month or two won't know what in hell happened to them. For one week little old Al here'll know. I'm taking Ike's advice. Locking myself up in a room with my sweet little woman. I'm hoping I won't survive and that'll solve my unemployment problem. I'm more concerned about what Chuck's going to do considering he's all rusted up."

"Not to worry about me. I'm borrowing money from the bank to buy me a car. Travel, on land."

Ike led the song:

I got myself a Ford machine and filled her up with gasoline
I cranked her and the darned thing ran away
It didn't wait till I got in and now I own a pile of tin
But every month I walk right up and pay.
Up and pay--- Up and pay
So much down and so much every certain day
It didn't wait till I got in so now I own a pile of tin
But every month I walk right up and pay.

"You guys laugh. The company my dad works for has a spot open for me. Every month I'll walk right up for my paycheck."

"You guys talk-talk-talk a blue streak but let's face it. You're all tuckered out. Al, I'll bet you can't even get it up anymore and you, Ike, won't be any good for your woman for at least six months yet. But then, she may have had it better anyway while you guys were saints on board."

"Chuck, watch who you're slandering, you sanctimonious prick! It's the women we love you're talking about. By the way, Moss, how about a heavy dose of eggnog starting right about now?"

"It'll take more than ten gallons of eggnog to straighten you out, Al."

"I wasn't thinking of myself, Moss, for God's sake! It's Chuck Boy I'm concerned about. He's gonna need some kind of magic rust remover. Could be the eggnog would help to blast him loose." Al got up and started off toward the engine room. 1620 hours. "Cool enough to work down there now. Give me a shout when grub's on again."

No other crew member was concerned about fixing the engines. At anchor in the St. Lawrence a few hours below Quebec City was not all that bad a spot for fixing an engine. If Al didn't get the engines fired up for another week that was just fine.

Ike, surprised, glared at the huge portion of roast beef, mashed potatoes and gravy, canned peas and figgy duff on his tray. Good Lord! He obviously was wrong to have thought Moss had run out of cattle in the food locker. Through clenched teeth he vowed to disown anybody who served him roast beef during the first five years after discharge. He joined the others on upper deck. Al and Chuck, eagerly shoveling it in, complimented each other on the delicious grub, hoping for a continuation of the good stuff at home.

Ike shifted to a spot forward where he could eat in peace. Alone. Avoiding a discussion about inconsequential nothings. Such as the one at lunch. Too easy to get your shit hot about issues over which only the big nuts had control. Seclusion. Not to be forced to think or participate. Relish the moment. The realization of approaching good garden country and remembering the taste of real, fresh peas, elevated his frame of mind.

Al's announcement interrupted his thoughts. Engines ready. The captain ordered anchors to be weighed at 0600 hours.

Ike picked up his reverie about food, good food, home-cooked food. Prepared by Mom and the girls, food the men folks expected to be delicious. Never gave any other possibility a thought as they sat down and ate. To be fair, he acknowledged that a diet made up largely of pork, as theirs had been, might become as tiresome as one of roast beef. Variety had made the difference. Spring rooster done western style in a pan, turkey and goose in the fall, or an old, fat hen at any time, boiled down into chicken soup for which the girls made egg noodles. The pigeon kill in the fall yielded a special ecstasy—a whole pigeon per person, pot roasted and served with potatoes smothered in cream gravy.

Staring at his un-touched tray, he wondered whether Moss had ever sunk his teeth into a properly prepared Manitoba winter-killed jack rabbit. Or been treated to a pot roasted Hungarian partridge picked off with a .22 in a minus 35 degrees storm. Or had fried pork brains with hash fried potatoes for breakfast. Did he know what a fried pork kidney looked like and why one licked the plate clean after it? And the varieties of fish they had enjoyed at home, even though they were more than a hundred miles from Lake Winnipeg. Frozen stone hard in the dead of winter. Some were thawed for flour-dusted pan frying. Others (such as the whitefish and tullibee) were hung in the smoke house. Best not to dwell on or try to recapture the response of a hungry man, sinking his teeth into a golden, crisp, skillet-cooked steak of Red River whiskered catfish.

While determined to cut beef out of his reflections, he admitted that boiled beef with lots of marrow bone would even now seem delicious. Or beef liver smothered in onions. No point in getting all worked up about all the other food, the milk custards, the vegetables, fruits, breads and pastries. Time to start afresh on all those goodies when he got home. He was uncertain whether Sara could cook, now that he thought about it. She'd learn. He was sure of that. Then again, maybe he shouldn't be so sure about her anymore. He'd mailed her a letter from Sidney, saying he wouldn't be home until he'd won the war in the Pacific too. What would she think of that?

Chapter 19
Quebec

The engines reciprocated exactly in accord with Al's repair schedule, propelling *Kamsack* gently up the St. Lawrence towards Quebec City where fresh water would be taken on. Meantime the crew enjoyed the view on either side of the river. Clusters of buildings on patches of cleared land between stands of green, green forest spoke of a kind of farming very different from that to which Ike was now returning. Pretty as a picture, he thought, but how could any family survive on the harvest from such small fields? Cattle grazed in lush pastures. Now and then someone ashore waved as K171 slid through the silky smooth water not far from the river's edge.

They docked at Wolfe's Cove at 1500 hours. The approach to the city was the most spectacular Ike had seen since he'd left the farm. They tied up at the historic spot where General Wolfe had performed the unexpected. Leading his army, he had scaled the cliffs to catch Montcalm by surprise. A perfect maneuver except for an early alert enabling General Montcalm to muster his army and line them up, fair and square, facing the Englishman.

Ike wondered who gave the critical signal for these two armies to move towards each other, obviously set on a do-or-die course. Both Generals, directing their men up front, were killed that day. Because there were more live Englishmen than Frenchmen left on the field that day the country changed hands. All over in about the length of time it would take to play a serious craps game.

Skipper had decided to lay over for the night and take the *Kamsack* to Sorel, her final resting place, next day. When she was moored, the entire ship's company, except for Ike and one officer, McCurdy, took shore leave. Ike was to stand a ten-hour boiler room watch beginning 1700 hours.

Chuck approached Ike on a payback. "Listen man I owe you a couple of watches. What you did for me in Bermuda. How about you standing watch till 2100 hours and I'll take over till 0600. That gives me about three or four hours ashore and still lets you take in a few sights during daylight and lots of night life if you want to."

"Sure, if McCurdy agrees. It sounds real good to me. I'll clear it with him and let you know."

The arrangement cleared without a problem and Chuck went ashore with the rest of the crew. At 2000 hours McCurdy informed Ike, "I'm stepping off for a short spell, a bit of a walk on The Plains. Are you all right here?"

"Yes, Sir. I can handle her. Have a nice time, Sir."

"Thanks, Ike."

"My pleasure, Sir. Don't mention it."

Ike, alone on board. Skipper. Number One. Made it. Finally. Without a commission.

Not much to do yet. In the boiler room he occasionally checked steam pressure and, if necessary, fired a burner, came back up and took in the sights from the best vantage point – the bridge. For supper Moss had left a plate of canned salmon sandwiches which Ike took up to the bridge to eat rather than invade the officer's wardroom where skipper normally took his meals. He was, after all, only a "straw skipper." The bridge was just fine. He'd suggest that Chuck try the sensation when he took over later. A sensation of having arrived, however late in the war.

He poured a small rum from a bottle in his locker and took it up to accompany the sandwiches. My God! What a bloody warm evening it was. He opened some portholes for better ventilation in the mess decks, especially for the stifling lower deck. On his way up he opened portholes in the officers' mess as well.

Rum and sandwiches for supper. Not bad, but then, by gosh, later when he got ashore he'd try some French food. With wine. Like the locals did, according to what he'd heard. He munched away, watching the sun sink over the ramparts that rose sharply behind the jetties. Perhaps he should sound the fuel and water tanks and then take on water. But what the heck. He might just leave that for Chuck to do. He was skipper now by darn, no need to be Upper Deck Stoker as well. Just be skipper. No worries. As he surveyed his ship, he noticed the hawsers tightening up and went down to give them more slack. Might just be a bit of a tide in Wolfe's Cove. He went back up to his bridge, meditating.

To be a real cat's ass Skipper you had to be an officer. With education. A university degree or at least a couple of years towards one. Quite different from being top dog on a farm. With little education his Old Man was running the farm pretty damn good. Operated a unit made up of men and machines with greater complexity, by damn, than it took to manage this tub. Unlimited variations of the elements to contend with. Horses, cattle, pigs, turkeys, geese, chickens by the dozen.

Also a plethora of different machines – cars, trucks, tractors, plows, drills, wagons, a threshing machine, a combine. No end to it. For harvesting, a dozen extra men to get the job done. Nobody ever for a minute suggested the job was too big for him. Or for any of his sons. They had all learned about being boss by doing the job right. Make a mistake and the advice was to the point. Use your head!

Sure thing. In the navy a man could aspire to be an officer and a Skipper by demonstrating ability to use his head. An examination, test, revealed this ability quickly. On the farm it took a bit more time for evidence. It occurred automatically when the older brother married and left. The next oldest boy was Boss. That is, "Straw-boss". The real Boss, the one sitting at the end of the table, money holder, car steerer, final Yes-or-No-Giver, disciplinarian, top-dog, cat's-ass, big-cheese, the one deserving a special way of being addressed, like "Sir" or "Ye" or such. That was a real Boss. Straw-boss took over the reins when King-pin was not around, had gone to town or was asleep on the couch for a mid-day nap.

Along with a promotion to Straw-boss came privileges. First call on the truck to go see a girl. A choice of who would go haying on a blistering hot day, the job more despised than any other, or who would stay back doing repair work in shaded comfort. An immediate one-position advance along the bench behind the dining table, a notch closer to the real Boss.

While sipping his rum Ike speculated on what the sensation might be like to dine in the wardroom seated beside skipper. Or next to some high falutin' society woman invited to dine. One who might object to loud farts and coarse language so common in a men-only stokers' mess or when on duty down in the boiler-room. Somehow, it seemed it would block out the constantly surrounding fear, would help to take a mind from ever-lurking danger without need of fogging up the brain with pusser rum.

He sipped his rum and vowed to polish up his language on his return home. Behave like a skipper. But to sign up as an officer in the navy, you had to prove you could use your head. Perhaps he should have told the recruiting officer that he was able to castrate pigs successfully. Or repair an engine blindfolded. No matter. Too late now. Screw it all anyway. He was skipper for another fifteen minutes, so why not relax and enjoy it. Chuck could sound the bloody tanks and take on the water, too. When you're skipper, have the menial tasks done by servants. Simple as that. Chuck will do it tonight.

"Ike, I'm back!" Chuck came on board. "You've got to get out there, Ike, and take a walk on Abe's Plains before it gets dark. A million steps straight up and you're there, but it's kind of breathtaking in itself. It's history up there. Go on up and take a look."

"Thanks, Chuck. Give me ten. That's how long it takes to change. You're to sound all the tanks at 1000 hours and take on some water. You know the routine. Meantime, you're skipper. The duty officer hasn't come back from his walk, so enjoy the feeling. See you later sometime."

Ike clambered up the steps. At first he moved quickly, but gradually the going got slower. Bloody long way to the top! Wolfe's men must have had cat's paws to be able to scale this cliff without any stairs. Either that, or they were too stunned to recognize that the cliff was virtually perpendicular.

He reached the top and stopped to survey the view. Think of it! Three hundred years of history on this very spot and here he stood, one foot in Wolfe's boot prints and the other in Montcalm's. He looked back at the way he had come and saw his ship. Somewhere down there Wolfe's fleet had been moored when his men disembarked to do battle. On the opposite side of this field, Montcalm's men had slept. When you go to sleep on watch, something's sure to go wrong.

For an hour he walked around the park the field had become. He found he could remember very few details about the famous battle. Only the results. That is what his mind dwelt on now. Had the battle turned out otherwise, Ike's forefathers might never have migrated to Canada. Pure speculation, of course. They might have migrated much sooner with more and better rights. Who could tell? For now, he just felt grateful at the outcome and thrilled to set foot on the fateful spot.

Ike walked into the city and wandered about, enjoying its particular charm and character. He did not have time to see very much, but its cobblestones and alleyways breathed of another time and a culture different from what he had seen before. He would come back some day to explore it more fully. Supper on ship had been scanty, mostly to save his appetite for something French. The restaurant he chose buzzed with both civilians and servicemen. He noticed a few RCNVR service patches but no familiar faces.

He selected a table. Eating alone beat making conversation with any half-cut serviceman he might encounter. The waitress asked him something in French and he replied, "I'm fine. How are you?" She handed him a menu. Entirely in French. She stood there, looking bored. He puzzled over the print for a while but could make nothing of it. "Madame, pork chops, wine, coffee." She picked up the menu and left. He sat there, feeling foolish for not being able to speak her language. Simply not possible to feel part of this country if one couldn't order a common pork chop meal. He hoped she had understood him.

She reappeared with a decanter of wine. A generous amount for him to empty by himself, but then he had not specified quantity. One glass is what he'd had in mind. She poured some into a stemmed glass. A bit of class that. And more civilized than what he had experienced in eastern Canada where they locked up the drinks in liquor stores. He took a sip. Different from the Bright's Catawba he and his friends used to buy back home for a buck twenty per gallon. So smooth. It went down very well.

He was into his third glass when she brought his pork chops. He looked up at her, smiled, "Thank you."

It cracked the marble. She smiled. "You're welcome. I hope you enjoy your dinner. I bring coffee later."

Ike ate slowly and ran over in his mind the peculiar cadence of her speech, the way she said "din-NER" and "la-TER" seemed fascinating. He looked around, enjoying the lively atmosphere. Talking and gesturing at the same time. Noisy but not out of hand. Nice place, this Quebec City. He would definitely come back again. Someday.

As he sipped his wine, he noticed the waitress eyeing him. Not a bad looking dame, that one. She brought the coffee. "Are you long here?"

"No, I am leaving tomorrow."

"Oh! A pity." She left to wait on another table.

He sipped through a blurry dilemma. He had made the first move. Back out now? She'd be an easy pick up if he wanted to, he was sure of that. But what did he have to offer? A walk? A movie? A hotel room? A park bench? Maybe she had a place. The wine sang in his head. He signaled her to come back to his table. "Another coffee, please. I must sober up a bit. You're beginning to look too good."

"Oh, I don't think so," she laughed and went for the coffee. When she came back she said, "I work until one tonight," and left. Ike felt the stir in his white duck trouser leg. Damn! But he needed a good lay for a change and she would be good, he was sure. He had been out on pasture for so long now that he was sure he could give her a taste of heaven. He had not noticed any couples on the grass on the Plains, but it had been early. It was the logical place for some lush screwing. Hell, he could give it to her right now, this minute, if the place wasn't so full of people. He was ready for it.

He forced his mind to think of the ship's boilers instead of her swaying hips. He'd hate to go off in his trouser leg before even getting into her! Goddammit, Ike! Think of rough weather and spewing your guts out!

She came back to the table with the check and as he counted out the money he said in a low voice, "At one, in front of the café. Your name? I'm Ike."

"Francine... see you."

As he got up, Ike stumbled against the table leg. Perhaps four glasses had been too much. The last cup of coffee had calmed him a little, but he needed air, lots of it, and fresh stuff. Once out the door, he took a deep breath and walked away quickly. You're drunk, Ike, but sober enough to know what the hell you're up to. His mind replayed the image he had of her as she moved between tables while he sipped his second cup of coffee. He sucked in more fresh air. Perhaps she wasn't so hot after all. He saw her differently now that he no longer had that big stick up. Actually, kind'a plain, dammit, like a million other women. Nothing special about her when he saw her from behind. Plain in the ass, in fact.

He paused on the corner, trying to sort out which direction to take. Was the Frontenac Hotel to the left or right? Couldn't recall which way he'd turned when he arrived. When the traffic light changed he crossed and kept on walking. His head fogged up with wine, with images of sweet ass in the grass, of doubts about what in hell he was up to, he plodded along not knowing or caring the direction. How long until one o'clock? Hours. No sweat at all to get her to agree to meet him. Push-over. Seemed too easy. Must've had dozens of hot shot salts stick it in to her already if she was that quick to stroll on the Plains. What was he getting into anyway? His mind turned to the sickly pallor of men with a serious dose. This whole thing was stupid. So close to going home. Damn fool to risk taking back a shiny green drop at the end of his pecker. Or worse yet, a case of syphilis. Or one of the dreaded, much-talked-about Caribbean, impossible-to-cure, diseases.

At an intersection, he caught a blurry-eyed glimpse of the steeply pitched roof of the Frontenac and turned towards it. Head back to the ship, Ike, and forget her. She may not be waiting for you anyway. Fuck! Her being that easy, someone's got to her by now. Hell, he had known Sara for almost a year before he'd had the courage to ask if he could walk her home. Come to think of it, he hadn't asked her. Somehow, they had just suddenly found themselves separated from the rest of their crowd that was strolling along after the dance at Penner's house at the edge of town. They had just turned down a side street without exchanging any words about it. He smiled when he thought about that evening of moonlight and hoarfrost and wonder. Something in his chest had exploded when he kissed her and the sensation came back to him now. Finishing the Japs shouldn't take long but he was almost sorry that he'd signed up for the Pacific rather than taking the chance to go home.

Gradually his head cleared. He stumbled upon a small green square with a few benches, sat down, leaned back and closed his eyes. The after image of a street light whirled against his inner eyelid, making his stomach churn. He opened his eyes quickly and started to walk again. He rambled aimlessly before finding his way down the steps at Wolfe's Cove. He kept his eyes steadily on the steps and, although he considered himself sobered up, he was careful not to inadvertently take the big, long step down.

Reaching the jetty safely, he came face to face with his ship. Oh my God and holy shit! Either he was still dead drunk or else she was listing heavily. Listing at least forty-five degrees to port where she was tied. Where in the name of sweet fucking Jehosafat was that idiot Chuck? Why was he trying to sink this useless tub? And here in Wolfe's Cove, of all places? Flipped his lid for sure.

"Chuck! Chuck! Where the hell are you? What's gone wrong?" No sign of Chuck anywhere on the upper deck. Ike saw that the hawsers were tight as a drum. He could hear portholes being slammed shut below. Chuck must be trying to keep water from flowing into the stokers' mess and the skipper's wardroom. Ike leaped to loosen the hawsers. It wasn't easy. Too god dammed tight. After a struggle he got the forward line to slip some on the winch and felt the ship straighten a little. He rushed aft to slacken the stern rope. She was coming around. The list diminished marginally. He stooped over the side to look at the portholes, but she still listed too much to be able to see them.

Chuck clattered up on deck. "Jeez, Ike, I'm glad you're here. I damned near sank this crate."

"What in hell happened, Chuck?"

"Ike, I didn't realize there was any kind of tide in here and ignored the hawsers. When I took on water and filled the port tank first, all of a sudden I was in trouble."

"Dammit, Chuck, it doesn't happen that quickly without noticing anything. You must have dozed off, you silly fucker!"

"Only for a minute, Ike. But that's over now and I've got a real mess to clean up and I'm not gonna stand here taking crap from you."

"Don't you get your shit in an uproar yet, too. I'll give you a hand. Where do we begin?"

"It's 0215 hours. How long till that duty officer gets back here, Ike?" Chuck asked anxiously.

"If we're lucky, he's found himself something nice and we'll have a couple of hours, but if not he could be back here any time now."

Feverishly they struggled with the clean-up. Chuck pumped water from Number Four tank into Number Five. He had made soundings of all tanks and logged the status of each before starting to take on water. "Double check," said Ike, "to be sure we have no more frig-ups." He went topside to look after the hawsers as the ship gradually came back to an even keel. In a very short time she had righted herself. She was level. No harm was apparent on the top deck. Thank God!

He rushed back down to confer with Chuck. Down in the stokers' mess the damage seemed to be negligible. They sloshed through water on the floor and opened drains to let it run into the bilge. Ike checked his starboard locker. Dry. Chuck lifted the lid of his locker on the port side. "Oh, Jesus!" he moaned. "This damned locker is full of water! This whole side must be full. What do we do now? These lockers don't have a drain!" He turned and sank down on the cushioned locker lid but jumped up quickly as it oozed water from every seam. "And I've got to bring the log up to date before that fucking officer gets back here."'

"The hell you do! I didn't record the fact that he left the ship to take a walk and I'll bet my mother's virginity he won't want to see any of this in writing anywhere. You'd just better damned well wait."

"Hadn't thought of that. Damned good thinking, Ike."

Dolefully they surveyed the locker problem. "Jeez H. Murphy! How in Hades do we get all the water cleaned up before Dingle Balls gets back? Where do we start?"

"Just can't clean it all up in time. Let's face it. The rest of the crew will start stumbling on board any minute now. It's 0345 hours now so drinking and screwing time has just about had it, so watch them come. Get the buckets and we'll start bailing the water over the front ledge of the lockers and just let it drain along the floor into the bilge. Thank goodness a lot of these are empty now that the crew's so small."

They were still hard at it when a shout came from above. "Ahoy, down there! Is there a watch?"

"Yes, Sir! Hogan here, Sir! Coming right up, Sir!" Chuck bounded up the ladder while Ike bailed more furiously than ever. There had been no time to check the officers' mess which, being amidships was even lower than the stokers mess. Since Charlie had not been able to enter the locked wardroom to close the porthole, the damage there couldn't be less.

Ike continued bailing. Had he stopped to lay it into that little dish, the lines would not have been released in time to right the ship. She would have sunk! Her final resting place, Wolfe's Cove. Drama for sure. Court martial kind. Bad enough as it was now. For certain another standoff between Chuck and McCurdy. A replay of the New York fire episode. They had been on bad terms from the time McCurdy came on board and though open conflict had been avoided, the relationship had always been a tinder box rattling around on an otherwise mostly happy ship.

Ike stopped bailing to check on how Chuck was handling the situation on deck. At 0425 hours, the ratings had not yet returned from shore leave. He heard McCurdy before he stepped over the coaming. "My God, Hogan, from what you say you could have sunk this damn tub! How could you do it? Where did you go wrong?"

"Well. Sir, I thought I could handle it myself or I would have called you. You know, I hated to wake you up."

Brilliant, thought Ike. Didn't know the boy had it in him. Thought he'd try to face down McCurdy, stand on principle as he did in New York. He'd learned a thing or two and was now playing his hand perfectly.

McCurdy caught the opening Chuck had left him. "Why don't you go to clean up the stokers' mess while I review the situation with Ike here. Before you go, tell me, are all the lines in order now?

"Checked and in order, Sir." Chuck headed for the ladder.

"Did you want to see the log, Sir?" Ike asked, handing him the book.

"Yes, I'd like to check it. What has been recorded about taking on water?" he asked, leafing through the pages quickly.

"Sir! The log shows that the ship took on water at 1340 hours, that port tank Number Four was filled and half the contents were transferred to Number Five starboard tank. Sir! The log does not show that you were not awakened. Is it necessary?"

"No, no, Ike. That's a trivial matter." He turned to go down to his mess.

Ike wondered how he'd react when he opened the captain's cabin. He could just picture it. The porthole had been open and must have shipped a generous amount of fresh St. Lawrence water, all of which would have run down the port bulkhead into the captain's locker. When that filled up it must have overflowed onto the deck of the cabin and eventually found its way under the door to the wardroom. He heard his name being called and went down.

McCurdy was standing in the cabin doorway with his best shore leave shoes in two inches of water.

"Sir! Friedlen here."

"Oh, yes, Ike, tell me, can this water on the deck be drained?"

"Oh, yes, Sir! No problem. I'll do it immediately." He went down to fetch a spanner and returned to find McCurdy still standing as if in a trance. He opened the drains quickly and watched the water on the deck gradually disappear. He glanced at McCurdy. He was staring into space like a shipwrecked sailor desperately searching for someone to take him off his stark little island. Ike came to the rescue at the top of his voice. "Sir! Sir!"

McCurdy came to himself with a startled look. "Yes, Ike. Oh, yes, how is the water draining?"

"Fine, Sir. But the lockers in the cabin must be full of water. They'll have to be bailed out immediately. Should I start?"

"Yes, Ike. Do what has to be done as fast as you can. I'll help."

Ike heard boots and voices coming on board. For a few moments no unusual sounds. Pissed to the eyebrows. Well, they would bloody well sober up in a hurry. McCurdy went out as the first yell of complaint went up. Ike could hear him putting them to work to clean up as if this were any other routine. Five men had lockers on the port side, as did the skipper, where all clothing, bedding, cushions and personal items were awash.

Carried up on deck, the wet gear was wrung out by hand. They fixed a line from high on the stack to the Oerlikon gun platform on the ship's stern and another from bridge to prow, where it was tied to the railing for the skeleton crew to hang up, clamp, and tie the soggy clothes to dry. Moss broke the unusual silence, "Just you guys wait'll skipper comes aboard. Bloody hell to pay, that's what".

But skipper took the news quite calmly. No real damage had been done, except to the men's personal belongings and to his own mahogany chest. It had always stood in its place on the deck of his cabin. Now it lay topside to dry out in the sun. The heavy carving on top and front indicated its origin in some faraway place, some place where palm trees swayed over sandy beaches while woodcarvers sat in their shade. A dark band around the bottom marked the level to which the water had risen. Whether it would need refinishing was hard to tell. Skipper's problem. For now he was as busy as the rest of the crew, wringing out his clothes to add to the assortment on the lines.

So it was that *Kamsack* cast off and steamed out of Wolfe's Cove flying an undecipherable pennant, colors of officers' braid and stokers' pusser underwear.

Chapter 20

Sorel

Let the "sinking" affair be left behind. Put it to rest. Enjoy the view of glowing green pastures, serene farmsteads and shaggy, dark wood-lots along the shore. Too few hours of it before the graveyard. While the entire crew resisted the very thought of Sorel, at 1500 hours there was no escaping its reality. In clear view, more than 350 ships lay abreast like so many masted coffins. "Jeez!" Moss murmured, leaning on the rail beside Ike. "I knew we'd put out a lot of ships, but gad, I never dreamed it was that many."

"Yeah. Hardly a ship five years ago and look at all this...." Ike's sentence trailed off. Difficult to express his feelings. "We started with bugger all. Give it a few days and we'll have the navy disappear. Makes you wonder about the whole show. Goddamn right it does."

"Dutch, you old prick, we did what we had to do. It's over. That's how I see it. No use getting all worked up about it." Moss spat over the side.

"I know what you're sayin', still...." He paused thoughtfully before continuing. "No matter what anybody says, though, it couldn't have been won without corvettes. Without the goods in convoys getting over there in all those goddam storms they'd have been up shit creek in England and Europe. We know that. For Christ sake, Moss, look at 'em now. A pile of junk, that's what. Given to scrap dealers. To make money. That's all I was thinking. On with the show."

Gloomily they watched while K171 eased her way between rows and rows of sterile hulks, their guns covered in canvas, smoke stacks cold, decks utterly silent. Already traces of rust noticeable on some. A depressing image of how their home of many long months was about to be treated. She would lie here, abandoned.

Corvettes were ranged in rows of six to ten, one at anchor and the others tied alongside. Skipper had orders to fit Kamsack in. Somewhere. Gently he maneuvered her alongside eight sister Corvettes and ordered her tied down. For the last time. No gravestone. No monument. No memorial service to acknowledge her contribution to winning a war. No formal acceptance of a defeated admiral's sword. No orders to chisel in stone a declaration that this war had been won by a sailor, a First Class Stoker, not quite Canadian yet but Dutch-Canadian, for whom the inscription could be in Low German.

The order from the bridge was clear. Except for navigational equipment specified on the posted list, she was to be gutted and ready for abandonment at 1700 hours next day when all bulkheads and hatchways would be locked, boilers at zero pressure. On that day her last meal was scheduled for 1200 hours.

Along with the rest of the crew, Ike went below and crammed navy gear into his sea bag. What couldn't be fitted in he set aside for tossing overboard. McCurdy emphasized that absolutely nothing was to remain on the ship. Heavy gear not listed—firefighting equipment, spare hawsers and such—was to be dumped. Dishes, pots, pans, all moveable galley gear to go the way of Davy Jones' Locker. Buckets, soap, toilet tissue, cleansers, brooms, foodstuffs, whether fresh or canned or dried, coffee, cheese, jam, butter, meat. Overboard.

Small boats manned by local inhabitants swarmed around K171's hull as the crew came on deck to jettison the gear. They shouted upward asking if they had anything to sell, shoes, clothes, food, blankets. Polite but eager to make a deal, they pulled out dollar bills to show they could pay.

Skipper had delegated McCurdy to order the boats ashore and he did so, loudly and sternly. But the civilians in these boats were not to be cowed by orders from the military. The war was over. Having seen this procedure many times before, they rowed a short distance away from the ship and waited, anxious to see what could be salvaged.

Enroute from Quebec City, skipper had briefed ship's company on the official policy regarding disposal of government property still left on board upon reaching Sorel. Under no circumstances were servicemen permitted to sell, give, or barter any goods whatever to local inhabitants. These goods were to be destroyed, including personal items belonging to crew members. Sailors always accumulated extra gear during their time on board, shoes, scarves, sweaters, blankets, books. Each man had more gear than he could fit into his sea bag and hammock roll. A considerable amount of gear abandoned by the ninety men who had left the ship in Halifax and Sydney was still on board, ready to be pitched overboard. Sailors caught in an act of selling or giving away goods would stand to lose their Active Service War Gratuities. Citing several examples where men who had violated regulations had been charged and punished in accordance with that policy made an effective impression on the crew.

Losing gratuities was a serious matter. Loss of gratuities was the punishment that went with a dishonourable discharge. For some personnel, gratuities represented the difference between having a few nickels to rub together or to be flat broke when walking off the ship into civilian life. Each month on Active Service earned a man a few extra dollars that were held back until his service terminated. Some resented the term "gratuities" as an implication that the money was a kind of gift for which a serviceman was expected to be grateful. Actually, it was earned wages withheld until service terminated. Whatever the label, it would be the height of folly to risk that amount now in the last hours of service. So there would be no bartering, no selling, no giving stuff away.

Two deck hands responsible for clearing rubbish from the upper deck messes feverishly set about their task. Later they would assist McCurdy and skipper with stripping the officers' mess and bridge. Al did the dirty work in the engineers' mess and ship's stores. Chuck and Ike cleaned out the stokers' mess. Moss gutted the galley. They worked in silence in an atmosphere of intense drama, like the moment in the plot when an admission of guilt is expected from someone, and nothing comes. Finished with collecting the goods on the main deck, they waited for darkness and the order to proceed pitching stuff overboard.

Moss served chili con carne at 2000 hours. What goods still remained were the few items required overnight—toilet tissue rolls, the ends of soap, the last few dishes. Crouched among the rubble, the crew ate supper. Skipper and McCurdy joined them there. Too bloody demoralizing to eat down in the mausoleum that the wardroom had become. No one on official watch. None needed. The engines dead, the boilers on hold. The bridge had ceased to function.

No dignitary would be piped on board tonight. No beautifully dressed women could visit the officers' mess for dinner. And perhaps linger on a bit. No beer would be smuggled on board by the crew. No traders waited on the jetty to buy bottles of 160 over-proof rum from seamen hard up for cash. No Dirty Gerties on the wharf, lurking in the shadows waiting for the right moment to offer a quick piece of ass for a buck or two. No nothing! Only this godforsaken junk and a plate of chili con carne.

"Sir!" Ike looked at the skipper. "Why are we waiting until after dark to dump this stuff?"

Skipper chewed his supper for a moment, "Those are our orders, but you can see what'll happen if we start now. Look at the boats coming at us from all around."

"Holy Shit!" exclaimed Moss. "See there in the distance? There must be a dozen coming. Hell, they're coming from all directions. What do these bastards think they're doing?"

McCurdy could hardly wait to answer. "You throw one piece of stuff overboard and if it floats you'll have all those boats alongside in no time flat. Dammit! They want this stuff for nothing and they're not going to get it!"

"Fuckin' right, they're not!" said Moss vehemently. "We'll sink every last bit of it even if we have to tie rocks to it."

"The damned Frenchies are a funny lot," mused Al. "They didn't want to go to war and now they expect to get this stuff for nothin.' Fuck 'em, I say."

"Yeah, to hell with 'em all. I can see why we wait until dark. What time do we start, Sir?" Ike asked.

"We begin at 2200 hours. There is no moon tonight so the darkness will be in our favour." Abruptly he left for his cabin.

McCurdy lingered on with the men for a while longer, picking at the last of his food, obviously in need of company this night. Content to be with ordinary seamen and stokers.

Moss wasn't satisfied that their talk had brought out the real problems of the country. "Look, you guys. We've got a funny country. So many crackpots want special privileges. These bloody Frenchmen need to be taught a lesson. Look at them down in their boats over there. Do you call that fighting for your country? The hell it is! It's shit, and we've got to clean up this mess sooner or later."

"That's right," McCurdy agreed forcefully. "We're getting every kind of riffraff into this country. And, to top it off, these sons of bitches here won't even learn the language, the language of the country, the Empire, the King's English. I don't like to say it, but fuck 'em all. That's how I feel. And they're not getting one bloody bit of this stuff tonight!"

"They're worse than the Jewish junk dealers," agreed Moss. "Screw 'em."

"Those cocksuckers need to be treated like we treated the Japs. We shoulda put 'em all in concentration camps and made 'em produce for us, hoe sugar beets and stuff."

"Damn right," said Al, "or like these conscientious objectors. Put 'em out of circulation. Hide 'em out in the bush."

Moss had worked up some real steam by now. "We're just too bloody soft in this country, allowing too many of these Bohunks in. My God! We've got Swedes, Poles, Ukes, Jews, Japs, Chinks, Krauts, it's gettin' outa hand. That's a lot of horse shit that's gotta stop. We just can't control 'em anymore!"

Al got up abruptly, "Ike and Chuck, give me a hand with getting the firefighting equipment ready, would you?"

"Sure, Al," said Chuck evenly. "What do we do?"

"Well, if we dump this in the drink the way it is now it won't sink. Too much rubber hose with air in it. So what we have to do is tie a heavy weight to it."

"Gotcha! Where's the weight? Want a four-inch gun?"

"I've gathered two buckets of pipe fittings and there are a half dozen iron pipes in stores. Go get it to lash to this equipment. That should do it."

Meantime, upper deck hands tied similar weights to bundles of small gear lying on deck.

2200 hours and pitch dark. Skipper and McCurdy came on deck. Skipper made a cursory inspection, peering over the dark night water, looking in all directions for rowboats. None could be seen. "Ship's company! You may begin dumping. Throw stuff overboard on both sides. First the clothing and such and then allow the stuff to sink before you throw in the heavy items."

Working with efficient determination, McCurdy saw them first. "Sir! Sir! They're here! They're all around us! There must be fifteen or twenty boats. What now?"

The crew stopped dumping and peered into the distance. They noticed the stuff being grappled and fished out of the water with oars, with sticks, with special grappling hooks brought for the purpose.

"Fuck off, you bastards!"

"We'll kill you, you sons of bitches!"

"Get the hell away from here or we'll blow you out of the water, you French pricks!"

Heavy objects were being thrown at the boats along with more invective. They hurled spanners, heavy bolts, pipe fittings to drive them away from the ship, away from this precious junk that had to be sunk, by God it did.

"Sir! Do we continue?" McCurdy asked the skipper.

"Not yet. How far out are they?'

"We can't see them clearly, Sir. Maybe two or three hundred feet. Shall we proceed?"

"No!"

McCurdy walked over to consult with skipper on the foredeck. In a few moments he came back and went below. On return he held a flare pistol in his hand.

"Fire 100 yards!" came skipper's order.

McCurdy fired. The brilliant flare illuminated every boat in the water and seemed to land in one of them. "Most of them are concentrated to starboard of shot, Sir, about a hundred yards."

"Aim 100 yards to starboard and fire!"

The flare lit up six to eight boats directly in the line of its firing.

"Fire again!"

"Aim 20 yards farther off and fire! –Fire! -Fire! –Fire!"

Moss was excited, "By God, skipper, Sir! The scrounging bastards are on the run. Well done, Sir!" He raised his arm and shouted "Hurray!" echoed by the rest.

McCurdy remained to oversee the disposal of the rest of the goods, but skipper retreated to his cabin. Most of the stuff left was metal and sank quickly. With some difficulty they heaved the firefighting equipment over the rail. While sinking, gurgling bubbles broke the water as air inside fought the weight of the ballast. The bedding and clothing they had held back before was last to go. Nobody there to retrieve it. A few all wool, white, pusser blankets left by the earlier crew floated on the water for a while as if regretful at parting from ship's company. Ike had noticed the names stenciled on the edges as he chucked them overboard. Laroux and McCaffrey.

At 0100 hours Ike and Chuck went down. They spread their cotton-padded hammock mattresses on the wooden lockers fixed along each side. At each foot end lay a matted heavy white woolen Hudson Bay Company blanket. No pillows for this night. Only the factory built-in lump at one end of the war issue mattress. They both had had down feather pillows. Sent from home. The kind that refused to sink readily. The ones out there floating away. Their two sea bags stood about at half mast, a bath towel lay here, a dickey there. A depressing sight.

"God, I hope some bloody Frenchie gets the feather pillows. Damned comfortable they were. Just imagine sleeping on this laughable, crappy little bump."

"One night won't kill you, Ike. If I can stand it, you can too. Quit bitching."

"It's odd, Chuck, that skipper hasn't notified us about our destination yet. Who knows? We may both have our heads on a crumby mattress pillow for a long time yet."

"Not me, Ike. I just know I'm going home. Skipper doesn't know who's going where yet. He couldn't. No navy boat's been alongside since we pulled in. We can't expect to find out until late morning. Shut up now."

They settled down under their blankets. Ike reflected on the day's events. A feeling of disgust came over him. He heard Chuck turning over on his locker. Still awake. "Chuck, was that really us up there tonight? Why the hell did we treat those people the way we did? We don't even know them. They didn't really hurt us did they?"

"Damn right, we were up there, and don't you start worrying now about not knowing any of them. Did we know the Krauts? The Italians? The Japs? The hell you did. Man, you've been keen to get a crack at them for years. Now suddenly you can't see the enemy." He was quiet for a long time and Ike thought he had fallen asleep. Then he sighed deeply. "Ike, I thought we had some guts. It's shit in our blood, that's what. Neither of us had guts enough to say. 'I'm not in on this. It's wrong!' Hell, let's just go to sleep."

Ship's company with sea bags, hammocks, and suitcases, was neatly lined up on the port side where a launch was scheduled for pick up at 1425 hours. As they stood there in the warm sunshine, they noticed a small rowboat approach the ship. It came nearer, a man and woman in it, both pulling on the oars. When within earshot, they dropped their oars. The woman stood up, waved her arms and shouted something loudly in French. On K171 no one understood what she was shouting about but they could see she was crying. She pointed downward to the hole in her skirt. Then the man spoke, pointing to the skirt. She lifted it to her waist and pulled up the leg of the blue bloomers she wore underneath. Even at thirty yards, ship's company clearly saw the large, purple bruise near her groin.

With grateful eyes they saw the motor launch approaching, leaving a sizeable wake as it sped toward them. The small row boat, struck by the turbulence, bobbed violently. On deck no one had said a word. Someone along the rail cleared his throat of something stuck at the root of his nasal passages and spat over the side. "Bitch!"

With the launch came orders to abandon K171 at 1500 hours. Ship's company would be picked up, taken to a bus on shore for transport to HMCS Hochelaga in Montreal to receive their discharge papers, all except Friedlen. He would be transported to the railway station in Montreal to proceed to *Stadacona*, Halifax, and there await orders for further sea duty.

Moss dished up soup, sandwiches, canned peaches and tea. Each man, as he finished this last meal, tossed his dishes overboard. Ike stood and watched his plate sink down slowly, crazily, toward the murky bottom, never to be retrieved. Out of sight, it left no trace. He checked the immediate area where he had eaten for any tell-tale vestige of his existence. Nothing. A spotless void. Momentarily he wondered if others too were inhabited with this empty feeling. No one offered a remark that might start off an argument. No one said much of anything. No compliments or complaints about the food. No comments or congratulations about the orders they had received. No...hip... hip...hip for good old *Kamsack*. Blankly, they climbed into the launch and eyes steady forward, headed for shore.

No time for goodbyes when the bus dropped him at the CN station. Ike was grateful for that. He had little time to wait before climbing aboard the train for Halifax. HMCS *Stadacona*! The last place to which he had expected to be transferred! Why wasn't he going to the west coast? The war in the Atlantic was over, for Christ's sake! He had put his name down for the Murmansk run long ago but had heard no more about it. Surely there was no longer any Murmansk run in operation. After VE Day, he had signed up for the Japanese theater of war. Now Halifax! Of all the rotten, goddam luck!

He stumbled along the lurching corridor to the diner for supper and ate it in silence. Two other servicemen and a civilian woman joined him at the table, eating without conversation. Probably their lives were crashing around them just as his own seemed to be. A moment though of modest rejoicing: a menu with multiple selections. He ordered chicken.

At Moncton they heard the big news. An ammunition dump had exploded in Bedford, just across Bedford Basin from Halifax. Buildings had been flattened, windows shattered, and a large part of the area had been evacuated for fear of further explosions as the fires spread. It called up memories of the great explosion of 1917 when the heart of the city had been destroyed. This time, however, the railway lines and the station seemed to be out of harm's way and there would be no delay in service. Nothing would halt Ike's inexorable return to HMCS *Stadacona*.

Naval transport at the station took Ike to the base. On reporting, he was advised to proceed immediately to Naval Dockyards, Jetty Number 9. There, report for duty to HMCS *Westmount*, a minesweeper. It could have been worse, he supposed. From what he had seen of the navy, there would still be boilers to clean even if there was only a fraction of the fleet left. A minesweeper couldn't be as bad as boiler cleaning, but he doubted it would have to sweep for mines in the Panama Canal or anywhere else where palm trees swayed.

Dragging his sea bag, hammock and suitcase over another ship, he descended the ladder into *Westmount's* stokers' mess. He had done all this before, he reflected, so there was no excitement, no sense of anticipation. With some trumped-up enthusiasm he introduced himself to the Leading Stoker who in response exchanged greetings in a somewhat curt matter-of-fact manner. He had been expected, his bunk was number four, and his duty watch was 0800 to 1200 hours and 2000 hours to 2400 hours. That was it.

Unpacking his gear, Ike's thoughts turned to *Kamsack* shipmates, traveling homeward with their discharge papers in their pockets. His own fortune would have been different, too, had he chosen a different course. He might have been with them on the way home. Considering the enormous amount of territory still under Japanese control the war there might go on for years. A posting, even temporarily, to this bucket sweeping east coast shipping lanes of enemy mines was a deep disappointment. He dreaded writing the letters he now had to send. Sara had not written since he'd told her about signing on for the Pacific.

Westmount went to sea by 0400 hours next day, heading for a mine field somewhere on the Atlantic coast. Ike went up on deck after his first watch to witness minesweeping in action. The sweeping gear trailed aft at a considerable distance. Good! If it picked up anything, it wouldn't explode under the ship if it was triggered by the gear. He wondered, however, how the *Westmount* could sail into the field without bumping one of the mines with her bow. He questioned a seaman standing near the winches.

"Well, we don't plow straight into the field, y' know. When we launch the gear the skipper maneuvers the ship so it veers to one side. Then we approach the field almost at right angles so we can sweep our way into it without too much danger. Mind you, we damn well don't know for sure where the field begins and where it ends. All we know is where ships have been hit. Makes you feel great, eh?" He laughed harshly and Ike went back down below. Might as well get some sleep.

For weeks *Westmount* continued to comb the waters for any mementoes the Germans might have left behind. Occasionally, she went back to port for refueling and re-provisioning. Several new seamen, recently taken on, were given a hands-on introduction to the intricacies of handling the minesweeping gear. Because of the dangers in the actual field, the ship staged a practice run in safe waters.

Ike felt lucky to be off watch when the procedure began. He hadn't seen any mine being swept so far and looked forward to the experience, especially so since they were about to sweep for a dummy. The upper deck crew laid their practice mine. Then they launched the sweeping gear and the ship carefully maneuvered into the "mined field." Back and forth, back and forth she swept, while her crew watched in anticipation for the pop-up. Her past record for sweeping was good except that Ike had been on watch each time it occurred and so had missed the real show. The gunnery crew stood at the ready to "explode" the dummy at first sight. Ike was ready to raise a cheer along with the rest of the crew. Back and forth, back and forth, but nothing happened. An hour passed. Ike didn't stick around for results and hit the sack fully dressed.

Excited voices interrupted the sweeping trials and Ike's sleep. Had they hit something? No, someone was cheering. He opened his eyes and peered over the edge of his hammock. The mess was a babble of talk. A bomb! A new bomb had wiped out a whole goddamned city in Japan. "The Japs are finished!" someone exclaimed.

"Can't be. Not with one bloody bomb!"

"With one, single bomb, I'm tellin' ya. The Americans dropped an atomic bomb! I just heard about it on the upper deck."

"What the hell's an atomic bomb?"

Ike decided it was time for him to follow the others rushing up the ladder to hear more. Not much more to hear. Only that the Americans had dropped one bomb that was equal to a thousand ordinary bombs.

"It must be big if it was big enough to destroy a whole city."

"If it's that big, how the hell did they carry it?"

"It's a new atomic bomb, I'm tellin' ya. One that packs as much TNT as a thousand ordinary bombs."

There weren't many details available until the ship got back to Halifax. Newspapers filled front pages with descriptions of the new weapon. Fuzzy pictures of a mushroom cloud that had sucked up a whole city. What a terrific job! Surely, the Japs could not hold out much longer. You had to hand it to the Yanks. Always ahead with important useful inventions. Some way to win a war! Damned right.

Japan surrendered on Ike's 22nd birthday. Two days later he headed west with discharge papers, medals, gratuities, railway pass. Before boarding the train he dispatched a telegram to his parents to meet him. Since he hadn't heard from Sara for so long he hesitated about sending one to her. Doubtfully, he sent her the date of his arrival.

An overriding question seemed to dominate conversation on the crowded passenger car heading west on Canadian National Railway's tracks. "What'll you do in civvies?" Some claimed assurance of university studies. Others had a job waiting for them. A few boasted of directorships, of positions ready for them to take on in "father's business." For infinite miles of uninspiring spruce tree landscape, Ike, however, heard from so many more like himself, men who had only a blurred, fuzzy vision of their future. No answers to "What's waitin' for ya, eh buddy?" Stunned, fingering loose change and dollar bills in their money belts, they sat staring through dirty window panes expecting, perhaps, a break, a ray, from the green landscape.

Hours on end, except for a trip to line up for the heads, Ike sat burdened with a sense of futility, a feeling of emptiness. On reflection he suddenly realized what was missing: his usual comfortable opinion, attitude, arrogance, about how this war had been fought, won, single-handed. That complacency had vanished. Gone completely. Where, when had he lost it? Perhaps, when he queued up for his discharge. Darn it, yes, receipt of that little baggie with medals like those handed to so many ahead of him in line had dampened his ego. An image of himself as a child and a bag of candy handed out at a picnic. For coming.

For long stretches, he deliberately shut his eyes to the unfamiliar world around him, men and women, strangers. All, he reckoned considering their behaviour, pre-occupied with uncertainties. Were they, as he was, unprepared for the sudden return to civvies? For finding the means to pay for pusser cheese and Red Lead and Bacon? Or finding the pad on which to put one's head down for a night? Or did they dread a return to civvies for fear of unconsciously blurting out uninhibited profanity, that macho bravado response to constant danger? After some time, Ike opened his eyes. To face the realities before him. No need now for gross vocabulary where he was heading. Where soft voices beseeched men to search for reason, root out blasphemy, and bend the knees.

Ike's spirits shot up as CN passed through Manitoba flat farm land on its approach to Winnipeg. Impossible to lose a kinship to good land in a few years away from it, fighting a war. Swathers, combines, trucks, men and women busy everywhere on the fields this August day. He could tell there would be no celebration. Tomorrow he, too, would be on a combine. He had serious doubts about his father meeting him at the station, considering the fine harvest conditions out there. After completion of autumn field work he would look up Sara. He just had to.

Disembarking, Ike decided to leave his possessions, sea-bag and hammock in baggage until he knew with certainty that transportation was waiting. He scanned the arrival area. From the entrance, he searched for a familiar car from home outside. Nothing. He'd leave his gear and thumb a ride.

Then he saw her.

Endnotes

1 Globe and Mail, June 9, 1943, p.1

2 Op.cit., p.1

3 Globe and Mail, July 26, 1943, p.1

4 The Globe and Mail, Fri., Sept 3, 1943, p.1

5 The Globe and Mail, Tues., Feb. 8, 1944, p.1

6 The Globe and Mail, Wednesday, April 19, 1944, p.1

7 The Globe and Mail, May 8, 1946

Printed in Canada